A Great Lady Lies Near Death . . .

"It's really her whole body," Rod said. "She's just wearing out, son."

"How can that be!"

"Because she's a quarter elven," Rod answered.

Magnus's mind spun furiously through the chain of facts, trying to catch up with what his father had spent months absorbing. Some unwitting telekinetic long ago had told tales of the Wee Folk, and blobs of fungus in the nearby forest had pulled together, shaped themselves into a form that could stand and walk, then turned more and more into an elf, one who could beget its own kind, one who had . . .

"Genes!" Magnus stared at his father. "The elves can reproduce, so their fashioning must have worked on so deep a level that the tele-sensitive fungus even formed chains of DNA!"

"Yes," Rod said softly. "And when that re-creation interacted with real human genes, it only modified them so that they became extremely long-lived . . ."

"So the elves live forever! Then should not mother . . ."

Rod watched him carefully, saw the realization in his eyes, and nodded. "When the witch-moss genes are outnumbered two to one, it seems they eventually break down. You might say they become overwhelmed by reality."

Magnus stared back at him, chilled. "She waited for me."

Rod nodded . . .

D0958893

THE
WARLOCK'S
LAST RIDE

2981 4586

CHRISTOPHER STASHEFF

Stayton Public Library
515 North First Avenue
Stayton, Oregon 97383

ACE BOOKS, NEW YORK

If you purchased this book without a cover, you should be aware that this book is stolen property. It was reported as "unsold and destroyed" to the publisher, and neither the author nor the publisher has received any payment for this "stripped book."

This is a work of fiction. Names, characters, places, and incidents either are the product of the author's imagination or are used fictitiously, and any resemblance to actual persons, living or dead, business establishment, events, or locales is entirely coincidental.

THE WARLOCK'S LAST RIDE

An Ace Book / published by arrangement with
the author

PRINTING HISTORY
Ace mass market edition / June 2004

Copyright © 2004 by Christopher Stasheff.
Cover art by Matt Stawicki.
Cover design by David Reinhardt.
Interior text design by Julie Rogers.

All rights reserved.
This book, or parts thereof, may not be reproduced in any form without permission. The scanning, uploading, and distribution of this book via the Internet or via any other means without the permission of the publisher is illegal and punishable by law. Please purchase only authorized electronic editions, and do not participate in or encourage electronic piracy of copyright materials. Your support of the author's rights is appreciated.

For information address: The Berkley Publishing Group,
a division of Penguin Group (USA) Inc.,
375 Hudson Street, New York, New York 10014

ISBN 0-441-01176-4

ACE®
Ace Books are published by The Berkley Publishing Group,
a division of Penguin Group (USA) Inc.,
375 Hudson Street, New York, New York 10014
ACE and the "A" design
are trademarks belonging to Penguin Group (USA) Inc.

PRINTED IN THE UNITED STATES OF AMERICA

10 9 8 7 6 5 4 3 2 1

Prologue

THE CONCERT MASTER WAVED HIS BOW TO TIE up the last note, and the orchestra fell silent. Then the organ began its murmur, stumbling now and then, causing Rod to bite his lip.

Gwen placed her hand over his. "Patience, husband. The musician had other matters arising in his life than practicing these pieces you brought him."

"Considering he'd never seen anything remotely like Bach before, I suppose he's not doing a bad job," Rod admitted.

They stood at the back of the cathedral in Runnymede, waiting for their entrances.

"Think instead upon how well our sons look."

Rod looked up at the three tall young men standing at the side of the sanctuary, his sons and their lifelong friend the crown prince, resplendent in cloth-of-gold doublets and gleaming white hose. It had been difficult prying Gregory out of his usual monk's robe for the occasion, but Gwen had prevailed. At the thought, the scene blurred, and

he saw Gregory as he had been before he fell in love with
Allouette and went on a crash course of bodybuilding: thin
and pale, seeming almost anemic.

Then the three young men came back into focus, and
Rod marveled how much the lad looked like his muscular
brother, though Gregory was still brown-haired and Geoffrey golden.

As his brother Magnus had been when he was small . . .

Gwen's hand touched his arm, rested there in reassurance. "I would he were here, too, husband, healed and beside them—but we must settle for three rings, not four."

Rod covered her hand with his own, still marveling at
how clearly she could read his mind—even without using
her telepathic powers. "Just so he's healed some day, dear—
and this certainly is reason enough to set my heart singing."

Nonetheless, the old anger awoke and burned—anger at
Finister, the woman who had not merely broken Magnus's
heart with her ferociously powerful psi powers, but man-
gled it, then done so again and again in different guises. As
always, though, he schooled himself to forgive, for her
malice had been the result of systematic brainwashing and
emotional abuse by her foster parents—agents of the fu-
turian enemies of the royal family who sought to forge Finister into a weapon to be used against the Crown and its
main support, the Gallowglass family, and had succeeded
far too well—but Cordelia and Geoffrey had been proof
against her plots, and Gregory, though he had fallen in love
with her, had still managed to defend himself against her.
Gwen, seeing his despair and knowing how deeply her execution would scar him, had examined the woman's mind
in depth, seen the sweet child buried under all the machinations, found the kernel of goodness that could be nour-
ished into health, and in a marathon, exhausting night of
telepathic psychotherapy, had healed her well enough to let
her see the world as it really was, to cast off the false personality her tormentors had grafted onto her and, at last,
discovered the name given her as a baby—Allouette.

Gregory knew it would be a life's work helping her to
develop her own true personality, but had already made
great strides—so great that she had finally been willing to

wed him publicly, even side by side with his brother and sister, instead of being forever content with the quiet, almost furtive, ceremony performed by a monk in a tiny village.

Trying to put the thought aside as unworthy, Rod looked around at the assemblage gathered in the cathedral, what he could see of it from the rear. The nobility of Gramarye filled the pews—with one very notable absence. Sadness tugged at him.

Gwen noticed. "What sorrow?"

"That the whole family isn't here," Rod said. "Alain's uncle and cousin should be watching him marry."

"Aye, but an attainted traitor cannot come nigh the Crown." The thought was the one shadow on a glorious day.

Rod saw, and was sorry he'd brought up the issue. "Maybe the kids will be able to make peace even if their parents can't, dear."

Gwen smiled at the thought, then turned all her attention toward the central doorway of the cathedral, waiting for the brides.

Guards lined the central doorway and the path to it, as much to keep the common folk from blocking the way as to protect the brides. The commoners clustered at the other two doorways, eager for a sight of their future king and queen. Shafts of colored light filled the air above them, a shifting array of colors from the stained glass windows along the sides of the nave and the great rose window above the choir loft. The noblemen and their wives seemed to vie with one another for the glory and extravagance of their costumes, shifting restlessly now and then, hungry for a sight of the brides.

So was Rod.

Anxiously, he scanned the three young men waiting eagerly and apprehensively at the stairs to the altar, then turned to look back into the recesses of the foyer. "We shouldn't have left the girls to dress themselves!"

"They have three maids apiece to help them, husband," Gwen said sternly. "We brought them here, after all. We can allow them some measure of independence." Nonetheless, she was tense enough herself—poised, no doubt, to dash to answer a daughter's call, to resolve last-minute misgivings.

Then the organ broke from Bach and stilled. The orchestra began again, a joyous but stately promenade, as the queen herself stepped down the aisle escorted by her younger son, Prince Diarmid. She was spectacular in embroidered silk, but wore only a few gems, her notion of not outdoing the brides. She paced the length of the aisle in stately fashion, stepped into the larger of the two carved and gilded chairs by the altar, and sat as her son went on to stand beside his childhood friend Gregory—interesting that he was best man for his friend instead of his brother, who had to make do with the young Duke of Savoy.

It should have been Magnus . . .

Rod threw off the thought and turned to watch as the bridesmaids came down the aisle like a train of spring flowers, all members of Quicksilver's former outlaw band—and needed, for Quicksilver, Cordelia, and Allouette would all have served as each others' maids of honor, if they hadn't been marrying at the same ceremony.

Then came the ring bearer, proud of his place at seven years old and carrying the satin cushion as though it were the crown itself; after him came five girls of the same age, strewing rose petals. As they came to the head of the aisle, their mothers steered them toward the altar.

Then ten trumpeters brought their long straight horns to their lips, and the fanfare flared out over the crowd. As its strains died, the organ pealed out the opening notes of the "Wedding March," and there they came, a trio of veiled young women in shimmering white, Cordelia in the center and a little ahead. Rod knew her by the way she walked, the way she held herself, by the hundred and one little signs he and Gwen had learned over the years of rearing her. Behind and to her right, Quicksilver marched with head held high, almost defiantly. To the left, Allouette matched her pace, but with a diffident, hesitant stride, seeming almost to question by her very carriage whether she deserved to be there.

Rod erased that doubt from his own mind as he fell in beside his daughter, beaming down at her, then over her head at Gwen as she took Cornelia's other arm. They exchanged a brief glance that made the rest of the world seem to go away for a moment. Then, resolutely, Gwen turned to pace the aisle with her daughter.

Rod lifted his head as the "Wedding March" filled the cathedral, albeit with a few small errors that he was sure only he noticed. With avid eagerness, the nobility turned for a glimpse of their future queen.

In stately procession, the three young women paced down the aisle, bouquets clutched tightly in their hands, Quicksilver flanked by her mother and little sister, now almost as tall as she; each seemed awed and awkward despite her finery, shooting anxious glances at the grand people about them, for they were, after all, only a squire's wife and daughter, and unused to such pomp and ceremony.

Allouette had no one but Gregory—they had never managed to find her true parents, from whom she had been kidnapped as an infant—so beside her came the king himself, Tuan Loguire, for, ever quick to prevent embarrassment when he could, he had claimed the right of escort as her liege lord.

Quickly Rod faced front again, trying to give some reassurance of his own by his mere presence. Cordelia walked with head erect, with pride, but he could feel her hesitance.

Then the young men stepped out to the center of the sanctuary, and Cordelia almost stopped, staring at Alain's magnificence. Rod gave the lad a glance, saw his eyes wide in amazement at the most beautiful sight of his life, and with a covert smile urged his daughter forward. Up the steps they went, up to Alain, who proffered his arm with a look that said he wasn't worthy.

Privately, Rod agreed, of course—no man could be good enough for Cordelia. But he knew she was really in love with the prince and had decided not to hold his royal blood against him. Not without reservations of his own, Rod let her walk from his arm and Gwen's, to take Alain's. He stood beside his wife for a moment, drinking in the sight of bride and groom, then held out his arm to Gwen. She laid hers on top of his and turned with him to walk back down the steps to the pew that awaited them. As they entered, she exchanged a tremulous smile with Queen Catharine across the aisle. For a moment, their eyes held, old friends in league again, and Rod would never have believed the dozen confrontations the two women had had, over the details of the wedding, Gwen politely and tactfully holding firm for Cordelia's choices through every one of Catharine's tantrums.

Then Toby stepped up beside Geoffrey, and Quicksilver's mother joined them in the pew as Tuan took his place beside Catharine in the lesser gilded chair. They turned back to the sanctuary, where the archbishop was coming down from the high altar, resplendent in gold and white of his own—a gilded chausable over a snowy alb, his high-peaked mitre also gilded, so that Rod wondered how the man could hold up his head with all that weight. Maybe he was really leaning on the elaborate crozier, the very ornate shepherd's crook that is a bishop's staff of office. The three couples drew up before him, Cordelia and Alain in the center, Gregory beside Allouette at their left, fairly oozing reassurance, and at the right, Geoffrey offering his arm to Quicksilver, who took it but returned a challenging glance. Her reply was a look of adoration, and she whipped her gaze back to the archbishop, almost totally unnerved.

Gwen was murmuring to Quicksilver's mother, hand in hand, projecting reassurance of her own. Rod exchanged a glance with Tuan; as one, both smiled, then turned back to the altar.

The archbishop intoned the old words in a voice that carried through the cathedral. Rod had offered a tiny microphone and public-address system, but the prelate had refused them. Somehow the words blurred in Rod's mind—he could tell only that the archbishop shifted from English to Latin and back—and felt a sudden aching wish that he could have given Gwen a wedding like this. Unfortunately, he had been a wanted man at the time, scarcely daring to show his face in a village church, let alone the cathedral of the royal capital. He squeezed her arm, gazing at her with apology—but she gave him a look that was almost merry, and he knew that she regretted nothing. She might have been married by a wandering monk instead of an archbishop, but she'd had a flower-filled glade instead of a cathedral and a crowd of elves instead of nobility. Her dress had been stitched by a score of elf-wives and had outshone even her daughter's royal gown, and the King of Elves had given her away.

Rod wondered if, in spite of all his precautions, she had guessed that Brom O'Berin was her father.

Rod glanced around, wondering if Brom was here to see his grandchildren wed—but there he was by the king and queen, of course, for his elfin nature was secret; they took him for a mortal dwarf, and he who had been jester to Catharine's father had become her privy councilor. Rod knew the gray in his hair was carefully contrived, for Brom, like all elves, would still be living when the rest of them had been a century in their graves.

He turned back to the altar, determined to banish so melancholy a thought—just in time, for the archbishop had stepped up by Cordelia and was asking, "Who gives this woman to this man?"

Last-minute panic rose in Rod, but he overrode it to say with Gwen, "My spouse and I!"

Then the archbishop moved on to Quicksilver and asked again, "Who gives this woman to this man?" and her mother and sister answered, "We do!"

On the archbishop went to Allouette, who stood rock-firm but with a trembling bouquet, and intoned, "Who gives this woman to this man?" and Tuan and Catharine answered, "As her liege and sovereign, we do!"

Then the archbishop returned to stand between the line of young women and the line of young men to ask, "Do you, Cordelia, Quicksilver, and Allouette, take Alain, Geoffrey, and Gregory for your lawfully-wedded husbands, for better or for worse, to have and to hold, to love and to cherish, in sickness and in health, till death do you part?"

Cordelia's answer pealed forth: "I do." Quicksilver answered a beat later, "I do!" Allouette swallowed thickly but glanced at Gregory and froze, her gaze on his as she whispered, "I do."

Gregory seemed to glow.

The archbishop turned to the three young men. "Do you, Alain, Geoffrey, and Gregory, take these women Cordelia, Quicksilver, and Allouette, to be your lawfully-wedded

wives, for better or for worse, to have and to hold, to love
and to cherish, in sickness and in health, till death do you
part?"

Alain stammered, "I do!"

Geoffrey, his gaze burning through Quicksilver's veil,
said, "I do!"

Gregory, unable to take his eyes away from the veil that
hid the face he loved so well, breathed, "I do."

"Then I now pronounce you husbands and wives."

The three couples stood, unbelieving, for a few seconds.

Gently, the archbishop explained, "You may kiss the
brides."

The women lifted their veils, radiant; their husbands
stepped close. As their lips touched, twelve trumpets
pealed their joy. The archbishop cleared his throat and
turned away, taking off his mitre and handing it to an
acolyte, then trudging back up the stairs to the high altar to
begin the nuptial Mass, as more acolytes brought out six
kneelers for the brides and the grooms.

Either the Mass was short—which Rod doubted, since
it was a solemn high Mass—or his time sense had slowed
down, making everything a blur; it seemed only minutes
until the three couples were standing, the women relaxed
and joyful with their veils folded back, and the organ burst
forth in Mendelsohn's notes of rejoicing, as the three
grooms, laughing and chatting with their brides, descended
the stairs to the aisle and fairly floated down that long avenue to the great oaken portal.

THERE WAS MUCH more, of course—a banquet in the
Great Hall of the royal palace for all the nobility; dancing
afterwards, with the three young couples leading and Rod
having his first waltz with Cordelia since she had grown
too big to stand on his toes; the wine flowing freely and the
younger nobility becoming rather rowdy, on the verge of
bearing the three couples away to a bridal night that would
have had spectators—a must for royal weddings in the middle ages, when virginity was vital to be sure the heir was really of the royal line. But at that point, Gwendylon wound
her way magically through the throng and assembled all

three couples on the dais that held the high table. The brides-maids and other young women lined up facing them, chattering eagerly, forcing the young men back a little, and the throng began to count: "One . . . two . . . three!"

All three brides tossed their bouquets high, and the young women pushed and shoved to catch them. Then, the ceremony of the garter not having spread to Gramarye, the three young couples waved at their contemporaries, calling their thanks and farewells—and with the resounding of triple firecrackers, disappeared.

The hall fell silent for a moment, for even the people of Gramarye were still unnerved by teleportation, or any of the other psi powers they thought of as witchcraft.

Besides, they'd been robbed of the erotic riot they'd been planning.

So talk began, gathering anger—but King Tuan stepped forth, smiling with good cheer, hands upheld, and the crowd grew silent. "Each bride has gone with her groom to the love nest each couple has selected," he explained, "but there is wine aplenty and sweetmeats besides, so though they may seek their beds, there is no reason why you should. Musicians, play!"

A sprightly tune sprang up from the musicians' gallery, and the nobility turned, not without a little grumbling, to the quick steps of the dance. In minutes, they had forgotten their disappointment at having been robbed of their shivaree and were cheering with gladness.

"It is done, then," Gwen said, her hand on Rod's arm. "We have spirited them away to privacy, thank Heaven!"

"Not without quite an input of psionic power from their mother," Rod said with a knowing smile.

"I may have helped in some small way," Gwen admitted. "Lead me back to our place at the high table, husband, for I am rather weary."

"Not surprising, with months of planning and fixing and defending," Rod said, gazing down at his bride, with a look that echoed those his sons had given their brides. "And capped with a day that must have been the most strenuous of your life."

Gwen gave a little laugh, then said, "Well, there was

that night when Magnus was ten, when he woke with the nightmare, and Gregory had colic and was screaming, and woke Cordelia who joined him, and Geoffrey was determined to have his share of attention . . ."

"Yes, but there were two of us to sort that out," Rod said. "This you pretty much had to do alone."

"Not without a great deal of moral support, husband," Gwen said, with a look that renewed her wedding vows.

But she stumbled as she climbed the steps to the dais. Rod steadied her with his arm and tried to laugh it off. "More tired than you thought!"

"That may be," Gwen admitted.

But she stumbled again as they were leaving the castle, stumbled only on the single step down from the drawbridge, and this time Rod had to catch her, not steady her, and she couldn't make her legs bear her. He held her in his arms while footmen ran for a coach.

" 'Tis only weariness," she told Rod.

"You mean exhaustion," he said, "and you're right—total exhaustion. A few weeks' rest will restore you."

But it didn't.

One

ALEA CAME INTO THE LOUNGE AND FOUND IT
empty. Impatiently, she looked around, irritation growing,
then put the feeling into words and smiled with amusement
that was tinged with self-mockery. She was feeling, *How
dare Magnus not be here when I'm wanting company?* as
though his only purpose in life were to amuse her!

Well, of course it wasn't. He was there to provide her
this wonderful spaceship with its luxurious furnishings and
gourmet food and drink, and to guard her back in battle.
What else was a man for?

Loving, something in her seemed to say, but she shied
away from that. The parents she had loved had died and left
her alone and defenseless; the neighbors she had thought
her friends had turned against her to gain her inheritance.
The boy who had proclaimed his undying love for her and
seduced her had then mocked her and spurned her. What
need had she for love? Much better to have a shield-
companion like Magnus, a true friend who was unwavering
in his devotion, even though that devotion was so much less

than a lover's—and what did she want with love anyway? There hadn't been any pleasure in it, only pain. Oh, there had been pleasure in knowing she was making her lad happy, there had been pleasure in his passion, in the intensity of his longing for her, his need for her—but no pleasure for her body.

Magnus, though, with the sensitivity under his impassive shell, with the leashed fire of the emotions that he focused only on The People, whatever people they might be at the moment . . . if he were in her bed, might not love-making become . . .

She shut the thought off with anger. The bards lied, the poets lied, there was no pleasure in love! Besides, why jeopardize the solidity of their friendship for a romance that might turn sour?

Or might grow to greater heights all their lives . . .

Poetic falsehoods, she told herself angrily, and went to look for Magnus, already angry with him for leaving her the victim of her thoughts and feelings. Of course, she could ask Herkimer, the ship's computer, but somehow she thought she knew. If Magnus wasn't in his stateroom and wasn't in the lounge, he would probably be on the bridge. What need to ask?

So she strode down the companionway, a tall slender woman wearing loose shipboard coveralls to hide the curves beneath, long-faced with eyes too large and a mouth too wide, with a nose too small for the chiselled planes of a warrior's face, a latter-day Valkyrie born to a mortal man and woman rather than to the gods, in token of which her long yellow hair was coiled atop her head in two long braids, as though to cushion a helmet.

Up the spiral stairs she came, into the hush of the bridge. It was dark, of course, with only pools of light at the never-used consoles, to let the projected stars show in the dome overhead, that the pilot might see toward which star he coursed. She looked up herself, caught in the majesty and grandeur of the galaxy. She gazed for minutes, longer than she had intended, before she lowered her gaze to the solitary figure silhouetted against the powder-trail of the Dragon.

She gazed at him for a few minutes, marvelling that his seven-foot form with all its bulk of muscles should seem small against that starry grandeur, then looked more closely, feeling his unaccountable sadness, letting it soak into herself until she shared it, wondering.

Wondering? Why? How should it be unaccountable? For as badly as love had treated her, it had treated Magnus far worse. She didn't know the details, honored his privacy too much to try to read the depths of his mind, but from a careless word dropped here and there, she gathered that some young she-wolf had tortured his heart, whipsawing his emotions from love to utter humiliation not once, but again and again, for the sheer pleasure of abasing him. At least her lad had done it only once, and then more to taste the pleasures of her body than of her grief, and when he had spurned her, it was to make sure he wasn't burdened with a great lumbering lass, not for the purpose of tasting her pain.

Though he had seemed to enjoy that, too . . .

She shook off the memory of him angrily, concentrating fiercely on the great hulk in the acceleration chair, head back, eyes fixed on the stars. What need had she of the memory of a traitor when she had the reality of a friend who cared for her far more than any but her parents ever had? And what right had he to be gazing at the stars and wallowing in his misery when she was here, lively and vital, to distract him? She stepped forward, angry words rising to her lips to rouse him from his lethargy, to jolt him back to the life they shared—but as she came close, she saw the unutterable grief in his eyes. She slowed, letting her gentler emotions well up, sympathy and concern, and asked, very softly, "What hurts you, Magnus?"

His head tilted, gaze coming down, seeming to wander over the fittings of the bridge until it found her face, then rested a minute before he said, "My little brother."

Words of anger leaped to her tongue again, anger at the younger man who would hurt his own brother so, but she contained them, pushed them down, knowing that the younger d'Armand, the titanic telepath so distant on their home world, would scarcely spend the vast amount of energy necessary for his thoughts to reach Magnus over so many light-years unless there were good reason. "What news could a brother have to so sadden one of his own blood?" she asked softly.

"News of our mother," Magnus answered. "She is dying."

ALEA SPOKE BUT little in the days that followed but was never far from Magnus, trying to reassure and comfort him by her mere presence. She remembered well the death-watch as her mother lay dying, remembered the greater pain of her father's last days, greater because there was no one with whom to share it, no one whose pain dwarfed her own.

She never thought that it was unfair that Magnus should have the comfort of a friend when she had not—she was only glad that he did not have to face this long journey home alone.

In moments of honesty, she had to admit that she was also glad he finally needed her in a way neither of them could deny.

So she sat by and waited, watching his profile against the stars or watching him sitting in the lounge in the cone of light from the hidden lamp, saw him looking up now and then, startled to see her sitting and reading across from him, remembering his manners enough to ask how she fared, trying to engage in conversation, and she tried to be reassuring and positive then, smiling and talking of inconsequentialities, but ones in which she knew he had an interest—art and literature and science—though before long, his attention would fade, his gaze would wander, and she would let her own conversation lapse and return to her reading.

Reading! She hadn't even known how, when he met her on the road, on her home planet of Midgard, where only the nobles were literate. She hadn't known how to fight when she had run away from slavery, had survived a night or two alone and friendless in a world torn by war and ha-tred, in a forest filled with wolves and bears. Magnus had—well, not taken her in, though it felt like that. She was sure he hadn't thought of it that way, either, though she suspected he knew he was giving her protection. He hadn't said so, though, only that he was glad of a travelling companion. So he had walked the roads with her, teaching her how to fight and how to use the talent for telepathy that had been buried inside her all her life, and that she had never known. Together they had braved the perils of her world and set in train a course of events that would prevent her own people from their continual attempts to tyrannize the other peoples of Midgard.

Then, done with the task he had come to do, he had called down his starship, and she had stood rigid, knowing she would be deserted again—but Magnus had taken her aboard, given her a new life when her old one had collapsed, taken her to strange and amazing worlds where people labored in need as great as her own. They had fought off wild beasts and wilder people, guarded one another's backs, labored to save the weak and the oppressed, come to know each other's needs in battle, then in daily life—and never once had he put out a hand to try to touch her or uttered a honeyed word to try to coax her into his bed.

It was almost an insult, really, except that she knew now he had known it would violate the fragile bridge of trust growing between them—that, and that he didn't really seem to have much interest in her as a woman, or in any kind of intimacy, for that matter. Now, though, the trust had grown, become solid in spite of her tantrums and insults, and she found herself wishing now and again that he *would* put out a hand to her—but when she caught herself thinking that, she was aghast. She'd had enough of that sort of thing with the one young man who had used her and spurned her! The friendship she had with Magnus was far better than that!

Though perhaps it could be even richer . . .

This was not the time to think of it, though, with Magnus so sunken in gloom, so afraid he might not reach home in time—so she sat and read, or cleaned and oiled her leathers, then sharpened her blades, or read, fetching a cup of tea for him when she brewed one for herself, accepted the cups he absentmindedly brought her in return, chivied him gently into eating, and didn't let him see how frightened she became when he lost his appetite.

In fact, she did all that a good travelling companion should, all that a battle-mate could, and gradually, little by little, he began to talk, first a phrase or two, then in sentences, and finally in long rambling monologues about his childhood, his early travels, his parents, his brothers and sister—but he always cut short when he realized he was beginning to talk about that last adventure, about the woman who had hurt him, about the reasons he had left home.

"I couldn't be my father's son, you see." He stared straight into her eyes then, as he rarely did anymore. "I couldn't be an extension of him. I had to be myself, my own man, and I could never be that at home unless I turned against him, fought against him—so I left instead."

And Alea listened and nodded, eyes glowing, drinking up all the information about Magnus the boy, Magnus the wounded lover setting off on his travels, Magnus the son and brother—Magnus the person, the human being, as she had yearned to know him for three years and never had.

In return, when he asked her what it had been like growing up as the tallest girl in a Midgard village, one far too tall in every way, she couldn't very well refuse to answer, no matter how sharp the hurts the memories brought—but telling him, she discovered that the pain had dimmed, that she could cope with it now, that she could look at her memories and treasure the good ones and resolve the bad ones. Oh, they were still pain-filled, but they no longer had the power to cripple. She knew she could stand against them now, against any one of the people who had hurt her, could stand against the whole village with Magnus beside her—and knew he would always be there, even without the lure of sex to keep him, that she had come to matter to him as deeply as that—and paradoxically, it made her yearning for his touch grow so sharp that it was almost unbearable, even though she knew that sex hurt, that the feelings that went with it gave pain far sharper—but the conviction grew that with Magnus, it would not be so. She told herself that she only wanted to share his bed so that she could be sure of him, and that wasn't necessary at all, for she could be far more sure of him as a battle-companion, that their steadily-deepening friendship was far surer and more meaningful than romantic love could ever be, that she didn't need the baring of souls that went with it, that the intimacy they were sharing now was far more meaningful than the confidences of lovers, that she could be closer to him as a true friend, now when worry and grief made him more vulnerable than he had ever been.

But something deep inside her refused to believe it, any of it.

So the starship shot onward through eternal night, bearing two people who were finally coming to know one another as they never had.

A SCREAM RANG through the castle's hall, and Rod started up, then looked back at Gwen's pale face on her pillow, framed by the long flows of red hair streaked with white. She opened her eyes, reading his anxiety and smiling. "Go to her, worried father. I shall still live when you return."

"I know. I still don't want to leave you unless I have to." Rod sat back onto her bed, cradling her hand in his. "But it's hard having you ill while our daughter's giving birth."

"I shall linger awhile, I assure you," Gwen said with a smile that suddenly blazed through her illness. "However, this is women's work, and it is better if you leave it to Cordelia and her midwife."

"Yes, I guess so." Rod managed a smile. "I had to live through you giving birth four times and face the fact that I couldn't do anything to lessen your pain. You think I'd be used to it by now."

"It has been many years," Gwen conceded. "Then too, 'tis different with a daughter than with a wife." For the first time, her own worry showed in her face. "Finally I too must face that helplessness. At least I can share her pain and give her some strength."

"You haven't any to spare!" Rod caught her hand in a panic. "Don't tax yourself!"

"My body may have weakened," Gwen told him, "but my mind is yet strong."

Another scream tore through the hall.

Rod looked up with a shudder, but Gwen said quietly, " 'Tis the last such. The babe is born."

Rod's head snapped around to stare at her. "You mean . . ."

"Wait." Gwen's hand tightened on his. "We shall see soon enough."

Nonetheless, it seemed an hour before the midwife appeared at the door, holding a blanket-wrapped bundle that emitted a gurgle.

Gwen held up her arms, suddenly vital again. "Give me!"

The midwife came and laid the blanket in her arms. Gwen cradled it and beamed down, her whole face lighting up with an intensity of pleasure and wonder that almost scared Rod. Tentatively, he reached out to open the blanket in the crook of her elbow a little wider—and looked down himself at the dark-haired, wrinkled, pink-and-red little face with the eyes solemnly shut. He marvelled at the wise, even profound expression and wondered all over again what wisdom souls forsake in order to be born, in that bright world from which new souls come.

Then he looked up at his wife and was awed all over again by the look of near-adoration and exaltation that suffused her face. Could it be that the baby alone would keep her alive?

"Now I have lived most truly and completely," Gwen said softly. "What greater joy could life hold for me than this?"

Rod hoped it was his imagination that gave the words a very final ring.

FINALLY A DOT of light in the dome of the bridge grew brighter than all the others, finally it swelled into a little circle, and Alea knew they were coming home—at least, to Magnus's home; she doubted it could ever be hers, or would need to be. As the disk swelled, Magnus grew even more tense; he began to snap at her if she said the wrong thing. She managed to stifle the retorts that rose to her lips, telling herself that he would be able to relax when the trauma of his homecoming was over, that he would be sorry for the things he had said. She throttled her anger at his not even seeming to notice her, so preoccupied was he with meeting

the family he had left ten years before, and though she
adamantly resisted the temptation to read his mind, she
could tell his thoughts anyway:

How would they have changed, the family he had deserted? How betrayed had they felt by his leaving? Was
there still any welcome there for him, any love? He had
told her many times that "You can't go home again," and
she had believed him—so what must it be like for him now,
coming back when he knew that the home he remembered
was lost in the mists of the past?

Then, in the perpetual evening gloom of the lounge,
Magnus looked up at her, his eyes suddenly focusing on her,
and warned, "Gregory says we're clear to land—on the night
side, of course, so that we won't frighten the peasants."

"Our usual approach." Alea dared to try a smile.

Magnus stared at her a moment, then smiled in return
with a warmth that surprized her and reached out to catch
her hand, and something melted within her.

Then he let go and turned his eyes forward to the
viewscreen where the huge cloud-streaked disk floated, and
advised her, "Better web in."

The arm of the lounge chair popped open, the anchor
rod rising up. Alea pulled it across her body and pressed it
against the back, where it fastened and clung with a grip
that couldn't be shaken even if the ship were smashed to
filings. She could feel the pressure of descent, feel that
pressure lift as Herkimer countered it with artificial grav-
ity, felt the tug-of-war of natural forces against synthetic
ones, as the huge disk on the screen expanded past its
edges and was somehow no longer in front of them, but below, rivers and mountain chains streaking past, the night
rolling across to engulf them, then only the glint of moonlight reflected off clouds until daylight rolled in to dispel
darkness. Now as they raced across the surface of the
planet, she could make out the patchwork of fields and relaxed into the familiar feeling of approach on a medieval
planet, forgetting for the moment the tension that would
come on their landing, of meeting people Magnus knew,
but who might have grown and changed into strangers.

Night rolled across the screen again, but this time there were lights here and there from towns, lights that disappeared as night deepened, and when daylight came back, she could make out roads threading from one cluster of roofs to another. They drifted across the screen much more slowly as the starship shed its speed, slowing till it might land without churning up a whole forest. When night came a third time, she could see individual houses very clearly, barns, and even the dots that were cattle in the fields. A dark blot on the screen became treetops silvered by moonlight that drifted so slowly they scarcely seemed to move, then suddenly swelled and went racing by, the speed seeming greater as the ship swooped lower, and Alea's heart rose into her throat, as it always did, the primitive peasant within her unable to believe that they would not fall out of the sky and slam into the earth, to be squashed like flies. Her whole body tensed, pushing against the webbing as though she could slow the ship by her own strength, even as she scolded herself for a foolish barbarian.

Then the racing treetops began to slow, ceasing to be a blur and becoming individual masses again, a mass that opened into a huge ragged circle of a clearing with the silver trail of a river down one side, a circle that seemed to float into sight, then to swell so much that the trees drifted out of view at the edges, that the cluster of dots at the top of the screen grew into people who swam out off the bottom in their own turn. Then there was a jolt, ever so slight, and the dark mass below resolved into individual grass stems, unmoving, and Magnus was releasing his webbing, was rising to his full height, tense and braced, saying, "We're home," and turning toward the airlock as though he were about to face an army.

Two

ALEA WAS OUT OF HER WEBBING IN AN INSTANT and by his side, matching him step for step as he paced toward the airlock. As they stepped in, she snatched up the two staves that leaned against the wall and pressed the longer into his hand.

Magnus stared down at it. "What would I want with this? I don't have to be ready to fight—I'm home!"

She didn't believe the middle part, couldn't when his whole stance belied it, but couldn't say that either.

"I'm not a cripple, you know," he told her. "I don't need something to lean on."

She didn't believe that either, but said only, "I do. You don't want to embarrass me, do you?"

Magnus looked surprised, barely started to mutter a denial before the outer door opened and the ramp stretched down before them, a silver gleam in the moonlight that showed the cluster of people moving up to its foot.

Magnus steeled himself, though she suspected only she would have noticed it, then seemed to relax completely and stepped out onto the bridge to his home—stepped faster and faster, until with a grin and cry of joy, he swept three of the people up in a bear hug.

Alea followed more slowly, giving him time, giving them time, hoping desperately that they would take his seeming affection in the spirit in which it was offered.

As she stepped off the ramp, one of the figures let go her stranglehold on Magnus's neck and managed to disentangle herself from his arm with a wide grin, staring up with shining eyes as she said, "Welcome home, brother."

She was petite, she was slender and shapely, she was beautiful, and Alea's heart sank. *She's only his sister*, she thought wildly, *only Cordelia, his sister*. But now she knew the standard of beauty with which Magnus had grown up, knew it was everything she was not, and her heart sickened.

Then the other two stepped back from their brother's hug with equally wide grins, showing themselves to be two young men, one broad-shouldered and lean, the other slender and large-eyed but with an aura of power.

Magnus turned to the slighter one in the long robe, and Alea could see him restrain the words that came of themselves.

So did Gregory. He laughed. "Come, say it! 'How I have grown!' "

"I left you a stripling," Magnus said diplomatically, "and find you a man in full." He turned to the more muscular young man in doublet and hose. "And there is also somewhat more of you than there was when I left, Geoffrey."

"And of you." Geoffrey grinned up a foot at his older brother, his grin shading into a challenge. "Have you gained skill in fighting to equal it?"

A shadow darkened Magnus's face. "Many fights, brother, too many—though I cannot claim skill in their outcome."

Geoffrey stared in surprize, and there was a moment's awkward silence. Into it stepped a stocky young man, taller than Geoffrey but far shorter than Magnus, clasping Magnus's free hand in both of his own, saying, "Welcome indeed, brother-in-law."

But what was this? How could this great bulk of a man,

this indomitable warrior, this Magnus, HER Magnus, be bowing and saying, "My liege."

The blond's face twisted in pain. "Not your king yet, thank Heaven, Magnus. Come, rise and be my friend as ever you have been."

So this was Prince Alain, Alea noted. She surveyed the other three, naming them with information learned only in the last few weeks. Gregory was not so slender as Magnus had led her to believe—ten years had worked wonders indeed. Geoffrey was every bit as she had imagined him, muscular and seeming to be leashed mayhem even here with his family—but Cordelia was far more beautiful than Magnus's description had led her to believe.

In desperation, she turned to the two young women who stood by watching, but there was no relief in the sight of the brothers' newly-wed wives. The redhead stirred impatiently, and her skirt swirled, parting and revealing a flash of hose-clad thigh—the warrior, then, dressed so that her skirts should not get in the way when she mounted a horse. That meant that the one whose hair seemed white in the moonlight was . . . Alea braced herself, trying to hold down a growing anger.

Magnus straightened and embraced his old friend the prince. Alea realized he had made his point with skills hard-won, but of diplomacy, not fighting. As he stepped back, Cordelia caught Alain's arm and pressed against his side, saying, "Aye, embrace him as your brother, Magnus, not your prince."

"A year earlier and I could have come in time for your weddings," Magnus said, chagrined. "But at least . . ."

There was an awkward silence as everyone else filled in the words he had cut off: *At least Mother lived to see it.* The gloom of the occasion settled over the delight in Magnus's homecoming. Then Cordelia forced a smile and said, "I am not quite so badly outnumbered any more, Magnus. You have three sisters now." She turned to the other two women. "She with the fiery hair and the temper to match is Quicksilver."

The redhead stepped forward to take Geoffrey's arm with a proprietorial manner but extended the other to Magnus. "Welcome, brother."

Magnus took the hand with a flourish and pressed a kiss to it. Quicksilver's eyes widened with surprise, and Geoffrey's darkened, but before he could protest, Magnus released the hand and stepped back to look them up and down with a growing smile. "Well-matched, I should say—and a handsome couple indeed. I hope you shall be blessed with daughters, for they shall be paragons of beauty."

"What, brother!" Geoffrey said indignantly. "Will you wish me no sons?"

"As many as your lady can manage, Geoffrey," Magnus assured him, "for I doubt not they will be as turbulent as they will be handsome."

Quicksilver smiled. "Let them be holy terrors! I think I can deal with half a dozen at least."

Geoffrey looked at her in surprise, but Gregory cleared his throat, and Magnus looked up, then seemed to become still within his body, his smile a little more firm, even rigid, and Alea wondered if any but she realized he was bracing himself.

"Brother," Gregory said gravely as he led forth the stunning vision with the cloud of golden hair, "meet my bride, Allouette."

She stepped forward hesitantly, very hesitantly, seeming almost ready to run, eyes wide with apprehension. "You need not speak to me if you do not wish. We have already met."

Witch! Alea clamped her lips shut to keep the word in. This was she, this was the tormentor of her Magnus, the one who had tortured his heart, who had humiliated and shamed him. She was glad she did not know how the woman had maimed him, for she was having trouble enough keeping herself from rushing forward to strike the she-wolf down where she stood.

"Met you? I never have." Magnus took her hand, albeit somewhat stiffly, and her fingers lay in his palm as though they were lifeless—but his smile, though fixed, was still in place, and he actually managed to summon some warmth into his eyes. "I never met you with no guise but your own, and I must say it is far more fair than any illusion you projected."

Allouette blushed and lowered her gaze, and Alea knew

enough of men to realize that the gesture made her even more appealing—but Magnus seemed not to notice. She looked up, looked him squarely in the face. "Gregory has told me that when logic dictated my death, yours was one of the voices that spoke for mercy. I thank you for my life."

"And I you, for giving my brother the happiness that I thought would never be his." But Magnus still stood stiffly.

The silence was brief but awkward.

Then Magnus raised his head, looking around the little group, and asked, "Our father . . . is he . . ."

"By Mama's beside," Cordelia told him. "Not even for your homecoming would he leave her now—but I know he is almost as anxious for sight of you as he is for each breath of hers. Come, brother."

She started to turn away, but Magnus caught her arm. "No, wait. You must all meet my shield-mate." He turned to Alea with a smile of relief, but his eyes were haunted, pleading. She stared at him in shock, not understanding, but he only said, "How have you managed to find a shadow to cloak you, even here?"

"By full-moon light, when there is so much of you to cast that shadow?" Alea demanded. "How hard could that be?" She stepped forward nonetheless, gripping her staff to keep her hands from shaking, looking from Geoffrey to Gregory to Cordelia, and pointedly not at the ladies. "I am Alea, whom he took in from charity."

"Say rather, from an instinct for self-preservation!" Magnus protested, and explained to his sibs, "She has saved my life a dozen times at least."

"And you mine," Alea retorted.

"Ah, then," Geoffrey said softly, "there is already a deep bond between you."

Alea turned to him in surprise. Already? What did he mean, already? But Quicksilver was nodding, and Alea met her gaze. They stared straight into one another's eyes for a moment, and warrior recognized warrior. No, more—each knew how important the other's honor was to her, and knew in that instant that they would be able to trust one another in battle for the rest of their lives, no matter how much they quarreled in peacetime.

For they would quarrel, Alea felt sure of that—they would quarrel as naturally and easily as fox and hound. But she would never quarrel with Allouette, for if she once began, she would tear the witch apart.

Quicksilver laughed, a low, melodious, and somehow very reassuring sound. She reached out for Alea's hand, saying, "Come, battle-woman, for I think we shall be comrades in arms, you and I."

Alea thawed and stepped forward to take the offered hand, feeling a smile grow that she hadn't known had started, and turned to walk with the warrior.

"That staff is ash, or I miss my guess," Quicksilver said. "Did you season it long, or find it already sound?"

"I chose it from a fallen tree," Alea answered, and the two of them were off comparing aspects of weapons. Cordelia followed with a barely cloaked smile and caught Allouette's hand through the crook of her elbow, patting the fingers in reassurance.

But Gregory turned to Magnus, his face becoming grave. "Come, brother. Our mother awaits."

WHILE THE GALLOWGLASSES and their fiancées had been distracted with greeting, it had been easy enough to distract them a little further, to project a thought assuring that they would only notice one another, not a strange animal, and certainly not an alien—so Evanescent, stowaway from a distant planet, with a huge globe of a head and a catlike body far too small for it, padded down the gangway and scooted into the shelter of the surrounding trees. Once hidden, she turned to direct a thought at the spaceship's computer, wiping a segment of its memory; it would never remember her dashing down the ramp. She had deadened the sensors along her route between the hold and the airlock so that the computer hadn't been aware of her exit, but it never hurt to make sure.

That done, she folded her stubby legs beneath her, settling down to watch the humans' reunion and tasting the welter of their emotions. She was a very powerful telepath, easily more powerful than either of her two humans, even more powerful than Gregory—a trait that had served her species well in its scramble up the evolutionary ladder. Telepathy had warned them when enemies were coming; teleportation and levitation had made it possible for them to flee; telekinesis had made it unnecessary for them to develop hands. So she watched the humans' antics with amusement, enjoying the richness of their feelings. What constant diversion they supplied! How strange and delightful were their angers and hatreds and loves and delights! How subtle were the shadings of one emotion into another, how delightfully paradoxical their ability to feel several different urges at once, how admirable their ability to control them!

Joy was dominant in this reunion, but beneath it lay unease, not from Allouette alone but from each of the Gallowglass siblings as well—unease that Magnus's homecoming might shift the balance they had worked out between themselves, shock and concern to see how much he had aged in ten years, distress at the obvious ordeals he had survived, a lurking worry that those trials had made his vast mental powers even stronger than when he had left—and mystification at the tall willowy woman he had brought with him.

Evanescent smiled, amused as always by human foibles. She tasted the change in mood and marveled that the humans could become so somber simply at another's death, for her breed lost all interest in their sires and dams as soon as they were grown, barely mature. In turn, their mothers and fathers lost all interest in their offspring once they were past kittenhood. They wandered away from one another, and if they met a few months later, scarcely remembered who each other were.

So she lay watching, intrigued all over again by the strange emotions of these foolish people and wondering at their intensity. They cared so much, these silly two-legged creatures! Why did they let so many things matter to them so deeply? Didn't they know that life was brief, that nothing was of any real consequence when measured against the span of ages? She had probed the minds of her two and knew the answer—that they suspected how insignificant they were but refused to accept it and attacked life with all the greater determination.

She watched until the tallest one, the male whom she thought of as one of hers, turned to his spaceship and gave an order, whereupon the ramp slid back into the ship, the hatch closed, and the huge golden discus lifted silently from the earth, drifted up above the treetops, then shot away into the sky, dwindling to a dot, a point of light, then vanishing.

The humans strode away, but Evanescent lay still, following them with her mind, knowing she could trace them over hundreds of miles. She noticed that their apprehension deepened as they rode off—apprehension over their mother's impending death, but also over the new relationships they must forge with one another.

She decided she wanted to be closer to their destination and rose, stretched, then turned to trot after the riders—and stopped short, staring at the beings who confronted her, amazed that she'd had no slightest inkling of their approach. For the first time in decades, a worm of fear raised its head inside her.

Three

THEY LOOKED LIKE HUMANS, BUT WERE VERY
small, these strange creatures who faced Evanescent, vary-
ing from a foot to a foot and a half, and the one that stood
at their head was the biggest, both in muscle and in height.
He glared at the alien in anger and suspicion as he demanded, "What have you to do with my ward?"

Evanescent blinked, surprised by the creatures' sudden
appearance, then realized that she had been so intent on the
humans that she had missed the sounds and thoughts of
these small ones as they came up behind her. She smiled,
amused by their audacity. "Ward? How can so tall a creature as that be under your care?"

"Because he is my king's grandson," the small man
snapped, "and from the day the grandson was born, His
Majesty commanded me to watch and care for him—aye,
and for each of his sibs as they were born, too."

"An interesting command." Evanescent's smile widened.

"Do not show your teeth to me and think to cow me by
their threat!" the small one snapped, and the score at his

back chorused agreement. "I am the Puck, and all with any sense fear my whims!"

"If my smile displeases you, I shall veil it," Evanescent said equably. She knew that her shark-like teeth, once seen, were not easily forgotten, so did not mind closing her lips. "Still, I wonder how you could think to protect a man who is so much larger, and clearly much stronger, than yourself."

"By magic, of course." The little man and all his mates scowled intently as he aimed a finger at her.

A blow from an unseen hand rocked Evanescent back on her stub of a tail. She gasped, dizzy and frightened, her universe suddenly topsy-turvy. When it righted itself and stabilized, she knew it would never be completely firm again. No species but her own had ever been able to lash out at her with such force. "How . . . how did you . . ."

"By magic, as I said," the little man said impatiently, "magic of my own, and of the twenty-odd elves behind me. Be sure that I can do much worse, both in kind and in power—for I have more than two thousand years of knowledge and experience to draw on, and hundreds of thousands of elves to strengthen my spells. Tell me what you are, and from where you have come."

So they called themselves "elves" and guarded their minds well—Evanescent could barely catch a stray thought from any of them. But those thoughts were all of concern for the man they knew as Magnus, and anger at Evanescent for endangering him. She began to relax—they were only interested in the same thing, after all: Magnus's welfare. They were natural allies. She merely had to convince them of that.

Merely.

"I come from another world," she said, "one that circles a sun that is only a star among many in your sky. I came across your . . . ward . . . and his lady when they were trying to free the humans of my world from a would-be tyrant. I took an interest in them, for they were unlike any others—and saw that they were putting themselves in enormous danger. I followed to save them with my own—magic, if you wish to call it that—if it became necessary."

"Did it?" the little man demanded.

"Oh, yes." Evanescent smiled, then remembered just in time to keep her lips closed. "Necessary on that world, and on several others. I hid aboard their star-boat, you see, and went with them."

The little man frowned. "If you care so much for them, why did you not come down the ramp with them, rather than sneaking off like a thief in the night?"

Evanescent caught from his mind the image of a thief and had to throttle her own anger, remembering that to these little creatures, she was an unknown and threatening presence. "They do not know of me," she explained. "I have kept myself hidden from them, to keep them from relying upon my magic instead of their own cleverness."

"There is sense to that," a foot-tall woman said to Puck, and images escaped from her mind-shield, enough to show Evanescent that these little folk hid themselves from the humans, too, though as much from wariness as from refusal to be used.

But Puck was not so easily convinced. "You forsook your home and surely can have little hope of returning there. What kindled within you so great a liking for my ward and his leman that you were willing to leave all for their sake?"

"Fascination at their . . . efforts." Evanescent almost said "antics," but remembered in time that these small ones were prickly and that it behooved her to choose her words carefully. "It is quite unknown among my kind for a person to risk her welfare, to risk pain and even life for others— well, once they are no longer kittens—and is absolutely unthinkable to care in any way for people one knows not at all, to be concerned for them simply because they *are* people!"

"And thus did our Magnus?" Puck asked, frowning.

"Not simply that," Evanescent said. "He has gone from world to world, seeking out people who are miserable, almost as though he needs to have someone to care about!"

"So he does," Puck said slowly. "So do most of his kind. Still, even if such caring was a novelty to you, why would its attractions be so great as to make you leave your home?"

"But that is why," Evanescent explained. "Our home

means little to my kind. In fact, nothing means much to us, save food when we are hungry and mating in season and kittens when they are born."

An elf-woman shuddered. "What a dreary life!"

"So it is!" Evanescent turned to her, delighted that someone had seen the point; it would be far easier to explain. "When you've reared a litter or two, mated a few dozen times, tasted all the different meats our planet offers—why, you begin to grow bored and restless. We seek out more experiences, more sensations, even growing cruel in the pursuit—but after thirty or forty years, there seems little point even in cruelty or power. I wished to learn your ward's secret that keeps him so interested in life, so immune from my kind's ennui."

"Ssssooo!" The word echoed all around the glade in a hiss and a moan, and Puck nodded, face somber. "You joined them in search of relief from boredom, then. Do you truly wish to discover how to care about others?"

"Do you wish to keep living?" Evanescent countered.

The wee folk growled warning, spreading out to surround the cat-headed alien.

"I wish to keep living, too," Evanescent said quickly, "but I know I shall end my own life and its dreariness if I cannot learn what Gar and Alea know, what all their kind seem to know, perhaps even yours: how to find a reason for living, to find it in other people—yes, even people they do not know at all."

"And what will you do with this knowledge once you find it?" Puck demanded.

Evanescent stared, astounded that he should ask a question that had so obvious an answer. Then she shrugged. "I shall live."

"You shall do more than that," Puck said, "or you shall have learned nothing." He gave her a knowing smile, a nod, and turned away.

"We shall let her wander where she will, then?" an elf asked, frowning.

Puck nodded. "She is no threat to the folk of Gramarye, human or elfin, for she shall act only to keep Magnus and Alea alive—and will thereby help them achieve their goals." He looked back at Evanescent. "Is that not true, cat-head?"

Evanescent frowned. "True enough, bite-size. Indeed, there is some amusement in helping them without their knowledge."

"And since we know Magnus will not undertake any evil purpose . . ." The elf left the sentence hanging, still not happy.

"If he does, we shall speak to him most sternly," Puck returned, "though I cannot believe even ten years of harsh encounters can have changed our Magnus so much."

"You think rightly," Evanescent assured him. "He seeks only to help others and strikes out solely in his own defense—or to defend others. It is one more mystery to me—why he will strain so hard for goals that gain him nothing."

"Oh, he gains enough," Puck told her. "When you discover how his efforts enrich him, I shall be glad to discuss the asininity of it with you. You are welcome to the freedom of this land, star-farer. Do not abuse it."

Evanescent opened her mouth for a hot retort, then stared in amazement, for all the little people were gone, vanished in an instant. She closed her mouth and cocked her head, listening with a sense far more acute than mere ears and caught only fading chuckles, scraps of conversation. The Wee Folk seemed quite reassured now.

It was maddening, not to say insulting. There is, after all, something deflating about others deciding you're no threat.

THERE WERE HORSES waiting, so the Gallowglasses and their spouses rode out of the woodlands to the house that stood in the meadow beyond. Magnus drew rein in surprize. "They have come back to the cottage, then?"

Some cottage! Alea thought, mouth curving with irony. It was two stories tall with dormers peeking out from an attic, half-timbered and stucco-walled, with leaded windows that glowed with the light of a fire within, and candles on the floor above.

"Mama wanted to come back to the house where we grew up," Cordelia explained softly. "We were together for years here, after all, before Queen Catharine insisted we take the castle, and in spite of all the work and the exasperation we caused Mama, she said her happiest memories have soaked into the timbers of this house."

"I doubt it not," Magnus said softly, and urged his horse forward. "We were only in the castle for four years, after all, all of us together."

"Together, yes." Cordelia left it unsaid: *Before you deserted us,* but the sentiment hung in the air, and Magnus bowed his head as his horse carried him home.

Gregory pushed up beside him, murmuring, "Do not berate yourself, brother. Your absence gave Geoffrey room to grow."

He did not mention himself, Alea reflected, and could see from the ironic twist to Magnus's mouth that he realized it, too, though Gregory probably did not.

They dismounted at the door; hostlers appeared out of the shadows to take their horses. Magnus looked around at them in surprize. "Where are Puck and his kin?"

"About their nightly business, most likely," Gregory answered. "Come in, brother. The candle burns upstairs, and I doubt not that Papa is awake and watching even if Mama is asleep."

He opened the door and beckoned. Magnus followed, and it seemed to Alea that a mantle of doom settled over his shoulders. She stepped toward him automatically, reaching out to reassure, but Cordelia intercepted her deftly, steering her toward the sitting room and saying, "We must give them some minutes alone, must we not? Her first-born, after so many years."

"Yes . . . yes, of course." Alea let herself be led into the sitting room, turned to take a chair by the hearth, and sat gazing into the flames, mind and heart open to the young giant who walked up the stairs, alert for any call for support he might send—but none came. Finally she looked up at Cordelia—and at Quicksilver and Allouette. With a shock, she realized how neatly Magnus's sister had split her off to have her alone with the young women, and Alea knew at once what it meant. She braced herself for an interrogation, and for judgement.

Cordelia, however, only smiled gently and said, "Gregory has told us what Magnus has said of you, and of the rush of feeling that went with it. That seems so little, though, now that we actually see you."

"Rush of feeling?" Alea was instantly intent. "What feelings did he speak of?"

All three women exchanged a quick glance of surprize.

"Admiration," Cordelia said, "for your skill in battle, the sharpness of your tongue, and keenness of your wit—but also admiration for your face and form."

Alea gave a sharp, bitter laugh. "Face and form? A horsehead atop a beanpole? What could he admire in that?"

The women exchanged another surprized look, this one veiled; then Quicksilver turned back to Alea. "You know very little of yourself, damsel, if that is how you see your reflection."

"How shall I see my reflection," Alea asked bitterly, "when there is no mirror tall enough?"

"Almost as tall as Magnus, you mean?" Cordelia smiled. "Why would he want a minikin my size, when there is so much of him?"

Alea stared at her while she tried to quench a wild unreasoning hope, and had to lower her gaze to contain it. "No man wants a woman who's as tall as a tree . . ."

"Except a man who is a mountain," Quicksilver said, amused. "Besides, there is movement to mention."

"How?" Alea frowned. "What matters motion?"

Allouette made a small sound of exasperation.

"No, damsel, I do not know the workings of men's minds as you do!" Alea snapped. "I know only the result of your deeds—hurt that has burned so deeply that the wound can never heal and a heart locked away where none else can touch it!"

Allouette seemed to shrink where she sat, and Cordelia clasped her hand, saying to Alea, "That was unjust. It was not the woman you see before you who hurt my brother, but the she-wolf she was before my mother healed her."

"Indeed," Quicksilver seconded, "and we say that whom she assaulted, we from whom she tried to steal our beloveds."

"But failed!" Alea said hotly. "She did not fail in what she did to Magnus! I do not know what it is, I know only what I have guessed from the scraps of comments he has dropped now and again, but I know enough to gauge how deeply she has hurt him!"

"And how badly that has walled him from you?" Cordelia asked, her voice low.

Alea started to answer, but her voice caught in her throat and she had to shake her head angrily to clear the words. "I do not want that from him! Indeed, his loathing of sex, of any hint of it, was no doubt my protection in those first few months of our journeying together, when I was sure every man wanted to use me as his toy no matter how repellant I was, for I was at least female! To use but never to keep—and it took me long indeed to believe that your brother wanted my companionship and my welfare and finally my protection, but never my body! Aye, I suppose I should thank you for that." But her tone was bitter.

Allouette's eyes were wide and tragic, though, and she said softly, "One cripple healing another, then."

"Healing?" Alea snapped. "How can he be healing? Oh, I have tried, I suppose, much good it has done me—aye, much good indeed, when he has not healed a bit!" Then she stopped, staring in amazement at the words that had come from her lips.

"Do you wish him to be more to you, then, than a shield-mate in battle?" Cordelia asked gently, then answered her own question. "Of course you do, if you would see him fully healed."

"Aye, I wish it!" Alea cried. "But how can that be? I am not the sort of woman to be able to heal a man!"

"You are exactly the sort of woman to heal that man," Allouette said with certainty.

"To protect him, at least!" Alea turned on her. "Let none dare to strike at him again, for she shall meet two swords instead of one!"

"There is none here who will seek his hurt," Allouette assured her, voice low, but face composed with a serenity that discarded any possibility of fear.

By her very confidence, she struck doubt into Alea's heart, so that she spoke with more vehemence than she might have otherwise. "How can anyone be healed from wounds such as that!"

"By truth and kindness and forgiveness," Cordelia said, "even as our mother healed Allouette."

Alea turned to stare in surprize.

"She was most horrendously twisted from infancy on," Cordelia explained, "kidnapped from her real mother and reared by those who sought to fashion her as a tool for their own purposes—by people who knew exactly what they did and what pain they inflicted and cared not a whit, as long as it accomplished their ends. They twisted her and warped her into believing the world was far worse than it is, and no goodness possible."

"Twisted for their pleasures, too," Quicksilver said, her voice low.

Alea understood instantly what she meant, understood five possibilities on the instant, and winced at the thought.

"Do not feel sorry for me," Allouette said. "Do not pity me, for I deserve it not. What I did, I chose to do, and it does not matter that those choices were based on lies and on hatreds that were based on still more lies. It was nonetheless my decision, my choice, and I deserved every torture wreaked upon me."

"When the deeds came after the tortures?" Quicksilver snapped. "Be not so ingenuous, sister! You had not the ghost of a notion that you had any choice at all." She turned back to Alea. "Pity her indeed, for she was debased and humiliated so badly that I wonder she had any will to live. Forgive her, too, for when she learned the truth, remorse overwhelmed her, and threatens even now to drown her in spite of all the love and praise Gregory lavishes upon her."

Alea stared at Allouette, and the minutes stretched as Quicksilver and Cordelia held their breaths. Then, "I shall forgive you," Alea said, her voice cold, "when Magnus is healed."

"Do you see to it, then," Allouette said, "for only you can."

Cordelia and Quicksilver were still a moment more, then nodded, and Alea stared at the three of them, appalled and feeling completely helpless and inadequate.

A SINGLE CANDLE lit the room, showing the woman who lay propped up by pillows in the wide bed with the grieving, gray-haired man beside her, her hand in both of his, gaze never leaving her face. For a moment Magnus wondered who she was, then realized the shrunken, wrinkled face on the pillow was that of his mother. He froze in shock.

"Speak to her," Gregory said softly at his shoulder. "She will waken for you."

Magnus still stood unable to move as he heard the door close quietly behind him. At the sound, the old man looked up.

Four

ROD LAID HIS WIFE'S HAND ON THE BLANKET
and rose with a smile of welcome and pleasure stretching
the lines and creases of his face, a smile at the sight of his
eldest son—but a muted smile, struggling to emerge
through sadness, and through wrinkles that his son had
never seen. Rod Gallowglass held up his arms, and Magnus
leaned down to embrace his father.

After a few minutes, Rod's hold loosened; he stepped
back to gaze up at his son with pride. "You came," he said
softly, "you came in time."

"Praise Heaven." Magnus was surprised to find his own
voice shaky. "Are you . . . are you well, Papa?"

"As well as can be expected," Rod said sadly, and turned
to lead Magnus to the bedside. "Sit down, son, and tell her
you're home."

Magnus sat. For another moment, he felt he was looking
at a stranger again; then he saw the familiar features beneath the ravages of disease and took his mother's hand.
But such a frail hand, so wasted and bony! The eyes

opened, though; she frowned, puzzled, as she looked up at the hulking stranger beside her bed. Then she recognized her son, and her smile transformed her face. For a moment, the years fell away, and she was as he remembered her from his leave-taking. "You came," she said in the voice he recognized. "You came back." With great effort, she raised her arms a few inches.

Quickly, Magnus slid his arms under hers and leaned close to press her into a very gentle embrace.

Rod hovered near, anxiety warring with joy as he gazed upon his eldest and his wife. For a moment, his eyes clouded as he remembered the boisterous golden-haired toddler bouncing off the walls as he learned to levitate and the anxious young mother who rushed to collect him. Then the reality of the present became more important than memory, and he gazed upon the two with fond concern.

When Magnus let his mother go and laid her gently back on the pillow, she beamed up at him with pride and said, "Tell me, now. Tell me all that you have done."

"But you know it," he protested. "Gregory must have told you."

"Told me where you have been and what you were doing, yes." She seemed to tire simply with the effort of speaking. "How can a few hours' talk speak of years? He could not tell me how you were feeling, nor of the people who filled your life."

Slowly, then, Magnus began to tell her—not about the people of Melange or Oldeira or Midgard, but of the emotional ordeals he had passed through on their accounts, of his fellow disillusioned bachelor Dirk Dulaine, of their shared trials and triumphs, of Dirk's falling in love and staying behind as Magnus's ship lifted off to find yet another planet of oppressed souls to free, and finally of Alea and their growing friendship.

His mother listened, her hand in his, opening her eyes now and again to meet his gaze at a particularly telling remark, but always with that little smile of peace and pleasure in his presence—and Magnus knew she was listening as much to the emotions and images that crowded his mind as to the words he spoke. When he could see how badly she was tiring, though, he said, "Well, enough for now. I'll talk to you again tomorrow; there will be time."

"Perhaps." Her eyes opened again, looking directly into his, and for a moment he felt again the old power, the authority of this amazing woman who had borne, birthed, and reared him. "Bring her," she commanded. "This shield-mate of yours, this Alea. I must meet her."

Magnus knew she must be over-tiring herself. "Tomorrow . . ."

"There may not be a tomorrow, my son." She had to work hard to say the words. "Bring her now."

Magnus stared at her, feeling another wave of the tide of grief, but he thrust it back and closed his eyes, nodding, then reached out with a thought.

In the room below, Alea felt his plea and broke off in mid-sentence, staring at the sisters-in-law before her, then rose and rushed to the door without the slightest excuse or apology.

The women watched her go, then exchanged smiles. "We cannot blame her for lack of ceremony," Quicksilver said, "when he needs her so badly."

"Yes, but does he know that?" Cordelia asked. "He calls for her aid, but does he know he has come to need her?"

"Does she know she has come to need him?" Allouette countered.

"She will not admit it to herself if she does." But Cordelia was still smiling.

Quicksilver met that smile with one of her own. "She has come a long way toward healing, whether she knows it or not."

Allouette nodded. "She is ready to risk loving again."

"But is Magnus?" Cordelia's smile grew into a grin as she relished the thought of teasing her big brother.

But Allouette's face darkened with guilt. "Will he ever be?"

GEOFFREY ROSE AS Alea rushed out, and paced with her to the stairway. "First door on the left," he told her. "Godspeed."

"Thank you," Alea snapped, and rushed up the stairs, wondering why he bothered to wish her well.

She burst into the room and froze at the tableau that met her gaze—at her friend and shield-mate sitting hunched on a chair that was too low for him, holding the hand of the old woman in the bed, and the aged man who stood hovering across from Magnus. She realized they must be his parents, then dismissed them as unimportant and went to Magnus, light-footed and cautious.

He looked up at her, sensing her presence, and his gaze was a naked plea even as his voice said, "Alea, I would have you meet my mother, the Lady Gwendylon. Mother, this is my shield-mate Alea, who has fought beside me time and again and always given wise counsel."

"A pleasure, milady." Alea turned to the old woman. "Your son has been my . . ." There she froze, for the old woman's gaze held her own, the dim old eyes turning youthful and vibrant again, holding Alea in a bond that should have sent her screaming within herself, fighting to tear free—but there was something so soothing in those eyes, so understanding and sympathetic, that Alea almost welcomed the intrusion.

And intrusion it was, for Alea felt Gwendylon's mind blending with her own, reading the history of her life, of the anguish of her lover's desertion, the misery and grief at her parents' deaths, of the terror and rage at the treatment of the neighbors to whom the judge enslaved her, of fear and panic as she ran from them, and her wariness of the young giant who befriended her, a wariness that waned over the five years they traveled together as Alea learned to trust again, but never completely, never without the fear of betrayal, even though they saved one another's lives time and again, even though he withstood her tantrums and replied with reason and patience to her attacks and arguments . . .

Then the vibrance of the eyes faded, and they were only the rheumy old eyes of a dying woman—but the smile that blossomed beneath them seemed to enfold Alea in a gentle embrace even as Lady Gwendylon said, "I am glad my son has found so true a companion—and I thank you for his life."

"He has thanked me by saving mine," Alea assured her,

then wondered why she cared about the feelings of this stranger.

Lady Gwendylon turned to her husband; her fingers twitched in a shooing gesture. "Off with you, with both you men. We must talk of women's matters."

Alarm surged through Alea at being left alone with this stranger so soon after meeting her—but Gwendylon turned to gaze at Alea again, and Alea realized that the woman was anything but a stranger.

Rod came around the bed with a sigh, beckoning to Magnus. "Come along, son. There are times to argue with your mother, but this isn't one of them."

"But . . . but she is . . ." Magnus couldn't bring himself to say the word "weak."

"I shall find strength enough for this," Gwen assured him, and her voice was strong again. "Be off and tell your father what you have learned."

Magnus turned anxiously to Alea. "If there is the slightest need . . ."

"I will call you on the instant," Alea promised. "Remember, I have learned medicine in three different cultures. Trust me, Gar."

"I will." He pressed her hand.

She almost pulled away, for he seemed to speak of trust beyond caring for an invalid—but she held firm and even managed to smile into his eyes. Then his father took him by the arm and led him away. She watched them go, marveling that this dotard could have fathered a son whose head rose a foot and a half higher than his. Of course, he had probably been a few inches taller once himself, and Gar did tower over his brothers.

"Gar?" the old woman asked.

Alea turned back to her, feeling guilty that she had let herself be distracted. "He calls himself that when we land on a planet—Gar Pike. He began it to confuse spies from his former employers."

"SCENT, yes." Gwen's smile seemed to enfold her again. "I am glad he left his father's organization, though I could wish he had stayed at home. Still, he would not have met you, then, so it is well that he left."

"I am not so special as that," Alea protested, but she sat on the chair Gar had vacated anyway.

"To him you are," Gwen told her. "Tell me, how is his heart?"

Alea stared, frozen by the question—and its implications. She was only a friend! What should *she* know of Magnus's heart?

She could not say that to a dying mother, though. Instead, Alea chose her words carefully. "I can only guess, milady, for he is scarcely one to wear his heart on his sleeve."

"He was till he left here," Gwen said sadly, "but even in those few hours before he left for the stars, he had become . . . very private."

Alea leaned forward, frowning. "What had happened to him, milady?"

"You must hear that from him," his mother sighed, "for I shall not violate his confidence."

"I think I know some of it," Alea said, "and that it has to do with that witch downstairs."

Gwen smiled with gentle amusement; it seemed to require great effort. "All women in this house are witches, Alea, at least in local custom."

"Is that what your people call espers?" Alea nodded. "Gar has told me something of that—scarcely surprising, for people who know not how folk fly on broomsticks or read others' minds. Still, it is Allouette of whom I speak."

"Do not blame her for her beauty," Gwen said, still with the gentle, labored smile. "She is not now whom she was then—a murderess named Finister. I learned much of the mind in a few days, then labored mightily to show her how her life had been twisted by lies."

"I shall try to forgive her," Alea said, tight-lipped, "as Gar has—though I think not in his heart."

"He cannot, until his heart is healed," Gwen said sadly. "You must see to that for me, damsel, for I no longer have the strength."

Alea caught the meaning the old woman did not say— that she would not be here to do it. Still, the charge alarmed her. "I cannot finish your work for you, milady!"

"No, but you can finish your own." Gwen's hand stirred on the coverlet, reaching for Alea's. Almost against her will, Alea took it. There was some quality about this dying woman, some gentle authority that compelled obedience—almost like her own mother . . .

Alea purged the thought and said, "I can finish my own work, lady, but not yours."

" 'Tis work that only you can do," Gwen contradicted, then added, "I ask only that you finish what you have begun."

Alea frowned. "What have I begun?"

"To do for him what he has done for you," Gwen said simply.

Alea fought down unreasoning alarm to answer. "He has given me much of healing, aye, but he has done it by treating me as an equal, by teaching me what he knows."

"Only that?" Gwen asked, her voice a bare whisper.

Alea knew what the old woman was asking but refused to say it. "He has been a friend, a stalwart friend, and has given me some feeling of worth again, by . . ." She bit the words off.

"By treating you as though you are precious to him?" Gwen's head stirred in a faint nod. "Have you given him to know the same?"

"Surely he must . . ."

But the old woman's head stirred again, from side to side. "Men have to be told, damsel, or they will deny what they see and hear."

Well, Alea had to admit the truth of that. "A friend," she argued, "a precious friend, and nothing more."

"Go where your heart tells you," the old woman whispered, "or you shall never know the fullness of happiness."

"My heart tells me nothing," Alea snapped.

"Only because you will not hearken to it." The old eyes closed; Gwen sighed faintly. "You must learn to listen."

Alea felt anger and defiance at the order, but could not bear to speak it to a dying woman. Gwen knew her thoughts, though; a faint smile touched her lips, and her eyelids flickered in a knowing look, then closed again.

"Who tells me I must?" Alea challenged.

"Destiny," Gwen breathed, then relaxed so completely as to say without words, *Forgive me, but I am very tired and must rest now.*

How had Alea known that?

Perhaps Magnus's lessons in telepathy had worked better than she knew—or perhaps this old esper's mere presence increased the strength of Alea's talents. Either way, she knew the time for silence when she saw it—but she wasn't about to leave this new-found friend, either. She sat by the bed, the old woman's hand in her own, clinging to her for strength and warmth in the few hours left before Gwen should be taken from her.

AS MAGNUS CLOSED the door, he whispered to his father, "Why is she not in the most modern hospital on Terra?"

"Because her poor body won't take the acceleration of liftoff," Rod said sadly. "That's the opinion of the two best physicians in Gramarye."

Magnus frowned, puzzled for a moment, then asked with a touch of mockery, "You mean Cordelia and Gregory?"

"Yes, but Brother Aesculapius came from the monastery and confirmed the diagnosis," Rod said. "So did the Mother Superior of the Order of Cassettes."

"I thought Sister Paterna Testa refused that title."

"She did, but the convent's official now, so she has to be, too." Rod shook his head. "Under the circumstances, I'll trust her diagnosis more than his."

"What? A woman who specializes in psychiatric disorders?" Magnus's frown turned dangerous. "You don't mean . . ." Then he caught the implications of his own words and lifted his head, eyes widening in horror. "It's her nervous system!"

"That's part of it," Rod agreed, "but it's really her whole body. She's just wearing out, son."

"How can that be!"

"Because she's a quarter elven," Rod answered, and waited.

Magnus's mind spun furiously through the chain of

facts, trying to catch up with what his father had spent months absorbing. Yes, he knew his grandfather (who would never admit to the relationship but had been the darling of his childhood anyway) was half-elven, so his daughter was a quarter of the Old Blood—which in Gramarye, meant one-fourth witch moss, the strange local substance that could be molded by the thoughts of a projective telepath. Some unwitting telekinetic long ago had told tales of the Wee Folk, and blobs of fungus in the nearby forest had pulled together, shaped themselves into a form that could stand and walk, then turned more and more into an elf, one who could beget its own kind, one who had . . .

"Genes!" Magnus stared at his father. "The elves can reproduce, so their fashioning must have worked on so deep a level that the tele-sensitive fungus even formed chains of DNA!"

"Yes," Rod said softly, "and when that re-creation interacted with real human genes, it only modified them so that they became extremely long-lived . . ."

"But the elves live forever! Then should not mother . . ." Magnus's voice trailed off as a terrible suspicion occurred to him.

Rod watched him carefully, saw the realization in his eyes, and nodded. "When the witch-moss genes are outnumbered two to one, it seems they eventually break down. You might say they become overwhelmed by reality."

Magnus gazed at him, mind still reeling through possibilities. Then he said, "But couldn't Cordelia . . . I mean, if the genes have become faulty, couldn't she . . ."

"Remake them?" Rod nodded. "We thought of that—but by the time we did, the elven DNA had deteriorated so much that we couldn't be sure what they had been like."

"Then copy the human ones!" But Magnus had begun realizing the result before he finished the sentence.

Again, Rod nodded. "Which human ones—her mother's, or her grandmother's? In either event, what emerges might be viable, but it wouldn't be your mother."

"No, I see." Magnus's gaze wandered. "So her choice is to die, or to live, but not as herself."

"And you can be the one who tracks down a philosopher to ask how that's different from dying." Rod shook his head. "For me, all I know is that I'm losing the woman I love—but at least she gave me fair warning."

"As though she had any choice!"

"Didn't she?" Rod locked gazes with his son, and for a moment, his eyes burned with his old fatherly authority. "You think it's an accident that she was still alive when you landed?"

Magnus stared back at him, chilled. Then he said slowly, "She waited for me."

Rod nodded, not taking his gaze from his son's.

Magnus broke the lock and turned away, feeling numb. "Have I made her linger in agony, then?"

"No, she doesn't seem to be in any pain," Rod said, "just very tired—and that can be taken care of by long and frequent naps. Always terrifies me, though, because I never know for sure if she'll awaken . . ." His gaze wandered to the bedroom door. "She's been conscious for an awfully long time, now . . ."

Magnus gazed off into space, his mind touching Alea's. "No. She's sleeping again, and Alea won't let go of her hand for a second."

"I know how she feels." Rod's smile could almost have been one of fondness. "You choose your companions well, son. Come on, though—we'd better relieve her." He went back to Gwen's chamber.

Magnus followed, knowing that his father was in a rush to take his wife's other hand.

THE DOOR OPENED—and Alea looked up to see a dwarf enter. She stared, because he had the head and upper body of a big man, but very short arms and legs.

He met her glance with a grave nod. "God e'en, damsel."

Alea realized her rudeness and gave herself a shake. "Good evening, sir. I am Alea, Magnus's battle-companion."

"Road companion too, if Gregory's report holds true." The little man sat down opposite her. "I am Brom O'Berin, long a friend of this family."

"I am honored, sir."

"I, too." But Brom looked down at the sleeping woman, and his face creased in lines of guilt. "My fault," he muttered.

Alea frowned. "How can that be?"

Brom glanced at her in irritation. "Because her whole life is my fault!"

Five

NOW ALEA DID STARE AT HIM, REMEMBERING ALL
Magnus had said about his mother—only a sentence here
and there, but Alea had remembered them all and put them
together. "If that is so," she said slowly, "she must also thank
you for a very happy life and four wonderful children."

The little man stared at her, amazed, then slowly nodded. "There is truth in that—and aye, I may have had
something to do with her meeting a good man. Who
charmed your tongue, damsel?"

Alea blushed and looked down at Gwen. "It must have
been you, sir, for left to myself I am sharp-tongued and
shrewish."

"A shrew who digs toward the truth, then."

The door opened again, and they looked up to see Rod
coming into the room. He gave her a reassuring smile and
Brom a bob of his head; the little man stood, leaving the
chair for him. With a nod of thanks, Rod sat opposite
Alea, taking Gwen's other hand. "Thank you for watching,
damsel."

"My pleasure." Alea caught her breath at the irony of the word.

Rod smiled, seeming to understand. "A pity you couldn't have come a few years ago—but you were just meeting Magnus then, weren't you?"

Alea nodded, not trusting herself to speak.

Rod glanced at her keenly. "How long since you've slept?"

"Oh . . ." Alea counted backward in her head. "Eighteen hours."

"Better find a bedroom," Rod advised, then when she started to object, "We may need you later. I can't watch her the clock around by myself."

Flattered, Alea relinquished Gwen's hand. "Good night to you, then."

"And to you." Rod's smile was far warmer than a stranger should see. "See if you can get that big lug in the hall to lie down, too."

Alea couldn't help smiling. "He usually recognizes good advice."

"Gets that from his mother." Rod nodded sagely. "Sleep well."

"And you, sir." Alea turned away.

The dwarf laid a fatherly hand on Rod's shoulder. "Be of stout heart, lad. Her life has been good because of you."

Rod stared at him, then smiled sadly. "Wish I could be sure of that."

"You have always been slow to believe truth."

"Only when it comes to myself," Rod said, "but thanks, Brom."

"It is your due," the little man said, and turned to go with Alea. "If you begin to doze off, lad, call for another to watch in your stead."

Rod's voice stopped Alea at the door. "Damsel, by what name does my son call himself when he's planetside?"

"That depends on whether or not he thinks he's made a mistake," Alea answered. "Why? Did you change your name for each mission?"

Rod nodded. "I always tried to fit in with the local culture—that's why I chose the name 'Gallowglass' when I landed here." He smiled. "Never thought I'd use it for the rest of my life. What's Magnus's *nom de guerre*?"

"Gar Pike," she answered.

Rod gazed at her a moment, then nodded. "Appropriate."

Somehow, Alea knew he wasn't thinking of the fish. "His real name . . . it is d'Armand?"

"No, that's *my* real name." Rod still smiled. "His is 'Gallowglass.' Does he go by 'd'Armand' now?"

"Only if I press him."

"Do that more often," Rod advised. "Good night."

Alea stepped through the door, closed it softly behind her—and stared as the dwarf went over to Magnus, patting his hand and murmuring in a reassuring tone. Then Alea realized she was being rude and transferred her gaze to the young giant.

He looked up with a grave smile. "Your Majesty, this is Alea, my companion."

"We have met," the little man told Magnus.

Magnus nodded as though that made no difference. "Alea, this is Brom O'Berin, King of the Elves—and my grandfather."

The dwarf's head snapped back. "How didst thou know!"

"We figured it out before I was twelve," Magnus told him, amused.

"The Puck told you!"

"No, but he didn't deny it when we asked him." Magnus shrugged. "It made sense. Why else would you have visited so often? Especially on holidays . . ."

"Never tell thy mother!"

Magnus's smile faltered. "Wrong phrase just now, Your Majesty. Besides, she figured it out long ago."

Brom stared, amazed. "How many years?"

"I think it had something to do with the look on your face the first time you saw me," Magnus said.

"You were only twenty minutes old then!"

"Yes, but I saw the way you looked at Gregory when he was born, and I can imagine how much stronger it was the first time."

The conversation had allowed Alea time enough to

recover from the shock. She curtsied as she said, "I am honored to meet Your Majesty."

"Most excellently done," Brom said with approval, "and you must never do it again, for no mortals know me by that title—save those in this house, of course. To all others, I am only the queen's jester."

Now Alea did let herself stare. "Jester? But how . . ."

"Actually, they all know he's her privy counselor," Magnus explained, and turned back to Brom. "I don't think anyone has thought of you as a jester for thirty years."

Now Alea began to understand why Brom had thought his daughter's death was his fault. After all, he bore at least half the responsibility for her being alive in the first place, and if she hadn't lived, she wouldn't now be dying, would she?

Pure sophistry, of course. She wondered why a king would desire to take so much blame on himself, especially one who was king of elves, then realized that every good king had accepted responsibility for all his people's welfare, all his life. "It seems, Your Majesty," she said slowly, "that I must thank you for my life, too, and certainly thank you for saving it from ruin."

Brom stared, taken aback. "Why, how is that?"

"Because this young man wouldn't be alive without you." Alea nodded at Magnus. "He's the one who saved me when I was running for my life, fed me and taught me to fight and to read, and took me along to visit half a dozen new worlds."

Brom relaxed and looked Magnus up and down with approval. "You have done well, lad."

"Very well indeed," Magnus agreed, "for she has saved my life at least once on each of those worlds, not to mention the one on which she was born."

"Oh, I didn't save you there!"

"I seem to remember a pack of wild dogs, and the two of us standing back to back with our quarterstaves whirling . . ."

"Oh, *that*." Alea dismissed it with a wave. "He also realized I was a latent telepath, Majesty, and taught me how to use my talent—or at least, he has made a good beginning."

Brom stared at her, eyes glazing for a moment, and Alea felt his own thoughts brushing hers. Before she could object, the touch was gone and Brom was nodding. "Only a beginning indeed. This young woman can learn very much, Magnus."

"Then I have brought her to the right school," Magnus said with a smile.

"You have, and I will leave you to your lessons." Brom turned back to Alea. "He has not slept in thirty hours, has he?"

"Only in fits and starts," Alea admitted.

"On tenterhooks hoping you would not come too late?" Brom gave Magnus a penetrating glance. "Well, now you know you are here in time. Sleep, lad, and be sure we'll wake you if there is danger."

Magnus bowed his head gravely. "I thank Your Majesty."

Brom gave him a curt nod in reply and turned away, striding down the hall. Alea thought she heard him grumble, "Majesty, forsooth!!" before he turned a corner and was gone from sight.

Alone with Magnus, she couldn't keep the exhaustion from showing. "Have I a chamber of my own, Gar? I admit to feeling rather weary."

"Of course." Magnus offered his arm and led her to the end of the hall. "This is only a cottage, though a rather large one. At the castle, you would have your own suite, but here there's scarcely room. Don't worry, I'll sleep in the parlor."

It won't worry me if you don't, Alea thought in exasperation, then caught herself in horror. But it disappeared in an instant, for she noticed that Gar's arm was like wood, so tight was his self-control. Yes, definitely she needed to close a door between him and the rest of the world.

At the end of the hall, Magnus led Alea into a slope-ceilinged room with a narrow bed, a table and chair, and a wardrobe. The tapestries hiding one wall depicted knights in battle; another showed a scholar at his books, while behind him, the wall faded away into a view of an enchanted realm in which unicorns grazed and Pegasus flew. A third tapestry showed the ornate, powdery pinwheel of a spiral galaxy. She turned slowly, staring at the decorations, then realized that the hairbrush on the dresser was only a rectangle of wood, though polished and waxed. "This is the room where you grew up?"

"Till I was a teenager and we moved to the castle, yes."

Well, that explained why there was no crudely-drawn portrait of a pretty girl—though the presence of younger brothers and a sister who would surely have delighted in teasing might have explained it well enough.

With relief, Alea detached herself from Gar's arm and closed the door behind her.

Gar sank into one of the chairs and went limp.

Alea repressed the urge to kneel at his side and give what comfort she could; she knew that would only snap him back into his shell of self-control. Instead, she moved to the foot of the bed and sat opposite him, glad that the room was so small as to keep her near him. "It isn't just the lack of sleep."

"No," Magnus admitted. "It's all a bit of a shock, seeing my mother and father so much older, my little brothers and sister complete adults, and married . . ." His voice trailed off; he leaned his head back against the wall, closing his eyes.

He had never let that much weakness show in her presence—nor, she suspected, in anyone else's. More, she could feel him reaching out to her for reassurance, even the simple comfort of knowing he didn't have to face this ordeal alone.

It shocked her, though it only confirmed what she had known all along—well, after their first month of journeying together: that Magnus was only human, that he wasn't really a man of iron with no emotional needs, but a man who had locked himself into an iron shell—and that shell had cracked open now. *Careful,* she warned herself. An angry word, even a hint of mockery, and that shell would slam closed so tightly that she'd never be able to pry it open again. She didn't ask herself why she didn't want that—she only said, "I know it feels as though you're standing on the brink of an abyss, Gar—but you're not, really."

"Is that how you felt when your mother lay dying?" His eyes opened again.

Alea remembered that horrible day and shuddered. "That, and worse. But there was my father, that strong man so thoroughly terrified by the thought of losing her, so I had to hold myself together to be there for him."

"Yes." Magnus's eyes softened with compassion, and she knew he was thinking how horrified she must have been a few months later, when her father had died, too. "Yes, a grief-stricken parent is a lifeline for the daughter, isn't he? Or the son."

"We're not completely alone, no." Alea glanced at the door with a rueful smile. "Not that you would be in any event, with three siblings to keep you company." She started to mention their spouses, then remembered that one of them had been the cause of his leaving Gramarye, and stopped.

"Yes." Magnus followed her gaze. "It's odd to see them grown—but odder still to feel they're so much younger than I."

"Well, you have had a bit wider experience."

"Yes, but I can't say it's all that much more than they've had." Magnus shrugged. "Who knows what they've been going through?"

"I thought Gregory kept you abreast of the news."

"Yes, when he could establish a mind-link—an hour or so three or four times a year, if I was lucky. He let me know everything he thought important—but how much happened that he thought too minor to mention? Now here he is, no longer the teenager I've been seeing in my mind's eye— never mind that I knew he must have grown; that's how I remembered him."

Alea nodded. "It must be quite a shock to see him a young man now."

"Twenty-two—and that's quite mature in a medieval society."

"Yes, I know," Alea said drily.

Magnus frowned, suddenly aware of her needs again. "That's right, you were that age when we met, weren't you?"

Alea could have cursed; she wanted Magnus talking

about himself for a change. "No, somewhat older. I was twenty-four—your sister's age, now, isn't it?"

"No, if I'm twenty-eight, Cordelia is twenty-six," Magnus said.

Alea breathed a sigh of relief that the topic had shifted back to his family. "Then Geoffrey is twenty-four."

"Yes, and it makes me feel positively ancient."

"Old man nearing thirty, eh?"

She was rewarded with his old sardonic smile. "Yes, a doddering antique." Then his face clouded. "I should have been here to help, been here to insist Mama go to a hospital while there was still time!"

Alea frowned. "You don't know that much about medicine, do you?"

His face twisted, and his eyes hardened with the most intense anger she had ever seen in him. Frightened, she braced herself for a fight—but the anger faded as quickly as it had come, and Magnus bowed his head. "No, I've never been interested in more than a few field cures. Certainly I wouldn't have known what to do about such an exotic disease—and Papa told me that it seemed nothing but fatigue, at first . . ." His voice trailed off.

Alea waited, still shaken by his moment's anger but resolved to show the same patience that he had shown so often with her—though surely her anger could have been nothing like his own!

Could it?

She pushed the thought away and asked, "Why did you leave home, anyway?"

"To become my own man." Magnus raised his head, looking into her eyes again. The intensity returned, but now imploring her understanding.

"My father's very important here, you see," Magnus said, "the most prominent man in the kingdom after King Tuan, and my mother's perhaps even more important. It's hard to think much of yourself with them towering over you. I had to go away where no one knew me, didn't even know my name, and find what my own talents were, test my abilities, find out how much I could do by myself, without their having paved the way for me."

"And you couldn't do that here, where everyone knew who you were," Alea said slowly.

"Two feet taller than most men? I am rather hard to miss," Magnus said sourly. "So I went home to Maxima, the asteroid where my father was raised, to meet the relatives and find out what kind of people I'd come from."

"They must have been delighted to meet a kinsman they'd thought lost."

"No, they were afraid I'd come to claim part of the estate as inheritance," Magnus said sourly. "When they found out I hadn't, they gave me Herkimer out of guilt. I found the nearest red-light district then and went on a binge. I woke up in jail, then blundered my way into the very organization that my father belongs to."

Alea's breath hissed in. "Out of the frying pan . . . No, wait! That gave you the chance to find out how important he was off-planet!"

"Yes, it did—and he turned out to be one of their heroes." Magnus shook his head ruefully. "But I went along with it, absorbed their training, went out on a mission— and found I couldn't accept their trying to subvert the planet's government into their own form of democracy, whether or not it was right for the people there."

Alea lifted her head. "So you decided to go free people from bondage, but to help them develop whatever form of government was right for them."

Magnus nodded. "I've become fairly good at it, too, though I haven't become famous, the way my father had when he wasn't much older than I."

"No, you haven't." Alea smiled. "If you became famous, that would mean you'd failed, wouldn't it?"

Six

MAGNUS STARED AT HER A MINUTE, THEN BROKE into a genuine smile. "You're right. I am a secret agent, aren't I? And a secret agent who's no longer secret, isn't much use."

"No, he isn't." Alea shared his smile. "But you have built an amazing record—nine planets having developed stable governments of their own—governments that guarantee human rights."

"Well, eight," Magnus said. "You can't count Oldeira, after all."

"No—theirs wasn't our doing," Alea admitted. "A secret government is still a government, and it even guaranteed their rights. So you'll have to settle for having reformed eight worlds so far."

"Eight worlds—eight revolutions." Magnus nodded. "I suppose that's not such a bad record after all."

"Nearly superhuman, if you ask me," Alea said. "I see what you mean about becoming your own man. You've done different work than your father did, but done it just as well."

"Thank you." Magnus bowed his head, acknowledging the compliment—and angering Alea by his return to formality. It helped that he gave her his sardonic smile again. "Of course, my father was intent on turning every planet onto the path toward democracy, and each of the eight I've touched is developing its own local variation of democratic government."

"Yes, well, you've only succeeded in finding out that any government that guarantees civil rights is going to develop some way for its people to govern themselves," Alea said. "No, all in all, I'd say you've done quite well with your time away from home."

"It does seem to have served the purpose," Magnus admitted.

"But not for your brothers and sister," Alea said, frowning. "Hasn't your absence given them the same problem, left them in your parents' shadows?"

"One shadow." Magnus raised a forefinger. "My parents work so closely together that I've never been sure whether Papa was only successful because he had Mama behind him, or whether she wouldn't have made any difference to this land at all if he hadn't inspired her."

Alea felt her pulse quicken with hope and did her best to ignore it. "All the more difficult for your siblings to find out their true nature."

"That really seems to be more a problem for the eldest than for anyone else." Magnus gazed off into space, his smile turning nostalgic. "I remember when I was a teenager and my brothers were straining at the bonds of childhood, bursting into young manhood, that I felt a burning need to prove I knew more than they did, every time, every day—at the slightest sign of their having any knowledge beyond grammar school."

Alea's eyes rounded; she already had some notion of the younger Gallowglasses' abilities. "How long did that last?"

"Until I saw Geoffrey lead a troop of soldiers for the first time," Magnus said, "and until I overheard Gregory discussing the theory of magic with one of the monks from the monastery."

"Cordelia?"

"Well, she wasn't a boy, so I didn't feel her to be challenging me," Magnus said with a bleak smile. "Silly, isn't it? But I learned the truth of it when she healed me—or gave me the first stage of healing, I should say."

Alea could sense the revulsion, the turning away from the memory of the need for that healing, and knew it was something vital, something she would have to ferret out of him sooner or later.

Later. "So you can accept them as equals now?"

"Well, the impulse to argue and prove I know more is still there," Magnus admitted, "and probably always will be—but I've learned to fight it. I can accept the fact that Gregory has more knowledge of magic than I do, and Geoffrey more knowledge of war—and women."

Alea tried to ignore the anxiety the words raised. "And Cordelia?"

"More about people, more about healing, more about telekinesis," Magnus said, "and the list goes on. It isn't pleasant, but I've accepted it."

"You know more about subverting governments, though," Alea pointed out, "and about rebuilding them—with all the other kinds of knowledge that involves."

Magnus was still, staring into her eyes. Then he nodded slowly. "Yes, I do, don't I? Thank you, Alea. Thank you very much."

"My pleasure." Alea smiled, and finally dared to lean forward and catch his hand. "Who should know better than one who has learned with you?"

For a moment, they shared a smile, gazing into one another's eyes. Then that moment passed and Magnus stirred, looking away and breaking the connection as though it had become too strong for comfort. "It's late, and we're both drained. I must let you sleep."

Alea sighed with regret but forced a smile. "And I you. Good night, Gar. I hope you find a soft bed."

"Gar . . ." Magnus stopped in the doorway to turn back. "It's good to hear that name in this house—reminds me of who I have become."

"So long as you don't forget who you were," Alea said,

"or that the two together make up who you are. Good night."

The door closed behind him, and Alea sat alone in his boyhood sanctuary, surrounded by the mementos of his childhood ideals, feeling closer to Magnus in that moment than she ever had. In the last half-hour, he had told her more about himself than in the whole of the four years she had known him.

"MAGNUS, NOW!"

Magnus sat bolt upright in his pallet by the fire, heart hammering, whole body thrumming with the need to fight or flee. Then he felt the call, too—alarm and terror, and knew it was his father's. He threw back the quilt and scrambled to his feet, catching up a robe as he ran for the staircase.

Alea hovered outside the door of Gwen's room, not sure she should intrude. Through the open door, Magnus could see his brothers and sister kneeling by the bed—sleeping on the second floor, they had come seconds sooner than he himself. He caught Alea's hand as he passed, saying merely, "I need you."

Alea blinked, then hurried with him.

Gwen lay limp, hands on her breast, breath rasping in her throat. Magnus looked for a place to kneel, then stepped up behind his siblings and saw the grief already hollowing his father's face, saw the trembling hands, and moved quickly around the bed to kneel beside him.

Alea hovered at the foot of the bed, unsure of her place. She heard cloth rustle and turned to see Quicksilver come up beside her, knotting the cord around her robe, and Allouette beyond her.

A pang of fear turned her head toward the bed again, fear of loss that she knew came from Magnus. Gwen hadn't moved, but Alea saw her hand twitch as though trying to rise, saw Cordelia look up staring at her mother's face, then Geoffrey with eyes brimming, then Gregory, dry-eyed but trembling.

Magnus's head swiveled from Rod to his mother in surprize. After a moment, he nodded, reaching out to touch Gwen's hand.

Suddenly, Alea felt Gwen's mind in hers, heard her

voice, and knew that, though the body lacked strength to move, the mind could still quest. *Take care of him,* the thought said, and with a rush of emotion that almost overwhelmed her, Alea answered, *Madam, I shall.* Then she couldn't hold it back any longer; her own panic welled behind the thought: *Don't leave us!*

Gwen's children glanced at her in amazement.

I would I did not have to, the dying woman answered; then her touch was gone.

Magnus and his siblings stared at their mother.

Rod lifted his head, gaze fixed on her face, tears welling, hands clutching hers, and Alea knew he shared one last thought with his wife.

There was no visible sign, no sudden slackening of the body, no rattle in the throat, but Gwen dwindled as though she receded into distance, and was gone. There was one less person in the room, one less presence, one less soul.

Cordelia bowed her head over her hands, sobbing. Tears ran freely down Geoffrey's cheeks and finally welled from Gregory's eyes, though he knelt as stiffly as though carved in marble.

Alea felt Magnus's thoughts fasten to hers, felt the sudden clawing need, even as he turned to his father, arm out but not touching.

Rod knelt dry-eyed, though, face strangely empty; then his lips moved, and Alea could tell the thought: *Till I see you again.*

THERE WAS A great deal to do, and Magnus's siblings turned to it with the air of people carrying out plans already made. A hundred times Magnus had to bite back questions, then finally retired to a chair at the side of the house's central room, only able to watch. Alea realized it on the instant—she had been watching him like a hawk since he had come forth from Gwen's room—and sat by him, touching his hand. "Who is with your father now?'

Magnus looked up at her, startled, then nodded and went to the stairs, Alea right beside him.

Rod sat by Gwen's bed, gazing at her motionless face, his own almost as still. He looked up as Magnus entered, then reached out with a faint smile. "Thank you, son. I could use some company."

Magnus pressed his father's hand, then pulled up two chairs. He sat, and Alea sat beside him.

"It's good to have you here again," Rod said, "so good."

"Thank God I came in time, Papa!"

"I do." Rod nodded. "I do."

Then his gaze strayed to Gwen's face again.

Magnus and Alea sat in silence.

Rod sighed, shaking his head. "So many years wasted."

Magnus stared, scandalized.

"Twenty-eight years of my life, before I met her," Rod said. "Even if you don't count the first eighteen, that's ten years when I could have been with her but wasn't."

"None even knew of this planet then, Papa," Magnus reminded gently.

"True." Rod nodded. "That doesn't make those years any less empty, though." He shrugged. "I'd given up hope of ever falling in love with a woman who would fall in love with me—showed a horrible knack for falling in love with the wrong ones, in fact. Then I met your mother."

And the two sat quietly, listening in fascination as Rod told the story of his meeting with Gwen, of the slow realization of how much she had come to mean to him, of the sudden discovery that he was in love with her, and of their life together as a young couple.

Magnus listened intently, fascinated by all that he had never known of their early days, and Alea drank it all in, wanting every scrap she could have of this friend she had met too late.

THE COFFIN TOUCHED bottom, the pallbearers pulled up the silken ropes, and everyone waited for Rod to throw down the first handful of dirt, but he only stood, hands folded, musing as he gazed down at the oaken box. Finally, Magnus reached down for him, scooped up a handful of dirt, and threw it down.

Pebbles rattled on wood, and Rod looked up, startled, then nodded slowly and said to Magnus, "Thank you, son."

"My right," Magnus answered him, "and my honor. Come away, Papa."

Rod looked up at him with an amazingly peaceful smile. "Why not? After all, she'll always be with me no matter where I go."

A choked sob came from the mourners; Alea wondered if it were hers.

"Even so." Magnus turned his father away from the grave and began walking with him, back toward the house. "Bide with us, then—we who need to mourn, Papa."

"Of course." Rod nodded. "Not that it's really necessary, mind you—but it's fitting."

So they went down to the gate of the churchyard, where Magnus hovered watchfully as Rod mounted the tall black stallion that had carried him there. Magnus mounted his own horse, and the siblings and their spouses fell in behind him, then the rest of the entourage behind them.

Alea rode with them, as near Magnus as she could be, and wondered at the man and woman who rode in the black-draped coach with the gilded crown carved on the door.

SHE FOUND OUT who they were in the great room of the family cottage, where the mourners gathered for warmth and reassurance. Only a quarter of those who had come to the funeral stayed for the reception, of course, but that was still enough to fill the cottage's room. Alea threaded her way though to the kitchen, looked about for a tray, found one with glasses and a bottle, and took it to serve the guests, but Cordelia came through the door just as Alea approached it and smiled, stopping her with a gentle hand. "Leave that to the elves—they wish to honor their king's daughter, and their work is their tribute."

Alea sighed as she put the tray down. "I must have something to do!"

"Then stand by Magnus," Cordelia advised. "He will need you now as much as he ever did in battle."

Alea looked into her eyes for a second, saw there was far more there than Cordelia put into words, and nodded. "There is sense in that—but what will I say?"

"Whatever comes to mind. You've dealt with the grieving before, or I mistake quite."

Alea remembered sitting by the bed of a dying matriarch and nodded. "Yes, I think I can. Thank you."

She threaded her way back to Magnus and found him talking to the man and the woman from the coach. They were dressed in black, but their coronets gleamed all the brighter for it. Prince Alain stood beside them and looked up as Alea came near. He smiled with the warmth that would make his people love him and took her hand. "It is well you could be here, damsel. Mother and Father," he said, turning to the man and woman, "I would have you meet Magnus's companion, Alea."

"Welcome, damsel." The elegant woman with gold and silver hair held out a regal hand.

Before Alea could touch it, Alain said, "Damsel Alea, my mother and father, Queen Catharine and King Tuan."

Alea froze, staring at them, then dropped a curtsy, very glad that she hadn't touched the queen's hand. She did now, long enough to kiss it, and said, "I am honored to meet Your Majesties." She hadn't realized Magnus was so well connected.

"We were childhood friends," Magnus explained to her. "In fact, Alain came once to rescue us when we siblings had wandered off and become lost."

Queen Catharine's eyes sparked. "There may be such a thing as taking a friendship too far."

"Never, Mother," Alain said instantly. "After all, they have saved my life as often as I theirs."

"Yes, I'm looking forward to hearing those stories," Magnus said. "Gregory always glossed over the interesting parts."

"Such as our peril at the whirlpool of the afanc?" Alain smiled. "But how could I have been in any real danger with two doughty warlocks beside me?"

"The danger of a monster with sharp teeth baring them at you," Queen Catharine said instantly.

"Better that he has learned to face danger before it has come to war." King Tuan placed a mollifying hand on her arm, then turned to Magnus. "Though, if rebellion raises its many heads again, I trust you will be by his side."

The question caught Magnus off guard "I . . . I will if I am on this planet, Majesty."

Queen Catharine frowned. "Surely you will not be off on your travels again!"

"I . . . I had assumed that . . . of course, I would be about my work . . ."

"There is your labor." King Tuan nodded toward the fireplace.

Turning, Magnus saw his father standing alone by the hearth, an untouched wineglass in his hand, staring into the flames.

"I mistrust his composure," King Tuan said. "Be sure that I will do all I can for my old friend—but I must be far from here, in Runnymede. Surely the claims of blood are stronger than those of your mission."

"Especially since it is one you appointed for yourself," Alain added.

"Well . . . we haven't discovered the next planet that needs us . . ."

"Or have we?" Alea touched his arm, then stepped away and slipped between people to stand by Rod's side.

The room was full of bright chatter and muted laughter, people reassuring themselves that life could still be fulfilling without a friend they had always relied on. Rod was an island of silence there. Alea stepped up beside him and followed his gaze into the fire. "What pictures do you see in the flames?" she asked softly.

Seven

ROD LOOKED UP, SURPRIZED BY COMPANY, THEN smiled. "Those I saw when I was a child, damsel—fairy castles and shining knights fighting dragons."

Alea smiled, too. "Do you still cheer for the knights?"

"It depends on the dragon," Rod said. "I suspect you've faced your share of them."

"Literally? Only on one planet, and they were scarcely a few feet long—wyverns, really, not true dragons."

"A local life-form?" Professional interest quickened Rod's tone, and Alea wondered how much he had given up to remain on Gramarye.

Far less than he had gained, no doubt—but enough for nostalgia. "They were, but the colonists had tamed them—not that their descendants remembered, of course. Only a few still had the skill of writing."

"Typical retrograde colony." Rod nodded. "But the oral tradition held?"

"Yes, but in its usual garbled form." Alea said. "Space-ships were incomprehensible, so their legends only told that their ancestors had come from the stars and didn't say whether or not they had brought the wyverns with them."

"Medieval?" Rod asked.

Alea nodded. "I'm beginning to realize why Magnus understood the people so well."

"Yes, he grew up with knights and wizards on every side," Rod said, "but with Newton and Einstein and Hawking in his books. I think he was twelve before he realized that not everyone was reared with that blend."

"He wasn't caught between the two cultures?"

Rod shook his head. "Never saw the slightest conflict—but then, he had a very good tutor."

"Really! I would like to meet her. Who is she?"

"A him—sort of," Rod said. "My horse, Fess."

Alea stared at him, suddenly wondering if grief had unhinged him.

"He's a robot," Rod explained, "with a very powerful computer for a brain. In fact, when I was between stars, he piloted my ship."

"Oh!" Alea laughed with relief—and saw Rod's smile widen. "But if it's a robot, why do you say it's masculine?"

"It's the tone Fess takes." Rod shrugged. "Probably because I'm male, and all but one of his previous owners have been, too. Besides, it'd be a little awkward if you fell in love with your robot—though there are stories about my grandfather."

"Such as?" Alea was beginning to feel that the old man was trying to impress her in some way and was surprized to realize she was enjoying it.

"He went a little dotty in his dotage," Rod explained, "and started seeing the world as a medieval romance. He must have thought the serving robots were wenches, because he started making passes at them."

"Not really!"

"I've always wondered about that," Rod said, "after I grew up, anyway. Was he really delusional or just putting us all on?"

"When you grew up? What did you think of him when you were little?"

"That he was an awful lot of fun." Rod's gaze strayed to

Cordelia. "I hope my grandchildren think of me the same way." But he saddened.

Alea hurried to change the subject. "May I meet this cybernetic horse?"

"A.I., actually." Rod pulled his gaze back to her. "He's an artificial intelligence—though sometimes I wonder about the 'artificial' part. I'm sure he'd love to meet you. Maybe give you a ride, too."

"It wouldn't be the first time a male has taken me for a ride."

"Oh, really!" Rod frowned. "I think I'd better have a stern word with that son of mine."

"No, the problem with him is that he'd never even think of taking me for a ride."

"That's not entirely reassuring."

"Oh, you want him to think about it but not do it?" Alea rushed on so that she couldn't think about what she'd said. "You have every reason to be proud of him, *especially* in his conduct toward me."

"I suppose he does make you feel safe." Rod still seemed concerned.

"Dare I say he's a good boy?"

"Not if he's listening, you don't."

Alea laughed and spent the rest of the evening chatting with Magnus's father. When the guests had left and he bade her good night, then went to his room, Magnus took her aside and said, "Thank you for taking care of him."

"Taking care?" Alea asked in astonishment. "I thought he was keeping *me* company."

"Really!" Magnus seemed surprised.

"If he hadn't, I would have felt very awkward amidst all these strangers."

"Surely you didn't feel you were in the way!"

"Not with your father talking to me." Alea frowned. "It's surprizing how comfortable I felt with him."

"Yes . . . He was in good spirits, wasn't he?" Magnus frowned toward the stairs, brooding.

"He was putting on a good face." Alea's tone sharpened. "You don't think there's anything wrong with that, do you?"

"If that were all it was, no . . ."

"You don't think he's grieving enough?"

"You could say that." Magnus turned back to her, face creased with worry.

Alea stared at him in surprize, then realized what he wasn't saying. She touched his arm gently. "It's denial, Magnus. It will wear off."

"I hope so." Magnus turned to the stairs again. "I do hope so."

IT LASTED THE rest of that week, at least. The siblings agreed it would be better that Rod not stay in the house where he and Gwen had been young parents, so they moved back to the castle. It had happy memories, too, but they weren't so overwhelming. Rod seemed quite cheerful, quite relaxed about the matter, friendly and amiable, and went right to the room he had fitted out as a study (it had been the tower magazine). On his way, though, he told one of the servants to set up a bedroom for him in the room next door.

Other than that, he seemed quite content, poring over his books, adding a few lines to his history of Gramarye, or wandering around the castle with a very peaceful, contented look.

Magnus didn't like it. "You don't suppose he's gone back into shock, do you?"

Alea frowned. "He passed that almost at once and went into denial."

"He still is," Cordelia said. "One of us must speak to him and make sure of it."

Magnus didn't wait to be appointed. Dreading the conversation, he fell into step with his father as he wandered through the great hall. Frowning about, he said, "We must be thinking about Christmas."

"Christmas?" Rod blinked up at him. "It's scarcely September!"

"Aye, but the Yule log should be cut soon so that it may season well. Did we not always do that at the end of summer, Dad?"

"No, we usually waited till October," Rod said, but not with any sign of nostalgia, simply reporting a fact.

That gave Magnus gooseflesh. "Dad—I am glad that you are so peaceful . . ."

"But you wonder why?" Rod gave him a keen look. "It's because I know she's not really gone, son."

Denial! "But, Dad . . . she is no longer here . . ."

"No, she's gone away—but I know where."

Magnus stared at him. "You do?"

"Of course—to Tir Nan Og. Everybody knows that."

Magnus froze, as much as he could while still keeping pace with his father. Then he said, "Well, yes, every Celt knows that the dead go to the Land of Youth—but they stay there, Dad."

"Exactly! So all I have to do is find Tir Nan Og, and I'll have found Gwen." Rod's gaze strayed from his son's. "We only know it's in the west. I've been working through the old legends, but that's all I can find out about its location."

Magnus struggled within himself, weighing the kindness of letting Rod keep his illusions against the possibility of a "cure," of putting his father back in touch with the real world by confronting him with the truth—that his mother was dead, gone no doubt to Heaven, not Tir Nan Og, and couldn't come back. But he saw the look of peace on Rod's face, remembered his past spells of delusion, and opted in favor of sympathy.

When he told his siblings, Cordelia nodded with satisfaction and said, "The dream will sustain him until denial passes."

"Yes," said Gregory, "but then comes anger, and he is likely to seek her out to scold her for leaving him."

"A possibility," Geoffrey admitted, "but let us see him across that bridge when he comes to it."

So, when all was said and done, they did nothing—but they kept a close eye on their father while they did it.

So did Alea, reminding Rod that he had promised to introduce her to his horse. Agreeably, Rod took her on a tour of the stables and brought her to the stall where his oldest friend spent his time with mechanical patience.

The black stallion stood with his head over the stable door, munching a mouthful of hay. Alea stared; if Rod hadn't told her what Fess was, she would never have guessed.

"You can stop the charade, Fess," Rod said. "She knows what you really are. He doesn't swallow the hay, Alea—just lets it fall out of his mouth. Horses aren't known for their table manners."

"One must keep up appearances, however," the black stallion reproved him.

Alea had to fight to keep from jumping out of her skin. Even forewarned, it was a shock to hear a horse speak.

"Ever concerned for the honor of the family," Rod sighed. "Fess, this is Alea, Magnus's companion."

"I am honored to meet you, Damsel Alea. I have heard of you from Gregory's reports."

"Well, I'm here to set the record straight." Alea managed a smile. "This kind gentleman tells me you were Gar's tutor—excuse me, I mean 'Magnus.' Gar is the alias he assumes when he lands on a planet to start another revolution."

"A wise precaution, and one that preserves the family's reputation," Fess agreed. "I was indeed Magnus's tutor and found him an excellent student."

"But as naughty as any little boy?"

"Rarely," Fess said. "He was aware that he had to set an example for his younger brothers and sister. In fact, one might say he seemed to feel responsible for their behavior."

Alea frowned. "I'll have to make sure he doesn't feel that way any more."

Rod smiled. "Good luck. Habits of thought that start that early are awfully hard to shake."

"Surely he realizes they're grown now!"

"Yes, but I do not think he acknowledges that they have become capable of assuming responsibility for their own lives," Fess told her, "especially since, when he left Gramarye, they were all still adolescents."

"He wasn't much more than that himself." Rod shook his head. "How could I ever have let him go?"

"Did you have a choice?" Alea covered a laugh. "I can imagine anyone trying to keep Gar from doing what he thought right!"

"It would have been counterproductive," the horse agreed. "You speak as one who knows."

"Oh, I've never known him to do anything he knew was wrong," Alea said. "Foolish, perhaps, but not wrong."

"And you attempted to stop him?"

Alea remembered Gar's exasperated search for a government on a planet where there seemed to be none. "No. But I did try to explain why it wouldn't do any good."

"Did he listen?"

"Of course not! But he found the facts for himself."

The horse nodded. "He is still Magnus, under the layers of experience he has accreted."

That, Alea was glad not to dispute—but the more they talked, the more she learned about the child who had been Magnus, and how much of that little boy was still there, carefully hidden and protected, inside the giant she knew.

As they discussed Fess's memories, though, Rod began to look nostalgic, then sad. Realizing that immersion in the past might not be the best thing for him at the moment, Alea ended the conversation and left the stable, telling Rod of her first meeting with Magnus. He was fascinated, so she went on to detail their wanderings on her home world of Midgard—and realized that it wasn't the wonders of the giants and dwarves that interested Rod, but the deeds of the boy who had grown into a very effective social engineer.

OVER THE NEXT few days, she had a chance for a conversation with each of Magnus's siblings and their spouses—though she kept avoiding Allouette. Rod strolled about the castle with a distant gaze and a soft smile; she came across him several times and, not liking his look of not being quite there, engaged him in conversation to bring him back to the here and now. Rod always proved capable of drawing laughter from her, and she returned the favor.

On the third evening, when the others had gone up to bed, she and Magnus sat by the fire talking a little longer—or rather, Alea talked, trying to draw Magnus out of brooding. Finally, exasperated, she said, "You're really not the most cheerful companion right now, Magnus. What's wrong?"

"I'm worried about him," Magnus told her, "about Papa."

"Yes, I know what you mean." Alea frowned. "He doesn't seem to be quite here all the time, does he?"

"No—and he's far too happy being wherever he is."

"You're worried that he might decide to stay there?" Alea shook her head. "He has children here, Magnus. Each of you gives him a stake in the real world. But he does have to work his way through his grief."

"Yes, if it doesn't unhinge him," Magnus said. "I hadn't thought to mention it, but he hasn't always been of excellent mental health."

"You mean he's had bouts of insanity?" Alea stared. "Surely not!"

"His psyche has taken a real battering over the years." Magnus's gaze strayed to the fire. "The worst was when his enemies managed to feed him a chestnut made of witchmoss."

Alea froze in horror.

"We all ate them," Magnus said, "but a quarter of Mama's genes were made of witch-moss anyway, and ours were an eighth, so it did us no harm. With Papa, however, it sent him into delusions, and it took Mama a while to figure out how to cure him."

"He . . . he wasn't dangerous, was he?"

"He could have been, I suppose," Magnus said, "but we had elves watching him wherever he went, and I was old enough to shadow him and come running when I was needed. Mama restored him to his senses—she was always a very stabilizing influence."

"And she's not here any more," Alea whispered.

"No. I'm not sure Papa realizes that." Magnus held up a palm. "Oh, I'm sure he won't become a danger to anyone—but I don't think it's good for him to be lost in the past."

"Give him time," Alea counseled. "Give him time."

THE NEXT MORNING, a mental clamor awakened Alea. She sat bolt-upright in bed, hearing Magnus and his siblings exchanging emergency cries: *He has saddled Fess! He rides toward the gatehouse! Stop him!*

Alea scrambled to pull on a dress, rammed her feet into her boots, and ran down the stairs.

She came out into the courtyard in time to see Magnus dashing to the gatehouse tunnel just in time to cut off Fess. The great black horse drew to a halt.

Alea ran to join him. Cordelia and Quicksilver beat her to it, but not by much. Alain, Geoffrey, and Gregory came up right behind her with Allouette behind them.

"You've come out to see me off!" Rod smiled around at his children and in-laws. "That's awfully good of you."

"Not at all, Dad," Magnus panted. "Planning to . . . be gone long?"

"As long as it takes." Rod reached behind and slapped a bulging saddlebag. "Don't worry, I've packed the necessities."

"Yes, and you're quite adept at hunting and camping, I know." Magnus glanced at his brothers and sister, all trying to hide their alarm. He glanced back at Rod. "So if you've packed that much, you must be planning a long trip."

Rod shrugged and said again, "As long as it takes."

"May I . . . ask your destination?"

"Tir Nan Og."

The siblings froze and Alea shared their horror. Tir Nan Og may have been the Celtic Land of Eternal Youth—but it was also the Land of the Dead.

Rod saw their fear for him and leaned down with a gentle smile. "She's out there somewhere, children. She's gone to Tir Nan Og, and someone somewhere among the living will know where it lies."

Cordelia's thought fairly shrieked: *Denial!*

Magnus was very still for a moment. Then he said, "Of course."

Cordelia whirled to glare at him in disbelief. Quicksilver looked to be on the verge of rage, and the brothers stared at Magnus as though he'd taken leave of his senses—but the alarm faded from Alain's face. He lifted his head slowly, then nodded.

Magnus darted a look of appeal to them all that clearly said, *Trust me,* then turned back to his father. "Yes, of course, you have to go search for her. It's fitting, after all."

Rod frowned. "Fitting?"

"Of course," Magnus said, "You spent the first thirty years of your life looking for her. It's appropriate that you spend the last in the same search."

Rod nodded, pleased. "I'm glad you understand."

"It does give your life a certain symmetry," Magnus said. "You will—write home often?"

"Oh, of course." Rod frowned, concerned, and leaned down to rest a hand on his son's shoulder. "Don't for a moment think that I'm leaving you." He turned to his other children. "You know I love you all very much, and if you have the slightest need of me, I'll be back in a second—but I have to do this."

Allouette stifled a sob, and Cordelia swallowed tears, but they both nodded.

"How shall we reach you if we need you?" Quicksilver asked.

"By telepathy, of course," Rod said, "and you can always ask the elves where I am. I'm not foolish enough to think that I can go wandering through Gramarye without a pixie having an eye on me every step of the way."

"The Wee Folk have always been your allies," Magnus agreed, and stepped aside, reaching up to clasp his father's hand. "Go well, Dad."

"Stay well, son." But Rod held his hand fast, anxiety creasing his face. "You'll take care of them for me, won't you? The people of Gramarye, I mean."

Magnus froze. His siblings' heads whipped about to stare at him in shock.

"I won't try to foist off a democratic government on them," Magnus warned.

Rod nodded complacently. "That's all right, son. I only ask that you protect them from any other agents who are trying to steer them into governments that are wrong for them—particularly the anarchists and totalitarians."

"Well, of course," Magnus said. "I mean, if I want to protect them from democracy if it's wrong for them, of course I'll protect them from anything else that's wrong, too."

"Why Magnus, Papa?" Cordelia demanded. "Why give him the job?"

"Because he's had more than ten years' practice over-hauling governments." Rod touched her hand. "I know you have every concern for the people's welfare, darling, and Geoffrey, you'll protect them from any kind of armed inva-sion . . ."

Geoffrey nodded stiffly.

". . . and Gregory, that you'll figure out how to fend off any magical attacks—but governments are Magnus's spe-cialty now."

"I hadn't thought of it that way, Dad," Magnus said slowly.

"I was a bit late acknowledging my own abilities, too," Rod told him, then leaned down to kiss Cordelia and straightened up to clasp Geoffrey's hand, then Gregory's. "You know I'll be thinking about you constantly. If you need me, just spare me a thought."

"We will, Papa," Cordelia said, voice thick with tears.

Rod nodded, satisfied. "I'll be home for Christmas, if I haven't found her by then. Take care of each other, chil-dren."

"We will, Papa," Gregory assured him.

Rod gave them all a radiant smile, then turned his head forward and kicked his heels into Fess's sides. The great black horse stepped forward, saying, "Excuse me, Magnus."

"Yes, of course." Magnus stepped aside. "Godspeed, Dad."

"Godspeed," everyone called.

Rod waved and rode into the gatehouse tunnel.

Cordelia whirled to a nearby guard, snatched his spear, leaped astride it and rose circling toward the battlements.

Alea stared; she had never seen such a sight.

Gregory threw his arm around Alouette's waist; Geof-frey caught up with Quicksilver. With twin claps of thun-der, they disappeared.

Alea stared. "What happened to them?"

"They've teleported up to the battlements," Magnus told her. "Would you like to ride the way Quicksilver did, or would you prefer to run?"

"I'll go the slow way, if you don't mind," Alea said, "but don't let me keep you."

"Thank you," Magnus said, and disappeared in a minor explosion of his own.

Alea darted for the stairs to the battlements and ran up. She came out, gasping for breath, to see the brothers, sister, and spouses lined up by the battlements. She managed one more sprint to Magnus's side and watched the lone figure riding toward the woods. Dimly, she heard the sound of plucked strings.

"He's still not much of a musician," Geoffrey said.

Magnus smiled. "Your talent, brother, not ours."

"He has slipped into delusions again, of course," Cordelia said.

Magnus nodded. "There's no reason to think he'll be dangerous, though—neither to anyone else nor to himself."

"I think not," Geoffrey said, frowning. "After all, he's quite sane—except for this delusion that he can find Mama somewhere out there."

"The wandering will do him no harm," Gregory said, "and if this is his way of working through his grief, all well and good."

"It's really none of our business," Magnus said.

"*Everything* having to do with him is our business," Cordelia corrected him, "but it's not our place to tell him what he can and can't do."

"No," Magnus agreed. "He is a grown man, after all, and in good health—almost."

The tiny figure turned back to wave just before the road went into the forest and the leaves swallowed him up. The whole party on the wall waved back until their arms drooped in dejection. Then Geoffrey turned to Magnus, jaw jutting in defiance. "And will you seek to rule us now?"

"Of course not," Magnus said. "After all, I haven't had much luck with that since you turned twelve."

Geoffrey stared at him, then slowly smiled. "Not that it kept you from trying."

"Give me credit for having gained some maturity in my travels, brother." Magnus returned the smile. "Besides, I'm quite well aware that I am, shall we say, rather behind in recent history as it has happened in Gramarye. You surely know your own tasks better than I."

Gregory frowned and said to Geoffrey, "He says it too easily."

"Dad only told me to fend off foreign agents who might try to subvert Gramarye into following their own forms of government," Magnus reminded him. "He didn't say a single word about giving you orders."

"I'm glad you see that." But Cordelia frowned, searching his face, then turned to Alea in exasperation. "Does he mean it?"

"I can't honestly say that I've ever seen him do much in the way of giving orders," Alea said slowly. "Suggestions, yes, and he can be very persuasive—but outright orders, no."

Gregory and Geoffrey looked somewhat reassured, but Cordelia didn't look at all convinced—nor did Quicksilver, and Allouette seemed doubtful.

Magnus turned from face to face, then settled on Alain's. Slowly, he knelt.

Eight

"WHAT DO YOU DO!" ALAIN CRIED. "ON YOUR feet, man!"

"*Your* man," Magnus said. "I swore fealty to your father ten years ago when he knighted me, and I swear it now to you, Prince of Gramarye. I am your man and will answer to your commands, no matter the cost to me. Call me at will; I swear my loyalty to you, by Oak, Ash, and Thorn."

They were all very still for a moment, staring at Magnus—and at Alain, for his gaze was locked with his subject's as the softness faded from his face, faded until he was deadly serious as he nodded. "I am your liege lord, and will provide for you and protect you at need. Rise, Sir Magnus."

Magnus stood up, tall and straight before his future king.

No one said it, but all of them realized that Magnus had committed himself to staying on Gramarye. Like it or not, he was home for good.

* * *

"THIS IS NOT the kind of issue to use as a plaything," Geoffrey said.

"Not a bit," Gregory agreed, "and Magnus knows that far too well to use it as a persuasive tool. He would not mock so solemn a ceremony or give a frivolous oath. He meant what he said."

The two brothers sat in the sitting room of Gregory's suite, alone together for a few minutes, the bottle that was their pretext for going aside sitting uncorked between them, their goblets half-full.

Geoffrey nodded. "Of course, that means that when Alain becomes king and Cordelia queen, Magnus will take orders from her."

"His kneeling was as much a declaration of that as of obedience to Alain," Gregory agreed, looking very thoughtful. "I think he meant to reassure us on that very point. It will stick in his craw; he will hate the taking of orders from his little sister, but he will do it. He is sincere in what he says; he will not try to command us."

"Perhaps," Geoffrey said, "but I think I had better make sure."

AS ROD RODE into the forest, he had the feeling of a huge weight lifting from his shoulders. The kingdom was no longer his care. "I'm a free wanderer again, Fess."

"Yes, and the best kind," the horse answered, "one who has a castle for a home whenever he wants it."

"Do I infer a charge of hypocrisy there?"

"More likely a statement that you are playing at resuming your youthful life," Fess said.

"Touché." Rod winced. "And there is the little problem of having dumped that load of responsibility on my boy."

"He is a grown man now, Rod, and equal to the task."

"And I'm not?" Rod said. "Well, I suppose I am a little over the hill."

"I am sure Magnus will call upon you if he has need of advice," Fess said complacently, "but having engineered revolutions on eight planets, I scarcely think he will."

"Yes, but this is his home world." Rod frowned with a trace of anxiety. "That might impair his objectivity."

"Not a bad thing, so long as it doesn't impair the clarity of his vision," Fess said. "Besides, giving him the charge was the only way you could be sure he wouldn't leave again."

"Well, I do want him around until I find Tir Nan Og," Rod admitted. "Something secure in knowing all your children are in shouting range when Christmas comes."

"You also have the young lady in mind, have you not?"

"Yes." Rod nodded, feeling part of the weight settle back on his shoulders. "They're so right for each other, but both bound and determined not to see it."

"They are ready for the final stages of working through their recovery, Rod."

"Been doing a little mind-peeking, have you?"

"I am not a telepath, Rod; though I can communicate with you and your offspring, I can broach no one else's mind. No, I have simply listened to every word that was said and remembered them all."

"And put them together into patterns the two of them thought they were hiding? I can't criticize that." Rod gazed off into the trees. "I know what maimed Magnus—but I wonder what trauma made Alea so shy of romance."

"Whatever it was, Rod, it taught her that men are not to be trusted—though Magnus seems to have taught her that he, at least, is."

"The exception that proves the rule—but she only needs one." Rod nodded. "Of course, she's still denying her own beauty—but nobody ever accused Magnus of being handsome. Not after he grew up, at least."

"Ugly men are no less apt than handsome ones, to fall in love with beautiful women."

"Or plain women with handsome men," Rod agreed, "not that that has anything to do with these two. Whatever is attracting them to one another, it's not physical beauty."

"No, Rod, I think Magnus admires Alea for her character—courage and steadfastness, perhaps even compassion."

"Yes, but whether she knows it or not, she has her own kind of classical beauty, and I don't think Magnus is immune to it."

"I beg to differ, Rod. I do not think your son admits to the physical attraction he so obviously feels."

"Obvious to you, maybe," Rod countered, "not to some of us who don't notice the miniscule clues you seem to find. Okay, so there's some physical attraction between them, but I think most of what binds these two is shared danger that they've survived together."

"And in the process, learned that they can depend upon one another absolutely," Fess agreed.

"They have no doubt that they can count on one another when the chips are down." Rod nodded. "It's when the chips are *up* that they might have trouble."

"Perhaps, Rod, but that is no longer your concern."

"You kidding? The kids will *always* be my concern. However, I will admit there's nothing I can do about it right now." Rod shrugged the invisible weight off his shoulders and plucked another chord on his lap-harp. "I think I could manage another chorus of 'My Only Jo and Dearie-O.'"

"Why not?" Fess asked. "Only the wild things are listening."

"Look, I'm trying not to think about Magnus and Alea. At least the birds won't be critical." Rod began the rolling strum that underscored the words and began to sing, very softly and almost on key,

" 'Thy cheeks are of the rose's hue,
My only jo and dearie-o . . .' "

Truly enough, the birds did not criticize. Some of them, however, did remember urgent business elsewhere and left the vicinity.

IT BEGAN AS a rather somber breakfast, and Alea noticed that Magnus pointedly did not take the chair at the end of the table. His brothers and sister must have noticed it, too, because they seemed to be very wary, poised and waiting for him to try to order them about. She had a notion of the shouting match that would ensue and braced herself for it.

But Magnus said very little, only spreading preserves

on a roll and cutting his meat, glance flicking from one face to another, seeming relaxed and alert. Alea wondered that his siblings failed to notice how tense he was underneath the calm exterior—but apparently they did not; there must have been some rule in this family of telepaths that they not read one another's minds the least little bit without invitation or dire necessity.

Gregory turned to Magnus, and the mildness of his voice belied the tension in his body. "I take it you do not approve of the care Cordelia and I gave our mother, Magnus."

Alea sensed the anger that surged through Magnus at Gregory's impudence and the reminder of their mother's death, but felt also the immense tide of guilt that welled beneath it. None of that showed in his face, though. He was calm and urbane as he answered, "You did all that you could, my sibs, save to talk her into going to an off-planet hospital, and I'm sure that was not for lack of trying."

Slowly, Gregory nodded. "Mama could be most stubborn when she wished."

Geoffrey watched all three like a cat about to pounce.

"Besides," Cordelia said sharply, "what could an off-planet hospital have done? They knew nothing of witchmoss."

Magnus nodded. "If they had even caught the deterioration of her genes, they would have had no idea what to do about it—and when she died, they would have fought to keep her body as a specimen for research."

Cordelia shuddered, and her brothers winced.

"No," Magnus said softly, "I cannot fault your care in the slightest, nor her determination."

Brother and sister looked up in surprise. Then Cordelia frowned. "Why this attitude of blaming, then? Whom do you censure?"

"Myself," Magnus said, "for not being here."

Instantly, Gregory relented. "You would have caused strife by your mere presence, brother. After all, you could not have accepted Papa's authority as easily as the rest of us."

Magnus frowned, unsure what he meant but quite sure he resented it.

Cordelia's voice was low. "Even as you say, you could have done no more than we—but you would have ranted at Papa to do something, anything, and wasted Mama's strength with your pleas."

Magnus sat immobile.

Silence stretched taut in the room. Geoffrey grasped the edge of the table as though to vault over it—but Magnus finally nodded. "Perhaps I would have."

Cordelia reached out to place her hand over his. "We missed you sorely, brother—but we all understood your need to seek your destiny."

Magnus gave her a weary smile and nodded. "How ironic it will be if it turns out that destiny is here!"

Cordelia glanced at Alea but as quickly glanced away and said, "It could not have been, if you had not brought it home with you."

Magnus frowned, not understanding, but Geoffrey laughed softly. "Perhaps Papa is right—that your years of helping people rid themselves of tyrants and learning how to govern themselves have equipped you to ward the people of your homeland—even when that warding is simply to watch and do nothing."

This time it was Magnus who glanced at Alea; she managed a tremulous smile for him. He took that smile and gave it to his brothers and sister as he said, "Yes. I have, at least, learned some patience between the stars."

They all laughed then, and began to discuss the gossip of the day as they ate. They seemed to relax more and more as the meal went on, even beginning to trade quips.

"We shall have to see elf-sentries posted throughout the kingdom," Gregory said.

Cordelia laughed, a light and skipping sound. "They are already there, brother, all over. We have but to tell them what to watch for."

Geoffrey turned to Magnus, and there was an edge to his voice as he asked, "How think you we should deal with Papa's wandering, brother?"

Alea could feel Magnus's urge to give an order and the effort it cost him to bite it back. "I think he is no danger to himself or anyone else, Geoffrey, and is old enough to take care of himself. If I am wrong, I have no doubt the elves are capable of dealing with any difficulties until one of us can arrive."

"Surely they already know to keep watch over the Lord Warlock," Gregory agreed.

"Yes, and to pass word of his misadventures back to the Puck," Cordelia seconded.

Alea frowned. Had they so little faith in their father as that?

Then she remembered what Magnus had said about Rod's earlier spell of mental illness, about his children's agreement that he had slipped a cog during the funeral, and thought there might be no disrespect in their concern.

Then she found room to wonder what "the Puck" was.

Geoffrey noticed Magnus's silence, and his voice took on a challenging note again as he asked, "What think you, brother?"

Again, the urge to command and the effort it cost to quell that urge. Alea wondered if she were feeling Magnus's emotions with him or simply reading them from microscopic tremors in the muscles of the face she knew so well, perhaps better than his brothers or sister did.

No matter which—she knew his feelings, as his sibs apparently did not. They saw only the smooth, bland face he showed the public—and her own heart cried out at the wrongness of it. To have to guard oneself from one's sibs! If she had ever had a brother or sister, she would have treasured them dearly, made them confidants of her innermost secrets, as she had always longed to do! That was what brotherhood and sisterhood meant!

Wasn't it?

Magnus met Geoffrey's gaze, then slowly shook his head. "I think I have been away a long time, brother, and that much has changed while I have been gone."

"Surely not." Cordelia frowned. "Unless you think that I have aged!"

Magnus laughed softly. "Grown up, rather. When I left, you were still a teenager."

Cordelia stared in surprize, then laughed with him.

Geoffrey shook his head. "What could Mama and Papa

have been thinking, letting you go off on your own at such a young age?"

"I don't remember that I gave them much choice," Magnus said slowly.

Cordelia frowned at the willfulness in his tone. "Perhaps, but they did not have to be so encouraging!"

"Ah, but by encouraging, they made sure that I left with Fess to watch over me." Magnus raised a finger. "They saw me off with every advantage I could have—including my old tutor who, I doubt not, sent daily reports on my wellbeing and who was quite capable of defending me from any mess I might have worked my way into."

"Yes, but Fess was home before his messages arrived," Gregory pointed out. "His starship travels much faster than a tachyon beam, and he did not stay with you long."

"Not physically, no," Magnus said, "but when our cousins gave me Herkimer, Fess gave him a download of our complete family history before he left."

The others stared, then broke into laughter.

Magnus smiled, a small but satisfied curve of the lips.

"You didn't tell me that!" Alea protested.

Magnus shrugged. "I hadn't even thought of it again, until this conversation reminded me."

Alea's thoughts whirled, wondering how she could contact Herkimer for a complete account of Magnus's childhood and adolescence.

"How like Fess!" Geoffrey said. "The mother hen to the end."

"And does Herkimer remind you to carry your umbrella and wear a cloak in autumn?" Cordelia asked.

"No," Alea said, "I do that," then bit her tongue, wondering what she was doing intruding.

But the family laughed all the louder, and Quicksilver nodded. "Well done, damsel! Keep on!"

"I do think my brother needs a great deal of reminding," Cordelia said. "He never was overly careful to look after himself."

Magnus managed another small smile, but Alea could tell how much it cost him and tried not to shrink back in her chair. Then she reminded herself that if Magnus was really displeased, he could manage by himself—but was surprized at the surge of panic the thought brought.

The moment passed, and Magnus gave a fair imitation of actually enjoying her presence. "It was very lonely, after Dirk jumped ship and before Alea came."

"Yes, Gregory mentioned this friend Dirk." Cordelia frowned. "What was he like?"

Alea tried to hide her curiosity. She had wondered often about Dirk Dulaine and how close his relationship to Magnus had been.

Magnus shrugged. "Only another disillusioned, discontented bachelor like myself, sister."

Allouette was the one who seemed to shrink this time, but it was Quicksilver who said, "Then I suspect you whiled away the time between planets by discussing the perfidies of women."

"No, strangely." Magnus gazed off into space, mulling over a problem. "I suppose there was a tacit agreement not to discuss our attempts at romance. Besides, Dirk had a great deal more cause to be disillusioned than I had."

"How so?" Gregory asked, and Allouette stared in surprize, then was quick to look away.

Quicksilver turned to Gregory with a frown. "Did Magnus never mention this Dirk when you shared thoughts over light-years?"

Gregory shook his head. "There was little time and much to discuss." He scowled at Magnus. "You never did say much about your adventures, brother—only wanted to hear all that had happened at home."

"Of course," Magnus said. "Exiles always do."

"Say 'expatriates,' rather," Geoffrey corrected. "You left by your own choice. Certainly it was never ours!"

No resentment showed in Magnus's face, but Alea could feel it.

"And you did not think your own escapades were important?" Quicksilver demanded.

"Not to me." Magnus shrugged. "I already knew how they came out."

His siblings laughed, but Alea did not—she'd had altogether too much of Magnus's unwillingness to share his memories.

"Well, they are of interest to us," Alain said, "of great interest. Therefore tell us why this Dirk was disillusioned."

"Because he had devoted his life to helping free his people," Magnus said, "and had sacrificed all normal experiences to that goal. He never mentioned having fallen in love before we met, for example."

"That does not mean he did not," Allouette said.

"No, but it means he never tried to act upon it," Magnus answered. "He was only in his twenties, but he had been studying and working to free his people since he was eleven."

"As the two of you finally did," Gregory said.

"We did—and he found those very people had no place for him. He had lived off-planet, in the modern world, learning the skills he needed as a revolutionary." Magnus shook his head. "Learning—and working in the shipping line that amassed the wealth needed to fight the lords of Melange, his home world. The vast majority of his people had stayed planet-bound, downtrodden serfs with no education and no concept of the modern world."

"He came home and found it was no home for him," Allouette whispered, wide-eyed.

For once, Alea agreed with the witch. "Appalling, and most unjust! Surely there were others of his kind, though."

"Yes, and they all realized the most important work they could do for Melange was to keep up contact with the outside world," Magnus said, "to keep the supply of modern medicines and interstellar money flowing in."

"They were exiled for life!" Gregory exclaimed.

Magnus nodded. "Either that, or bound to the life of a common peasant—very hard for a man to accept, when he has lived in glittering cities and piloted a starship."

"No wonder he left his home to wander with you," Cordelia said.

"Yes, but even less wonder that when he fell in love, he was willing to stay on his lady's planet and make her home his," Magnus said.

"Of course, since he must have longed for a home of some sort," Gregory agreed.

"But it must have been very lonely for you," Quicksilver said.

Magnus nodded. "I was very glad to meet Alea."

Alea wasn't sure that was all that much a compliment under the circumstances, especially since Magnus did not reach out to her in the slightest way, not even to touch her hand when he said it—but she felt the fondness radiating from him, and under it, a desperate need so strong that it shocked her. Had it been there all along? She was amazed that none of his sibs seemed to notice—but perhaps they were all too polite to acknowledge it.

Or could Magnus somehow direct it only at her?

Or—stranger still, enough to make her heart flutter— was he even aware of the emotions that came to her?

THEY DISPERSED AFTER breakfast, each to his or her own duties—or if they had none, to leisure. For his part, Magnus opted to roam about the estate for a while, to visit the scenes of his youth. Alea recognized the excuse for what it was and came with him.

They wandered out through the gardens, Magnus telling her his memories of being a teenager there, Alea's gaze fastened to his face as she drank in every word—but when a row of lilacs screened them from the castle, he sank down on a bench and seemed to go limp.

Again, Alea knew how much it meant that he was willing to relax so much of his control with her, of the trust it proved—and the need for compassion. She sat beside him, hands in her lap, waiting.

Finally, Magnus said, "It's like walking a plank."

Alea waited, and when he said nothing further, asked, "Do you really feel they're all waiting for you to make one misstep?"

"Waiting for me to try to give an order, or to correct them or remind them how to behave, as I used to do when I was eighteen and Gregory twelve," Magnus said, "and ready to scold me or challenge me if I do, to prove they are grown and that I no longer have authority."

Alea frowned. "Perhaps it's because I've never had a sister—but isn't it obvious that you consider them your equals now?"

"I've read a book or two on the subject," Magnus sighed, "and apparently that isn't usually obvious to an older sib. I probably wouldn't have realized it myself if I hadn't read about it."

"But you have," Alea said. "Surely they have, too!"

"They haven't had empty hours weighing on them as they travelled between stars," Magnus said. "I gather their lives have been very full, every day." Sadness, bitterness, and envy showed in his face and were gone.

Alea felt it as a stab, that he still did not trust her enough to let such emotions show for more than an instant—but having seen him with his family, she realized how much even those flashes of feeling told about his confidence in her. Warmed by the thought, she said, "Travel can be tedious, yes—but your life has been very full, too, whenever you've landed on a new planet."

"Full of events," Magnus said, "not relationships." He turned to her. "That has been my choice, though. I have no right to feel bitter about it."

"You have when your choice was determined by the events of your past." Alea felt her own anger begin. "When having feelings for someone only let them use you and humiliate you, of course you would choose not to let that happen again!"

Magnus gazed into her eyes, and for a moment, Alea felt she was shrinking, that his eyes were growing almost to encompass her—but he spoke and was only a man again, one with a very tender voice. "And you—was that not your case, too, attraction only a tool that let someone use you?"

Alea started to answer, but the words caught in her throat and she turned away. "That doesn't matter—what happed to me. That doesn't matter at all, now."

"It does to me." Magnus dared to let his hand rest on hers. "It matters most greatly to me."

He waited, and she trembled within, longing to spill out the story with the flood of emotions, of infatuation and pain and shame—but no, not yet, not when he had so much to contend with . . .

Not when she still didn't trust him enough.

After all, how could Magnus think she was important? She was only a gawky, homely girl grown into a woman with no talent or skill, a peasant from an insignificant town in the outlands of a planet no one could find on a star map.

When she did not speak, Magnus lifted his hand and sat back. Afraid she had hurt him, she darted a quick glance at him, but he seemed restored somehow, full of confidence again, his smile open and warm without the slightest trace of pity but a great deal of caring. "We are shield-mates, after all," he said. "I have trusted my life to you, and will again."

Alea could only stare at him, wondering at what he had said, but even more at what he had not.

"IT'S GOOD TO have you back, sir," the Home Agent for Savoy and Bourbon said with her most winning smile.

"And a sad thing that I have to be," the Mocker snapped. "A fine mess you amateurs have made of the planet while I've been gone."

The Home Agent lost her smile for a moment and bit back a retort—that the Mocker hadn't done so well himself, when it had been his job to organize a rebellion against the Crown. Oh, he'd organized it well enough, but when they were almost ready for battle, the Lord Warlock had led a commando raid of three, tied up the Mocker, and let that half-dunce Tuan Loguire steal the Mocker's whole army and turn it against the anarchists—not a bad idea in itself, but considering they'd been trying to overthrow the queen at the time, not the best either. The Mocker also seemed to forget that he had been removed from his command in disgrace, not promoted to a desk job in the coordinating office.

But she remembered her priorities—ingratiating with senior officers always came first—and forced the smile back into place, making it as dreamy as she could. "There have been a few setbacks," she admitted.

"Well, let's see about setting them forward," the Mocker said as they went in the door.

They came into a large panelled room occupied by a long table and decorated with pictures of the great dictators of history. When the Home Agent sat, all the chairs were filled except the one at the head of the table. The Mocker sat and let himself savor the feeling of triumph for a moment, of vindication. What mattered a failure he couldn't have prevented? But now that he knew what he was up against, he would clear it away in days! He would have his revenge!

Then he thrust down the emotion and turned to assessing the situation. He surveyed the faces around him—some expectant, some clearly hiding worry, some completely bland, more skillfully hiding their emotions.

He nodded and said, "Understand—for you, it's been thirty years since my last foray against the Gallowglass clan, but for me, it's been scarcely a month."

"We do understand that," said a portly, middle-aged man. "I was a young recruit in your peasant uprising."

The Mocker frowned. "Name?"

"Dallan," the man said.

The Mocker's face went neutral to hide the shock. "Yes. I remember you."

Dallan's face turned bitter. "I've toiled in the ranks for the decades you've been gone."

"And think you should have been appointed Chief, hey? But the job needs perspective, Agent, not just experience—and I toiled in the VETO ranks for thirty years before I was given this post. Would have overthrown the monarchy neatly, too, if it hadn't been for the interference of that backstabber Gallowglass!"

"It was the coalition he put together that was too much for your army," said a motherly woman in her forties, "mostly that witch Gwendylon."

"Yes, well, he's lost her now, hasn't he?" the Mocker said with bitter satisfaction. "And lost all the influence she brought with her."

"He's made some connections of his own," said a man who seemed young until you looked closely.

"Connections his wife made for him," the motherly woman returned, "who will stand by him out of loyalty to her memory."

"Let's find out just how far that loyalty goes, shall we?" the Mocker said. "Start by sending out agents disguised as forest outlaws, to circulate in the villages and remind the people how badly they're being exploited."

"We've tried that," a pretty older woman said. "Whenever we manage to build a movement and gather some steam, Gallowglass sends one of his brats to hypnotize the people into thinking they're well-treated."

"Gallowglass, or his wife?" the Mocker asked with a sour smile. "Send out the agents and tell them to be ready to fade into the greenwood quickly if Gallowglass does send in his goons—but I don't think he will."

Dallan frowned. "Why not?"

"I don't think he'll have the heart," the Mocker said, "not with his wife gone. Who did you lot think was really running this land, anyway?"

WHEN HE WOKE the next morning, Rod chewed a heel of bread while he cooked the eggs he had found the evening before, and with them the strip of jerky that had been soaking all night. Breakfast done, he saddled Fess and rode down the woodland path. They had not gone far before Fess lifted his head, nostrils spread wide.

Rod knew the robot-horse didn't have a sense of smell as such—just an ability to analyze air molecules and detect anything that shouldn't be there. "What's wrong?"

"The smell of blood," Fess said.

Nine

ROD DREW HIS SWORD. "WHAT KIND OF BLOOD?"

"It is difficult to say when the molecules are so thinly spread," Fess answered, "but I am fairly certain that it is not human."

"Won't hurt to make sure. Follow your nose."

"I can scarcely do anything else, Rod, since it is so much farther in front than the rest of me."

"A point," Rod agreed. "Follow your scents."

"Technically, Rod, a robot has no sense."

"Nor do I, half the time," Rod sighed. "At the moment, though, I'll rely on your tracking ability."

They turned off the beaten track and broke through a screen of brush into a small clearing, where a boar lay on its side, blood spreading from a rip in its abdomen.

"It would seem we have found the loser in a fight over a female," Fess said.

But Rod dismounted and knelt beside the boar, inspecting the wound. Then he rose, shaking his head as he remounted.

"It was no tusk that made that wound, Fess. It was a blade with a serrated edge."

"Only a boar hunter, then?"

"If so, he was a very clumsy one—hunters meet a boar's charge head-on, or step aside and stab for the ribs and the heart. This poor beast must have staggered for hundreds of yards before it finally collapsed."

"Perhaps, then, the hunter is tracking it."

"Could be—the kill is fresh enough, only beginning to draw flies." Rod started to sheathe his sword, then thought better of it. "If that hunter is coming this way, I'd better be ready to meet him."

"People who hunt boar, Rod, generally do not hunt people."

"With some notable exceptions. England's William the Second was killed when he was out hunting, after all."

"With an arrow, not a boar-spear—and as I recall the incident, he was hunting deer at the time."

"Yeah, but his nobles were hunting him."

"It could have been a Saxon peasant who loosed that arrow, Rod."

"Or a nobleman who wanted it to look like a peasant's work."

"The peasants did have much to resent, so soon after the conquest," Fess mused.

"Yeah, but so did the noblemen, even if they were part of the invading force. William Rufus wasn't the wisest or most moderate of rulers."

So, happily bickering, they went back to the trail and on down it. After a while, Rod decided they must have passed the hunter, if he'd been tracking his prey—and the thought that he hadn't bothered gave Rod a chill; he didn't like men who killed solely for sport.

To banish the gloom, he took out his harp and plucked out a melody in a minor key as he rode, remembering other such journeys in his bachelor days, when he had been looking for something worth doing, looking for a woman he could fall in love with who would fall in love with him—and knowing he never would, that he was far too unattractive.

Incredibly, he actually had found such a woman. Even more incredibly, she had actually fallen in love with him. He marvelled how little had changed, for here he was riding down a woodland path alone, searching for her again.

A cawing broke into his reverie. He frowned, looking up into a tree at its source—and was astonished when the cawing shaped itself into words.

Three ravens sat high in a tree, where the branches thinned enough to let them survey the forest around them. "RAWK!" croaked the first. "I see a tasty morsel!"

"And I," cawed the second. "But we must wait for him to die."

"How, though, shall we decoy his hound?" a third asked. "Even his horse stands guard over him!"

Rod frowned. Someone lay dying? Not if he had anything to say about it. "Off to the right, Fess—that's the direction they're looking."

"As you say, Rod." The robot horse stepped off the path and picked his way between saplings and rotting stumps into a small clearing.

"CRAWK!" The third raven cried in alarm. "There comes a human doe!"

"As heavy with child as she may go," the second said in disappointment.

"Patience, brothers," said the first. "Perhaps the hound will drive her away."

But Rod came into the clearing in time to see the hound run to the woman, saw her stroke its head with words of praise even as she made her way toward the young man who lay, blood oozing from the shoulder joint of his armor, eyes closed and face pallid.

The young woman sank heavily to her knees with a cry of distress. She was indeed in the final weeks of pregnancy. "Oh, my Reginald!" she cried. "Live, my love, live! Do not leave me now!"

The young man's eyelids fluttered; he looked up at her a moment before his eyes closed as though the weight of the lids were too heavy a load for him to bear. The young woman gave a long, keening cry.

"Mayhap she will die with him," the first raven called hopefully.

Rod rode toward them, and the second raven saw and gave a loud, long caw of anger. "Brothers! A vital one comes within!"

"CLOSE THE DOOR," Durer said.

Aethel stepped through and shut the portal. The three other agents exchanged a glance, wondering why the rest of the cadre was shut out.

"Too many people make a discussion too cumbersome," Durer told them. "Everyone wants to say something, and nobody wants to listen. The five of us should be able to come up with a useful idea."

"An idea for what, Chief?" Aethel sat down with the others.

"A rebellion, of course! A coup to thrust that little snip off the throne and put our man on!"

Again the others exchanged a glance; the "little snip" was in her fifties.

"Not a chance of succeeding without one of the twelve great lords to lead it," Stan said, "and they're all too willful to let us guide them."

"Except the king's brother," Durer countered.

The others sat very still. Anselm Loguire had been the figurehead for Durer's last rebellion against Queen Catharine. The agents didn't even have to look at one another; they knew they were all thinking the same thing: *How long will it take him to stop living in the past?*

"Anselm Loguire isn't a lord any more," Orin said. "He's attainted—stripped of his title and estates."

"I know, and that witch Catharine gave them to her younger son," Durer snapped, "but the other lords all know that Anselm is really the rightful Duke Loguire and heir to all its estates."

"Maybe," said Aethel, "but they all know what happened to him, and that it was only because King Tuan counselled mercy that Anselm is still alive."

"Alive—and bitter," Durer pointed out. "He's probably long over his gratitude at being left alive and in charge of a small estate. He'll be angry with his brother and the queen—angry and wanting revenge."

"And wealth." Stan knew it didn't pay to argue with the boss for long.

"For his son," Aethel added.

Durer nodded, pleased to see them falling into line. "But we need something to push him, something to turn bitterness into action, something so strong that he won't care whether he lives or dies as long as he has a chance of bringing down the monarchy."

Everyone was quiet, each glancing at the others. Then Aethel hazarded, "A threat to his son?"

"LET US HOPE it is the knight's enemy," the first raven said.

"Aye, and that he will slay the fellow, then drive off his hound and take his horse," said the second.

"No such luck," Rod called back to them and hoped the young woman couldn't understand their words. He dismounted even as Fess stopped beside the fallen knight.

The young woman looked up in terror, then leaned across her husband to protect him, crying, "If you have come back to finish what you have begun, know you shall have to slay me, too!"

The hound crouched, baring its teeth and growling, and the horse stamped its hooves and neighed a warning.

"I did not begin this," Rod assured the young woman, "and I have some knowledge of healing. May I come near?"

Wild hope filled her eyes, and she struggled to straighten up. "If you can staunch the flow of his blood, aye!" She stroked the back of the hound's head, crooning, "Aye, you are a brave guardian, but, I hope, not needed now. Let the good man approach, Voyaunt, let him come nigh."

The hound sank to the ground; its growl receded deep into its throat, but it watched Rod with suspicious eyes.

Rod took his first-aid kit from his saddlebag and went to kneel on the other side of the knight. He unbuckled the shoulder-piece, asking, "What is his name, young woman, and your own?"

"He . . . he is Reginald de Versey, goodman, and I am his wife, Elise."

"I am Sir Rodney." Rod flashed her a smile. "No, I don't look like a knight, not in these travelling clothes, but I am one nonetheless." He pulled out his dagger.

The hound's growl rose as it did, rising ready to pounce.

"Easy, fellow," Rod crooned. "I draw the blade to save your master, not to slay him. Dame Elise, reassure him, if you will—I must cut away the cloth beneath to find the wound."

"Gently, Voyaunt, gently." Elise stroked the hound's neck but didn't sound too sure herself.

Fess stirred, and his words filled Rod's head through the implanted earphone. *If the hound springs, Rod, I shall block his way before he can reach you.*

"Nice to be able to concentrate on my work without worry," Rod muttered. "With luck, the wound won't have begun to, with *thanks, Fess*-ter."

"Pray not!" Elise said with a shudder.

Only my duty, Rod, the horse assured him.

Rod laid aside the padding and the blood-soaked linen shirt beneath. The rip was long and ugly. Rod frowned. "It was no sword that made this wound, Dame Elise, unless it had a serrated edge. Who did this knight come to confront?"

"He . . . he said he merely wished to patrol the park, Sir Rodney, for he thought there might have been poachers about."

"And he went against them without his game wardens?" Rod shook his head as he pulled out a cloth and a small bottle that looked as though it contained brandy but really held iodine. He poured some on the cloth and pressed it into the wound as he said, "A knight wouldn't wear armor to brace a few poachers."

"So I thought, but he said he must not become too accustomed to riding without the weight of steel plate." Elise's voice quavered. The hound growled at her anxiety, but she stroked it to calmness.

"If he meant to exercise, he would have gone to the tilt-yard." Rod placed over the wound a cloth that had been impregnated with antiseptic and clotting agent, then began to wind a bandage around it. "We'll take him home, and when I'm sure the flow has slackened, I'll stitch him up."

"Stitch?" Elise asked, wide-eyed.

Rod nodded. "Just as you would a torn garment." He realized that the young woman had been watching him carefully not just out of fear that he might harm her husband, but also to study how he cured the wound. He began to unbuckle the rest of the armor. "However, it won't help him to be carried back with this weight on him."

"Ahhh! He shells the sweetmeat for us!" cawed a voice high in a tree.

Rod cawed back, projecting thoughts with the sound. "Yes, but then I'm stealing him from you, greedy ones. Go seek a dead polecat for dinner!"

"Faugh! How unmannerly of you, to insult us so!"

"Oh, all right," Rod said, relenting. "I passed a dead boar half a mile back. Go stuff yourselves with pork." Even as he said it, he wondered if the same blade that had killed the boar had also wounded this knight.

"Ah! Many thanks for this kind information, human!" The ravens raised their wings.

"Wait!" Rod called. "A favor for a favor, information for information! Do you know the road to Tir Nan Og?"

"Tir Nan Og?" The third raven turned a blank stare to his mates.

"I have heard of it," the second said. " 'Tis the Land of Youth, the place the Wingless Ones think they go when they die."

"Fools! They come only to us." The first clacked his beak in contempt.

"Aren't ravens supposed to know everything that moves in Middle Earth?" Rod called.

"Belike, for there are ravens in every county," the third replied, "but how are we to know what a raven a thousand miles distant has seen?"

"He speaks of fable," the first said, and turned to Rod. " 'Tis not ravens you seek, bare-skin, but crows."

"Aye, two crows!" the second agreed. "Their names are Hugi and Munin, and they sit on the shoulders of the All-Father Odin."

"No, those aren't quite the feathered wizards I had in mind," Rod said with a smile. "Well, let me know if you do learn of that road from one of your friends."

"We shall, but we see them rarely," the first raven told him. "Where shall we find you, soft one?"

"Prithee let him be," said the second, "for with nonsense like his, he shall come to us soon enough."

"Or we to him," the third agreed. "Go your way, human, and be assured we shall find you when the time has come."

Rod managed to keep the smile in place. "Better make sure no one beats you to that boar, hadn't you?"

"Indeed!" All three ravens leaped into the air, beating their wings to rise above the treetops, then coasting down the wind toward the dead boar.

Shaking his head in disbelief, Rod turned back to the knight and his wife to find her staring at him in amazement. "I could almost have thought, sir, that you spoke to those birds!"

"I'm good at bird-calls," Rod told her, "and it worked—I got them to go away."

The lady shuddered. "I am right glad you did, for they are truly birds of ill omen!"

"Just creatures trying to make a living, like the rest of us." Rod inspected the bandage around the knight's shoulder. "His wound has clotted enough to make it safe to move him. Let's finish taking his armor off."

"A wise thought." The lady turned to husking her husband so efficiently that Rod knew she had done it many times before. He only wondered if it was her husband's armor she had removed, or her own.

He managed to push the knight up onto Fess's back, then leaned him against the horse's neck and tied him into place. "Walk by him, lady, on one side, and I'll walk on the other." Rod gave her a glance of concern. "Though you shouldn't be walking far just now."

"I've a cart at the edge of the wood," she told him with a grateful smile. "Be sure I have no wish to lose Sir Reginald's son!"

Or daughter, Rod thought, but only nodded. "Not too

long a walk, then—and the cart will be a better place for him than horseback. Let's go."

Fortunately, the route the lady showed him didn't go past the dead boar.

THE MOCKER STRODE through the house, snapping, "Meeting! Now! News!"

Each agent stopped what he or she was doing, stopped to stare at the retreating back of their new and former chief. They had each wondered what news the dusty messenger had brought; now they were about to find out. They rose from their desks and hurried to the keeping room.

They found the Mocker already seated at the head of the table, drumming his fingers in impatience. As the last agent came into the room, he snapped, "Right! News has come! Gallowglass has left his home!"

"Left!"

"Gone off?'

"Where?"

"Why?"

"As to 'gone off'—yes," the Mocker said. "As to 'where,' he seems to be wandering through a forest with no particular purpose in mind. As to why, I assume it's his way of dealing with grief."

The agents were silent a moment, staring at their chief. Then one said, "What happens now?"

"I don't know," the Mocker said with a certain degree of relish. "This isn't the way things happened in the timeline I just left."

"You mean he's changing the future?"

"Right. In history as I know it, that gawky eldest son of theirs left the planet again as soon as his mother was buried—some sort of argument with his siblings. The Gallowglass stayed with them—for comfort, we've thought; at least, that was the historians' verdict."

"Now it seems that the comfort was theirs, not his," a woman said.

"Perhaps, although I scarcely think that hulk of a boy could have given much reassurance in his place."

The room fell silent for a moment, agents glancing at one another, then glancing away.

"What?" The Mocker glared around at them. "What information are you withholding?"

"Not really information," another woman said. "Just a guess . . . from the reports our agents inside Castle Gallowglass have been sending, we'd wondered if . . . well . . ."

"Spit it out!"

"That woman that's with the eldest," a man said. "She seems to be horrendously insecure, but maybe that's a comfort to the Gallowglass heirs in itself. Certainly, by intention or accident, she seems to be able to prevent friction."

"An empath?" The Mocker frowned.

"Maybe a projective empath," the first woman said. "The accounts make it clear she visits with each of them, and they feel more confident afterward."

"That's simply the effect any weakling has on people who are unsure of their own importance!"

"The reports don't paint her as a weakling," the second woman snapped.

The Mocker glared at her until she lowered her gaze.

"She definitely is a telepath, at least," the man said.

The Mocker sat back, thumbs in his belt. "Then perhaps we need to remove her from the equation."

Nobody looked particularly happy at the idea. The Mocker frowned, wondering why, then shoved the idea aside. "We'll table that. We can always send an assassin later. For the moment, we'll have to split up the siblings, set them against one another."

Everyone nodded at that. After all, it was obvious; the second generation of Gallowglasses were virtually unbeatable, as long as they all worked together.

"The Mist Monsters . . ." another man said.

The Mocker frowned. "I read the reports. Difficult to believe, I admit, but on this benighted planet, anything could happen."

"It did," the agent assured him. "It seems they need to be invited in, and the advance guard of illusions they sent were doing a fine job of wangling that invitation until the Gallowglass brats interfered."

The Mocker nodded slowly. "Send an agent to persuade the peasants to work themselves up to inviting monsters in, eh?"

"It worked once," the man said, "though we weren't behind it."

"You should have been! All of that will take time, though. Meanwhile, I think I had better contact our enemies."

"The High Warlock?" a third woman gasped. "But he'll recognize you!"

"Not him—SPITE!"

They all sat back, appalled. "That *is* consorting with the enemy," a second man said.

"We can use them to help us get rid of the Gallowglasses, then chop them down." The Mocker's gesture made it seem a simple matter. "We'll have them spring their coup at the same time that we engineer our peasant uprising."

The agents looked at one another in surprize; then one nodded in reluctant approval. "It could work—but what do we do with SPITE afterwards?"

"There won't be any SPITE afterwards," the Mocker said, "at least, not on this planet. We'll have agents among the palace guards assigned to shoot down their agents right after they've done in the Gallowglasses."

"It would be nice to have revenge on them at last." The third young woman gazed off into space.

Even the Mocker decided he didn't want to know what scene she was imagining.

SIR REGINALD WAS only a knight, not a lord, so the dwelling Elise led Rod to was a manor house, not a castle, though it was clearly fortified, and they rode on a drawbridge over a moat to come to its front door. Servants and men-at-arms came pouring out as soon as the cart rolled into the yard.

"Take your master to his bed," Rod told them, "and bear him gently; I'd rather his wound didn't open again."

"We shall indeed." But the steward cast a doubtful look at Rod, unsure of his right to give orders.

The lady saw. "How are you called, Sir Knight?" she asked Rod.

"Rodney," he answered.

"Sir Rodney came upon us in the forest," the lady informed her steward—and the rest of the servants who were listening.

They paused in the act of pulling the knight onto an improvised stretcher, staring at Rod. Then the steward nodded in respect. "As you bid us, Sir Rodney. Quickly, lads! Bear him to his bed!"

The soldiers took the stretcher and paced quickly up the stairs and into the house.

"Had it not been for him, your master would have bled to death on the road," the lady informed the rest of the soldiers and servants, "if I could have pulled him into the cart myself."

"Lady, you should not have gone alone!" an older woman chided.

"You were right to tell me so, Nurse, for I . . . Ahhh!" The lady doubled over with pain.

"It is the child! All this parading and worry has brought it before its time!" The older woman bustled up to the cart, arms up to catch. "Some of you stout oafs help your lady down!"

Three footmen jumped forward and lifted as much as helped the lady down into the nurse's arms. Scolding the servants and soothing the lady, she helped her into the house, one painful step at a time. The next spasm took her on the threshold, but the lady throttled her reaction to a groan.

"Upstairs and into your bed," the nurse said severely. "The child must be born in its rightful place and time!"

They went on into the house, the footmen following anxiously in case they were needed to carry their mistress up the stairs.

The steward turned back to Rod. "Will you take some refreshment, Sir Rodney?"

"Not a bad idea." Rod dismounted. "After I'm done sewing up his wound, that is."

The steward goggled. "Sewing?"

Ten

"I DO VERY FINE STITCHERY." ROD TOOK HIS first-aid kit out of the saddlebag again and turned to follow the steward. "Show me his room."

Rod came into a room, which, by its barrenness and the narrowness of the bed, was clearly not used much; the footmen had had the good sense to take their master to a spare chamber. A single tapestry softened one wall, and the windows onto the courtyard did let in sunlight to brighten the cold stone walls. A chest stood against another wall, a table and two chairs against a third. The footmen had finished undressing the knight and put him in his bed. He lay with a sheet pulled over him, still unconscious—and, in medieval sleeping style, naked.

Rod pulled up a chair beside him, laid the kit on the bed, and took out a needle pre-threaded with sterilized gut. He unfolded the cloth that attempted to keep germs out and told one of the soldiers, "Hold the wound closed when I take off the dressing."

"Aye, Sir Knight." The soldier stepped close, still a little alarmed for his lord—and very interested.

Rod unwound the bandage and inspected the wound. The bleeding seemed to have stopped under the clotting, but slight pressure set it oozing again while, with teleki-netic touches, he made sure there were no bits of metal hidden in the flesh. Rod nodded, satisfied, and took another sterile cloth to wipe the wound again—with alcohol. "Push," he directed the soldier, and began sewing, as, with telekinesis, he began to knit the muscles together.

When the wound was stitched and bandaged. Rod sat for a minute or so, studying his patient—and not really probing his thoughts, but certainly paying attention to any images that floated to the surface of his mind. Probably unnecessary—there was no reason to think the man wouldn't regain consciousness—but just in case . . .

At last he stood up, stretching, then folded up his first-aid kit.

The steward, who had hovered nearby, said, "There is rest and refreshment near, Sir Knight."

"Good idea." Rod nodded. "I could do with a stoup of ale, and there's certainly no shortage of people to watch over him." To the nearest soldier, he said, "Call me as soon as your master is awake."

"I shall, Sir Knight," the man assured him with a little bow.

Rod returned it with a nod and followed the steward out of the room. As they came to the top of the stair, a quavering cry, half-gasp and half-moan, echoed down the hall. Rod paused, frowning at the double door at the end of the corri-dor, then started downstairs after the steward, telling the man, "Send word to the women—that your mistress should go ahead and scream. This is no time for self-control."

The man stared at Rod as though he had come from Elfland but said, "I will, Sir Rodney." It didn't take telepa-thy to see that the man was wondering how this knight knew anything of women's matters.

He took Rod into a small chamber near the kitchen—a pantry, at a guess, but Rod wasn't about to protest; the solar was on the second floor, and the lady should at least have some privacy this day. A bowl of fruit stood ready by a mug of ale. Rod sank into an hourglass-shaped chair with a sigh, took a sip, then looked up at the steward again. "Tell the women to call me at once if there is any difficulty in the birth."

"I shall, Sir Knight." The steward bowed and departed, clearly amazed at the notion that a man should know anything about birth.

Alone in the pantry, Rod gazed at the grid of light on the bottle-glass window and mused, thinking over the events of the morning and wondering what the missing piece was that would make the whole pattern take shape. A knight had gone out alone—in the darkness before dawn, probably, considering how early was the hour in which Rod had found him. He had clearly expected battle, or he wouldn't have worn armor—but his wife had known nothing of his going. From what threat had he sought to shield her? And what enemy would require single combat without the presence of even a squire?

There was no assurance the other guy wouldn't have brought a small army—which meant the knight was either going to meet a blackmailer (but why the armor?), answering a challenge to single combat, or going after a suspected threat that he wasn't sure existed.

Rod decided on the third.

"Sir Rodney." The steward was at the door. "Sir Reginald is conscious, but tosses as though with a fever."

"Delirious," Rod interpreted. "Well, I can do something about that." He stood, picking up his first-aid kit. "Lead on. By the way, steward, what's your name?"

"Michael Duff, Sir Rodney."

"Figures."

A full-throated scream rent the air as they reached the top of the stairs; Rod nodded with satisfaction.

"How long will the labor be, Sir Rodney?" the steward asked nervously.

"No way to tell, Michael Duff."

The steward glanced over his shoulder at the guest and risked informality. "Most call me Mick, Sir Rodney."

"Mick you shall be," Rod promised. "Let's see your master."

The knight tossed in his bed, mumbling incoherently—unless he rolled onto the wounded shoulder, in which case the mumbling turned into a cry of pain. Rod sat beside him, frowned down at the man for a moment while his thoughts probed his patient's delirium, then laid a hand on his forehead and said sternly, "Sir Reginald, awaken!"

The knight stilled as Rod's thoughts calmed his; then the pain bit, and his back arched as he pulled in a long, shuddering gasp.

"It will mend," Rod assured him.

Another scream echoed down the hall.

Sir Reginald tried to sit bolt upright. "What . . ."

"Only your lady in the labor of birth." Rod pressed a hand against his chest. "It's perfectly natural, and there's no reason for worry."

"I must . . . must . . ."

"Go to her?" Rod shook his head, smiling. "The women would chase you out, Sir Reginald. The last thing they need on their hands right now is a hysterical husband. Besides, you're wounded, in case you hadn't noticed."

The knight turned to look at his shoulder; the pain bit through the adrenalin his wife's scream had summoned. He clamped his teeth, gasped again, then asked, "What . . ."

"I was hoping you could tell me," Rod said.

He didn't have to eavesdrop; the flood of images in the man's mind were so vivid Rod would have had trouble shutting them out: a bright slash of daylight bordered by darkness above and below—the slits in a knight's helmet, through which he saw three foresters in dark green, two with bows bent and arrows aimed at his helmet as the third thrust upward with a blood-encrusted sawtoothed pike.

The shield dropped to block the pike, and the hound charged the villein who held it, barking furiously, but the bows thrummed and the dog leaped aside at the sound, as he had been trained to do. The shield jumped up to ward off the arrows—and pain seared the knight's shoulder, as the pike jammed under his pauldron; the shield dropped down as his own cry of pain echoed in the helmet. But his sword flashed across and down, and the villein fell back holding a shortened pole with no head and pressing a hand to his arm, where blood welled. The hound was after him, barking like a whole pack. The two archers lifted their bows again, but the knight charged them; the arrows leaped up, then passed him, as the varlets scrambled aside—but not quickly enough for one of them to avoid the sword. He dropped his bow, bellowing pain.

"Coward!" the pole-bearer shouted. "Come at us without armor or horse!"

The knight's voice echoed in the bell of his helmet: "Come alone, and I will." Then he was charging down at the man, and the villein lurched aside, then fell and scrambled to escape the horse's hooves. On his feet again, he stumbled away into the forest. Turning his horse, the knight saw the archers making their escapes too. Panting, he felt the exaltation of victory, of vindication, for he had beaten off three who had set upon him without cause.

Then the pain in his shoulder flared, the world blurred, and the blur lurched, ending with a jolt. Dimly through thoughts gone murky, Sir Reginald realized he had fallen from his horse.

Memory came in flashes after that, enough so that Rod realized the knight was fading in and out of consciousness, managing to drag himself up out of the darkness of blood loss to meet threats—the first being a return of the pole-arm villein, a bandage around his arm and one archer behind him—but Sir Reginald saw him through the arch formed by his warhorse's legs, which rose out of sight while his head filled with the charger's battle-scream, and the foresters backed away hastily. The archer nocked an arrow, but the hound burst from cover, barking madly. The archer swung his arrow to the beast and loosed, but again the dog leaped aside, then came on, baying madly, and the archer ran. The dog stopped at the edge of the wood and turned back—to find the pole-armed villein with his pike lowered and centered on the hound. The beast came on, barking and growling as it leaped to this side, then that, evading the pike-point, and the villein gave ground—too much, for he came within the horse's range, and the charger screamed as it lashed out with its forehooves, knocking the man over.

The dog leaped in, but the villein brought his blade around in time and the dog dodged, then leaped in and out, in and out, as the man scrambled to his feet and backed away. The hound stopped when the trees had swallowed him, but stayed stiffly on guard as the man called, "Come alone yourself, knight!" then crashed away.

The last picture was the dog's head, filling the knight's vision and whining anxiously, then turning away and barking with gladness as the lady sank heavily to her knees by him, weeping even as she loosened his helmet, and frantic worry kept the knight awake despite the pain, worry for her when she was so heavy with child—but his strength ebbed, and darkness came again.

"Valiantly fought," Rod said, "but what made you think they would be there?"

"Signs in the wood, and words of worry from my tenants." Then Sir Reginald gasped at a spasm of pain, but went on through clenched teeth. "They said outlaws had come by many farmsteads in many manors, telling the peasants their masters were using them as beasts of burden and cared nothing for their welfare. But I have always dealt fairly with my peasants and have done all I could to make sure they are well fed and well housed, so they brought the word to me instead . . ."

Another cry echoed down the hall, a ragged tearing cry this time, and Sir Reginald jolted upward to answer, but met Rod's palm pushing him down again. "If that wasn't the birth, it's very close," Rod said. "Nothing to worry about, not that knowing it will stop you, or any young husband at a first labor—but you'd only be in the way. Trust me—my wife went through this four times, and it always took two or three people to keep me calm."

"Praise Heaven you are come, then!" Sir Reginald said.

"We're all the same in this hour," Rod told him, "and all need the reassurance of a man who's been through it before, having to stand by and do nothing when his wife's in torment . . . So you didn't know these three were going to be out there hunting knights?"

"Belike they only sought to trouble my people," Sir Reginald said, then clamped his jaw against pain.

"It will fade eventually," Rod told him, "as the wound heals. Then it will begin to itch most abominably, but you mustn't scratch it . . . So that's why you didn't bring any men-at-arms; you were afraid of looking foolish if all you found was a boar."

"Aye," Sir Reginald gasped. "Yet when I found a boar dead and saw the wound in its shoulder, I knew there were strangers in the wood." He frowned, focusing on Rod. "What manner of outlaws are these, who seek to stir up even happy peasants against their lords?"

"Ones who will never stop causing trouble, I fear," Rod sighed, "but whom I think I . . ."

The nurse came in, holding a squalling bundle in her arms—and Sir Reginald's relief and sudden awe and massive urge to protect nearly bowled Rod over. He came around to put an arm under the young knight and lift him up to sit so that the nurse could put the baby into his arms, saying, "Here is your daughter, Sir Knight."

"She is beautiful," Sir Reginald said, huge-eyed, and held the baby as though she were made of glass, then looked up at the nurse with anxiety. "My lady . . ."

"She is quite well, though weak from her ordeal—and immensely happy," the nurse told him.

"I must go to her!"

"That's not impossible," Rod said, "but it will be painful."

"The devil with the pain!"

"Where it belongs, no doubt," Rod agreed. "Very well, then—up with you."

But the knight still clung to the baby.

The nurse reached down for her, saying in a tone that would brook no argument, "You may not have her long, for she needs her mother." She lifted the child out of his arms and turned away—which was just as well, since Sir Reginald emerged from his bed naked and Rod had to call a man-at-arms to fetch a robe while he steadied the knight on his feet.

* * *

HE RODE AWAY an hour later, basking in the reflected glow of the young couple's joy and love—but as the leaves closed about him, he remembered the "outlaws" and frowned. "We'll have to be ready for attack, Fess."

"I always am, Rod," the robot replied.

Of course, Fess was epileptic, as much as an electronic brain could be, so he couldn't fight for more than a few minutes without having a seizure—but Rod could be sure no one could take him by surprize while Fess was near.

"I think I recognize the modus operandi," Rod mused, "the jolly boys from VETO."

"Their rhetoric does have the ring of the totalitarians," Fess agreed, "and their fondness for stirring up peasant rebellions."

"Or trying to," Rod said. "Catharine and Tuan have ruled with the best interests of all their people at heart, so VETO's agents are going to have to stir up discontent before they can exploit it. Y'know, this almost sounds like the work of my old enemy the Mocker."

"Not impossible, Rod, considering that he was a time traveller. Indeed, as I remember, we heard nothing of him after he escaped from the royal dungeons again."

"You mean he could have jumped forward in time to this moment?" Rod frowned. "Why now, though?"

"His organization has been in decline since its last defeat," Fess pointed out. "It could be a last desperate measure."

"I suppose his bosses could have sent him off to the fourteenth century, or some such time, in disgrace," Rod said, frowning, "and be calling him back because they don't have any better guesses—but why now?"

They rode a moment in silence. Then Rod said, "You're thinking it's because of me, aren't you? Because I've retired."

"The idea has some merit," Fess agreed. "The totalitarians have been suspiciously inactive for ten years. They could have realized that you and your family are insuperable obstacles."

"Yes, because we combine medieval loyalty with tremendous psi power and modern knowledge." Rod frowned and forced the next words out even though they tore at him. "But with Gwen gone . . ."

"Half your strength went with her," Fess agreed, "not only in her own ESP talent, but also in her influence with others."

"Yes, starting with her own children but expanding to Queen Catharine and the Royal Witchforce." Rod turned somber as memories rose around him. "And I suppose my retiring doesn't help any."

"They could think they see a moment of weakness and the opportunity that accompanies it, yes."

"If that's so, then they don't know my kids," Rod said, grinning, then frowned again. "Though it will take Magnus a while to re-establish his own influence, and expand it . . ."

"You know he will not seek to command his siblings, Rod."

"Yes. He did when he was seventeen, but he seems to have learned a bit on his travels—mostly that manipulation is far more effective than bossing," Rod said, "especially considering his training as a secret agent."

"Your central office did give you some difficulty about his resignation, as I recall."

"They called it a defection." Rod smiled at the memory. "I pointed out that he couldn't have defected because he hadn't joined the other side—and he hadn't."

"But that made him a loose cannon, a wildcard, and in some ways a greater threat than a turncoat."

"Which he certainly proved to be." Rod nodded. "It was just good luck that he never landed on a SCENT planet again—good luck for them."

"Now he has, though, Rod."

"Yes, well, he was born and reared here," Rod said, "which I think gives him a somewhat stronger claim than my old organization can have. But he will need some time to consolidate his position."

The robot was silent a moment, choosing his words carefully. Then he said, "It will take you some time to find Tir Nan Og, Rod."

"Yes, and if I manage to bump into some VETO cells and wreck their games, that should take some of the pressure off

Magnus." Rod sighed. "Well, I suppose Gwen will forgive me if she has to wait a little longer."

"But she would not forgive you if you abandoned your children before they could manage by themselves."

"No, she wouldn't, would she? Well, let's see what we can find in the wildwood, shall we?"

"Whatever awaits, you will find it more easily if you make some noise."

"Or let it find me, huh? Okay, I can take a hint." Rod pulled out his harp. "Though I do take umbrage at your calling it 'noise.'"

"I was not necessarily speaking of your attempts at singing, Rod."

"Attempts, huh?" Rod gave a snort of mock indignation and began to pluck at the strings.

The birds braced themselves for a quick retreat.

THE ANARCHISTS' BASE was modest, as manor houses go, but was nonetheless respectable by the standards of the gentry, in case any of the noblemen who were their targets ever found it. A person coming from that big tranquil-seeming ivy-covered house would be acceptable in polite society, for she would be a lady or he a knight. Even a duke would talk with such a person, though he might not make her his friend.

Of course, the agents who worked and visited there had elaborate safeguards in place to make sure none of the lords ever discovered the estate.

One of the Home Agents knocked at the door of the solar, then opened it. An old-seeming man was seated at a table in the fan of sunlight from the tall windows behind him. He looked up as the Home Agent came in. "News, Dierdre?"

"Yes, Chief." Dierdre handed the old man a scroll of paper.

The Chief Agent took it, broke the seal, and unrolled it. He stared.

"What is it, Chief?"

"A letter from my old enemy the Mocker." The Chief Agent looked up. "He proposes a temporary alliance."

Eleven

"ALLIANCE? WITH TOTALITARIANS? CHIEF, THEY stand for the worst in everything we detest!"

"True—but they could be useful." The Chief Agent laid down the scroll and turned to look out the window at the gardens. "Also, it seems, they've done just as our future Central Committee did—sent back the Chief of Mission who directed things when that confounded Gallowglass first came."

"You would have succeeded in your palace coup if he hadn't interfered." The young woman had read SPITE's official history. "Then it would have been only a matter of time before you had all the noblemen fighting each other."

"And exterminating the Mocker and his gang." The Chief Agent turned back to her, nodding. "We didn't realize then that the Lord Warlock was a bigger enemy for each of us than we were for each other."

"He put you in jail, Chief Durer."

"Yes, with the Mocker in an adjoining cell." Durer gazed back into memory—for him, only three months earlier. "Of course we spent the first week going at it hammer and tongs through the bars, but in the second week we started comparing notes. By the time we were ready to break out of there, we both understood who the real enemy was."

"Meaning the Lord Warlock."

"He was neither a lord nor a warlock at the time," Durer told her, "at least, as far as any of us knew—including him."

The young woman stared. "You mean he didn't know he had ESP powers?"

"If he had, he would have used them." Durer pulled a volume to him and pointed to the open page. "According to my successors' journals, he had a rather extended visit from a monk, after which he demonstrated a wide range of talents."

"Brother Aloyuisis Uwell." Dierdre nodded, again demonstrating her knowledge of recent history.

"I have a message into headquarters checking on him," Durer said. "I suspect he taught the Lord Warlock how to live up to his title." He sighed, paging through the book. "Three Chief Agents after me, and none of them had any better luck than I—but I have their hard-won knowledge to help me now, and a better idea of what the Gallowglasses can do."

"Now that the Lord Warlock is off on his own, maybe he's more vulnerable."

Durer shook his head. "His children can teleport to him in an instant. No, we have to remove them first. *Then* we can take care of my old enemy." His eyes gleamed.

That gleam chilled Dierdre—and surprized her; usually the old man seemed so nice.

Durer turned back to the book, leafing through the pages and frowning. "Not much here from the traitor."

He meant Finister, the last Chief Agent before the one he had replaced.

"She wasn't Chief Agent very long before she changed her name and turned her coat to marry the youngest Gallowglass." Dierdre's tone was sharp with spite.

Durer shook his head. "I don't know what possessed Chief Agent Lewis to appoint that witch as his successor just before he died."

On Gramarye, the term "witch" might have been merely descriptive, referring to someone with extra-sensory talents—but Durer chose to interpret it as an insult.

"I don't think he had much choice about it," the Home Agent said. "We all knew Finister was a powerful esper, but we had no idea *how* powerful."

Durer turned to her with a frown. "You mean she bewitched Lewis?"

"In more ways than one," the Home Agent said. "I'll admit he was using her for his own . . . amusement . . . so she may have thought she was justified in using him in return."

"Using him in what way?"

"She projected a very beautiful and voluptuous image, but we're pretty sure she manipulated his emotions telepathically, too. Why else would he have given the order that she be his successor? And considering that he died the next day . . ."

"The autopsy?"

"Showed no reason for death—his heart simply stopped."

Even Durer felt a chill. "I take it this Finister was telekinetic, too?"

"She had all the ESP talents except levitation and teleportation," the Home Agent confirmed.

"I'll have to meet her—with my most advanced weapons," Durer said with a smile.

Dierdre nodded. "You might want to consider a quiet little assassination for her before that."

"Oh, no! Our revenge on the Gallowglass heirs comes first," Durer said. "Then I shall have my own revenge on the young woman who usurped my office and betrayed our Cause." He gazed off into a dream future, his eyes kindling. "My revenge on this Finister-Allouette will be delicious and prolonged."

Dierdre stared at the look on his face and shuddered. How could she have ever thought this man was kindly?

Durer made a quick gesture that banished his vision. "When I'm satiated, I'll be generous and give her a quick death." He turned back to Dierdre, all business once more. "After all, she was Chief Agent once, no matter how briefly, nor what skulduggery she used to get the job. We do owe her *some* respect."

THE SUN WAS rising when Cordelia came out onto the battlements, where the servants had told her she could find Magnus. Sure enough, there he was, strolling along the eastern wall, stopping to chat briefly with each sentry, then standing still in the center of the parapet to watch the great orange disk rise.

Cordelia came up behind him. "How now, brother— have you become a Zoroastrian, that you must rise to pray to the light as it returns?"

Magnus looked down with a fond smile. "Not at all, sister. It is simply that it is beautiful, and a promise that some of the world, at least, is clean of humankind's more sordid doings."

Cordelia wondered what had happened to the cheerful, optimistic big brother of her youth, then reminded herself that two years' difference in age didn't mean much between adults. "You rise early only for this moment of contemplation?"

"It would be worth it." Magnus turned back to look at the sun. "But I wake early without meaning to now. I've become accustomed to rising with the sun on my travels, and my body does it whether I wish it or not."

"This is your idea of sleeping late, is it?" Cordelia turned to gaze at the great glowing ball, too. She let a few minutes pass, steeling herself to confrontation, then asked, "And do you mean to become the sun to us stay-at-homes, expecting us all to revolve around you?"

Magnus's shoulders shrugged with a stifled laugh. "Scarcely."

"I mean it, brother." Cordelia's voice gained steel. "You have little knowledge of what has passed on this world in this last ten years. You are in no position to give orders, no matter what Papa has said—and neither Alain nor I would obey you if you did!"

"Dad did not say to give orders."

Cordelia's eyes widened in surprise.

"He told me to take care of the land and people of

Gramarye," Magnus went on. "He did not say that I had to command a cadre of officers in the doing of it."

"Surely you do not think you can answer every challenge alone!"

"If there is an emergency to which I must respond, Alea may choose to come with me."

"Well . . . so shall I, if it comes to that." Cordelia turned to look at the sun again. "But that is a matter of choosing, Magnus, not of responding to order."

Magnus nodded. "It will be your choice, Cordelia, not mine."

Cordelia snapped a sharp glance up at him, frowning. "Do I hear overtones of emotional blackmail in that?"

"If you do, they are of your own making." Magnus smiled down at her, amused. "You may infer them, but I do not imply them."

Cordelia stared at him a moment, frowning. Then she said, "So you will go kiting off on the spur of the moment to answer some fancied challenge and expect Alea, and the rest of us, to come chasing after you."

"I shall not expect that." Magnus locked gazes with her. "I shall not expect anything."

Cordelia frowned, trying to puzzle him out. "Do you think you can meet all threats alone?"

"Not really. But I have no right to command anyone who has not elected me to the task. I have authority only over myself, so I shall go to meet every challenge by myself."

"Is it thus that you overthrew governments as you careered through the stars?"

"No," Magnus said. "I began alone, truly enough—on Melange, and again on Midgard. On all other planets, I had Dirk Dulaine, then Alea, for companions, and redoubtable they were, I assure you."

"And the two of you were proof against all encounters?" Cordelia didn't try to keep the skepticism out of her voice.

"Not alone, no." Magnus turned to gaze at the sun again. "We generally found a local refugee or two to advise us, then gradually built up groups of disaffected people and found some way for them to communicate with one another. Twice there was some event, some unusually harsh burst of arrogance from the local lords that triggered an uprising, and we rose with them and made sure of their victory. More often, we put the individual cells of resistance on the road to eventual victory and left them to grow and flourish."

Cordelia stared, appalled. "You shall never know whether you condemned them to defeat or assured them of victory?"

"I don't suppose we'll ever have it confirmed," Magnus acknowledged, "but we never left until the crisis had passed and the machinery was in place to guarantee their eventual triumph. It is better, after all, for a system of government to grow rather than be grafted; it has a stronger chance of survival."

Cordelia frowned, searching his profile. "There is no need for revolution here, brother."

"No," Magnus agreed, "though SPITE and VETO may still foment discord and attempt upheavals, each in its own style. If they do, I shall do all in my power to thwart them, for I've no more wish to see totalitarians impose a dictatorship on our people than for Dad to foist on them a democracy that would be wrong for them."

"But democracy is not wrong for them!"

Magnus turned to her, amused. "Is it the future queen who speaks?"

Cordelia's lips pressed thin. "A constitutional monarchy can become a form of democracy, Magnus. You know that!"

"Yes, I do." Magnus met her eyes again. "Sharing power between a parliament and the crown is a way-station on the road to democracy, and I have no wish to block that road. In fact, I'll do all I can to make sure it is open for the people to travel." He frowned, suddenly intense. "But it must be a living thing, this democracy—it cannot be a corpse animated like a puppet. And to live, it must grow of its own and take what form is natural to it."

Taken aback by his intensity, Cordelia said, "That is all I wish, brother."

"And Alain?" he demanded, still intent.

"He, too," Cordelia said. "How could you think otherwise?"

"Because I have little knowledge of what has passed here these last ten years." Magnus relaxed and turned to face the sun, now risen. "Little knowledge, and I shall not be foolish enough to try to act without it. Be sure, sister, I shall go my own way and trouble no one—unless armed conflict arises."

"No one?" Cordelia frowned.

Magnus shrugged. "I may wander about the land to catch the temper of the people and tell a few stories—tales of heroes who overthrew despots, or of peacemakers who reconciled warring factions—but nothing more."

Cordelia, however, was sharper than most Magnus had dealt with. "Building your cells again?"

Magnus turned to her, smiling with pleasure. "You have lost none of your quickness, I see. Yes, I may plant cells throughout this land—but they shall all respect the Crown and the commonweal."

"The will of the people, and the burdens they bear in common?" Reluctantly, Cordelia said, "I cannot quarrel with that."

Magnus nodded, turning to the east again, but without speaking.

Watching his face, Cordelia saw that he was really gazing at the mist rising from the meadow. After a few minutes she said, "Magnus . . . when Alain becomes king and I queen . . ."

"I hope to be first to kneel to you at your coronation—and be sure that I shall obey my sovereigns in every order they may give."

"Unless it goes against your conscience."

"I cannot conceive of that," Magnus said—with no delay.

Cordelia knew by that sign that he had given the matter careful thought. The implication, of course, was that if she and Alain ever did become tyrants, Magnus would fight them tooth and claw—and she had no illusions as to just how formidable an enemy he could be. However, she couldn't conceive of either herself or Alain turning into despots either, so she felt warmed by her brother's pledge of loyalty. She stood beside him, watching the mist burn off in the sun's heat, and after a while, she slipped her hand into his.

GEOFFREY ALWAYS LIKED coming down to town. Oh, the castle on the hill was a fine place to live, after his parents' renovations, but it could still be socially claustrophobic to be around the same people day after day—and always being surrounded by walls went against the grain of a man who was in his element when he was in field and forest. So, if there were no fields or forests close at hand, the town on the lower slopes of the castle hill would do nicely as a change of scene.

He reined in as he came to a tavern, jumped down, and beckoned to a hostler standing near. "Hold my horse, lad, and there will be coin for you when I come out."

The hostler came over and took the reins. "Does he need currying, my lord?"

"Only 'sir,'" Geoffrey corrected. "I am a knight who hopes never to be a lord."

"Oh, aye—for now that your elder brother is back, it is he who will inherit the title, will he not?"

Geoffrey looked more closely at the man, frowning. He hadn't realized the townsfolk followed the goings-on at the castle so closely. "The title is not hereditary, goodman. It was bestowed on my father only for his lifetime."

The hostler nodded, stroking the horse's neck. "Yet surely your brother-in-law will raise one of you to the title when your father passes away—and as surely, it will be the eldest."

"There is no promise of either." Geoffrey's frown deepened. "Nor any cause to expect it."

The man feigned surprize. "You do not mean it could be you who would be raised to lordship!"

Frankly, Geoffrey had never thought about the issue, but he was nettled by the man's bland assumption. "It could be. If there is war, I may well earn the honor in battle."

The man grinned, showing yellowed teeth, one broken. "Come, my lord! All the land knows that it is your brother who will command, now that he has come home!"

"Then all the land knows falsehood!" Geoffrey snatched the reins back and mounted again. "My brother gives me no orders, nor do I take them from him!"

"Surely, Sir Knight." But the hostler's smile said he knew better than to believe so obvious an untruth.

Really angry now, Geoffrey turned his horse toward the road back to the castle.

"But the tavern, my lord! Your pint of ale!"

"Drink it yourself!" Geoffrey slipped a coin from his purse and tossed it back over his shoulder.

The hostler let it lie in the dust, grinning as he watched Geoffrey ride back up to the castle.

GEORDIE WALKED OUT under the early sun, enjoying the coolness of the morning and the feeling of cleanliness that always came with dawn. Long shadows striped the land, dew clung to the grass, and his tenants were already abroad. Geordie drew in a deep breath and rejoiced. He was young, in his mid-twenties, with half his father's estate to manage and, most importantly of all, a beautiful, intelligent, spirited wife, and they were very much in love. No matter what went wrong in the world, everything would be right when he came home to her. Life was good.

Good for his tenants, too, it seemed. The earth was green with the sprouts of the new crop, and children were driving the cows out to pasture.

But their parents were hurrying from their homes to the granary when they should have been out to the fields. Frowning, Geordie quickened his pace; what had gone wrong?

In minutes he was twisting his way through the throng of peasants inside the shadows of the barn, lit by stripes of sunlight where the boards failed to meet; Geordie's shadow walked long before him as he said, "Room, Willikin, there's a good lad . . . Good morn to you, Corin, and let me by . . .

The peasants opened a lane for him in the coolness and fragrance of the barn—but the aroma was wrong; instead of the richness of stored grain, he scented something sour, acrid.

" 'Tis the garnered grain, my lord," old Adam said. He

lifted a hand, letting the kernels sift through his fingers—
but only powder came out, and it was far darker than it
should have been.

Geordie stared. "What rot has struck?"

Old Adam shrugged. "One I've never seen, my lord . . ."

"Don't call me that," Geordie said with the weariness of
one who knows it will do no good. "My father was attainted."

"A lord you are by the way you walk and bear yourself
toward others," the old man sighed, "and there's naught the
king can do or say that will change that."

The throng of men muttered assent for the fiftieth time,
nodding agreement.

"But if it will please you better, I'll call you squire," old
Adam said, "for such you are, in the heed you pay your
lands and the concern you give your people."

"Concerned I am," Geordie said with a frown, "for
we've a summer to live through before the new crop
comes. Is all the stored grain like this?"

"All, my lord," said burly, grizzled Tavus, "save for the
last layer of kernels that cover it—and I'd not dare to eat of
them."

"No, of course not." Geordie scowled, brain racing.

"What shall we eat, my lord?" one of the men asked,
voice low and heavy.

"The first carrots and turnips will be grown in a few
weeks," Geordie said. "We'll have to plant more. Till then,
we shall have to manage off what we can scavenge in the
forest."

The people muttered, for the forest was as all forests
were—the property of the Crown and the hunting preserve
of the nobility.

"There's no law against our gathering nuts and berries,"
Geordie called over their voices, "or anything else that
grows from the earth there."

"But the keepers will think we are poaching, my l . . .
squire," said Hobin.

"We'll all go gathering together, and I'll speak with the
keepers for you," Geordie told them.

Relief washed over the people's faces, but the older

ones still looked glum. "There can't be enough wild oats and squirrel's hoards to keep us until the harvest, squire."

"True enough," Geordie said. "We'll have to stretch it with porridges and stews."

"Stews need meat, squire," Old Adam pointed out.

"So do you, all of you, even if it be only an ounce or two a week—and aye, even slaying so much as a badger is poaching, I know. Still, if the beasts come *out* of the wood, they're ours."

The peasants muttered their misgivings, and Hobin said, "Don't know what the keepers will say to that, squire."

"Let me worry about the keepers," Geordie said. "Take your children and go searching the hedgerows first—we'll certainly find there enough food for the day." He turned and stalked away.

The peasants watched him go, every face grooved with worry.

"What will he be doing, Adam?" Corin asked.

"What any good lord would do if his people starve," Adam said grimly, "feed them."

"The keepers will take him then!"

"That they will," said Adam, "and he's not noble no more. We'll have to keep a watch on that lad."

"Aye, and keep him from doing something foolish," Hobin agreed.

But they all knew how skilled a woodsman Geordie was, and wondered if they could find him to guard him if he didn't want to be found.

GEOFFREY WAS STILL seething as he rode through the gatehouse. He dismounted in the courtyard and tossed the reins at a hostler running toward him, then strode up the stairs to the keep's double door. It was time to have it out with Magnus for once and for all.

He strode toward the stairway, and a footman came running. "Is there aught you wish, Sir Geoffrey?"

"Nay, unless you know where Sir Magnus is."

"Why—in his chamber, I should think."

Geoffrey started to say, "Yes, you should," but caught

himself in time. He wasn't one to take out his bad temper on his subordinates. He gave the man a curt nod and a "thank you" instead, then all but ran up the stairs.

He had no need to knock at Magnus's door; it was wide open, and his brother was at work with pen and ink, on a table in front of the wide window.

"What have you there?" Geoffrey demanded as he came into the room.

Magnus looked up in surprize. "Some notes on Alea's homeland, brother." He laid aside his quill and leaned back in his chair. "You seem agitated."

"You might say that." Geoffrey shut the door with a bit more force than necessary.

Magnus raised his eyebrows at Geoffrey's anger—and at the obvious insistence on confidentiality. "Sit down, why don't you, and tell me what has set you off this morning."

Geoffrey wasn't about to take even that much of an order. He strode up to Magnus's desk and demanded, "Do you know that the word is all over the town that you shall be master of us all, now that Papa has gone off wandering?"

"Is it really!" Magnus exclaimed. "No, I didn't know."

"It is not true, brother," Geoffrey snapped. "He may have won from you a promise to care for the people of this land, but he did not give you authority to command me!"

Twelve

"EVEN IF HE HAD, I WOULD NOT," MAGNUS TOLD him. "I have no right to command any of you."

That brought Geoffrey up short. He stared; then his eyes narrowed in disbelief.

"I have trouble enough of my own, trying to become used to my homeland again," Magnus said. "I am quite content to leave command of the army to you."

Geoffrey turned his head a little, eyeing Magnus sideways. "You, who have commanded legions? You do not wish to command them again?"

"I never really commanded any army," Magnus corrected. "I may have advised those who did, but I did not myself command more than a company."

"Oh, aye, and they did not follow your advice to the letter!"

"More often than not," Magnus admitted.

"Do not think I shall, brother!"

"I do not," Magnus said, and spread his hands. "I may

have a gift for warfare, Geoffrey, but you have a positive genius for it. I know my own limitations."

"But Papa made you promise to care for the people," Geoffrey protested. "You gave him your word you would ward Gramarye from its enemies."

"So I shall—but our old adversaries of SPITE and VETO are not often countered by force of arms."

Geoffrey lifted his head slowly as understanding sank in, lifted until he looked down his nose at his brother. "So you shall be commander in chief; you shall retain civil command! You think to tell the generals where to go and when!"

"No," Magnus said. "That authority is Queen Catharine's and will someday be Alain's."

"But King Tuan cozens the queen into wise deployments, as you think to cozen your brother-in-law Alain."

"Cordelia would have my head if I even tried," Magnus said. "Indeed, she is all the advisor that Alain will really need."

Geoffrey scowled at him, trying to puzzle out what he was not saying. "And if Alain asks your opinion?"

"I shall give it to him honestly," Magnus said, "but I shall wait to be asked."

"And shall not cozen him into asking?" Geoffrey asked sourly, then answered his own question. "Cordelia will know it if you do!"

"She will indeed," Magnus agreed, "and will counter me most effectively. No, if Alain asks my advice, it will be his doing, not mine."

"With Cordelia's approval." Geoffrey frowned. "You do not think he will ask your advice, do you?"

"Oh, I think he may ask," Magnus said, "but he will make his own decisions. Alain has as much a genius for good judgement as you have for warfare."

Geoffrey stared in surprize; then his brow furrowed in thought as he studied the careful neutrality of his brother's face. "I had not thought of it in those terms," he admitted, "but I have realized his good sense and given my word to heed his commands when he becomes king."

Magnus nodded. "As have I."

They were silent as Geoffrey absorbed the implications of that simple statement.

Then he sat down, crossing his legs, eyes narrowing again. "So you do not mean to command your sibs or manipulate the Crown. What then *do* you plan to do in this land? Sit here and write your memoirs, and rot for the rest of your life?"

"Well, not for all of it," Magnus said, "and I suspect there will be problems enough arising that I can lend a hand in solving—but for the moment, perhaps even for a year, a long rest sounds very attractive."

"I thought you'd had ample time to rest between the stars."

"So had I," Magnus said frankly, "but I find, now that I am here where I grew up, and suddenly have no responsibility, an amazing lassitude has taken me."

"Depression?" Geoffrey's voice sharpened with concern.

"No, it is very pleasant, actually," Magnus said, "rather like a waking sleep."

"Then beware of dreams."

"Well cautioned." Magnus nodded. "I find myself mulling over the events of the past ten years, trying to make sense of them."

Geoffrey's frown deepened; he didn't understand.

"Is there a purpose to my life?" Magnus asked. "Perhaps even only a pattern? You have no need to ask yourself that question—you have Quicksilver, after all, and a blind man could see that she is all the purpose you need, at least for the present."

Geoffrey was reluctant to admit that. "A battle now and then would be pleasant."

"And I've seen you drilling the troops to be ready for it." Magnus nodded. "After all, you must always be prepared to fight off an attack, must you not?"

Geoffrey finally smiled. "Enemies do not usually send warning."

"No, the honorable old custom of declaring war seems to have fallen into disuse," Magnus agreed. "Somehow I feel sure you will have all the opportunity you need to practice your profession."

"Well, it would be better for all that I did not," Geoffrey said with a sigh, "so I am seeing to building a tournament circuit that will keep men in fighting trim even should peace prevail—and may leach from them the need for war."

"For which we both devoutly hope," Magnus said, "but it certainly answers your need for purpose."

"Well, Papa has handed you one, whether you like it or not." Geoffrey was surprised to realize the truth of what he said.

"True, brother—but like yourself, I must wait for the opportunity and hope it does not come."

"Perhaps it would be well if it did not, at least for a year or so, if you are as much in need of rest as you say."

Magnus nodded. "Of rest, and of trying to understand the land of my birth."

"What is there to understand?" Geoffrey frowned. "We are a most simple nation, when all's said and done."

"But I have not been here to hear it said, nor to watch it done," Magnus pointed out. "Believe it or not, brother, it will take me some time, and considerable study of the recent history of Gramarye, before I have the feel of my native planet again."

"Surely you cannot have become so much an alien!" Geoffrey protested.

"I keep thinking I have not; I look about me at familiar sights, hear familiar sounds, walk through a peaceful town and think all is as it was when I was a youth," Magnus said. "Then something will happen, someone nearby will speak of some event that I know nothing about or of some public figure whom I've never heard of, and I realize all over again that the land has become strange to me."

Geoffrey frowned, still not understanding. "Gramarye could never be strange."

"More than you know, brother," Magnus sighed. "Thomas Wolfe was right in saying 'You can't go home again.'"

Geoffrey's frown deepened. "You *are* home."

"Yes, but in the years I've been gone, home has changed, and I have changed, and it will take some time for me to find myself a new place and become a part of the kingdom again."

Geoffrey decided that, all in all, Magnus finding a new place, rather than trying to bull his way into his old one, might not be a bad thing. "How shall you find that place, then?"

"By approaching Gramarye the way I approached any planet on which I landed—as a new world, one which I'll have to study before I try to do anything. I've always taken a few months to get the feel of a place and learn the basics of its culture before I ever thought of any kind of action."

"What sort of action might that be?" Geoffrey asked, on his guard again.

"Well, first, to discover if my interference was warranted, or if things were all right as they were," Magnus said, "but I had judged well from such historical records as I had, and from my reconnaissance in orbit; only one of those planets did have a government that suited the people, though it was very hard to discover."

"And the rest?" Geoffrey demanded.

"I set out to overthrow their tyrants, of course," Magnus said, "and to make planets proof against SCENT's machinations. With the sublime audacity and supreme arrogance of youth, I never stopped to think that I had no more right to meddle than SCENT had—but, like them, I was certain I was doing it for the people's own good."

"Supreme arrogance indeed." Geoffrey frowned.

"At least I chose planets on which the bulk of the population were clearly oppressed," Magnus said. "The first solo I tried was on a planet called Melange, where the colonists had made their own try at the ideal society—essentially an eighteenth-century culture, periwigs and kneepants, paniers and pompadours—and had cloned the few servants they had brought along into a massive underclass. Having made them, of course, they feared them, and ruled them with iron oppression. They kept modern technology, but only for themselves."

"Which rather negated the advantages of any gadgetry you might have brought along!"

Magnus nodded. "Therefore I went down to the planet

with only a peasant's clothes on my back and my spaceship in orbit."

"Foolishly strolling into danger, brother!"

"Of course," Magnus said in surprize. "Don't try to tell me you would have done anything else, Geoffrey."

Geoffrey stared at him a moment, then broke into a shamefaced smile. "Well, but that is *me,* brother. I would not see *you* imperilled."

"No more than I would you," Magnus returned. "After a week of skulking about like an outlaw, trying to learn the inside of the society and failing, I had the good luck to make a local contact—Dirk Dulaine."

Geoffrey frowned. "I thought you said he was a spacer."

"He was, but he had been born a churl—that's what they called their clones—and escaped as a boy, whereupon he had been recruited into an organization of other escaped churls, one that had been going on for more than a century. Their founders had managed to hitch rides off-planet, work their way up to riches, and buy a foundering interstellar cargo line, which bought out the supply rights for Melange—so Dirk was a local boy from a backward culture, but had a modern education. He was also a trained commando . . ."

"Like yourself," Geoffrey interjected.

"There were a few similarities," Magnus admitted. "We strolled the land looking for ways to overthrow the lords. Dirk told me the time was right; there was a prophecy that DeCade, the leader of a centuries-old rebellion, would rise from the dead to lead them again, and if he was ever going to wake up, the time was near. Unfortunately, I was captured by a lord who decided I would make a perfect gladiator . . ."

He went on, telling of his battle in the arena, and Geoffrey listened, enthralled, as his brother told a fantastic tale of a pitched battle between gladiators and lords, of automated hideouts for aristocrats and a sojourn in a madhouse—a horrible place for a telepath; it had driven Magnus into catatonia—and of Magnus himself finally becoming DeCade.

Thrilled and shocked by turns and appalled at the dangers Magnus had faced, Geoffrey cursed himself for not having been there to protect his big brother—never stopping to think that he had been far too young.

"A MINSTREL! THERE'S a minstrel come to the common!"

"New songs! News!"

Suddenly all the young folk were running back to the village, leaving the grain to stand unharvested another day. Diru dropped his scythe and went to run with them, but Hirol elbowed him in the ribs and Arker kicked a foot between his ankles, saying, "Keep your place, lummox!"

Diru stumbled and fell; Hirol and Arker laughed and ran on. Lenar and her friends ran past, giggling. Diru heard one say, "He can't even keep on his feet!!"

Face crimson, Diru struggled up and lumbered after, limping now. He managed to ignore the shoots of pain that went up his shin every time his left foot hit the ground; it wasn't really much, certainly less than the embarrassment of having the girls watch him fall—tripping over his own feet again, they probably thought.

Diru was a little shorter than the other boys but a great deal more bulky. It was all muscle—well, mostly—but it didn't look that way. Too much muscle—he was slow; all the other boys could punch much faster, and did. He was moon-faced with a snub nose, small thin-lipped mouth and narrow eyes with sparse, dun-colored hair—certainly no prize to look at, as his mother kept reminding him. He knew she was right, because the village girls looked right past him and never seemed to see him unless he was being more clumsy than usual.

He hated them for it. Hated the boys, too, for making fun of him and beating him if he dared talk back. Some day he'd find a way to get even, some day . . .

But not now. The young folk fell silent as they dodged between huts into the village common, and Diru could hear the plucking of strings. Way behind the others and only a little ahead of the grown-ups, he lumbered into the common, slowed, and stopped, gasping for breath but already listening.

"When the wind blows cold o'er the stream at night,
(All along, down along, out along lea!)
The Monster King gathers his swords for the fight,
Horsemen and pikemen and catmen with glee!

Then when the mist rises o'er the river at dawn,
(All along, down along, out along lea!)
His legions burst forth, every dire dreadful pawn,
Boneless and ogres and redcaps they be!

"But they cannot come nigh of their own desire,
(All along, down along, out along lea!)
Unless some fool asks them, they're bound to their
    mire,
Every fang-toothed and sword-clawed nightmare we
    see!"

The minstrel went on, describing the horrors that had
burst from the mist over their nearby river the year before.
He didn't mention how they'd been chased home—everyone
knew the Gallowglasses had defeated them, with the king's
army right behind to cut down the few monsters who had escaped. It was a tale that made Diru's blood sing, that called
up wonderful pictures of heroic young folk like himself—
but the minstrel didn't sing of that, he sang only of the
deed that had allowed the monsters to burst out of their
mist-bound realm, the foolishness of the villagers who had
sought to appease the hideous creatures by inviting them to
come, thinking they would be spared by showing friendship—but their leader hadn't; the giant cat Big Ears had
killed him where he stood before the wizards could send it
back where it had come from.

"So never invite, never think to appease," the min-
    strel sang,
"For the Monster King's favored ones swing in the
    breeze!"

But Diru was suddenly fired with inspiration. That
wasn't true, couldn't be true! Anyone these spiteful villagers feared had to be Diru's friend! And a way to gain revenge on them all . . .

He shuddered and thrust the idea from him; even they didn't deserve to be torn apart by nightmares. He paid closer attention as the minstrel began to sing a happier song and hoped the horrid vision would fade.

ALLOUETTE ROSE FROM lotus position and went silently away. Instantly concerned but delayed by the depths of his trance, Gregory let his consciousness drift upward until, minutes later, he surfaced and raised his head, frowning. He rose and went after his wife, soft-footed.

He found her by a window in their solar. "What troubles you, love?"

Allouette kept her back turned to him, only waving him away—but even without reading her mind, Gregory could feel the apprehension radiating from her. He came up behind her, arms open to embrace, but had the good sense not to touch her. "Is it Magnus?"

Thirteen

"YOU MUST NOT READ MY MIND IF I DO NOT invite you!"

"I do not," Gregory said, "nor do I need telepathy to guess the cause of your concern. Love, be sure—Magnus forgives you as completely as any man may. As he comes to know you, even this current . . . awkwardness . . . between you will pass."

"You cannot mean he will learn to trust me!"

"I mean exactly that," Gregory said, "for you are as unlike the woman who hurt him as any could be, save for your beauty and your spirit."

Allouette strangled a sob.

"Yes, I know you did not consider yourself a beauty then—but you were, even without projecting any idealized image. Still and all, you did project it, and it is that image he associates with hurt, not your true self."

"Then why is he still so chill toward me?" Allouette spun about, and Gregory saw her cheeks were wet and her eyes red. "How can we possibly go on in our lives with my unspoken guilt hanging between us?"

"It will pass," Gregory assured her. "It is only there now because, in all ways, you are a stranger to him."

"A stranger and a horrid memory!" Allouette finally came into his arms and buried her head on his shoulder. "Oh, Gregory, how shall we fare with your family now? I had begun to believe your sister and brother had really begun to accept me, and their spouses, too! This throws it all agley!"

"If I know them," Gregory said drily, "Magnus's dislikes will have no effect. His pain might, but you are no longer a cause of that."

"But I am!" Allouette raised her head, staring into his eyes. "He and Alea so clearly care for one another, but he will not admit it even to himself—and why? Because of the hurt I gave him ten years ago!"

"It cannot be your hurt alone that chains him," Gregory protested. "Besides, what of Alea? Why will she not admit her attraction to him?"

"There are signs." Allouette's own fears became secondary as she spoke of someone else's. "Even without reading her mind, I can see that she was hurt, and deeply— more than once, or I miss my guess."

Gregory studied her, frowning. "But they have journeyed together for four years. Would the hurt throttle her for so long?"

"Oh, yes! So I have no doubt it still troubles your brother." Her eyes brimmed again. "Oh, Gregory, he will poison the others against me, even if he does not mean to do so!"

"Against us," Gregory said firmly, "and if for no other reason, he will learn to like you for my sake."

"But if he holds true to his promise to your father, he will become chief of you all and turn Cordelia and Geoffrey away from me!"

"You and Quicksilver have become the sisters Cordelia never had," Gregory said firmly. "She will not give you up at Magnus's order—nor will he give such orders, for he knows that would set us against him. He may have ruled us when we were children, or thought he did, but he certainly will not now that we are grown."

"Gregory, the man has immense power, I can feel it! More than he did ten years ago, much more! And he has learned subtlety and manipulation on his travels. I shall not dare to go to court while he is there."

"Then we shall stay here in our ivory tower." Gregory pressed her closer. "You are certainly world enough for me. What need have I for anything else, so long as you are by me?"

Trembling, Allouette lifted her head. "Oh, you and this tower are certainly all I need, too. I have had enough of the world, and I shall let it have no more of me!"

They gazed into each other's eyes a moment, then kissed. Allouette closed her eyes and let Gregory's embrace be her universe, concentrated on nothing but the feel of his lips, his arms, his hands . . .

Hours later, when she was soundly asleep, Gregory rose from their bed and dressed quietly. He left a note assuring her he would be back the next day, only had to attend to a brief errand. Then he went down the spiral stair to the base of the tower and, with several floors between them to absorb the noise, disappeared with a bang of imploding air.

EVANESCENT BECAME AWARE of the sounds around her but lay still a while longer, probing her surroundings with her mind. Satisfied that there was no danger near, she opened her eyes and lifted her head. Stipples of moonlight floored the glade where she had chosen to sleep for the day. She admired the beauty of the scene until her stomach reminded her it was time to hunt. She rose, stretched, then padded out into the glade and stood, mind questing for something edible. Though her visible teeth were those of a carnivore, the molars behind them were adapted for plants. The small people were so very protective of their forest that she decided it might be the course of prudence to seek out some nuts and berries.

Not that she was afraid of those diminutive beings, of course—well, not much. Her own extrasensory powers were so strong that no single one of them, not even the one who called himself the Puck, would stand much chance against her—no, not even if he drew on the powers of five or six of his fellows.

The trouble was that he was apt to come with twenty or more.

No, the course of prudence dictated a vegetable diet for a while—at least, until Evanescent was more certain of the Wee Folks' intentions. She padded in among the trees, night-vision alert for anything that looked edible. Leaves, shrubs, fungi . . .

The alien stopped, frowning, to stare at a mound of something that looked like moss. She lowered her head to sniff; it didn't smell like moss. In fact, its scent was that of fungus.

Witch-moss! She remembered it from Magnus's thoughts. Wondering if it really was sensitive to telepathy, she aimed a thought at it, a memory of a large and luscious fruit from her home planet—and stared in wonder as the mound pulled in on itself, rounding on one end and pointing on the other, its color deepening to mauve, until her homeworld fruit lay before her.

Hunger rumbled again; she lowered her head to sniff and found its aroma exactly as it should be. She wondered if it would be good to eat but decided on the course of prudence.

She sat back on her haunches, head tilted to one side, considering the fruit. Was it frozen in that form now, or could she make it into something else? She stared at it, thinking of a stick she had seen the day before, one that had caught her attention because of its curious knobbed shape.

The fruit shrank in on itself, its color darkening, as it stretched, roughened, and turned into the stick.

Evanescent stared. Then she grinned and batted at the stick with a paw; it rolled over just as a real stick would do. In fact, it felt like a real stick. She tilted her head to the side again, thinking of Alea's dagger, then of a ball she had seen children play with on one of the planets they had visited, then a woman's mortar and pestle—and watched as the lump of witch-moss changed from one form to another.

Evanescent lay down, staring at the mortar and pestle intently. What of something that could move? She thought of an elf, and the lump began to change—but Evanescent realized the small people might be angry if she imitated them, or anything that had a mind. She changed her thought at the last moment; the lump sprouted legs and a chest, but nothing more. She decided to make it look like a stick again, then told it to move, and a little stick man marched up and down before her.

There was a rustling in the underbrush.

Evanescent was on her feet in the blink of an eye, whirling to face the sound—and saw half a dozen more stick men come marching out from the fallen leaves. She stared, then grinned, realizing what had happened—she hadn't limited her thoughts; other lumps of witch-moss had taken on the same shape as the one she'd been playing with and had come marching to the one who had thought them up.

More rustling; she whirled, and saw more stick figures marching out of a thicket. Rustling again; she spun about and saw another dozen striding out from some brambles. She lay down and grinned, thinking directions at them, and the stick figures came together, formed ranks, and marched out into the glade.

Hunger forgotten, Evanescent lay in the moon-shadow of an oak, watching her new-made toys march and counter-march in ever-more-intricate formations.

GREGORY APPEARED IN the solar of Castle Gallow-glass with the sound of a firecracker as his sudden presence compressed the air about him. He looked about him to discover no one there in the early morning, then strode down the hall to his brother's suite. No one answered his knock. Frowning, he opened his mind to the world around and found no other mind within the suite, but felt Magnus's presence above. He would have been ashamed to teleport so short a distance, so he ran up the stairs.

"HO THE CASTLE!"

The sentry stepped up to the battlement wall and waved to the man he had been watching ride up, then saw the shield slung at the horse's rump and the coat of arms emblazoned on it. He didn't recognize those arms, but it didn't matter—the man was a knight at least, possibly a lord. "Aye, good sir. I prithee attend while I take tidings of you to my lord."

"Well, be about it quickly," the stranger knight called back, clearly not pleased with the answer. "I've ridden long and would rest and drink."

The sensible thing would be to raise the portcullis and let the man in on the spot, but it wasn't the sentry's decision to make. He called his mate and ran off to tell the Captain of the Guard.

The Captain knew the forms, and the precautions with them; he bade the porter lower the drawbridge and raise the portcullis, then conducted the stranger into the guest chamber of the manor house. He was sitting at his ease with a glass of wine in his hand when his host of necessity came in. "Welcome, Sir Knight!"

"Lord Anselm Loguire!" The knight rose and bowed. "I am Sir Orgon of Needsham, knight errant."

He was clearly a rather unsuccessful knight, to be errant at his age—forty if he was a day. His doublet and hose were of good cloth but worn, and his boots, though well-polished under the dust of travel, were equally worn.

"You are welcome, Sir Knight." Anselm Loguire might have had the stranger thrust upon him, but he was by no means a reluctant host. News was rare and treasured, as was a new face—and if the man turned out to be unpleasant, why, he was only staying the night. "Have you travelled far, Sir Orgon?"

The knight sighed. "Over hill and dale, milord duke . . ."

"*Sir* Loguire, if it please you," Anselm said firmly, but bitterness tightened his face. "I am only a knight, like yourself, and was never rightly duke of Loguire."

"Well, no, but by rights you should have been, should you not?" The stranger knight gave him a keen glance, then dropped his gaze. "But I presume. Let me tell you the news of the capital, as I had it from the knight with whom I broke a lance outside the keep of Rodenge."

"I hunger for it," Anselm said, eyes bright, "as I think

you hunger for bread and meat. Come, Sir Orgon, let us find happier quarters than these. What of His Majesty?"

"Your younger brother is alive and well, though saddened by the loss of a friend." Sir Orgon fell in step with his host.

"A friend?" Hope brightened Anselm's eyes—or was it vindication? "Not the Lord Warlock, surely?"

"Nay, Sir Anselm—his wife."

Anselm stared in shock.

"It was neither sudden nor painful, they say," the knight began, and told as much as he knew of the event as he followed his host. He was remarkably well informed for one who had heard of it, not been there—he told of Magnus's return and of the funeral and the subsequent events as they dined.

They had finished their meal and were sharing a bowl of sweetmeats by the time he told of the Lord Warlock's departure into the wildwood, bound no one knew where.

Anselm had come alive with the description of Rod Gallowglass's trials. Now he leaned back, swirling the wine in his cup, and mused, "I have heard he has taken leave of his senses now and then. Perhaps he has done so again."

"I doubt it not, Sir Anselm—but by his going, he has left the Crown unguarded."

Anselm stilled. "What do you say?"

"Only that, if ever the lords wish to claim back their rights and powers, the time to strike is come." Sir Orgon leaned forward with glittering eyes. "But they will not rise without a leader, and who better to command them than the rightful duke of Loguire?"

Anselm sat frozen, not believing he was hearing talk of rebellion again after all these years—or how welcome that talk was, or how it roused a sudden yearning for revenge. He hated himself for it, but he listened all the more intently.

"The Crown has lost its two most stalwart supporters," Sir Orgon said. "There will never be a better time to rise."

For a moment, Sir Anselm's eyes burned; then he summoned the will to resist and forced himself to stand, pushing back his chair, and said, "I have no stomach for talk of treason, Sir Orgon. I will bid you good night."

He turned and stalked away, not waiting even to see Sir Orgon stand in respect—but the knight watched him go, eyes glittering, knowing that his fish was half-hooked. If he were not, if he were truly loyal down to his bones, Sir Orgon would have been clapped into irons on the spot and would have spent his night in a dungeon cell.

AS DARKNESS FELL, Rod found a stream, kindled a solitary fire for warmth, then went to the brook with his folding bucket, brought back water, and hung the bucket over the fire to heat for tea. Then he took jerky, cheese, and hardtack out of his saddlebag and sat down on a log to have dinner.

"That really is not adequate fare for an evening meal, Rod. You usually find wild vegetables and heat them with the beef as a stew."

"Yeah, but what's the point in cooking for just one, Fess?"

"Health, Rod."

"So what's it going to do—kill me?" Rod gave the horse a sardonic smile. "I'll gather vegetables as we go tomorrow—but right now, I'm tired."

A low growling began off to his right, swelling into a heart-rending moan.

Rod froze. "What was that?"

"A waveform of low . . ."

"Yeah, I could tell that much. What made it?"

"From the quality, Rod, I would assume it is a creature in distress."

Rod stood, came over to stuff his dinner back into the saddlebag, and led Fess off into the woods. "Can't ride—the trees are too thick. How far away is whoever made that moan?"

"It is difficult to tell with only the distance between my ears for triangulation, Rod."

The moan sounded again.

"Make a guess!" Rod said. "Whoever that is, they're in dire distress."

"Rod, you know my distaste for . . ."

"Okay, call it an estimate! Just tell me how far!"

Static crackled through Rod's implanted earphone—Fess's version of a sigh. "Perhaps two hundred meters, Rod."

"To carry this far, that would have to be a pretty loud moan. Let's hurry as much as we can, Fess—whoever that is, needs help in a bad way."

There was a little moonlight—not enough to show the roots or potholes that waited to trip Rod, but enough so that he could keep from blundering into tree trunks. As he went, though, the moonlight seemed to grow brighter. A little farther and he saw the cause—delicate strings of light hanging all about. With a shock, he realized they were branches, and the leaves that hung from them began to glow. Another few yards, and he found himself walking through a forest of crystal, adorned with berries that were gems and filled with the delicate silver glow of moonlight concentrated and refracted all about him. "What is this place?" he asked in a hushed voice.

The moan came again, much nearer. Rod turned to his right—and stepped across an unseen boundary. Everything about him was dark and dank; the branches hung bare, and mold squelched beneath his boots, filling his head with the stench of corruption. He found himself in a pocket of decay in the center of the crystalline wood. He half expected a skeleton to rise from the muck.

Not a skeleton, but right beside him rose a glowing figure hung with rags, its cheeks sunken, its skin withered and wrinkled, its eyes lost in the shadows under its brow, long trails of mucus streaking down its cheeks. It moaned, the sound so loud that Rod clapped his hands over his ears—but it drifted toward him, reaching out a skeletal finger to touch him.

Fourteen

ROD FLINCHED AWAY, BUT TOO LATE—HE HAD
felt that touch graze his shoulder, and his arm suddenly
weakened.

"Why come you here, foolish mortal?" the apparition
demanded. "What has brought you so far down this road?"

"Time." Rod lifted his arm to fend off the spectre even
as he backed away—but that arm seemed leaden, taking a
titanic effort to lift, and wouldn't rise more than half-way.
Rod gave it a quick glance and was shocked to see that the
skin of his hand was wrinkled, the muscles of the arm
shrunken. He backed away quickly, not stopping to wonder
how the creature had come to be—on Gramarye, there was
no doubt it was real, for all practical purposes.

"Turn aside," the creature advised, "for know that you
have come to the place of Decay, where you shall waste
away till you can neither walk nor lift, nor even raise your
hands to eat."

"There is always the mind," Rod said. His arm was in-
tolerably heavy; he fought to keep it high, but it drooped

steadily. He had to let it fall; he needed all his attention to avoid the creature's next lunge.

"Your mind too shall waste away," the spectre intoned. "Go back, human creature. You may not be able to choose your death, but you can surely choose not to have this one."

"Can I?" Rod met the hollow gaze with a level stare. "My road goes on past this place, Decay. I will not turn aside; the one I love awaits upon the farther side."

"Then you are a fool, for you'll not pass," Decay answered. "Your hips shall seize up, your spine shall bend, your muscles shall waste away." It drifted closer, finger reaching out. "Beware my touch."

"Good advice." Rod stepped aside.

The spirit turned and came after him. "Forgo this land, go out from this forest—for even that creature that goes on four legs in morn and two legs at noon must walk on three when coming here—and shall leave on four again, if it goes at all."

"A human." Rod sidestepped the touch and backed away again. "That's an old conundrum, spirit. Surely you can do better than that."

"I have no need," Decay answered, "for your mind shall fade so gently as to escape your notice. Can you not feel your acuity slipping even as you speak?"

"No, for if it were to fade so gently that I didn't realize, how could I feel it?" Rod sidestepped another touch. "Fess, come up behind this creature and pull it away!"

"I see nothing, Rod, except a small clearing in the woods, like any other. You must tell me where to bite."

Illusion! Rod realized. But was it in his own mind, his old delusions returning, or was it the work of a projective telepath? Or even a witch-moss construct that was visible only to living creatures? Rod had no idea how such a thing could be made but didn't doubt that it could.

"You are liable to me, as are all living things," Decay told him. "You cannot turn me any more than you can turn that invader who roars across the land and whom even the Crown with all its soldiers cannot divert."

"The wind," Rod interpreted, "and we may not be able to turn it aside, but we can certainly harness it with windmills. Will you do as much work for us as it does?"

"I shall work upon you." All at once, the spirit darted forward, lunging to touch.

Rod ducked and said, "I have it! You yourself are a riddle!"

"Foolish human, I am nothing of the sort," Decay answered, still drifting toward him. "I am inevitable, if you are born to meet me."

"Not since DNA surgery was invented," Rod said, "and since my great-grandparents all had it, I'm exempt from your domain."

"Do you mean to say you are not human?" Decay kept drifting even as it spoke. "Then you are truly a fool! But how can a man not be a fool and still be a man?"

"When he's dead and gone," Rod said, then leaped aside to avoid another lunge. "All men are fools in some way—the more so because we can't agree on which behavior is foolish. Some of us are fools about money, some are fools about power and status, some are fools over women . . . The list is endless."

"Then cease your folly and hold still to receive my touch."

"Ah, but that would be the greatest folly of all." Rod still backed away, feeling an idea germinate. "After all, it's clear you're trying to distract me with riddles so that I'll slip and let you touch me. I've no desire to waste into an imitation of you."

"How shall you avoid me, then?" Decay asked. "All living things must age, and age is wasting."

"Yes, but you're the spirit of wasting disease, aren't you?" Rod countered. "More particularly, of inborn wasting conditions." Out of the corner of his eye, Rod saw Fess standing stolidly opposite him and knew that he had come half-way around the clearing. What a sight he must have made, backing away from a nonexistent creature!

"All must wither, soon or late."

"Later, thank you." Rod leaped high and far.

The spirit lunged forward with a cry of rage in one last attempt to touch Rod and infect him, but he landed outside the circle of mold on the glistening ground amid the crystalline trees, out of the shadow and back in the light of the moon.

"You cannot truly escape!" the spirit cried. "You must come to me some day!"

"No I won't," Rod countered, "because I have a friend to transport me beyond your reach. Over here, Fess."

The robot horse paced toward him across the darkened circle. With a glad cry, the spirit of Decay surged toward him, reaching out to touch—then crying out in dismay and rage. "This is no living horse, but a thing of metal!"

"Beneath the synthetic horsehair, yes," Rod confirmed, "and he's built to last considerably longer than I am."

"Even things of Cold Iron must rust away!" the spirit threatened, and floated beside Fess, darting its touch at Fess's withers, backbone, flanks.

"Well, yes, but Fess's body is a rust-proof alloy," Rod explained. "He's only metaphorically of Cold Iron—and even then, when this mechanical body breaks down, we can always get him another one. The computer inside him may be long outmoded, but it's made of materials that don't erode."

The spirit made one more lunge at Fess's retreating form and cried in anger, "You have cheated me! But one day I shall have my due!"

"You already have," Rod said grimly. "You've taken my wife, and with her, my heart. Be assured, if I could find a way to rid the universe of you, I would—and my children just may learn how."

"None can defeat me! Even you and your contraption have only avoided me!"

"I know," Rod said. "You're an aspect of Entropy and are inherent in the universe itself. But we can make humanity immune to you—and some day, someone will."

"You speak like Tithonus, foolish mortal!"

"What, to be wanting eternal life and forget to ask for eternal youth?" Rod shook his head. "Other way around, haunt of humans. I ask to be immune from the ravages of age—but I don't exactly want to live forever." His laugh was short, bitter, and sardonic.

"You laugh at nothing, Rod," Fess pointed out.

"Or at something that will come to nothing," Rod said, "and try to take me with it. Come on, Fess. We have moonlight enough to find a road through this wood."

He mounted and rode off, leaving the spirit to gnash its teeth and wail.

NEARBY, A DOZEN elves sat spellbound among the crystal leaves, watching Rod ride away. Puck looked up at Evanescent. "Well done, strange creature. You have given him a foe to outsmart when he needed one. I did much the same myself, when he was young and had need of a dragon to combat."

"It was nothing," Evanescent answered. She certainly wasn't about to tell Puck that she spoke only but the truth. The illusion of the moonlight-filled, crystalline wood she had indeed made for Rod—but where Decay and its mouldering circle had come from, she had no idea.

GEOFFREY WENT OUT the door, and Magnus sat completely still for several minutes. Then he took a very long breath and turned back to the books and papers spread out on his desk. He studied them for half an hour with nothing registering; his mind kept going back to Geoffrey and their confrontation. He was finally beginning to be able to concentrate on the print instead of the problems with his siblings when he heard a knock. He sat very still for half a minute, then looked up at the sentry with a bland smile. "Yes, trooper?"

"Your brother, Sir Magnus."

Magnus stared, his thoughts still on Geoffrey, then smiled with relief as Gregory came in. Magnus stood, raising his arms—then lowered them as he saw Gregory's frown. He came around the desk slowly, smile still plastered on his face, and said, "Good morning, brother. Some tea?"

"Not now, I think, Magnus." Gregory took a chair without being invited.

Magnus took the point and sat across from him. Of course, Gregory couldn't know he was sitting where Geoffrey had only half an hour before. Well, actually, he could know, but he wouldn't—none of the siblings went in for mental eavesdropping without very strong cause; they'd been reared better than that. "You are well today, I hope—and Allouette, too?"

"I am well enough, brother," Gregory said, "but Allou-ette is very concerned."

So much for social pleasantries. "Concerned about me? I should be of no consequence to her—far away and un-seen."

"She fears that you shall begin giving me orders and drive a wedge between us."

Magnus gazed at his youngest sib with bent brows for a few seconds, then said, "She still does not understand the depth or intensity of your love, then."

Gregory blushed and looked away. "She is very inse-cure, brother. I have told you of her past; you cannot won-der that she is slow to learn to trust again."

"Then I think she has made remarkable strides, consid-ering how thoroughly Cordelia and Quicksilver have bonded with her."

Gregory nodded slowly. "They adventured together, and common enemies have a way of making faster friends quite quickly—as I am sure you know."

"Friendship grows slowly for me," Magnus said, "but I am fortunate in having made two close friends."

"Shield-mates."

Magnus nodded.

Gregory frowned at him, then said, "You seemed open enough to her until you heard her name, brother. Then, well though you tried to hide it, all of us could see how you hes-itated. Why?"

It wasn't like Gregory to be so direct, but Magnus had heard love could cause such changes. " 'Allouette' was also the name of the woman who recruited me into SCENT, brother—not entirely by reason alone."

"Her beauty?" Gregory asked.

Magnus nodded. "I would scarcely say I was swept away, but I was very much aware of the attraction. Finister did that much for me, at least—that I became very slow to fall in love."

"Which is to say that you never have." For the moment, Gregory was full of sympathy. "I cannot tell you how deeply Allouette regrets what she did to you, brother. Whenever she thinks of it, she is filled with anguish again."

"Then it is a wonder she can bear to look upon my face." Magnus smiled. "This scarcely needed telling, Gregory—but I am glad that you did."

"I do not merely *show* concern," Gregory said anxiously. "I *am* concerned for your emotional welfare, brother."

"I have always managed to keep my wits about me," Magnus hedged, "so I was well aware that the other Allouette meant to use me and was enraged when I disobeyed orders and did what was right for the people of the planet I was supposed to subvert, rather than what was right for SCENT."

"So," Gregory said softly, "two women to whom you were attracted, hurt and abused you. No wonder you chilled on the sound of the name."

Magnus nodded. "But it is certainly no fault of your bride's, nor do I hold it against her."

"But her actions toward you ten years ago?"

"I can forgive, Gregory, and have. In time, I am sure I will forget them completely."

After a moment, Gregory nodded, though reluctantly, then sat forward, suddenly even more intent. "Understand, though, brother—even were you to attempt to command us, neither of us would obey."

"Then I shall give no orders."

Gregory's brows drew together; his intensity sharpened. "Do not think to use us as your magical tools, Magnus. You cannot know anything of our research."

"Absolutely nothing," Magnus admitted cheerfully, "and for that reason, I would not dream of telling either of you what to study and what not."

"And would not ask us to study certain uses of magic for the Crown?" Gregory asked suspiciously.

"I think the Crown can do its own asking," Magnus said. "After all, you are not exactly unknown to our sovereign and her husband, not to mention their younger son. Is your friendship with Diarmid still close?"

"We have drifted somewhat apart," Gregory admitted, "though we still share the occasional game of chess."

Magnus nodded. "Then I am sure he could mention any

problems his parents thought needed investigation before he said 'Check.' "

Gregory smiled. "Before the game, rather. Studying the next move would drive it completely out of his head."

"Ever the scholar," Magnus said, amused, "both of you. I wonder how he manages as Duke of Loguire."

"Quickly, as I understand it," Gregory said. "He is very efficient, clearing up administrative details before midday so that he can spend the afternoons in study."

Magnus raised a skeptical eyebrow. "And his peasants are none the worse for it?"

"He has an excellent steward," Gregory said, "who is always out among the people—but I suspect Diarmid's tenure lacks the personal touch."

Resolved that easily, the conversation passed to updating Magnus on events in the kingdom, and Gregory finally accepted tea. When the cup was empty and he rose to go, though, he paused at the door to look back, suddenly intent again. "I have your word on it, brother? That you shall not try to command us, nor to come between us?"

"My word of honor," Magnus said gravely, "and I shall swear an oath to it if you feel the need."

Gregory gazed into his eyes a few seconds, then nodded. "I do not think we will. Good night, brother." He went out the door.

Magnus stood immobile a minute, then lowered himself carefully into his chair and placed his hands on his knees. After a few more minutes, he tilted his head back against the upholstery and closed his eyes.

ROD LET FESS choose their path and concentrated all his attention on pumping strength back into that withered arm. Its maiming had to have been an illusion, though a very powerful one; whatever latent telepath had unwittingly created Decay to embody his worst fears, had made it projective, too, and if the mind could be convinced that the body was wasting, why, waste it would.

So Rod's first purpose was to convince himself, very thoroughly, that his arm was sound and healthy. He fell into the trance he had learned early in his training as a secret agent, working downward to the bedrock of his beliefs and discovering anew that, even at the most fundamental level, he knew Decay to be only an illusion. Unfortunately, all his emotions between that foundation and the superstructure of intellect believed the spirit to be real.

So Rod began to work on convincing himself that the illusion was only that, an illusion, and nothing real—further, that his arm hadn't really withered, that the illusion was only an extremely convincing projection.

When morning came, his arm was whole again, and he was so exhausted that he barely managed to spread out his blanket roll before he fell on it and slept.

MAGNUS WAS STILL sitting in the same posture when Alea strode into the room. "Are you still poking into mouldering books, Gar? It's high time . . ." She broke off, staring at him, reading the great soul-weariness of his posture. She studied him a moment, then brought the straight chair from the desk to sit beside him. Gently, she covered his hand with her own.

Magnus opened his eyes, saw her, and slowly lifted his head.

"As bad as that?" Alea asked softly.

Magnus studied her a moment, then glanced at the door; it swung to and closed quietly. He turned back to Alea and acknowledged, "As bad as that." He shook his head in exasperation. "They've all grown up; their powers are mature. They're equal to any threat. Nothing can stand against them—if they all work together!"

"Then the first thing any enemy will do, will be to try to split them apart."

"Oh, I don't think he'd have to—they're bidding to do a fair job of it themselves!" Magnus sighed as he leaned his head back again. "Why do they all think I'm going to try to boss them around?"

Alea chose her words carefully. "Perhaps because you did when you all were little."

Magnus lifted his head, frowning at her. "How did you know?"

"I didn't; I guessed," Alea answered. "Why else would they all be so worried about it now?"

"Because Dad asked me to promise to take care of Gramarye and its people." Magnus shook his head. "Whyever would he do that?"

"Because he knows you can," Alea said instantly, "knows you can fight off any enemies that come, from inside or from outside. But bossing people isn't your style, Gar." She smiled ruefully. "No, I suppose I should say, 'Magnus' now, shouldn't I?"

"You shall call me anything you please." Gar locked gazes with her a moment, covering her hand with his. Then he looked away with a sardonic smile. "But as to bossing people, I've done my share on occasion."

"Yes, but only when there was no one local you could maneuver into it."

"Well, of course." Gar frowned. "After all, they were going to be there for their whole lives. I wasn't."

"You will now." Instantly Alea regretted saying it.

Magnus sat still and somber, gazing at the window. "I suppose I shall," he said at last. "Not so bad a thing, after all. I've longed for home these last ten years. Now I shall have it again." He turned to her with concern. "But you won't."

"I don't have one," Alea snapped.

"I could take you back." With a sudden heave, Magnus pushed himself up. "Back to Midgard to stay there with you—and leave this nest of infighting factions and jealous siblings behind!"

Alea's heart skipped a beat, but she knew he'd spoken more truly the first time. "Back to that nest of bigots and sexists? No thank you, Gar! I don't have a home there any more—I haven't since my parents died! I'll stay here and find some way to make it my home, thank you very much!"

Gar turned back to her, frowning with concern again. "Are you sure you wouldn't rather tramp the spaceways for the rest of your life? Always a new planet, new sights, new customs . . ."

Alea shuddered. "I think not. Oh, it's been good in its

way, but I'd rather stay put. At least there are people here who know you—and are being friendly toward me."

Magnus gave her another long stare, then nodded and sat down again. "Here we stay, then. After all, if I get really sick of it, we can do as Gregory's done—go out into the mountains and build our own house away from them all!"

Alea stared, thunderstruck by his assumption that they would spend their lives together—but she pushed the issue aside, and smiled with relief; she knew one challenge from a real enemy would be all it would take to kindle his enthusiasm again. "There's always that. Of course, we could tramp the roadways here for a while, as we have on three other planets. You'd be building a network, planting ideas, making everything ready in case it's needed."

"A very attractive idea," Magnus said with feeling. He turned to smile at her and squeezed her hand. "Yes, I always have that, don't I?"

"Of course." Alea returned the smile. "That's always been your way, while I've known you—pulling the strings unseen, strings that most people don't even know exist, manipulating where even other telepaths wouldn't realize it. If you need to take command at all, it won't be for very long."

"Yes, I have had some experience with that." Magnus nodded, gaze straying to the window again. "I've done it on so many other planets—why not on my own?"

"Why not indeed? If you have to, you'll be able to weld your siblings into a unit." Alea stood, holding out a hand to him. "But all this emotion-charged talk must have built up a ton of stress in you. Time for some martial arts practice, Ga . . . Magnus."

"I said call me what you will." He scowled up at her.

"I will call you Magnus." Alea returned glare for scowl. "If it's your real name, it should come naturally to me. Now are you coming to practice, or do I have to carry you?"

"Practice would be just the thing." Gar smiled, and from his mind, Alea caught a picture of himself draped over her shoulder. "I'll change and meet you in the courtyard."

Alea chose to dress for kendo, white top and long black trousers, so fully-cut that they wouldn't scandalize the

medieval people who might see. She was down on the clay
floor ten minutes later, but Gar was there before her in similar clothing, punching at the air in quick combinations,
dropping to a fencer's lunge and bouncing to stretch the
long muscles of his legs, up to punch again, then leaping
high to kick at an imaginary enemy while the sentries
watched in awe.

So did Alea; seeing Magnus come alive with action
made her catch her breath. He was so strong, so vital! But
within the man of war, she knew, was the soul of a poet—
and a man who cared far too much for the welfare of others. Watching him make a ballet of fighting, Alea
wondered if he would break from the stress his family had
heaped upon him. She would never let him know how concerned she was, of course.

No, not concerned. Watching him whirl and leap, Alea
finally admitted to herself that she was really, fully in love
with the man, and knew a moment's despair, for surely he
could never fall in love with so plain and gawky a woman
as she. Oh, he cared for her, she knew—as a friend.

Perhaps it was just as well that he couldn't see she was
in love with him.

Sighing, she went to become his sparring partner again.

OVER BREAKFAST THE next morning, Sir Orgon told
the tale of his travels, of the list of noblemen whose hospitality he had accepted—and who chafed under the rule of a
queen who would not let them lord it over their peasants as
they had been accustomed to.

Anselm listened quietly, but his eyes grew steadily hotter. When Sir Orgon had finished the list, Anselm
protested, "Surely these lords will not rise against their
liege."

"Not unless you are of their number." Sir Orgon locked
gazes with Sir Anselm and sat back, waiting.

Sir Anselm said stiffly, "I am not. I have no reason to resent Their Majesties."

"You have every reason," Sir Orgon contradicted. "She
attainted you, barred you from inheriting your father's castle and lands and title! She cast you into this exile in a

house not fit for a baron!" He carefully did not mention the queen's husband, Sir Anselm's brother.

"She did rightfully and mercifully," Sir Anselm said. "I was a traitor who had risen against the Crown; I deserved death on the block, not mere attainder."

"But your son does not," Sir Orgon said.

Fifteen

SIR ORGON KEPT HIS GAZE FIXED ON ANSELM'S and waited a few seconds for the thought to sink in—no one had ever claimed that Anselm Loguire was quick-witted—then went on. "Your son should have inherited the duchy of Loguire in his turn. What shall he have now? Only this poor castle, or the manor in which he dwells!"

Anselm's eyes burned with barely-suppressed anger. "Geordie and his good wife, Elaine, seem quite contented in their manor. His fields flourish; his peasants prosper."

"Indeed." Sir Orgon nodded. "Word has it that they are constantly out among their tenants, tending and healing and seeing that all goes well—as a steward should. I have even heard that at harvest, they are themselves in the field."

"So they would be even if Geordie were to appoint a seneschal," Anselm said roughly. "He loves the land and the people."

"That is well." Sir Orgon nodded sagely. "It is well they can be content with so little."

Anselm sat and glared at him, for even he realized what

had been left unsaid: that Geordie would never have anything more. Anselm's hatred for the queen and resentment of his brother was there in his face; perhaps it was well that only Sir Orgon could see it. But Anselm said, "I would remind you, Sir Orgon, that the queen is my sister-in-law, and that I would not willingly hurt my brother."

"Would you not?" Sir Orgon asked in feigned surprise. "But he was quick enough to attack you, thirty years ago!"

"Tuan did no such thing," Anselm snapped. "He defended the queen against my own uprising, nothing more—and he was right to do so, for I had broken the law."

"Had you?" Sir Orgon said quickly. "Or did you only seek to defend your age-old rights and privileges that she sought to usurp? Appointing priests on the lords' estates, sending her own judges to try your cases—woeful breaches of ancient custom indeed! No wonder you led the lords to rise in protest."

"And here is the result of that treachery," Sir Anselm snapped, "this manor, and this quiet life, rather than the headsman's axe and a narrow grave. I shall never fight against the Crown again, Sir Orgon." But envy and hatred were clearly eating him alive.

ROD CAME OUT of the woods onto the crest of a hill and pulled up, gazing down into the valley. Far below lay a tidy village, embraced by the hills whose sides were terraced into fields for farming. Those fields were green; maize already grew tall there, and at mid-morning Rod would have expected to see at least a few people out hoeing—but there was no one there, and no one moving in the village streets, either.

"Something's wrong here, Fess."

"Are there people inside the huts, Rod?"

Fess might be able to transmit on human thought-wave frequency, but he couldn't read minds unless thoughts were directed at him. Rod probed the village and found nothing. "Not a soul—and come to think of it, I don't see any smoke from the chimneys, either."

"If the hearths are cold, they have been gone for some time," Fess said.

Fire wasn't all that easy to kindle in a medieval society; peasants banked live coals to last the night and puffed them alive in the morning. Rod nodded. "Something scared them away—and not just a few hours ago, either."

"You are going to insist on riding down there to investigate, aren't you, Rod?"

"Sure am." Rod grinned, beginning to feel like his old self again—well, maybe his young self. "If there's somebody in a coma down there, we might be able to help—and if whatever scared them away is guarding the place, we should be able to draw it out of hiding."

"To fall on us with fang and claw, no doubt." Fess emitted the burst of static that served him as a sigh. "If you say we must, Rod."

"We must." Rod knew Fess was far more concerned for his rider than for himself—not that there was much that could dent the alloy body under his horsehair hide, anyway. But there were things from which he might not be able to protect Rod.

Rod intended to make sure he didn't have to. He readied his crossbow with the laser hidden in the stock. "Let's see what moves, shall we?"

Reluctantly, Fess began the plod down into the valley.

They rode slowly through the town's single street, seeing only leaves and sticks blowing in the occasional puff of wind and hearing only the banging of shutters that had come loose. "No sign of what drove them away," Rod said.

"Perhaps inside one of the houses?"

"Maybe, but I don't see any open doors, and even now I'm reluctant to break into somebody's house."

"Scruples well-advised, Rod—but there are loose shutters. You would be able to look in, at least."

"Still seems wrong," Rod grumbled, but he dismounted and walked up the beaten earth to the doorway of a peasant hut. There was no lawn, but the tenant had planted a few flowers, and Rod was careful to place his feet between the stems as he stepped up to the window. Looking in, he saw a single room with a rough table and benches near him, and in the outer wall, the fireplace that served as both heat source and stove.

"What do you see, Rod?"

"Only a tidy, well-kept room, Fess. Dusty now, though. I really should secure these shutters." He closed them, making sure the latch fell back into place as he did.

"There is another open window toward the back of the hut, Rod."

"Oh, so now I get to peek into the parents' bedroom, do I?" Nonetheless, Rod picked his way carefully around to the side of the house. There the going was easier, for the tenant hadn't planted flowers. Rod went back to the single flapping shutter, caught it as it swung toward his head, pushed it wider open, and stepped in front of it to look in.

The hag grinned at him, showing only two yellowed fangs left between leathery lips. Her hair was long, tangled, coarse, and would have been white if it had been clean. The same could be said for her dress. Her face was lined with a hundred wrinkles, and her eyes glittered with malice.

Rod recoiled, trying not to show his revulsion. "Oh! Sorry. Didn't know anyone was home."

"I am not," said the hag. "This is not my home—or at least, no more than any house."

Rod stepped closer, feeling considerably less guilty. "I hope you're not taking anything that belongs to the people who live there!"

"Only their peace of mind," the old woman said. "Only the harmony and sense of safety that used to fill this house."

Rod felt a thrill of fear—could this really be only an old woman? In the land of Gramarye, malignant spirits could take actual form—the spirits of malignity within ordinary people. He managed to ignore the fright, though, and the revulsion that came from the woman's neglect of herself, and asked, "Now, how did you do that?"

"That horse is old." The hag pointed at Fess. "See where his coat is wearing thin? Surely you can't depend on him to carry you much farther!"

Rod swallowed a smile. "Older than you think, beldame—but apt to stay in good condition longer than I will."

"Yes, your body will start to fail you in a year or two,

won't it?" she said with venom, then to Fess, "Why do you obey a master who ignores your welfare, beast? Know you not that he will ride you till you founder one of these days?"

Fess turned to give the woman a bland look, but inside Rod's head, his voice said, "I believe, Rod, that she spread these sorts of lies throughout the village."

"Aren't you a little transparent?" Rod asked the hag. "How could anyone believe such obvious lies?"

The woman's eyes sparked with anger. "Not lies, old fool, but saying large and loud the sort of things people wish to keep hidden—especially from themselves."

"Lies with a kernel of truth in each," Rod interpreted— and insight struck. "But you didn't tell them to the people themselves, did you? You told the husband his wife's faults and told her his. How many times did they scoff at you? So you made the lie even bigger when you told it to them again. How many times did you have to tell the same lie in different words before they began to believe you?"

"How many times have you shied away from your true nature?" the old woman snapped. "How many times have you overlooked your lord's highnosed ways and his heavy-handed treatment? The forests should be open to everyone! The deer are the property of the peasants, not the Crown!"

"Oho!" Rod lifted his head, leaning away from the gust of foul breath and fouler words. "So you didn't stop with setting husband against wife and sister against brother, did you? You tried to set them all against the Crown!" Then he frowned. "Or was that what you really meant to do all along?"

"The Count of Leachmere still forces each woman to his bed before she marries!" the hag raged. "The Earl of Tarnhelm flogs any peasant who dares go into the wood! Duke Bourbon turns his peasants out of their cottages when they're too old to work!"

"Only when they can't do the housekeeping any longer," Rod said. "Then he moves them into one of the one-bedroom cottages he's had built for his old folk, where he has people to look after them and take care of them."

"And despoil them of what little wealth they've managed to scrape together!"

"It doesn't cost them a penny." Rod gave her a sour smile. "He figures he comes out ahead because their children can do their work without worrying about their parents. And the cottages may be small, but they're clean and well-appointed; I've seen them."

"Oh, aye, while you were away from your wife! How many young women did you importune, knave? As many as the king, when he makes a progress without his wife?"

"And that's what you're really after, isn't it?" Rod gave her a shrewd look. "To turn the lords against the Crown and the people against their lords? But first you have to build up their discontent at home!"

"All folk have truths they wish to ignore!" the old woman shouted. "You more than any!"

Rod knew very well what his failings were—everything that had made Gwen unhappy, and that he had tried to change. Her memory made greater his anger at this woman who had made it her business to disrupt homes and break up a village. "What failings are you trying to hide, beldame?" he asked quietly. "What flaws of character have you managed to overlook by telling everyone else about theirs?"

"I am the Truth that lives at the bottom of every village well!"

"No you're not," Rod snapped, "because that Truth is naked, and you would no more dare look upon your own body than you'd look into your own heart! Who are you really—one of Morrigan's ravens who has taken on human form?"

The woman flinched but retorted, "Morrigan shall come for you, and that right quickly! She shall fan the peasants' rage and send them to burn and flay all you lords!"

"How does she know you're a lord, Rod?" Fess's voice asked. "You dress like a soldier on a journey."

Rod nodded. "Didn't realize you'd recognized me."

"Any would recognize a lord who tyrannizes his peasants! But you shall know oppression in your own turn, lordling! How long have you made excuses for the arrogance and tyranny of your queen?"

"Never," Rod said. "I've fought for her, but her public image is her own worry. You know that, though, don't you?

Well, if you're a raven in human form, you'll be attracted to bright and shiny things." He slipped a coin from his belt-pouch and flipped it.

The woman stared, following the silver's flashing with hungry eyes. She made a grab for it but missed.

"You really are a raven," Rod said softly, "feeding on the carrion of decaying marriages and drinking the anguish you have caused. But shape-changers on Gramarye are made of witch-moss and can themselves be melted down like wax in the sun." He stared at her, picturing her form blurring, features smoothing into a shapeless lump that melted into a puddle.

The woman shrieked and clutched her head, crumpling to the ground and rolling in agony.

Rod stared, horrified, and the image disappeared from his mind. The woman went limp, gasping for breath.

"You're real," Rod said softly, "a real woman who for some insane reason has decided to take out her unhappiness on the people around her—but my thoughts wouldn't have hurt you if you weren't a telepath yourself." He leaned over the windowsill to wrap his hand in the back of her tunic and haul her to her feet.

The woman flailed her fists at him, but her reach wasn't long enough; he stepped back, pulling her out of the window. "Let go!" she shrieked. "Blast you for a villain and bully, let go!"

"Oh, I will," Rod said, "when I've seen you safely inside the nearest dungeon."

The woman howled and writhed, trying to break free. "Tyrant! Ogre! Dire wolf! Have you no shred of mercy left in your heart?"

"Plenty," Rod said, "but not for a projective telepath who uses her gifts to cause other people misery. I think this village is on Count Moscowitz's estate. His dungeon should hold you long enough for one of the Royal Witches to come and collect you."

The woman shrieked, doubling over as he tried to drag her to Fess. Then she uncoiled, and something shiny flashed as she slashed at Rod. Pain burned through his arm, loosening his grip just enough for her to twist free. She shot off down the village street far faster than a woman her age should have been able to, black cloak billowing about her.

"After her!" Rod mounted and caught the reins. "We can't let a germ like that stay loose to spread a plague of lies."

Fess leaped into motion even as he said, "That wound must be attended to, Rod."

"It's only a scratch," Rod said impatiently. "It was the surprize that got me, that's all. Quick, Fess! If she makes it into the woods, we'll have lost her!"

But the billowing cloak steadied and spread wide even as the woman's form dwindled and lifted—and a huge raven soared up into the treetops, cawing in mockery.

Rod reined in, staring. "She must have been made of witch-moss after all!"

"Quickly, Rod! She is almost into the underbrush!"

"Underbrush? She's into the treetops! Didn't you just see her turn into a raven, Fess?"

"I saw nothing, Rod, except an old woman escaping—and she obviously is not as old as she pretended to be."

Rod looked down at the horse's head, frowning in puzzlement—then understood. "Of course! She's a projective telepath! She made me see something that didn't really happen—and I bit on it!"

"Whatever illusion she projected into your mind, Rod, it worked well enough to give her time to make good her escape."

"Yeah, it sure did, didn't it?" Rod said, chagrined. "Well, the least I can do is track the people who left this village to protect them from her—and tell them what she really is, so they won't believe her any more."

"You can still call in Toby and his friends from the Royal Witchforce, Rod."

"I suppose I can. They should be able to track her down—and even if they can't, they can leave a sentry here to nab her if she tries to come back. Come on, Fess—let's see if we can talk the villagers into taking their homes back."

Fess went toward the forest, saying, "There is the possibility that she is not the only one of her kind."

"A concerted campaign, you mean?" Rod frowned. "I

do remember thinking that our old enemies had been too quiet lately."

"They may think that you are incapacitated, Rod, and no longer a threat."

"They're right, too," Rod said. "I've got my own work to do now—my very own, trying to find Gwen again. We'll leave the totalitarians to Magnus."

Fess was quiet for several paces, then said, "So you don't intend to mount a campaign to ferret out these agents?"

Rod shrugged. "As I said, I'll leave that to Magnus—the boy's more than capable of dealing with something like this. Of course, I won't ignore anybody I stumble across."

"Yes, it does fend off boredom, doesn't it?"

"Are you telling me I need a retirement project?" Rod looked at his old friend and robot with a jaundiced eye. "Why should I, when such interesting things keep presenting themselves? There, Fess—that's their trail, where the grass is just beginning to recover. Shouldn't take us too long to find them."

GEORDIE CAME INTO the village with his bow and quiver on his back and a basket in his hand. The peasants looked up and smiled their greeting. Old Liz leaned forward from her seat by the door of her daughter's cottage. "Good day, my lord."

"Squire," Geordie said automatically. "Where's your son-in-law, Goody Elizabeth?"

Old Liz leaned back chuckling. "Elizabeth, is it? 'Old Liz' was good enough for you when you were no higher than my waist."

Geordie grinned down at her. "I'm somewhat taller than you now. Where's Corin?"

"Out to the fields with the rest of the young ones, Squire, digging to see if any of last year's turnips were missed— don't know why they bother; anything there would be rotted by now."

"Or have sent up shoots." Geordie set the basket down by her feet. "Well, see if you can divide this up among the families, then. It will go well with the turnips."

Old Liz stared down at the basket, then back up at Geordie. "Why, thank 'ee, your worship! Thank 'ee very much!"

Other seniors came up, surprized and interested, all adding their thanks to Old Liz's.

"You're my people," Geordie told them. "I'll not see you starve. Dine well."

They bade him good day as he strode away, no doubt to take another basket to the North Village. Then they turned to examine his gift. Old Sal laid back the corners of the cloth that covered it and gasped. "'Tis venison!"

They all exclaimed as they gathered around, for each knew the meat well—and had already used up that week's salt pork. Then the delight ebbed into concern, and they looked at one another with apprehension. Old Will it was who asked, "Where did he find it?"

"On the hoof, of course, and you know it well!" Old Liz told him. "Thank heaven the keepers did not find *him*!"

"Pray heaven he does not go hunting again! For they will catch him sooner or later!"

"Someone must tell him not to," Old Sal said. The others chorused agreement, all turning to look at Old Will.

"Aye," he said, as though the word had a bad taste. "'Twas I who taught him to hunt, so it's for me to teach him not to. Well, I'll have a go."

RAVEN CAME SPIRALING down to the safe house in the nearest town aboard the sorriest excuse for a broom anyone had ever seen. The sentry came to his feet, staring. "Where did you find that piece of rubbish, Raven?"

"Had to improvise it from a tree branch and a few handfuls of grass," the woman snapped, "after the High Warlock chased me off."

The sentry stared—partly in alarm, partly because, even dishevelled and upset, Raven was still a marvelous figure of a woman. Crow's feet and smile lines couldn't hide her beauty. "How did he find out about your campaign?"

"Sheer bad luck—I hope." Raven limped toward the stairwell, pressing a hand to the small of her back.

"Broomsticks are even more uncomfortable than they used to be. Where's the boss?"

"In his office." The sentry held the door for her. "Good luck."

Raven went downstairs, dreading the encounter.

Her stomach sank when she saw the door was open; she didn't even have knocking to brace her. The Mocker looked up as she came in. "Failure!"

"Bad luck." Raven wished she could sit down. "I thought Gallowglass had crawled into a hole feeling sorry for himself."

"He's on the move again—the word came after you'd gone out." The Mocker glared. "Don't tell me you let him chase you off!"

" 'Let' isn't the word—he was going to clap me in an esper's prison." Raven shuddered at the thought of a team of telepaths watching her night and day, even though her cell would have been well-appointed and roomy.

"You ran!"

"Not much choice, Boss—and he figured out that I was laying the groundwork for a peasant revolt!"

"Fool!" the Mocker raged. "You tipped your hand! How could you be so stupid!"

Raven shrugged. "I didn't know who the intruder was until I saw him. Then it was too late to pretend I hadn't."

"You told him!"

"I tried to throw him off by telling him all the lords were tyrants," Raven said. She was feeling worse and worse about this report. "It didn't take him long to figure out the rest."

"So you fled! Where has he gone?"

"He said something about finding the peasants and telling them it was safe to come back."

"Finding them!" The mocker shot to his feet. "He'll see the children and old folk alone and go after the rest of them! He'll talk them out of marching against their lord!"

"Maybe he'll forget," Raven said weakly. "His mind isn't all there these days, they tell me."

"What if he doesn't forget?" The Mocker glared at her.

"The plan depends on hundreds of village bands joining up to march on Runnymede!"

"This is just one . . ."

"But he'll seek out more! Worse, he'll tell those brats of his, and they'll bring out an army of emissaries to meet the small bands before they can gather and talk them out of their grievances!"

"I can go talk them back into bitterness. Turn husband against wife, wife against husband, make the kids take sides, and they'll want someone to blame because their lives are going rotten. I can make them think they're worse off than ever."

"Oh, you will, you will indeed!" The Mocker pointed a shaking finger at her. "If I didn't need every agent I have, you'd spend a week in a hotbox on bread and water to make you more aware of your duties—but since I can't spare you, you'll go off to the mountains and tell the people there that living in a forest away from the lords only means they've given up, that the lords are barring them from the really good life! Now go!"

Raven winced; being stuck out in the boondocks, in the middle of a forest where the trees were a hundred years old and there wasn't an inch of level ground, was punishment enough. But she knew it could have been worse, much worse, and went.

The Mocker sat down, seething, even though he knew Raven could be right. Raven! What an asinine choice for a code name! But she knew the state of the situation, he had to give her that—not that he'd let her know, of course. Gallowglass's memory and attention span were both dwindling, and there was every reason to hope he'd simply forget about the encounter—but the Mocker couldn't take the chance. He picked up the handbell on his desk and shook it. One of the older agents came hurrying in. "What is it, Boss?"

"The Gallowglass," the Mocker snapped. "Raven just ran into him at that village in the south. Send five of your best assassins with your best tracker to find him and lay an ambush. I want him dead!"

"Will do, Boss!" the man said, wide-eyed, then hurried out.

The Mocker sat back in his chair and cursed Rod Gallowglass for ten minutes straight, cursed him and his ancestors, cursed him for a fool who didn't know when to quit. He should have retired while he had the chance! But that opportunity was past, and now he would pay for having aborted the Mocker's revolution thirty years before—thirty years to him, but only weeks ago for the Mocker. Nine years of work, scrubbed out in a few months! Well, it wouldn't happen again. Laser pistols would see to that, and if Gallowglass managed to spike them somehow, there were always poisoned arrows.

The Mocker smiled, feeling charitable. If Gallowglass was so eager to join his wife, the Mocker would be all too glad to help him!

THE VILLAGERS HAD left a broad trail; here and there were small household objects that had fallen out of their packs on the way. Rod picked up a variety, including some wooden spoons, tallow candles, spools of thread, and an almost-empty sack. He caught up the last one and tucked the others into it, then followed the trail on foot, gathering odds and ends as he went—not many, but definitely important to the people who had lost them. Spools of colored thread were items of considerable value in a medieval culture, especially ones with needles still tucked into them; the peasants must have been in a desperate hurry not to stop to retrieve even such treasured belongings.

Into the woods they had gone, but still with no attempt to hide their trail. Most of the loose baggage had fallen out before that, so Rod mounted and followed in the saddle, still on the watch for fallen treasures—and since his eyes were on the ground, tracking, he had no warning when something slammed into his shoulders, knocking him out of his saddle. He tumbled to the ground, then looked up to see half a dozen people jumping on him and a dozen more standing behind them with grim faces and knotted fists.

Sixteen

FESS SCREAMED, REARING, BUT TEN HANDS caught his bridle to pull him down. Others were pinning Rod's arms and legs, one was slamming blows into his midriff, another was sitting on his chest, punching his face. He would have been in a very bad situation if any of them had been older than twelve or younger than seventy.

Fess screamed again, rearing and scattering peasants, then thudding down and reaching for a woman with his teeth.

"No!" Rod called. "Don't hurt them! They've been through enough!"

Fess turned to start on the group holding Rod down, but a woman's shrill cry froze everyone. She was pointing at the sack by Rod's hand; it had fallen open, and the odds and ends were strewn about. "Look!" she cried. "That's my oaken candlestick, I know it is!"

"So he robbed our houses and came after us!" an old man snarled.

"No! I know I packed it with the others I could not bear to

leave! He's brought us the things we dropped in our flight!"

The people holding Rod looked down at him, suddenly uncertain.

"True enough," he said. "I thought you might want them back."

"He's not come to hurt us!" the woman insisted. "He came to bring back our belongings!"

Suddenly the hands holding him down were helping him up. Rod felt an impulse toward honesty. "Actually, I was coming to tell you that you can go back to your homes now. The wicked woman who set you against one another has left."

"Left?" an older woman said incredulously. "But we could do nothing against her, even those of us who could see how her lies were turning husband against wife and child against mother. That Raven-woman only invented new slanders about us and accused her accusers of horrible deeds!"

"So pretty soon, nobody was willing to stand up to her? But you had to know what she was doing, or you wouldn't all have fled!"

Silence fell; neighbors looked uneasily at one another. "It was not her lies that chased us, squire," one of the old men said. "It was the word that ran through the town, that the queen had sent soldiers to the south and they would ride through our village—and everybody knows what soldiers do."

"But you never dreamed it was Raven who started the rumors." Rod looked about him, frowning. "Where are your able-bodied men?"

"Some of us are able-bodied yet," a graybeard growled, and the other grandfathers chorused agreement.

"That you may be, but you're not of an age to join the queen's army," Rod explained. "Did your sons hide in the deep woods to be sure the soldiers wouldn't try to put them in livery?"

The silence became distinctly uneasy. Villagers glanced at one another; none met Rod's gaze.

"Worse than that?" Rod frowned. "Wherever they've gone, they've been chased by lies! Tell me!"

"She told us how badly our knight was treating us, that

Raven," one of the women said, "and railed at our menfolk that they couldn't be worth their salt if they let Sir Aethelred bully them about and live in his big house while we had only cottages."

"Before that, none ever thought it bullying for Sir Aethelred to tell us what to plant in which field," an old man said sourly.

"But when Raven said it again and again and again, some of them must have believed her," a white-haired woman said.

"It was her telling them they had to prove their worth to their wives and sweethearts by marching on Sir Aethelred," another woman said, "and they wouldn't believe us when we denied it."

"They began to talk of it among themselves," the older woman said, "and when they were sure we were well-settled in the woods here, they went off to brace Sir Aethelred and demand that he share our burdens and we share his wealth!"

"Even though they knew Raven lied about everything else." Rod shook his head. "Thanks for letting me know, good people." He mounted again.

"And thank you for bringing back our bits and pieces, squire," an old man said, "but where do you mean to go now?"

"To finish what I began," Rod said. "I'm going to find your men and tell them Raven's gone and they can go home!"

In spite of the chorus of protests, he rode off into the trees.

DIRU STUMBLED; HIS mattock nearly fell off his shoulder. The boy behind him laughed. "Wake up, Diru! Are you still dreaming?"

Diru shuddered at the reminder. He had slept very little the night before, for whenever he had, he had dreamed of the horrors the minstrel had described—a giant cat with tufted ears and very long, sharp teeth; a shapeless, quivering mound of white jelly that absorbed anything it touched;

a giant beaver with teeth like cleavers and maddened burning eyes; and many others, all wheedling, all telling him that no one liked him, but they would be his friends if only they could come to visit. He might have believed them if the minstrel hadn't told the villagers in song what had happened to the ones who had invited the monsters in when last they had been importuning people for an invitation. Every time he had fallen asleep, those dreams had come, until he paced the floor to stay awake, starting at every creak of the old hut and shuddering at the thought of what prowled outside in the night.

"That minstrel gave us a good time, at least," one young man said.

"Yes," said an older, "once he was done trying to scare us with his tales of the Mist Monsters."

Another father nodded sagely. "I've dreamed of such horrors myself, telling me that they're really good neighbors and cajoling me to invite them in."

"Fat chance, after that minstrel's warning."

"It's boring," a young woman complained, "always the same warnings over and over. 'Don't invite the monsters in, don't invite the monsters in!'"

"And don't believe they're nice and friendly, even though they look so horrid," another young woman agreed.

An older woman frowned. "It's good advice, younglings! If they do come back, we'll be their meat!"

"Oh, everyone knows that, Auntie," the first girl said impatiently.

"Yes." Diru shuddered again. "Nobody would be foolish enough to invite horrors like that, in their dreams or awake."

"Oh, so you know everything, do you, Diru?" the first young woman snapped.

"Aye, tell us something we don't know, Diru!" the second young man jibed.

"Sure, Diru knows all about monsters." The first young man grinned. "Takes one to know one, after all."

Diru's face burned.

"Oh look, he's gone all red again," the first young woman said with a giggle.

Thankfully, the huts rose just ahead. "Good night," Diru mumbled, and went into his.

His mother looked up from the pot she was stirring by the hearth. "How was the reaping today, dear?"

"Good enough for everyone else," Diru snapped as he put down his rake.

"Oh, dear," his mother sighed. "I do wish you could get along with the others your age."

"I wish they'd try to get along with me! Maybe I'll be better if I can get some sleep." Diru bulled through the curtain that separated his pallet from the rest of the hut and threw himself down, hoping he wouldn't dream.

He didn't, for he didn't sleep. When he closed his eyes, all he could see was the taunting faces of the other young men and women. All he could feel was anger and shame— and hatred for his tormentors. It was almost enough to make a fellow wish the monsters would come back and gobble them all up!

THE NEXT DAY, Rod came to the top of a ridge, as the sun was nearing the horizon, and looked down to see a channel between the forest trees that marked a stream. Rivers made for easier travel in forest lands, so he wasn't terribly surprized to see men walking there, or at least the tops of their heads. What did surprize him was their number. This wasn't just the hundred men from one village—it was a thousand at least. Rod frowned. "How many villages did it take to send this many men?"

"Between five and fifty, Rod."

"Pretty broad range." Rod dismounted. "Well, if I'm going to talk to them, I'd better not look too affluent." He pulled the flat-folded tunic and leggins out of his saddlebag; he never travelled without a disguise ready. Some of the ideas from his training as a secret agent had stayed with him.

With Fess shadowing him deeper in the trees, Rod melted in with the mass of men who moved down the forest trail. He asked no questions, only kept his ears open. The other men paid no attention; apparently they were all used to strangers joining them as they marched along. Few of them could have known one another before they had joined this mob.

As they went, they talked. "I don't know—seems to me the lords ain't all that bad. Our squire wasn't, leastways."

"If you think that," growled the man next to him, "why be you here?"

"Seemed like all the other lords were rotten, when that peddler were talkin' 'bout them," the first said. "Once we was on the march with you lot, though, he went off to peddle his wares somewhere else, and it didn't seem so good an idea any more."

"You're fed, ain't you?" asked another man. "And the wife ain't here to scold or the squire to buckle you into the traces and set you to plowing or hoeing."

"Well, there's that," the first man admitted. " 'Tis a holiday, like . . ."

"Then take the good while it lasts, and quit whinin'," the second said.

Rod slowed, falling back to hear similar grumbling from other peasants. He wandered through the crowd, listening for word of the villagers he'd come to find, but hearing only misgivings and doubts. Whenever several men began to share those second thoughts, though, some other man always showed up to remind them of their grievances. Rod realized that there were a hundred agents or more working this crowd, keeping them motivated and on the road.

Road to where?

He glanced at the angle of the afternoon sunlight through the leaves and realized their direction—north and east. They were moving toward Runnymede—and rebellion.

THE SUN WAS setting, and Geordie was striding out toward the forest with his bow in his hand when he heard a voice call his name. Turning, he saw old Will hurrying toward him as quickly as his bad leg would let him. As the man came up, Geordie said with a grin, "Good evening to you, Will."

"God's e'en to you too, squire," Will wheezed. "And where might you be bound on so fair an evening?"

Geordie's smile faded. "To hunt, Will, as you know well."

"There's others will be hunting you, my lord." Old Will stared him straight in the eye.

Geordie's mouth tightened. "I'm not a lord, Will!"

"I'll use your true title when I tell you not to go into certain danger," the old man told him. "Poachers hang by the neck until dead, my lord. We'll manage somehow. The land and streams will yield us enough to get by."

But Geordie knew there were very few fish in the rivers this year, because of the previous year's drought. "I'll not see my people starve, Will!" He turned and strode away toward the forest.

Old Will looked after him, shaking his head and muttering. Then he turned and hobbled back to the village.

Old Sal looked up and saw him coming. "He wouldn't listen, would he?"

"Not a word," old Will said.

"He always was headstrong." Old Sal shook her head.

"Aye. You'll have to talk to his lady," Old Will advised.

It was the first really serious fight Geordie had ever had with his wife, and did not a hand's-breadth of good.

ROD DIDN'T FIND the men from Raven's village until night had fallen and the separate bands had settled down for supper and sleep. They were roasting a haunch of venison, and Rod wondered how much wildlife would be left in this wood after the mob had passed through.

One of the men looked up as Rod came by. "Hope you've something for the pot, if you plan to share in it."

"Happen I do be looking for a share." Rod swung his pack down, opened a flap, rummaged, and pulled out a dozen hardtack biscuits. "Bread to soak in the soup?"

Another man eyed the contribution. " 'Tain't no soup."

"I'll brew some, then." Rod pulled out his field kettle, dropped in all but one biscuit, and set it to catch the dripping from the roast. He broke the last biscuit, tossed one piece away, then dropped the other in with the rest. The villagers stared; one or two of them shuddered and tossed a morsel of his own into the night. They all knew one should always leave a token for the Little People, but had obviously been forgetting.

"Let the biscuits catch some of the drippings," Rod said, "and I'll add enough water to soften the bread. Though if you'd sooner I go . . ."

"How think you, Nicol?" the first man asked. "Send him packing?"

"Nay, Ruben," Nicol said. "Bread'll be welcome, even hard biscuit." He turned to Rod. "What's your village, gaffer?"

"Gaffer" was short for "grandfather;" Rod decided to take it as a title of honor. "Maxima be my town." Which was true enough, though it was technically also an asteroid.

Nicol frowned. "Never heard of no Maxima."

"It's small," Rod said, which was also very true. "What's your town?"

"Hardly a town," Ruben said sourly. "Maybe fifty families in Rookery."

Rod glanced at the fifty men gathered around a dozen campfires. "You've most of the fathers and brothers here, then."

"All over eighteen and under sixty," Ruben acknowledged. "Seemed like a good idea at the time."

"Not no more, though?"

"More than ever, now," Nicol growled. "Mind you, we set out to demand of Sir Aethelred that he treat us like men instead of beasts—but we met up with the men from Loudin Village, on their way to talk to their knight, so we joined with them. Then we met the men from Tilbury, and from Schoon and Dobry, and the more we talked, the more we came to see our quarrel was with the baron, not none of his knights."

Rod wondered which of them had been the VETO agent. "So you all set out to demand better treatment from the baron. How many of you?"

Nicol shrugged. "A thousand at a guess. But the next day, our path joined with a road, and we found ourselves marching with another band the same size, and the more we talked, the more we came to see 'twasn't the baron we had argument with, but with his master, Earl Dommen—so we turned our steps toward the castle, and the farther we went, the more bands we met."

Rod had a vision of five thousand men marching through the greenwood. "Dommen County's a ways behind us."

Ruben eyed him suspiciously. "Haven't you a like tale to tell?"

"Hasn't every man here?" Rod countered.

"Aye," another man grumbled, "and the more we've talked, the more we've come to see 'tisn't the earl who's ground us down, nor the duke neither."

"Aye; 'tis all of them," Nicol growled. "There oughtn't to be no dukes nor earls, no, nor knights nor squires neither."

"Nay," said Ruben, "only free men living in their villages, and no castles to overawe them."

Rod nodded. "But where's the root, hey? The dukes and earls are all branches of the same tree—but where's the root?"

"You know full well," Nicol snapped. "'Tis in Runnymede. Begin by haling down the queen herself and her lap-dog king, and the tree's uprooted."

"Then we can go about pruning the branches," Ruben said.

But there would be men giving orders, Rod knew—the totalitarian agents who had stirred up this discontent in the first place, and if the peasants did succeed in overthrowing the lords, those agents would become the governing officials, each gaining more and more power, until, if the history of other totalitarian revolutions were any guide, the people would labor under masters even harsher, for they would guide their subjects' every step.

He had a vision of twenty thousand unruly peasants marching on Runnymede and the Crown—and stripping the countryside bare of every shock of grain and cow and piglet on the way.

"Who's this?"

Rod looked up to see a face he knew well, and shock held him immobile for a minute.

"Only a gaffer from another village, Mocker," said Nicol. "He brought biscuit." Then to Rod: "You get confused about where we're going or what we're about, you talk to the Mocker, and he'll set you straight."

Rod was sure he would. The Mocker had been the chief VETO agent when Rod had first come to Gramarye—one of the enemies Rod had overthrown to keep the land and its telepaths from being conquered and trained to become weapons for a totalitarian government. The idea of a dictator being able to know what secrets people hid in their own minds gave Rod as bad a chill now as it had then—but the Mocker didn't look a day older than when Rod had seen him last. For a moment, the unfairness of it bit his soul—that he should have aged so, but the Mocker not!

On the other hand, the Mocker had looked ancient when Rod had first known him.

The Mocker stooped, peering into Rod's face and frowning. "I know you."

"You've never looked on this face before," Rod told him.

The Mocker's eyes widened. "Yes I have, though there were no wrinkles on it then, and the hair above it was black!" He spun toward the villagers. "'Tis the Lord Warlock come among you! Seize him! Bear him down! Let your tearing of the lords begin here!"

Seventeen

THE VILLAGE MEN STARED AT ROD, THUNDER-
struck; then they began to mutter fearfully to one another.

"What are you waiting for?" the Mocker cried. "Seize
him! Tie him up! Hang him high!"

"He's a warlock," one of the villagers explained. "He'll
freeze us with the Evil Eye, he'll turn us into toads!"

"He's only a man, like any of you!" the Mocker shrilled.
"They may call him a warlock, but he's nothing of the
sort—only a treacherous backstabbing spy!" He spun,
lashing a kick at Rod.

Rod pushed himself up, but only enough so that the kick
caught his shoulder instead of his head. Pain shot through
his left arm, but he forced himself to his feet and blocked
the next kick with his right, then countered with a feint to
the head and a quick jab to the diaphragm. The Mocker fell
back, clutching his belly but managing to cough out, "If he
had magic, I'd be a toad, not a punching bag! He has no
magic!"

"You're a little behind the times," Rod informed him, and projected a blast of pure mental energy at the man. The Mocker shrieked, seizing his temples and falling.

Rod let up as the tall black warhorse seemed to materialize out of the night. The villagers fell back with cries of superstitious fear. Rod mounted and turned Fess, looking into each one's eyes as he said, "Raven's gone from your village—I chased her away. She had magic of her own but couldn't stand against mine. I found your wives and children and parents and told them they could go back. Home with you, for I promised I'd find you and send you! Home with you, before some of you fall in battle with the Queen's soldiers and the rest rot in prison!"

"But . . . but the lords' tyranny . . ." the man who said it stared at the Mocker, limp and unconscious on the ground, and swallowed thickly.

"The Queen keeps the lords from abusing you," Rod explained, "but the lords have their council where they keep her from becoming a tyrant. Home with you, lads—this may be the Mocker's fight, but it isn't yours."

"What of all the rest of the men marching here?" Nicol asked with a dark frown.

"They don't care about you," Rod answered, "not the Mocker nor any of his men—they care only about breaking the Crown and taking the throne for themselves. They disguise it as the people's battle, but it's really a fight to see who will govern you. Stay out of it, lads. Go home." Then he turned Fess and rode off into the night.

GEORDIE BROUGHT HOME one deer after another, keeping the peasants busy dressing and smoking the meat, which they did even though they were worried for his safety. After the third one, Geordie didn't even bother skinning and disguising what he carried—he brought the carcasses home over his shoulders and left them for the peasants to skin and dress out, which they did—and again, after the third deer, they gave up trying to talk him out of it. No one could turn him from his course, and the meat should not go to waste.

But his wife worried. "You must stop this, Geordie! The keepers will catch you, and, squire or not, they'll arrest you—or bring the shire-reeve himself to do it!"

"Don't fret yourself, sweet chuck—I know how to hide my trail." Geordie reached out to touch her cheek in reassurance.

Rowena struck his hand away. "This is no jest, Geordie! I've not even born a babe yet, and here you'd leave me a widow! I've no wish to lose my husband!"

"Darling, darling, don't fret!" Geordie held out his arms. "None will find me, none will catch me!"

"The keepers can track as well as you can hide your trail, Geordie! You must give this over! We'll find other ways to feed our peasant folk!"

"There is no other way." Geordie's face firmed. "I'll not see my tenants starve."

"But you'd see your wife left alone, vulnerable to the importuning of any man who wishes to insult her!"

"None will insult you, either." Geordie stepped forward. "Be easy in your heart, love. All will be well. Come, let me embrace you."

"No! If you'll not heed me, you cannot love me! Sleep by your own hearth!" She turned away and ran to her room; Geordie heard the latch fall. He sighed, bowing his head in defeat, and stood gazing at the fire a few minutes. Then he lifted his head and set about finding blankets, to make a bed by the fire.

AS THE FOREST closed behind Rod, he told the robot, "Thanks for perfect timing—as usual."

"I simply fulfill my programming, Rod."

"And very well, too, though it's not always that simple." Rod glanced over his shoulder and decided there were enough trees between himself and the mob that he could stop for a few minutes. He reined in and called, "Wee Folk! Is there a brownie about?"

"Not a brownie, but a wood-elf," chirped a voice above him.

"Or two or three," crackled an older voice below and behind him. "What would you have of us, Lord Warlock?"

"Communication," Rod said. "Bear word, I pray you, to my son Magnus in the Queen's castle at Runnymede. Tell him that thousands of men are marching through the greenwood, to rise against the Crown."

"We shall tell him," the crackling voice assured. "Go now, Lord Warlock, and lose yourself in the depths of the wood, for the Mocker will have men beating the thickets for you in minutes."

"I'm going," Rod said. "Don't get caught, eh?"

"Not half, mortal, not half," the crackling voice said dryly, "though the searching peasants might have a nasty surprize or two."

"Not a one of 'em has left a crumb for a brownie," the chirping voice said with an indignant sniff.

Rod shook his head, tut-tutting in indignation. "Mustn't let them forget who really runs this land, eh, folks?"

"That is what they seek to do." The crackling voice turned grim. "Never fear, Lord Warlock—we shall remind them most shrewdly."

Rod shuddered and rode off.

GEOFFREY CAME OUT onto the battlements and frowned as he saw Magnus standing by a crenel, watching the soldiers drilling in the bailey. Geoffrey stepped up beside his older brother. "I had not thought you took any joy in watching soldiers march, Magnus."

"There is always pleasure in watching something being done well." Magnus turned to him. "However, I came because I knew you would be here to make sure of their practice."

Geoffrey frowned. "You can always find me at dinner."

"True enough, but an elf brought word in the night," Magnus said. "Peasants are marching on Runnymede from all directions. By the time they reach the city, there will probably be ten thousand of them."

Geoffrey stared in shock.

"Didn't your spies tell you of this?" Magnus asked.

That restored Geoffrey's poise; he gave Magnus a sardonic smile. "I am a general, brother, not a spy-master. I leave that to Their Majesties."

Magnus nodded judiciously. "A wise course of action—
except that they have never placed great emphasis on intelligence."

"How came the elf?" Geoffrey asked.

"Dad sent it," Magnus admitted. "I am no spy-master
either."

"No, only a master spy." Geoffrey's smile returned.
"Though that is not accurate, is it? On those other planets,
you did not ferret out information and bring it back to those
who could do something about it."

"No—I decided what to do about it when and where I
was," Magnus said frankly. "However, that was myself
with only one companion—first Dirk, then Alea. I can
scarcely lay claim to commanding a force of spies."

"But Papa has." Geoffrey looked out over the courtyard,
automatically noting slight flaws in the soldiers' marching.
"Though that is not true either—he has never set up a spy
ring of his own, only taken advantage of one already in
place."

"Yes, the Wee Folk were sending word of troubling
events back to Brom O'Berin before Dad ever arrived on
the scene," Magnus agreed. "So what will you do about this
growing mob, brother?"

"What Their Majesties will have me do, of course,"
Geoffrey said, "but if they wish it, I shall send a few peasants to join the crowd and bring word of what the marchers
do, and of who leads them."

"I was thinking of Toby's Royal Witchforce," Magnus
said. "Perhaps with their mind-reading, it would not be
necessary to send spies into danger."

"A good thought, but there are many things the eye can
see that the mind may not think important enough to notice," Geoffrey said. "Still, why not have the best of both?
I shall recruit my spies from Toby's telepaths. They may
observe on the spot and send thoughts back to Runnymede,
not words alone."

Magnus nodded with slow approval. "A shrewd choice."

"And exactly as you yourself would have done?" Geoffrey gave him a brittle smile. "Why do I feel I have been
maneuvered into this?"

"Because you are used to maneuvering." Magnus gestured at the troops below. "You excel at teaching those maneuvers to others, too. I, though, am a loner, brother—and one who is tiring of being a communication channel."

"You were never that." Geoffrey looked up with concern. " 'Tis true we rarely saw other children as we grew, brother, but we learned social skills quickly enough when the time came—even Gregory, when he had to. How is it you have not?"

"Oh, I can deal with people when the opportunity presents itself," Magnus said, "and would prefer to have others around when I can—but I chose the role of the lone rebel when I found I could not accept the means SCENT used to gain its ends." He shrugged. "What other course was there than to seek to do what I thought right, by myself?"

"You could have come home," Geoffrey said softly.

"Come home?" Magnus smiled without mirth. "You know I could not. Dad is a SCENT agent; if I could not endorse their policies, I could not accept his."

"But that is not the deepest reason, is it?" Geoffrey gave his brother a glance so probing that it left Magnus shaken. "Do not fear—I shall not pry—not that it would do me much good to try, so well are you shielded."

"Dad's SCENT policies are reason enough," Magnus maintained.

"They would be if he sought to impose democracy on a people for whom it was not right," Geoffrey said, "but they were on the road to constitutional monarchy before he came; he has only set them more firmly on that course by warding off SPITE and VETO, who sought to subvert."

"There is some truth to that," Magnus agreed, "and that is all I have promised to do—to prevent conquest, to protect the people from those who seek to imprison them in a government not of their own choosing."

"As Papa does."

"Yes, but that is more a matter of convenience than of choice." Magnus straightened and looked up at the dawn sky. "If they had not already set themselves on the road to democracy, he would have sought to subvert them into it."

"He would not have succeeded," Geoffrey said. "But

they were already on that road. He was the right person in the right place at the right time, brother." His gaze was penetrating and unwavering.

"As you think I am?" Magnus asked with a sardonic smile. "I hope you are right, brother. One thing is certain— I cannot merely wave my magic wand, overthrow a tyranny, and go my merry way this time. For once, I must live with the consequences."

"They could be worse," Geoffrey said softly—perhaps too softly for Magnus to hear. His gaze was distant, focused over the battlements to the land rolling away beneath the castle hill, as were his thoughts.

ROD SLEPT UNTIL he woke, found the sun high in the sky but nonetheless took his time over breakfast, then finally mounted up and rode through the woods, waiting for an elf to bring him a report of any action Magnus had taken to sidetrack the building peasant insurrection. "Maybe I should have taken word to Magnus myself."

"You could simply contact him by telepathy, Rod."

"I could, but his brothers and sister would overhear, and it should be up to Magnus to tell them," Rod said. "Besides, I don't want them to think I'm favoring him. There's too much of that already, what with my asking him to guard Gramarye."

"Understandably. He leaves you for ten years, and when he comes back, you appoint him leader for all intents and purposes—and for no apparent reason."

"Oh, there's reason enough," Rod said. "Who would know best how to guard against subversion than someone who's been building revolutions for ten years? Besides, it was the only way to keep him from running off again."

"Are you sure that is a desirable goal, Rod?"

"Very sure. This is his homeland. It's the only place he'll ever really feel he belongs."

"Has this nothing to do with your desire to keep him near you, Rod?"

"Me?" Rod shrugged. "I don't matter. Once I find Tir Nan Og, I'm gone."

"That is not a healthy attitude, Rod."

"No, but it's very natural. I know I'm in denial, Fess. It's a good illusion to get me through the worst of the grieving process."

They rode in silence for a few minutes. Then Fess said, "You say that too easily, Rod, as though you do not entirely believe it."

MAGNUS AND ALEA had brought two chairs and a small table up to the battlements to watch the sun rise. The sentries eyed them covertly, unsure what to make of such unorthodox behavior. Battlements were for fighting, not pleasure.

Magnus was listening, nodding thoughtfully, as Alea told him of her conversations with the peasant folk near the castle. She was speaking of the need to interest them in eating more fruit, when a young man in royal livery came up the inner stair. Magnus saw him and touched her hand; she turned to look.

The herald came up to their table and bowed. "Sir Magnus, Their Majesties send their compliments and ask that you attend them in Runnymede."

Alea frowned, wondering at the formality, but Magnus only nodded. "Thank you, courier." He turned to one of the sentries. "Conduct this young man to the kitchen and see that he is fed and rested before he begins his return."

"Yes, Sir Magnus." The sentry turned to the young man and jerked his head toward the stair; they went away.

"You've known them all your life," Alea said. "They're your sister's parents-in-law. Why the formality?"

"They have to send word somehow," Magnus explained. "They can't call me by satellite phone—but more to the point, I think they wish to make me understand that this will be official business. Do you fancy a morning's ride?"

"What, and waste the best part of the day?" Besides, something inside Alea quailed at the thought of meeting a king and queen face-to-face—and as though they were only the next-door neighbors. "You go. I need some time to myself anyway."

"NOT BELIEVE I'M in denial?" Rod smiled. "You're saying I'm denying denial?"

"I would not have put it that way, Rod, but I suppose there is some validity to the phrasing. Is it accurate?"

Rod shrugged. "I've always operated on two levels, you know that—the part that's very involved in the world around me, planning what to do and getting excited about whatever situation I'm in, and an aloof part of me that sits back and watches and tells me what a fool I'm being."

"Perhaps advisedly."

"Yeah, but sometimes it's too critical."

"At other times, though, it is right."

"Yeah. See that branch up ahead? Right now, my brazen side is telling me I should just push it out of the way, while my monitor-mind is telling me not to be a fool and duck." He leaned forward against Fess's neck, and the branch passed overhead. "Sometimes I listen to it."

Something whirred where his head had been. Rod stayed down but looked up quickly enough to see a tiny spearpoint arcing down to bury itself in the forest mold. "An elf-shot!" Rod threw himself off the horse and charged back ten feet. Something hurtled out of the road-side brush toward the woods, something small and fast— but not fast enough. Rod lunged and caught a diminutive collar. He yanked its owner high, amazed at his weight; he was very heavy for someone so small. He held the chubby elf even with his face and demanded, "What are you shooting at me for?"

The elf's form blurred; it grew amazingly, becoming very heavy very quickly. Rod dropped it, but it kept on growing—and changed form as it grew. In seconds, it towered over Rod, tall and cadaverous with a long white beard, whole body a mass of tremors. With shaking hands, it lifted the diminutive crossbow and levelled it at Rod's eyes.

Eighteen

ROD QUAILED WITHIN BUT SUMMONED THE courage to slap the crossbow aside. "Who are you, and why did you try to give me epilepsy?"

"Not the falling sickness, but the one-sided stiffness," the rasping, shaking voice told him. The ogre peered down at him through rheumy eyes.

"A stroke?" Rod shuddered at the thought. "But why?"

"Because you have come within my domain," the ogre-elf answered. "You are aged as much as most who die in this land, and you have no wish to live."

"That makes me subject to elf-shot?" Rod frowned. "Just because I'm sixty and grieving? I know most medieval people die in their forties and fifties, but that doesn't mean they have to have strokes!"

"They age quickly," the spirit reminded him. "It is a hard life, to be a mortal in a world where all work is done by hands and horses, and wars are fought with sword and spear."

"Okay, but I grew up far away, in a world where people had sound nutrition and medicine, and robots did everything

but the brain-work! I should be good for another twenty
years of good health."

"Logic may say so," the ogre said. "Your heart knows
better." It levelled the crossbow again.

"Now, stop that!" Rod slapped the weapon away. "Step
aside and let me pass! I don't want to have to hurt you."

"I cannot say the same." The creature stepped back, lifting the crossbow again. "It is my nature to loose my points
against your kind."

"Hold!" Rod raised a hand, palm out. "Remember,
you're made of witch-moss—and I'm very good at melting
the stuff down."

The creature swelled, its head shooting up twenty feet,
its body widening to fill the whole trail. "Do you truly
think you can melt all this?" it thundered.

"Sure, but why bother?" Rod mounted again and kicked
his heels against Fess's sides. "If you're stretching the
mass of an elf into the volume of a giant, you've made
yourself so tenuous that you couldn't stop a songbird."
With that, he rode straight through the ogre.

The creature cried out as Fess plowed through its legs.
Rod felt as though he were riding through a screen of cob-
webs—nasty clinging stuff that he had to brush aside.
"Cold Iron!" the creature screeched.

"Only sixty percent," Rod called back. "He's magne-
sium and tungsten, too—not to mention a lot of carbon
compounds."

He rode out the other side, and the creature's wailing
soared up the scale, until it seemed a marsh bird's piping.
Turning, Rod saw it shrink into an elf again—but also saw
the crossbow rising, heard the thrum as the creature loosed.
He threw himself down against Fess's neck, but not far
enough; pain lanced through his forehead, and his whole
right side went numb. "Run," he told Fess—or tried to, but
the words wouldn't come out right. "As fast you can!"

Fortunately, Fess's voice-recognition program was able
to accept substitutions and relate them almost instantly to
the sounds they were supposed to have been. He leaped
into motion and shot through the forest, and was far from
the shooting elf in minutes.

* * *

GEORDIE HEAVED THE dead buck up over his shoulders and turned his steps homeward—but he hadn't gone a dozen paces before a man in green tunic and brown hose stepped out of the leaves onto the trail ahead of him, a bow in his hands with an arrow nocked, but not drawn. "Hold, squire."

Geordie stared at the man, his heart sinking. Then he summoned his nerve and grinned. "Come, fellow, I've no wish to harm you. Step aside."

"You bear your guilt on your shoulders, squire. You must answer to the reeve now. Put down the buck and hold out your arms."

"If I put down my load, it shall be atop you," Geordie said evenly, "and if I hold out my hands, there shall be sword and dagger in them. Step aside—I have folk who will need this meat."

"They shall have to find it somewhere else."

Battle-lust rose; Geordie's friendly smile turned into a savage grin. "Do you truly think you can take me alone?"

"I do not think I will have to."

Branches rustled; two other men stepped up at either side, and Geordie could hear more stepping out onto the roadway behind him. His hackles rose, but he brazened it out. "You've not the right to arrest a squire, especially one born to nobility!"

"They have." The branches parted; a man wearing a black doublet and hose with crimson piping stepped out behind the first keeper. "But even if they did not, I surely do. As reeve of this shire, I arrest you in the Queen's name!"

Geordie stared into the reeve's face and felt his heart sink down to his boots.

FESS SLOWED, AND Rod slid down from his back—but his right leg buckled and he fell. He tried to stand again, but the leg wouldn't cooperate. He turned to catch the stirrup with his left hand and pulled himself up to his left knee, then with a titanic effort pushed himself up to stand. He started to fall but flailed at the saddle, caught the pommel, and managed to balance on his left foot.

"It is only projective telepathy, Rod," Fess told him. "Your muscles are doubtless as good as ever. It is merely your mind that has been convinced of paralysis, by the power of myth made seeming flesh."

"Maybe," Rod said, but his ears heard a hoarse caw that said, "Maeh-hih;" he shuddered. He directed his thoughts toward Fess. "Time to meditate again." He let himself fall into the trance—difficult, because of the uncertainty of meditating on his feet, but it was necessary this time. When he knew his hindbrain was at its most suggestible, he began to put weight on his right leg and withdrew it in a slow but regular rhythm, as though he were strolling. As he practiced the movements, he imagined the deadened area of his brain coming alive, beginning to regrow neurons, synapses firing more and more normally until it was restored to full function. When his right leg could feel his weight again, he knew the neurons had really regrown, that his brain had repaired the damage—if there had actually been any. It was, as Fess had said, probably only a very convincing telepathic illusion—but if it had been, it had managed to convince his neurons they were burned out. They had recharged now, recharged and were firing with every mock step, more and more until, greatly daring, he finally let go of the saddle and stood alone.

The leg held.

Rod gripped the pommel again and began to swing the leg as though he took a step with every shift of weight. At first it refused to budge, then twitched, then swung a little, then wider and wider. When he had achieved a normal length of stride, he began to put his weight on it at the end of the forward swing, then lifted and swung it back. When it held his full weight, he let go of the pommel and began walking in place, then stepped away from Fess and back, then away and around in a circle.

"Well done, Rod," the robot said. "You have recapitulated two years of physical therapy in an hour."

"Is that how long it's been?" Time seemed to pass differently when Rod was in a trance. "Now let's work on the arm." He heard his voice say, "Nahwehwhirahdah."

"Then you will begin work on your speech?"

Rod glanced at the sun's rays, where they laid their path through dust-motes to the leaves below. "Won't be time before dark. I'll have to finish that tomorrow."

By sunset, he had the right arm and hand back to full function and was quite unreasonably proud that he was able to brew up a stew of jerky and dried vegetables.

Speech took longer, though. It required much more fine-muscle coordination, so even after a night's sleep and a morning's work, it was noon by the time Rod was willing to take a break, drown the fire, and ride on through the forest. After an hour, he started practicing tongue-twisters again, and was speaking quite normally by the time he pitched camp that evening. For practice, he discussed the elf marksman with Fess.

"I did not notice any unusual amounts of witch-moss around his feet, Rod."

Rod nodded. "It probably all came from within—he was much heavier than anyone his size has a right to be. Even if he absorbed extra witch-moss as he grew, there must have been a lot of it in him to begin with. That was one very tightly-compacted elf."

"But you knew whatever mass he had would be, shall we say, stretched thin when he grew twelve feet in a matter of minutes?"

"Thin as cobwebs—which is exactly what he felt like when I rode through." Rod shuddered at the memory and spooned up some more stew—an action of which he was unreasonably proud at the moment. "He had become, if you'll pardon the phrase, a very insubstantial elf."

THE SENTRY AT the gatehouse looked uncertain as Alea approached. "Do you need an escort, milady?"

Alea bristled but hid it; she flashed him a smile instead and wondered why his eyes widened—but she said, "No thank you, trooper." She brandished her staff. "I have all the protection I need—unless there are wild lions in that wood that no one's told me about?"

"No, milady." Wide-eyed or not, the man still seemed doubtful. "There's wolves and bears, though we haven't seen 'em in a year or two."

"I'll take my chances, then," Alea said. "Sometimes you just need to be by yourself for a while, you know?"

"Yes, milady." The young man clearly didn't.

Alea knew she didn't have to explain but tried anyway. "I'm a stranger here, trooper, and sometimes I feel very much alone—but I don't when I'm in the forest by myself."

"Just call if you need help, milady."

"As loudly as I can." Alea gave him a bright smile as she turned away. "And I'm not the daughter of a lord, so you don't have to call me lady."

"Begging your pardon, milady, but if you're Sir Magnus's companion, you're a lady."

Alea sighed, recognizing a fight she couldn't win. She only said, "Thank you, soldier," and turned to walk through the tunnel and out under the portcullis.

The woods were as welcoming as Alea had expected; as soon as the leaves closed around her, she felt a burden lift from her. She wondered why—she had been on planets where she knew no one before. Here, at least, she had Magnus's brothers and sister.

Of course—that was why. She felt she was continually on trial, continually being judged for her fitness to accompany Magnus. Here, though, only the beasts and birds would judge her, and that was as a threat or merely an interesting addition to their world.

She strolled down a path, letting the thoughts gradually empty from her mind, filling it instead with birdsong and the rustling of leaves. She came to a little clearing with a large rock off to one side and sat down to enjoy the play of sunlight and shadow.

"It has taken you long enough to come out of that ugly stone shell," Evanescent said.

Alea looked up, surprised to see the cat-headed alien, then frowned. "It would help if you didn't keep erasing my memories of you after every encounter. How am I supposed to know you want to talk if I can't even remember you exist?"

"You might ask me how I like this new world."

"You might ask me the same."

"Very well." Evanescent tucked her paws under her

chest as she lay down. "How do you find this world of Gramarye, Alea?"

"Oh, the world itself is well and good," Alea said. "It's the people who are giving me difficulty."

"Really?" the alien asked, interested. "Which people?"

"Only Magnus's brothers and sister," Alea said with a sigh. "His father has gone adventuring, which is too bad, for he seemed very nice. All the servants and soldiers are friendly, though. A bit distant, since they seem to think I'm an aristocrat, but friendly nonetheless."

"You don't think you're a fine lady?"

"I'm a farmer's daughter," Alea snapped. "If I'd known Magnus was noble, I'd never have had anything to do with him!"

Evanescent tilted her head to the side, considering the statement, then asked, "Isn't the man worth more than his rank?"

"Yes, I suppose so," Alea conceded. "I'm just a bit upset at the thought of serving as his squire."

"That's not what people expect." Evanescent spoke as a mind-reader with no compunctions about mental eavesdropping.

"No, it's not. They all seem to expect me to marry him—never mind that he isn't in love with me!"

"Or you in love with him?" Evanescent asked. "I noticed you didn't mention that."

"Didn't, and won't," Alea snapped.

Evanescent sighed and stirred with impatience. "This emotion you silly two-legs call 'being in love' is rather exasperating."

"Don't I know it," Alea said with all her heart. "But why does it bother you?"

"Only because you all seem to want it so badly, but are so reluctant to tell each other about it," Evanescent explained. "Are you that much afraid of being hurt?"

Yes! Alea thought, and was surprised at her own intensity. Aloud, she said, "That's where we can be most easily and most deeply hurt. Magnus still hasn't recovered from the injuries that she-wolf Finister gave him years ago."

"Just as you haven't recovered from your own . . . what is your phrase for it? Heartbreak?"

"That's it," Alea said through gritted teeth.

"A most nonsensical phrase," Evanescent said. "Hearts don't break, after all, though they may stop working—and it's not your heart that does the feeling anyway, it's your brain!"

"Would you have us say 'brainbreak,' then?" Alea couldn't help smiling.

"I suppose 'heartbreak' is a good enough metaphor," Evanescent conceded. "Of course, mating is scarcely a guarantee it won't happen. I do find it amusing that a strapping young woman like yourself who can face sword-swinging warriors in battle is afraid of a man who has proved his loyalty."

"If I were foolish enough to tell him I loved him, he might still hurt me by saying he didn't love me," Alea said, her voice hard.

"Quite so—he'll face ten armed men in battle but is still afraid to look into his own heart," Evanescent admitted.

Alea frowned at her closely. "So. You've been eaves-dropping again."

"Why not?" Evanescent asked. "Your kind are so amusing!"

Alea was afraid to ask but forced herself. "So you know he doesn't love me, then."

"He's afraid to let himself feel it," Evanescent explained. "Every time he has before, he's been hurt. Why should he think you'd be any different?"

"He's braver than that!"

"Something in him isn't." Evanescent nodded toward the side of the clearing.

Alea followed her gaze, frowning, and saw nothing but dry leaves and, behind them, dark trunks and live leaves— and dust motes dancing in a ray of sunlight. As she watched, though, the motes thickened, doubling in number, tripling, becoming a sort of sunlit fog, a mist that billowed up seven feet, then drew in on itself, taking human form.

Alea found herself staring at a stout little man in a

bottle-green coat and battered top hat, with ruddy cheeks and a rum-blossom nose, who cried, "A rag, a bone!" then turned a very angry glare on Evanescent. "And just who do you think you are to call me awake out here in the middle of a forest?"

"Who do you think you are," the alien responded, "to go hiding in the depths of a man's mind?"

"That's where I was born, catface," the tubby little man answered. "That's where I live!"

"*Magnus's* brain?" Alea asked, staring.

"In his most secret depths." The man turned his glare on her. "Where you'd like to be yourself, wouldn't you, and evict me or make me cease to exist!"

"I . . . I bear you no ill will," Alea said, taken aback.

"No ill will, she says! When my home's becoming so crowded I can scarcely move, there's so much of you there already!"

"Is . . . is there really?" Alea asked, wide-eyed.

"Oh, there'd be more, if he could open his heart," the rag-and-bone man told her, "but he locked it away years ago, he did, in a box of golden, and can't open it!"

"Did he, now!" Alea's eyes narrowed. "With no help from you?"

The rag-and-bone man shrugged impatiently. "I'm just a figment of his imagination, a personification of his fears and desires. To say I did it to him is as much as to say he did it to himself."

"Are you sure that she-wolf Finister didn't call you into being?" Alea demanded.

"Oh, she did the most," the rag-and-bone man said, "but she wasn't the first and wasn't the last. He had a knack for falling in love with women who wanted to use him, he did."

"And . . . that's why he hasn't fallen in love with me!" Alea felt anger growing. "Because I *don't* want to use him!"

"No, it's because his heart is locked up, and he doesn't know how to unlock it," the rag-and-bone man said cheerfully. "Don't put on airs, young woman. Don't think you're more than you are."

"Meaning he isn't in love with me!" Alea said, seething.

The rag-and-bone man rolled his eyes over to Evanescent. "Bound and determined to believe the worst of herself, isn't she?"

"She's growing out of it," the alien said. "These humans seem to cling to their illusions, even when they're destructive."

"All right, then, if you know so much," Alea said, "how *can* I free his heart?"

"Ask the one who did the most to imprison it," the rag-and-bone man said. "Ask the she-wolf!"

"Never!"

" 'Never' can be a long time," Evanescent warned.

"I couldn't stand to ask anything of her! I'd rather die!"

"Well, then, you will," the rag-and-bone man said, "alone."

Alea rounded on him in a fury. "Who asked you?"

"You did," he answered. "Go ahead, don't listen to the answer. It's better for me if he lives alone all his life, anyway."

Alea stood with fists clenched, fuming but silent, searching for some scathing retort but finding nothing. It made her feel helpless, powerless, and her fury built in silence.

"I'd love to help you, if I could," Evanescent said, "but I haven't the faintest notion how to generate this emotion you call 'love.' "

Alea stared at her in disbelief. "Don't your kind fall in love?"

"No—we come into season and smell the other's interest," Evanescent said. "Once we know, we do something about it. It's enjoyable while it lasts, but it never distracts us for long."

"And of course, distractions are what you most need," Alea said with disgust.

"Of course." Evanescent gave her a toothy smile. "Most of us die of boredom, quite literally. You promise to give me a good long life, you and your male."

"He's not mine!"

"And you can't change that," the rag-and-bone man said.

Alea rounded on him. "You be still! You can disappear!"

"Can I really?" he asked, and turned away, turned soft

around the edges, soft all the way through, his form blurring, then thinning as it turned back into dust motes that blew away. A last whisper of beery voice cried, "I can!"

"That didn't accomplish much, did it, dearie?" Evanescent asked. "But I suppose you'd learned all you needed from him, anyway."

"Not a thing!" Alea said.

"Of course you had," Evanescent said. "You learned that it's no lack in you that keeps that silly male from—'falling in love,' do you call it? The fault's in him, not in you."

"That's no help!"

"Oh, it's help you want, is it?" the alien asked. "Well, I'll be delighted to do what I can. Your species' courtship ritual is quite amusing—you make it so much more complicated than it needs to be, especially you and Magnus."

Something in the statement rang false. Alea eyed the alien narrowly. "Have I really fallen in love? Or have you just been manipulating my emotions for your own diversion?"

"How could you think such a thing!" But the alien's toothy smile was less than convincing. "Your emotions are real—though I must confess I find them a great source of diversion. No, if I were going to manipulate anyone's emotions, it would be his—but you just saw what I'm up against."

"A funny little man and a golden box?" Alea frowned. "Scarcely daunting adversaries."

"They wouldn't be, if they were real," Evanescent said, "but when they're buried in the mind, it's another matter entirely."

Alea heaved a sigh and sat down on a stump. "Does it really happen? I don't just mean people falling in love—I mean staying in love, even after they're married!"

"Well, I know of one couple that will probably manage to be in love until death does them part," Evanescent said, "though I suspect they're cheating by making death come sooner. She's only twenty-six and he's twenty-eight, but he's about to hang for the capital crime of feeding his people. She's more in love with him than ever, so I think they'll make it through life—his life, anyway."

"But that's terrible!" Alea was back on her feet again. "Who are they? Where? How can I help them?"

"In the south," Evanescent answered. "She's bound for Castle Loguire to make one last plea for his life. His case looks clear, though. He doesn't deny he slew all those deer."

"The poor woman!" Alea said. "What is her name? Tell me how to find her!"

"You have only to ride the forest road that runs from the west toward Castle Loguire and follow the sound of sobbing," Evanescent said. "After all, the poor thing hasn't been trained to war, as you have."

"We have to find a way to help her!" Alea spun about, looking helplessly at the trees. "How, though? There must be lawyers on this planet!" She looked around at the empty clearing and did wonder for a moment how she'd come to know of the young man's arrest. Well, that was what came of practicing on other people, of trying to see how far away she could read minds. She deserved every bit of anxiety she was feeling.

But she had to find a way to help! She turned and started back up the trail toward Castle Gallowglass, never thinking for a moment that she hadn't learned of the young couple's plight by anything but her own telepathy—for of course, she didn't remember meeting Evanescent at all, nor even a hint of their conversation.

AS ROD RODE, the woods thinned out. By noon, Fess brought him out of the last trees onto a long ramp of grassland—but as they climbed, the grass grew thinner and more yellow until Rod rode across an upland of scrub and tufts. "We've come onto a moor, Fess."

"Yes, Rod, but it is surely the most barren moor I have ever seen."

"They're not exactly known for being fun places." Rod shivered as a sudden gust of wind chilled him. "Well, if it's barren, there's that much less to catch fire if my campfire shoots out sparks." Rod dismounted. "And if it's cold, I could use the warmth for a little while. Time for lunch."

"Where will you find wood to burn, Rod?"

"Good question—but as I remember, moors have pockets of peat." Rod scouted about. "Though we may have to ride a bit farther before we . . . Hey!"

Fess came closer. "Mud, Rod?"

"Mud that won't let go." Rod tried frantically to pull a foot loose. "And it's getting deeper!"

Nineteen

"NO, ROD—YOU ARE SINKING." FESS STARTED for him.

"Stop!" Rod cried. "I don't want you sinking, too!"

"But I cannot let you . . ."

"You won't! Go forward a step at a time, and if the ground goes soft, step back!"

Fess edged toward him, tossing his head to make the reins fly forward over his ears. "Catch the reins, Rod."

Rod flailed, missed—and sank another two inches. "Isn't there a branch . . ." Rod broke off, staring, as the mud began to bubble. "No! There can't be anything living in this!"

The ooze heaved upward, higher and higher into a sloppy sort of column. At its top, pockets appeared with a sucking sound, two holes of darkness over a much larger third that yawned wide and said, "Foolish mortal, to have dared come into the Barren Land!"

For a moment, Rod wondered crazily if he had stumbled into mud or a pool of witch-moss. Then he realized that it wasn't crazy at all if the bog could take on a face and talk to him. "What manner of spirit are *you*?"

"I am the Spirit of the Waste," the mud-monster intoned, "and I spread sloughs for the unwary."

"I'm not sure you can actually spread a slough." Rod looked down at the mud. "But I'm not exactly in a position to argue."

"Nay, nor to struggle." A muddy hand shot out from the monster's body to touch Rod on the forehead. He shouted and recoiled, trying to avoid the oozing finger—but the mud sucked at his feet, and he fell on his back.

Fess neighed a protest, and Rod felt the mud pulling at his back and hips, dragging him down—but he saw no reason to resist. When he stopped and thought about it—and what else could he do, lying on his back in a bog?—there was no reason to struggle. Sure, there would be a few minutes of unpleasantness . . . well, pain . . . when the mud choked his lungs and he could no longer breathe, but if he went into a trance here and now, he wouldn't mind all that much—and what reason was there to live? The kids didn't need him any more—they had their spouses, all but Magnus, and he had Alea, a devoted companion who would give him all the emotional support he was willing to accept. The Crown didn't need Rod, either—Tuan was still amazingly devoted to Catharine, and she to him—nor did the nation; Magnus would defend it as well as he ever could, especially with his brothers and sister to back him up.

And Gwen was gone.

So why not just lie here and let the bog take him?

Rod felt as though a thin black cloud had fallen over him, dimming everything about him—not that he could see much from this point of view. Even the broad and cloudless noonday sky above him seemed dulled, its blue almost gray. Dimly, he was aware that there had been reasons to live once, but he couldn't remember them now. No, he could—they had been Gwen and the kids, and protecting Gramarye from the futurians. Even before that, the dreams that had kept him going were freeing oppressed peoples and finding a woman he could fall in love with, who would fall in love with him, something he had come to believe could never happen.

Then he had met Gwen.

Gwen, it had always been Gwen—even before he met her, there had been the hope of finding her.

Now she was gone.

So why not let the mud take him? There was no purpose in life any more, no reason for living, and certainly no joy, not without her. Sink down and die, and see her much sooner!

Something slapped his chest. Rod scowled down at it, resenting any interruption, now that he had finally made up his mind to die. Dimly, he was aware of someone ranting and raging at someone else who was poking in where he had no business, but he didn't really care. He saw the two-inch-thick stick lying across his doublet; it took him several seconds to realize it would probably hold his weight. Following it back, he saw the robot holding the other end in his mouth; Fess had somehow managed to find a fallen branch after all. He smiled sadly; it was a nice idea, but kind of tardy, after he had finally come to realize where his life really stood.

"Take hold of the end of the branch, Rod," the robot's voice said through the earphone embedded in the bone in front of his ear. "It will bear your weight, and I will pull you to firm ground."

"Why bother, Fess?" Rod said. "There's no point in going on. Go back to Magnus; he needs you. Go back to the ones who have reason to live."

"That is not your own thought, Rod," the robot explained. "It is a projection of this earthen elemental who seeks to drag you down."

"A projected thought?" Rod frowned. "Why would it bother?"

"For the same reason it spreads bogs for the unwary, Rod. It detests all life and seeks to purge the earth of living things. It sees all life as corruption, as obscenities that should not exist, and it seeks to cleanse its own element of all that grows or moves. It is the Spirit of the Waste because it makes wastelands. It finds in them a kind of purity."

"In my present state of mind, that almost makes sense." Rod turned to frown at the bulge in the bog. "Are you sure it's wrong?"

"Quite sure, Rod, but you will not be able to evaluate the idea objectively as long as you lie within its power. Take hold of the stick."

But the mud had covered his ears now, was sending a tendril across his chest; he could taste a trickle of it in his mouth. "It would be so easy . . ."

"Easy, perhaps, but not right. There are still people who need you, work that only you can do."

"Can't think of any, at the moment."

"No, and you never will as long as you lie within that creature's power. Seize the end of the branch."

But the monster stretched out a tendril again, reaching for Rod.

At the cold and clammy touch, something mulish and stubborn rose up in Rod. His mind, at least, had always been his own—until he had chosen to let Gwen share it. With both hands, he laid firm hold on the stick. The tentacle of mud poised over his face, then slammed down, but Rod managed to twitch aside, and it slapped into the bog, merging with the rest of the mud and losing its shape. The monster bellowed, and the tentacle began to reform—but it was moving away from him now. No, he was moving away, and the roaring monster was too slow in refashioning its boneless arm. Rod was actually making pretty good time considering he was ploughing through mud. Then firm ground slid up under his head; he tucked in his chin and solid earth jolted under his back. When it reached his waist, he flipped over and pushed himself to his feet, his legs sucking loose from the tug of the bog—and suddenly the world seemed to brighten, his spirits soared, and life was good again. Gwen was still a dream, one he could actually attain, one worth searching for.

The monster howled in frustration. "You are mine, mortal, and shall return to me!"

"All that lives will return to the earth sooner or later," Rod agreed, "but not today." He frowned, directing a thought at the creature, thinking of it melting back into the slough from which it had come. The monster roared rage even as it dissolved; the last roar was only a bubble in the mud.

"I have never seen a bog of witch-moss before, Rod."

"Nor have I," Rod said. "We'll have to call Toby and the Royal Witchforce to come clean it up."

"Speaking of cleaning up . . ."

Rod looked down at his doublet and hose to find them slathered with mud. "Might not have to throw them away. Let's find a pond and see what happens if I take a swim."

"If I were you, Rod, from now on, I would be wary of immersion in any medium."

"Yeah, but if we all gave in to that kind of impulse, no one would ever write a book." Rod turned to mount, then thought better of it. "I think I'll walk until we find enough water to rinse me. Lead on, Fess."

"I have no idea where to go, Rod."

"To the west, of course! That's where Tir Nan Og lies, doesn't it?"

"I have not noticed it on any map."

"Quit caviling. If you don't know where to go, any direction is as good as any other, and I choose west." Rod stopped for a moment, then said, "And, Fess—thanks for pulling me out of one more bog."

"That is why I exist, Rod."

MAGNUS WAITED FOR the seneschal to announce him. The man came out and bowed him into the royal solar. He came in and bowed himself. "Good morning, Your Majesties." Then he straightened and gave his parents' friends a bland smile that hid his scrutiny.

Catharine stopped pacing long enough to give him a courteous nod, while Tuan rose from his chair and came to press Magnus's hand with a smile. "Good morning, Sir Magnus. How do you find your old home?"

"There is some feeling of strangeness," Magnus admitted, "but the strangest thing of all is that it looks so familiar."

Tuan laughed. "I remember such a feeling when I returned from my exile. Be sure, it will pass."

"I am reassured." Magnus returned Tuan's smile; it was

almost impossible not to. The man's good nature was infectious.

It was his first close meeting with them since the funeral, and he was in far better condition to study the changes in them—but there didn't seem to be any, if you didn't count the crow's-feet and other new creases in their faces, and a little more thickness to their bodies. For a couple in their fifties, Tuan and Catharine were in excellent condition.

"We are quite curious," Catharine told him, "and very eager to hear of the strange sights and stranger customs you have witnessed—but we shall wait for that until you are feeling fully at home again."

"I am quite willing to tell you." Magnus smiled. "Your problem will be making me stop."

Both laughed, neither believing him. "We would not disrupt your day only for such pleasantries," Tuan said, "but we have heard reports that disturb us."

"Really." Magnus resisted the temptation to read their minds. "Reports of what?"

"Of peasants who gather in ever-larger bands, marching toward Runnymede." Tuan's smile faded. "They bear only the tools of their labor, but I know how well flails and scythes can harvest soldiers. Have you heard aught of such?"

"I have," Magnus said, "and have already spoken with Geoffrey."

"I thought you might have." Tuan nodded, pleased. "But our spies tell us more—that the agents who foment discontent and lead these bands answer to our old nemesis—the Mocker."

"How dare he!" Catharine burst out. "Surely the man is neither commoner nor lord—how dare he seek to lead the peasants against us!

"Worse," Tuan said, with a perfectly straight face. "How dare he, who was certainly in his sixties at least, now rise again and look no older than when we saw him last?"

"Surely it is his rising that matters, not his age!" Catharine declared indignantly, but turned to Magnus. "Thirty years have passed! Surely he should be dead!"

"By the standards of this place and time, yes," Magnus said "or at least drastically enfeebled. Since he is neither, Majesty, it is clear he must have found a way to travel through time."

King and Queen stared. Then Catharine said slowly, "Your mother mentioned such a thing, when we were wondering what manner of men and women our children would become. It seemed only a fable at the time. Surely you do not mean to tell us it can truly happen!"

"My parents made it clear to me that it does," Magnus said, "and that, though the Mocker must only be seen using such weapons as we have, he may secretly have far worse."

"Of course—the future will have developed more lethal tools than we have, will it not?" Tuan said slowly. "Still, he cannot use them on any large scale, or the peasants will shy away from him as a witch."

"There is that," Magnus agreed, "but it makes him no less lethal if we meet him hand to hand."

"We would not ask you to take any great risk," Tuan said, still slowly, "but we dearly wish to learn what truth there may be in our spies' reports. Can you ascertain whether or not peasants are gathering to march on Runnymede?"

Magnus stared at him.

"Come, come, you cannot be surprized to hear us ask it of you!" Catharine said. "Your parents have told us that you yourself have skulked in the shadows and plotted to overthrow tyrants who oppressed their peoples!"

"Your mother with concern, your father with pride," Tuan said.

Now Magnus was surprized—he had assumed his democracy-fostering father would have been ashamed of a son who empowered any other form of government. Perhaps the good of the people had been paramount to his father after all. It was a warming thought. "I never overthrew a king or queen," Magnus said, "though there was one whose lords had already pushed him aside—and he had so weak a mind that restoring him would only have led to more of the same. Still, Majesties, my siblings are at least as capable as I, and far more current with matters on Gramarye. Surely it is one of them you should entrust with this mission!"

King and Queen shared a quick glance; then Tuan turned back to Magnus. "All are quite able, it is true—but Gregory is too idealistic . . ."

"Too naive," Catharine said bluntly. "He will not believe evil of anyone unless it is undeniable."

"That could be a handicap in dealing with a secret agent," Magnus admitted. "Geoffrey, though . . ."

"Your warrior brother, confronting someone who is sly, subtle, and underhanded?" Catharine said.

Magnus saw her point but protested, "He would be quite stern with any criminal, once he was sure of the man's ill will."

"If he did not discover it by finding a knife in his heart," Catharine said darkly.

"More to the point, he would give himself away by his anger," Tuan said, "the moment he witnessed an act of treachery."

"You underestimate him," Magnus claimed, though more out of loyalty than a desire for accuracy. "However, you cannot deny that Cordelia is subtle enough."

"True," said Catharine, "but she would tell Alain straightaway, and he would go to confront the man openly—and take a knife in his back for his pains." The mother's worry underscored her words.

"Besides, though your sister is capable of being subtle, she is also apt to explode into anger if she discovers treachery," Tuan said, "or kill the fellow out of hand when more might be learned from him. You, however, are both devious and patient."

Magnus couldn't deny it—but he stalled. "How can you speak so of my qualities, Majesties? It has been ten long years since you have seen me!"

"We knew you well enough as a boy," Catharine said, "and you comported yourself well in several demanding situations. Your father's boasting makes it clear that those sterling qualities have only grown."

"Scarcely sterling," Magnus said. "Perhaps pewter— but I must admit I have honed my skills. Very well, Majesties, I will set inquiries in motion, though you will understand I cannot make them myself."

"You would be somewhat conspicuous," Tuan said with a smile of amusement.

"Yes, the penalty of standing nearly seven feet tall," Magnus admitted. "I do hope, though, that you will not expect me to command my sibs simply because I am the eldest. They have made it clear they will not stand for my lording it over them."

"We would not expect any such thing," Tuan said, this time with a straight face.

"Of course not," said Catharine, "but if there is indeed a rebellion brewing, you might mention it to your brother Geoffrey when the time for action is ripe—without making it an outright order."

"I think Sir Magnus is tactful enough for that," Tuan agreed.

"No, Majesty, devious," Magnus said. "You had the right of it the first time."

Twenty

MAGNUS WAS WAITING WHEN ALEA CAME BACK
to their suite, and he held up a basket. "If you haven't had
too much of the outdoors, we might try a picnic."

Alea stared for a moment, then laughed. "As though you
and I had not eaten by a campfire more often than not!
Growing restless indoors, are you, Gar?"

"It's good to hear that name again," Magnus said with a
smile. He stooped to go out the door. "You're as insightful
as ever, Alea. In fact, I begin to grow weary of towns, not
merely the insides of houses! Let us find some honest trees
to shade us."

Alea waited until they were out of the gate and halfway
across the meadow before she asked, "Was the chat with
your parents' old friends so bad as that?"

Magnus's face twisted for a moment. "Simply a matter
of their wanting me to check up on some intelligence reports they've had—because I'm devious enough."

"I wouldn't have put it that way," Alea said slowly, "but

I suppose they're right. You certainly have presented yourself as things you aren't."

"Yes, a knight passing himself off as a trooper," Magnus
said wryly, "or a madman, or a sage."

"Or a wanderer who took a wounded lass under his
care." Alea touched his hand. "And never imposed on her,
even when she wished it."

Magnus darted a look of astonishment at her. Alea
laughed, perhaps a little too quickly, and took her hand
away. "Still, you've usually worked alone, Gar, or with
only one companion. Can you truly adapt to becoming a
spymaster?"

"That's not so much of a problem. We have a host of
spies here on Gramarye, all of whom owe allegiance to my
family. They'll report soon enough, I'm sure." Magnus
paused under an oak and looked around. "Will this spot do?"

"Perfectly." Alea took the cloth from the basket, shook
it open, and laid it on the ground.

Magnus helped her to straighten it, then to lay out the
food. "How was your walk?"

"Very refreshing; the woods always are." Alea sat and
took out her dagger to slice the bread. "I let my mind wander and let the cares fall away—no promises to keep, no
lists of things needing doing. It was a pleasant morning."
She frowned, pausing as she turned to slice the meat.
"Though somewhere on the way, I overheard someone
talking about a young couple in trouble." Her brow furrowed. "Now, who could have been saying that?"

"You relaxed your mind?" Magnus asked.

"Oh, yes! That was the most refreshing part of it—not
having to keep on my public face for the people I met, not
having to guard my tongue—or my thoughts."

Magnus nodded. "Then your mind was open and recep-
tive. You probably overheard the thoughts of some cot-
tagers nearby as they gossiped—or of a merchant on a
nearby road. What troubled this young couple?"

"He'd been caught poaching, and she was on her way to
his hanging," Alea said slowly.

"The forest laws!" Magnus said angrily. "Well, I'll have
to establish some influence here before I can work for their

removal. It's obscene that a peasant should be hanged for shooting a partridge!"

"Not a peasant." Alea's brow creased with the effort to remember details. "He's a squire—and it wasn't a partridge he poached, but a deer. Several deer."

"A squire!" Magnus's eyes widened. "He could have wriggled his way out of shooting a partridge—but not a deer! He's probably completely law-abiding except for that! I've half a mind to do something about that now! Where is this young man?"

"To the south," Alea said slowly, the details swimming up from the hidden part of her mind. "His wife has to go to Castle Loguire to see him hanged."

Something in the word "Loguire" rang an alarm in Magnus's mind. "Alain's brother Diarmid is duke there—by his right as son of the king."

Alea looked up, frowning. "Who did he displace?"

"His uncle," Magnus said, "who was attainted for treason—but he's Tuan's older brother, so Tuan interceded for him with Catharine. This was before they married, but Tuan had just led an army of peasants to help her soldiers defeat a rebellion, so she spared his brother's life, though not his title. Tuan appointed a steward to administer the estates until Diarmid came of age."

"While you were gone, of course."

"Yes." Magnus frowned. "I have missed a lot, haven't I?"

"Oh, you've found a lot, too," Alea said casually.

"Yes." Magnus smiled, gazing at her. "I have indeed."

Alea smiled back at him, then felt her face grow hot and looked back down at the meat she was placing between two thick slices of bread. "Here." She handed it to him. "Add some cheese to that and you'll have a meal. I'll have some cheese, too, if you don't mind."

Magnus was laying the yellow slice on her bread when a voice said, "How now, wizard!"

"I'll let you know when I find out." Magnus looked up with a smile, then saw Alea's dumbfounded stare. "Alea, may I introduce you to the real spy-master here? His name is Robin Goodfellow, but he goes by Puck."

Alea looked away, abashed, then back to Puck with a

smile. "Pleased to meet you, Puck. Excuse my stares; you reminded me of someone I knew."

"Several someones, actually." Magnus caught the image of the dwarves of her homeworld that rose in her mind, then sank again.

"A pleasure to make your acquaintance, lady," Puck said with a smile.

"Spymaster." Alea frowned. "Don't tell me you have word of a rebellion already?"

"I do indeed," Puck said, and turned to Magnus. "Men from all over the land are indeed trooping toward Runnymede, their scythes and flails over their shoulders. It is as it was the year before you were born, wizard."

"Let us hope we can detour them before it comes to battle, then," Magnus said.

"So many in company will not be deterred long by any of my pranks," Puck said grimly.

"No, but there are other ways. See if the Wee Folk can learn who the leaders are, will you, Puck?"

"We shall have you a list ere long," Puck said, "but I think you would be wiser simply to track their movements and prepare for battle."

"I would never argue with the oldest of the Old Things," Magnus said slowly, "but I must try persuasion first."

"You will pit yourself against masters."

"Oh, he's no mean adept himself," Alea said.

Puck turned to her in surprise. "I hope you speak from your own experience, lady!"

Alea stared at him a moment, then dropped her gaze, blushing again. "I'm afraid not—but I've certainly witnessed his efforts. The man could charm a pitful of snakes!"

"Let us hope," Puck said darkly, "that he can charm a field full of angry peasants."

AFTER SUPPER THAT evening and before the usual entertainments began, Magnus was able to take Cordelia aside for a few minutes' talk. After listening to a glowing report on the baby princess's progress, he said, "Let us hope she will remain so bright and sunny even if she has a little brother."

"What, one for Alain, and one for me?" Cordelia smiled, amused. "I hope we shall have more children than two!"

"Yes, I've always thought four was the right number, myself."

"Because there were four of us? Still, I would have liked to have had a sister—as now I do!"

"Quicksilver certainly seems to be completely in sympathy with you," Magnus said, amused.

Cordelia started to speak of Allouette but caught herself in time.

"You have another brother now, too," Magnus reminded her, "though I suspect you rarely see Diarmid."

"Rarely indeed, since he was sent to administer the duchy," Cordelia said. "Still, he is pleasant enough when he is here, once you grow accustomed to his quiet ways."

"Surely you are accustomed already, having grown up with Gregory." Magnus frowned. "Or is Diarmid more quiet than ever these days?"

"If we saw him, we well might find him so," Cordelia said, "for I understand he has to judge his first capital case and is rather upset about it."

"Surely it would give him an excuse to delve into some other old books!"

"Perhaps," Cordelia said, "but the verdict seems clear enough, and I doubt that any moldy old volumes will show him any excuse to pardon the young man. He was caught poaching, after all—more than one of the royal deer—and Diarmid is not looking forward to carrying out the sentence. Still, he knows that, as duke, he must witness the hanging."

"The poor fellow!"

"Which," Cordelia asked, "Diarmid or the felon?"

"Both. I trust Diarmid can postpone the matter for some months."

"Alas, he cannot," Cordelia said. "The young man must hang in four days." She shuddered and looked away, then brightened. "Look, the jugglers are about to begin! Let us watch and think of happier events!"

Magnus went with her, thinking furiously how he could manage to travel to Loguire to plead the young poacher's case while he was trying to find a way to forestall a peasant rebellion.

THE CLEARING WAS wide enough for Rod to see a few stars between the tree-tops. He had pitched his tent in the center, the better to see anyone—or anything—approaching. So far, though, the night had been quiet, only the chirring of insects around him and, in the woods, the odd howl or shriek of the night-hunters or their quarry.

Rod plucked his harp, gazing into the campfire and letting his thoughts wander as he tried to pin down the cause of his vague unease. It could just be a quirk in his brain chemistry, of course, but he doubted that. Better to rule out events in the kingdom—but he couldn't think what they would be. He reviewed recent happenings, then let them sort themselves at the back of his mind while he tried an old folk song; maybe the odd correlation would make itself if he didn't try to work it out by logic.

"As I was a-walking one morning in May,
To hear the birds whistle, see . . ."

He broke off, alerted by some change in the night's sounds. Whoever was coming was very good—Rod couldn't hear his steps at all, only track him by insects falling silent around him, then starting their concert again when he was past. Rod opened his mind to scan and was doubly alerted by emptiness, the lack of mental activity of a shielded mind.

Strumming, he turned to his left just a little and made out the silhouette blocking the stars, a silhouette in the shape of a head. Whoever it was, he or she was very tall. He smiled, letting the strings fall silent. Sure enough, the voice came out of the darkness: "A new song, Dad."

"New to you, yes, son. I don't suppose I've played it since you were a toddler."

Gwen sitting on a blanket spread over meadow grass with a picnic basket beside her, arms outstretched to the tow-headed toddler who was having great fun being obstinate about coming to her . . .

Rod winced at the pain of the memory of happiness and put it aside, sure he could recall it when he wanted. He concentrated on the living son who was here, allaying the ache of longing for the wife who wasn't. "Your stalking has improved; you're excellent now."

"I can't be, if you knew I was there." Magnus stepped into the firelight.

"Ah, well, you forget that I'm an excellent sentry." Rod moved over on the log. "Sit down and have a bite." He nodded toward the kettle of stew that hung near the fire.

"Thank you." Magnus took a bowl from Rod's pack and ladled it full, then brought it back to sit beside his father, toying with the spoon, then sampling the food and nodding approval.

Rod smiled, amused; he knew his own culinary limitations. "Someone taught you good manners."

Gwen, thirty-two and smiling as she showed her little boy how to hold his spoon, while his baby sister napped in her cradle . . .

The deep voice of the grown Magnus pulled him from the memory. "I just happened to be in the neighborhood."

Rod gazed at the huge dark man who had somehow grown out of that blond two-foot toddler and blinked his eyes clear. "Yes, I understand you have friends living down this way."

"Kin, actually." Magnus turned his gaze to the fire, frowning. "I suppose they are, now that Cordelia's married."

"Kin?" Rod frowned, then remembered Alain's uncle and smiled. "Well, the king may be your sister's father-in-law, but I'm not sure that makes his brother Anselm your uncle-in-law."

"A relative of an old family friend, then?"

"Yes, but I'm sure his feelings toward me aren't friendly."

"Because you were the key to defeating his rebellion? Or because you counselled mercy for him?"

"Both." Rod looked more closely at his son. "Not that you were coming to visit him—or is there trouble in the south?"

"There's trouble in all quarters of the land, Dad," Magnus

sighed, "but only vague mutters of discontent—nothing I can really pin down."

So he needed to talk about threats to the Crown. Rod felt oddly flattered, even though it was a little disappointing that his son hadn't sought him out simply for company.

On the other hand, it was nice to know Magnus hadn't come to check up on his delusional parent.

Had he?

"Nothing specific, then. Has Alea heard any gossip you haven't?"

"No." Magnus turned to him with a frown. "Why should she?"

"Men aren't always privy to women's conversations— or interested enough to pay attention." Rod took a stick and reached out to stir the coals; flame licked up. "Then too, being new to Gramarye, she might notice some things that you and I would look right past."

"So used to them that we dismiss them." Magnus nodded thoughtfully, his gaze following Rod's stick back to the flames. "We talk constantly, and I'm sure she would have mentioned anything that seemed odd."

"She must be mentioning oddities every night."

"Well, yes." Magnus smiled, amused. "She's not used to elves, or to so many people with psionic talents. I do have to reassure her as to what's considered commonplace here."

"*She* certainly isn't."

"What? You mean being so tall that she seems a freak?" Magnus turned to him with a frown; it was a topic with which he was all too familiar.

"No, her perceptiveness and sensitivity." Rod put down the stick and looked up at his boy. "A very intelligent woman, son."

"Yes. She is that." Magnus allowed himself a small smile.

"Just a stray who followed you home?"

Magnus laughed.

Rod blinked in surprize at the rare sound, then smiled, thinking that Alea might be better for Magnus than he knew.

"A stray, perhaps," Magnus acknowledged. "Certainly a fugitive—but she scarcely followed me. In fact, she took quite a bit of reassuring and coaxing."

"Oh?" It was a side of Alea Rod hadn't seen. "What had made her skittish?"

"Her parents died," Magnus said, "and the neighbors she had thought were her friends turned away from her. On her home world of Midgard, the 'normal' people were reacting to the abnormalities of inbreeding by enslaving those they could and fighting those they couldn't—and she was too tall to count as normal."

"So they enslaved *her?*"

Magnus nodded. "Her parents' lands were given to their worst enemies, who proceeded to beat her or whip her for the slightest disobedience."

"Trying to break her spirit. They didn't succeed."

"No, but they might have, if she had stayed. The first night, though, the son made advances—if you can call assault an advance . . ."

"So she didn't stay around for a second night."

"She felt that a quick death was better than a lifetime of abuse," Magnus said, "so she took the chance to run and hoped she could escape the slave-catchers. She took her risks with the wild dog packs and the giants."

Rod shuddered. "Harrowing enough."

"Yes, but there's something more." Magnus frowned. "She has never spoken of it, but I'm sure there was a heartbreak there—and whoever broke her heart did it in the cruelest way possible."

Rod looked up at him. "Only a guess, though?"

"A guess, but the symptoms don't leave me much room to imagine anything else—unless it's something worse."

"So she took her chances with the forest's monsters instead of the human ones." Rod turned to gaze into the campfire. "Think she would have survived by herself?"

Magnus was still for a minute, thinking it over. Rod was surprised that his son didn't seem to have considered the issue before. "Not a relevant question?"

Magnus shrugged. "She met me before she met the wild-dog pack. I had to pretend to ignore her except to leave food where she could take it but still have a head start if I tried to attack."

Rod nodded. "She couldn't know you were safe, after all."

"She must have had some suspicion of the sort," Magnus said. "She travelled near me for the next few days until she plucked up the courage to talk with me—and I had to be very careful not to say or do the slightest thing that could even seem to be threatening."

"But you were a stranger, far too tall to be one of her own kind," Rod said, "and, I take it, too short to be a giant?"

"For once in my life, yes." Magnus smiled.

"So it must have taken a great deal of courage to trust you at all."

"Great courage indeed." Magnus nodded. "That was what I first admired in her—her bravery in facing the wilds by herself: the savage animals, the unknown, the unexpected . . ."

"Including you," Rod said. "How well could she survive by herself now?"

"Oh, very well," Magnus assured him. "She knows how to fight, bare-handed or with a staff, and knows how to find food in the woods. Then too, she turned out to have some psi talent—how much, I'm still not sure . . ."

"Which means it must be considerable."

"Exactly. She has learned how to use her powers enough to be formidable in her own right—and she's sharp-tongued enough to scare off any animal that can understand speech."

Rod glanced up quickly, looking for signs that Magnus had suffered the sharp edge of that tongue, but the young man's face was tranquil as he gazed into the fire, giving away nothing. "No chance she's an emotional basket-case?"

"Not once she recovered from the shock of betrayal and the two days' abuse that followed," Magnus said. "She grew up in a loving and supportive home—or so I'd judge from the odd comment she has made about her parents. Apparently she was devoted to them because they were devoted to her."

"Not because she was starved for approval?"

Magnus shook his head. "If anything, her parents made her feel so special that she had no idea how cruel the world could be."

Rod wondered if he and Gwen had been guilty of that,

then remembered his own rages with greater guilt. Maybe it would have been better for them all if he had left—but no, he'd considered that at the time, even tried it for a while when the delusions hit. "Your opinion of her seems to have grown with time."

"Oh, it has." Surely it was the reflection of the fire that glowed in Magnus's eyes. "Herkimer dug up enough material on the healing process to give me some idea what to expect, so I was able to endure the months of anger and insult. Then on planet after planet, her courage showed clearly, then her loyalty and her willingness to try to understand the people we met, to learn what was best for them and work for it, and finally her aptitude for caring re-emerged, for trying to help other people. Sometimes I don't think she's even aware she's doing it."

Rod studied his son's impassive face, hoping for some sign of his feelings. "Added to which, she's a handsome woman."

"Once she recovered from abuse and exposure, yes. Once she was able to wash off the dirt and eat decently again." Magnus's voice sank low. "Very handsome indeed." Then quickly, as though he had revealed too much, "More importantly, she's a valiant shield-mate and fiercely loyal."

"Maybe that is more important." Rod's shield-mate had been beautiful as well as ferocious and fearsome. Then he realized that Magnus's was, too. "You can't really be thinking that she's only a travelling companion."

Magnus was quiet a moment, then turned to him with a frown. "I wouldn't say that a shield-mate was that small a thing to be."

"Agreed," Rod said. "But you must realize that you care about her much more deeply."

"I care about her immensely, of course," Magnus said, frowning, "but still only as the closest of my friends."

Rod studied his face and decided that he'd hit the point of diminishing returns. "Then you're planning to take her home."

"She doesn't want to go back to Midgard. She says that since her parents died, she has no home there."

"So you're planning to find her one here?"

Magnus turned away, shaken, and Rod saw that his son hadn't considered Alea's falling in love with someone else—but Magnus said gamely, "Of course."

"Well, then, you'd better pay attention to what she means as well as to what she says." Rod ignored his son's puzzled look. "Just don't forget that you can't accuse a friend of not being willing to give if you aren't willing to take."

"No, of course not," Magnus said, even more puzzled.

"Good." Rod filled himself a bowl of stew. "Care for seconds?"

Magnus stared, then laughed and shook his head. "No thank you, Dad. One bowl was enough to tide me over. I do have to get back to the castle." He looked up with a quizzical frown. "I thought I had come to ask your opinion about my siblings' insistence that I not give them orders."

"They're grown up now." Rod smiled. "Are you?"

Magnus laughed again, and loudly. He stood, nodding. "You're right—I'll treat them as I've treated all the other adults I've met on my travels."

"Meaning that you'll manipulate them with respect." Rod smiled and set his bowl down. "Instead, we talked about something that must matter more to you. I take it you're planning dinner with Alea."

"Of course." Magnus must have realized that he sounded domestic, because he said quickly, "Oh, and Dad—Alea picked up word of a little problem in Loguire."

"Yes?" Rod looked up with interest. "What kind of problem?"

"A poacher who's about to be hanged," Magnus said, "and it's Diarmid who has to pass judgement on him.

Twenty-One

"OF COURSE," ROD SAID SLOWLY. "HE'S THE duke now, so any capital case would be referred to him."

"I understand he's not terribly happy about it."

"Sure," Rod said with a bleak smile. "Who would be? But it's part of being duke—he has to carry out his responsibilities."

"The poacher's wife is on her way to plead with the judge—Diarmid—for her husband's life," Magnus said. "He's a squire, you see, and had a bad harvest, so he was bringing the peasants venison to smoke and store for the winter."

"Deer?" Rod looked up. "Plural?"

"Sixteen," Magnus said.

Rod whistled. "Not much chance of claiming it was an accident or a drunken prank, is there? Or of promising he won't do it again."

"Very little," Magnus agreed, "but it gets worse."

"Worse?" Rod stared. "He's a squire who has purposefully poached sixteen deer, and it gets worse?"

Magnus nodded. "He's Anselm Loguire's son."

"You mean Diarmid has to pass judgment on his cousin?"

"First cousin," Magnus said with a sardonic smile. "Thanks for taking care of it, Dad."

Leaves rustled and he was gone. Rod stared after him, feeling numb.

Then he sighed and turned back to the fire, but could see only a lovely face with flame-red hair in its place. He looked upward to the patch of sky visible between branches and thought, *Sorry, dear—it's going to take a little longer than I expected. Have to take care of the children, you know.*

His body warmed as though wrapped in a loving embrace, and he felt fond reassurance fill him. Then it was gone, but he knew that Gwen understood. Even more, he knew she was waiting.

ROD HEARD THE sobbing before he could see anything but leaves. It was off to his left, but moving. "Fess, how far into the woods is that woman?"

Fess turned his ears forward, triangulating from the space between them. "Approximately a hundred yards, Rod, but I hear also the sound of hooves—about a dozen horses, I would say—moving at the same rate as she, and in the same direction."

"So she's riding with a small band." Rod frowned. "Just an escort, or is she a prisoner?"

"I can only conjecture, Rod."

"Which I know you abhor." Rod smiled. "Okay, I'll guess that she's a gentlewoman at least, riding with an honor guard. If they were her captors, I'd be hearing lewd jokes and loud conversation." Rod frowned, turning his attention to the realm of thoughts; it still didn't come as easily to him as it did to his children. *Or their mother . . .* "Actually, she's a noblewoman with her guards, and something horrible has happened to her husband; she's on her way to see him. Do you hear crunching of leaves and twigs?"

"None, Rod."

"Then they're coming down a road that crosses ours.

Let's see if we can't get there ahead of them, shall we?"

Fess picked up the pace, extruding the rubber horse-shoes that let him move almost silently. "I can see the intersection, Rod. It is at an acute angle."

"Then let's step into that angle and spy through the leaves."

"Reconnoiter, Rod, please! I have always told you not to spy."

"Yes, Mama," Rod sighed. "Just so we can see what we'll be running into."

Fess stepped off the shoulder and found a path that required the least amount of brushing against branches or stepping on sticks. Through the screen of leaves, Rod could see a young woman riding sidesaddle with six liveried men in half-armor before her and six behind. He nodded and said softly, "Okay. To the intersection."

They rode out just before the first of the lady's guards reached the cross-roads.

"Ho, fellow!" barked the lead man.

Rod turned back in polite surprize, then smiled with pleasure. "Company! Where are you bound, soldier?" Then he lifted his head as though seeing the young woman for the first time. "Oh! Riding escort?"

"We are," growled another soldier, "and you keep a civil tongue in your head, for she's our squire's lady."

All the other soldiers rumbled agreement even though, strictly, a squire's wife wasn't entitled to the title of "lady." This close, Rod noticed that the livery and the armor didn't quite fit the men who wore it. That, and their devotion to the lady in question, gave him a notion he was dealing with volunteers—and enthusiastic ones at that. "Good day to you, lady! Where are you bound?"

"To Loguire, sir, to meet my husband." The lady lifted her veil to give him a close look; Rod caught his breath. The lady was gorgeous; her beauty was dazzling, even through the signs of recent tears. She seemed to decide he was relatively harmless. "And you?"

"To Loguire, also, to speak with the reeve about my taxes." Rod fell in beside her. "I take it your husband is doing the same."

"Nay." Her face clouded again. "Oh, he has gone there for the reeve, sure enough, but . . ." She choked on sobs and turned her head away.

"That sounds as though it wasn't all his choice," Rod said gravely. "What manner of trouble is he in?"

The lady seemed torn, wanting to speak of it but ashamed to—so a grizzled guardsman leaned forward and said, "Our people were looking at a winter of starvation, traveler. Our squire did as he should and sought to find ways to feed us."

"Poaching?" Rod stared, then turned to the lady. "But surely, if he had a good reason . . ."

"What matters that to the King?" she asked.

"The Crown isn't unreasonable," Rod said. "Surely with someone to plead your husband's case . . ."

"There is only his father," the lady said sadly, "and he is attainted."

"Attainted?" Rod scowled, "Well, I'm not! Tell me a bit more about the case, and maybe I can help."

The men muttered with interest, and the lady looked up at him as though afraid to hope. "If you are a knight, the reeve may hear you—but by your clothes, I would guess you to be only a yeoman."

"Just travelling clothes," Rod said. "A man doesn't have to wear his rank openly and, personally, I believe that quality shows through the clothes, for better or for worse. I am indeed a knight, good woman, and my name is Rodney."

"I am Rowena, Sir Rodney." Her face came alight with hope allowed. "Will you truly plead my husband's case?"

"I can't say without knowing the facts. What kind of creatures did he kill, and how many of them?"

"Sixteen," she said bitterly. "Stole sixteen of the King's precious deer, and must be hanged for any. Never mind that sixty good people were like to starve next winter if he did not!"

"Never mind is exactly what the reeve may do." At least this was the party he'd come to find. "If he were a knight or a lord, he might be able to plead privilege, but a squire has far greater cause to fear the rope."

"Not rope." The lady lifted her head with pride. "My

Geordie will be hanged with a golden chain." Then, as if to explain her pride, she added, " 'Tis not the chain of many."

"Yes, I know." Chains were reserved for nobility—but only someone related directly to the Crown warranted the dubious honor of being hanged with a golden one. "Your Geordie, then, is cousin to the Queen?"

"To her husband," the lady explained. "He is the King's nephew—and first cousin to the Crown Prince."

"A Loguire?" Rod nodded slowly. "Then there may be some grounds to plead privilege."

"Not when his father is attainted," she said bitterly.

Well, she hadn't married as a social climber, anyway. Geordie must be a very handsome young man to have attracted so lovely a bride when his prospects were so poor. "The harvest has been good this year, lady. Why would your people have been likely to starve?"

"Mold in the bins," she answered, and proceeded to tell him the whole tale as they rode. When she was done, Rod said what he could to reassure her, but he had a bad feeling about the case. Unless the judge was merciful, Geordie would hang surely, and his father would lead a rebellion that none would blame him for.

Of course, if Diarmid did grant mercy, someone was bound to cry favoritism and start a rebellion on the grounds of corruption.

Still, one crisis at a time. Rod drew Rowena out as they rode on, and by the time they rode into the town that had grown up around Castle Loguire, Rod had decided that Geordie had unquestionably broken the law—but had equally unquestionably had only the best of reasons for doing so. Too bad he hadn't applied to the reeve for an official exception—but maybe he'd known he couldn't make this particular reeve listen to reason.

Rod hoped he could.

THE LAST ROW of wheat fell, and the men dropped their scythe-bladed cradles with a whoop of joy, then turned to help with gathering the stalks into sheaves—and there would be many kisses shared as the sheaves were stacked, as there always were.

None for Diru, though. He found a place in the line and bent, spreading his arms wide to scoop up an armful of stalks, then took another to bind them together.

"If people could only gather as closely as their sheaves, eh, Diru?"

Diru looked up in astonishment. It was Ria, one of the girls of the village, actually talking to him! "Why . . . why, yes," he stammered, and cudgeled his brain trying to think of something to say. His tongue seemed to tie a knot in itself, though, even though Ria wasn't the beauty that Lenar and her friends were. Still, she was pretty enough, and it was an amazing pleasure to have her talking to him.

"Maybe we're all like stalks of wheat," Ria said, "no use unless we're all bound together."

"I . . . I suppose that's what a village is," Diru stammered.

"A good thought." Ria nodded with approval.

Approval! of Diru!

"But if we're a sheaf, then we ought to press against each other, shouldn't we?"

Diru couldn't stop staring. She couldn't really be flirting with him! Not with *him*! But he told himself that it would be rude not to answer and said, "I suppose that's what we all want."

"All?" Ria's eyelids flickered. "Folk say you're happier alone, Diru. Are you sure you want other stalks to press you?"

"Oh, very sure!" Diru said fervently, then realized he was being too forthright. He tried to pull away a little. "I mean, I wouldn't want to be a hermit living alone in the woods."

"How about a hermit with someone else living with you?"

Diru couldn't believe his ears. She couldn't be hinting that she found him attractive. No woman could—could she? "I—I suppose that if you have someone living with you, you're not a hermit."

"Still, it sounds lovely, being just two people alone out in the woods." Ria scooped up an armful of sheaves and went to carry them to the shock.

Diru scooped up his own sheaves and hurried to keep up with her. "It would be good enough if we could all pull together the rest of the year, as we do at harvest."

"But there should be some times when people can be alone together." Ria set her sheaves against the shock; as she turned away and Diru stepped up, her breast brushed against the back of his hand.

Diru stood frozen an instant. No woman had ever touched him, let alone a touch like that! Then he hurried to set his sheaves and turned to catch up with Ria. "I've felt sorry whenever I've heard of a hermit," Diru said. "People aren't meant to live alone."

"And they're not always meant to be serious." Ria turned to him with a smile, eyelashes flickering. "We're meant to do things together—aren't we, Diru?"

Diru's heart leaped. "Why . . . of course," he stammered, "things like the Festival tomorrow night." He screwed up his courage and burst out, "Will you dance with me there, Ria?"

"Dance with you?" He saw the delight in her eyes, and for a moment, his hopes soared.

They came crashing down as she threw back her head and laughed. The other young folk looked up at the sound, already grinning.

"Why, Diru!" she said very loudly. "Are you flirting with me?"

Diru tried to answer, his mouth moved, but no words came.

"Diru's flirting with me!" she called to the other young folk. "He's asked me to dance with him tomorrow night!"

Hoots of derision came from every side, howls of laughter, and Diru's face burned.

"Getting ideas a little above your station, aren't you, Diru?" Lenar came forward, eyes alight with merriment.

"Yes, Diru!" one of her friends said, giggling. "You should be asking someone with your own kind of looks. An elk, perhaps?"

"Oh, an elk's far too pretty!" another girl cried. "Diru should flirt with a bear!"

"Yes, Diru!" Hirol stepped up behind Lenar. "Maybe a

she-bear would let you cuddle up to hibernate with her!"

"Yes, somebody must want you to cuddle!" Arker stepped up beside Ria and slipped his arm around her shoulders. "Nobody human, of course, but somebody." Ria laughed with him, clinging to his arm and pressing against him, eyes mocking as she looked at Diru.

Diru's face burned, but he burned hotter within, standing there in the middle of a ring of mocking laughter and realizing how they had laid their trap, and how eagerly he had fallen into it. It had all been a joke, a great big joke, to see Diru make a fool of himself—the beginning of the Harvest Festival merriment. He could see it all—it had been Lenar or Hirol who had thought of it, but Ria had been quick to agree, since she wanted so badly to be part of Lenar's circle—all the girls did, and this had been her chance. Then they had told all the other young people about their wonderful jest, one destined to be famous in the village for a lifetime—how pretty Ria made a fool out of ugly Diru!

Wordless, he turned and blundered his way out of the circle, the laughter of mockery filling his ears. He stalked away, but they kept pace with him for a hundred yards as the anger within him swelled and swelled—but he knew what would happen if he lashed out, for the boys had given him beatings enough before. In misery, he waded through that torrent of laughter until the trees enfolded him with their blessed coolness and the sounds of merriment began to fade behind him. There was little point in following him into the woods, of course. One last taunt came behind him: "Oh, leave him alone! He's gone to propose to that bear we told him about."

And one last burst of laughter.

Diru ploughed ahead toward the depth of the woods, not really knowing where he was going or why, filled with misery and rage. Some day he would have his revenge, on Ria and Lenar and Hirol and Acker—on all of them, the adults who had always sneered at him, the youths who had mocked him since childhood. How, he had no idea, but he would have revenge!

Then the idea struck, and he froze, staring off into the

trees, realizing just how he could have that revenge—and not a year or more from now, but tomorrow! He set off through the woods again, but with a sense of purpose now, going as quickly as he could toward the river.

THEY RODE INTO the town square, a rough circle perhaps a hundred feet across, surrounded by half-timbered three-story houses, each with a shop of some sort on the ground floor—but all were shut, and the townsfolk glum as they gathered around the scaffold set in the center of the square, its raw wood rough and uneven. At its left end rose a set of bleachers, separated from the scaffold by ten feet of space and fifty men-at-arms, their spears bristling—but their liveries were not those of Loguire. They matched the rich colors of the robes of the men who sat on the board seats, fine clothing of satins and velvets that displayed their wealth and power, and the swords at their sides proclaimed not only their military training, but also their readiness to use them to start a war if they didn't like the verdict.

Rod drew breath, chilled as he realized a rebellion could break out right here—or a civil war; he saw a dozen knights sitting on their horses at the far end of the scaffold with a score of men-at-arms behind them and many more sprinkled throughout the crowd. The judge had taken military precautions, but his own armed force wasn't going to prevent a battle. Only clear thought and keen judgement could do that.

Between the judge's high chair at the one end of the scaffold and Anselm and his allies at the other, stood the gallows. The late afternoon sunlight glistened on the golden chain hanging from it.

Rod stared. "I hadn't known we had come to witness Geordie's execution!"

"Nor had I." Rowena slipped off her horse's back; several of her guards leaped down to help her, but she was already climbing the rough stairs. "I must plead for him!" She almost ran to the young man who sat in the seat of judgement and threw herself to her knees, head bowed—but Rod took one look at that young man and knew how slim her chances were. Diarmid Loguire was supremely

logical, and prided himself on his ability to banish emotion
in his consideration of a problem.

Rod felt a chill wind blow that did not stir the leaves of
the surrounding trees and had nothing to do with the
weather. If clear thinking and sound judgement were all
that could prevent a war from beginning here, they could
all be in deep trouble. Rod had faith in Diarmid's ability to
think clearly, but he wasn't so sure about his sense of
judgement. Diarmid was not a people person.

Quickly, Rod scanned the others who stood on the platform. Nearest him stood three older men, all looking grim.
In their center was a lean, clean-shaven, gray-headed man
with a bitter face. Rod recognized him—the King's elder
brother Anselm, attainted for treason, demoted to the rank
of squire, and doomed to live out his life in obscurity. Rod
had heard that Anselm had wed and would have loved to
have met his wife, to see the amazing woman who had
married a man doomed to a life of shame. She must have
really loved him.

Behind Anselm and his colleagues stood a dozen men-
at-arms in his livery. Rod felt his scalp prickle.

Then, looking toward the center of the platform, he saw
a young man standing bare-chested with his hands tied behind his back, beneath the golden chain—a black-haired
young man who was amazingly handsome. That must be
Geordie, and suddenly Rod could see why Rowena had
been attracted to him. Anselm's wife must have been a very
unusual woman indeed, one who could have married much
better than an attainted nobleman who could give her no
better life than any yeoman could—for she must have been
radiantly beautiful. Geordie certainly didn't get his looks
from his dowdy father.

"Mercy, kind judge!" Rowena threw her veil back, looking up at Diarmid with wide eyes that glistened with tears,
giving him the full benefit of her astounding beauty. "Have
mercy on my husband, I beg you!"

There was a stir and a murmur among the lords behind
Anselm—and another to answer it, among the men-at-
arms, even from the knights and troopers behind Diarmid.
In fact, the whole crowd seemed to breathe as every man

sighed with admiration and longing. Lady Rowena's beauty moved them all, and her tragic tears and vulnerability made every man there long to leap to her defense.

Every man except Diarmid. With a quick glance, Rod saw the young man's eyes widen, saw his hands tighten on the arms of the great chair—but his voice was cool and calm as he said, "Milady, he has broken the law."

"My love, do not humiliate yourself before this heartless man!" Geordie cried as though his own heart would break.

Diarmid's eyes narrowed; his hands tightened further.

"There is no shame in pleading for my husband's life!" Rowena cried. "O kind judge, give him any punishment but death!"

"I would the law allowed it," Diarmid said in a far more sympathetic voice than Rod had ever heard from him. "I would I could give him back to you, but the law is clear, and he has himself admitted to poaching sixteen of the Crown's deer."

"Deer that should have been his!" Anselm cried, as though the words were torn from him. "The great lords have always had the privilege of hunting in the royal forests, and it is Geordie who should have been duke of Loguire, not his mealy-mouthed cousin."

"So he would have, if you had not robbed him of his place by your treason." Diarmid lifted his head to give his uncle a stony glare, and his guards took their pikes in both hands.

The men beside Anselm leaned in to mutter angrily to him, and the lords behind him loosened their swords in their sheathes—but they glanced at the knights behind the young duke, who seemed to strain forward; they glanced again at the guards beside Diarmid, the others who stood to either side of Geordie, and the thirty more who stood below the scaffold, pikes and halberds ready—and Anselm could only clench his fists in impotent fury.

Diarmid turned back to Rowena. "He has stolen sixteen of the Crown's royal deer, and must be hanged for any one of them. This is the law, and he has admitted his crime. I cannot pardon Geordie."

Anselm cried out in anguish and gripped the hilt of his sword, and the man at his side leaned in to mutter more urgently—but the attainted lord only stood trembling.

"Kind lord, can you not remit the law?" Rowena cried.

"If laws are cast aside, the kingdom shall fall into chaos and all shall suffer," Diarmid told her.

"I am with child!" Rowena cried.

Anselm groaned, and Geordie let out a cry of his own.

Twenty-Two

"ALAS, THAT MY HUSBAND MUST LEARN OF IT thus!" Tears flowed down Rowena's cheeks. "But I am sure of it—I shall bear a babe in seven months' time! Must I birth an orphan?"

"Oh, my love! Geordie started for her, but the guards yanked him back. He turned on them with savage fury, bound hands or no, but one of them caught him in a wrestling hold, and he could only struggle and curse.

"I grieve for you," Diarmid said solemnly, "but so long as I am duke of Loguire, neither you nor your child shall want for anything. Go back to your estate, lady, and tend your babe."

She stood and turned away, sobbing, to Anselm, who embraced her and cried over her head, "Heartless prince! Can you show no mercy even to your own cousin?"

"It is because he is my cousin, my lord, that I dare make no exception to the law," Diarmid returned. "Shall the people say that there is one law for the common folk and another for the Crown and its relatives? Surely not! There must be justice for all!

"Justice, yes." Rod mounted the stairs, saying, "But sometimes the law must be tempered with mercy to yield justice."

"Gallowglass!" Anselm cried in anger and despair, and Rowena look up in horror to discover that her traveling companion had been her family's arch-enemy.

"Lord Warlock!" Relief washed over Diarmid's face but was quickly hidden. "How come you here?"

"To plead the cause of justice, Lord Duke." The relief Rod had seen in Diarmid's face reminded him how very young the man really was. "The forest laws are well and good, since they keep the deer from all being killed, and allow only enough hunting so that they don't gobble up their food supply and starve—but is not this enforcement too rigid? Is not the whole purpose of maintaining the deer herds so that they are there to feed hungry people if they are needed?"

"A sound rationale," Diarmid said thoughtfully. "History tells us the Forest Laws were made only to save the deer as sport for the great lords—but you give them far greater purpose, Lord Warlock."

Anselm stared, unable to believe Rod was pleading his family's cause—but Geordie stared, stunned, and Rowena looked at him with a sudden wild hope.

"Surely that purpose should be considered here," Rod said. "Is sport for the few more important than the lives of peasants?"

The crowd began to mutter, and the soldiers shifted uneasily.

Rod pressed the point. "Is the law more important than good governance?"

"The law is the key to good governance, my lord." Diarmid frowned, puzzled.

"Then good governance is the purpose?"

Diarmid lifted his head slowly, beginning to understand Rod's direction. "Aye, Lord Warlock, good governance is the purpose of the law."

"Then it is a purpose the law must serve." He turned to

Rowena. "Lady, has your husband ever failed in his duty?"

"Never, my lord!" Rowena said fervently. "He has always been diligent and just in his care of his peasants! He is ever about the estates assuring that all is well! The welfare of his people has ever been his constant concern!"

"Even to making her quarrel with him," growled one of her guards, in a voice too loud to be a mistake.

Diarmid turned to the man—and to the whole dozen of her escort. "Surely a wife will speak well of a husband she loves—but what of his retainers?" He saw the man's furtive glance at Anselm and sharpened his tone. "Come, man, you've naught to fear! You shall have a place in my own retinue; you and your family shall have cottages on my estates to shield you from the anger of Sir Anselm! If there is anything to be said against Squire Geordie, speak!"

"Not one word!" the grizzled peasant cried. "Not one word is there to be said against him, my lord, and everything for him!"

"Aye!" cried a younger man. "He is beside us even at the plow to be sure the furrow is straight! He marches out with the sowers to broadcast the seed!"

"Aye!" cried another. "When the harvest comes, he is ever beside us with scythe and flail! If a plowman is sick, it is he who sneezes!"

"We would follow Geordie to the death, my lord." The old peasant made it half a threat. "Call him to battle, and we will follow him all, man and boy, because we know that our welfare is his concern."

"It is for our sakes he is here!" cried the youngest. "When the grain rotted in the bin, he swore we would not starve though it cost him his life! I pray you, my lord, let it not do so!"

Now Anselm shook off the man who was whispering in his ear and stepped forward. "My son has always been an excellent steward of the land and governor of his people, Lord Diarmid. If it is justice you seek, you should reward him for his diligence and care, not take his life!"

"There's truth in what he says, my lord." Rod turned to Diarmid. "People are more important than deer."

"They are, Lord Warlock." Diarmid was beginning to

show a touch of excitement which, for him, was amazing.
"But by your own argument, if we do not enforce the Forest
Laws, how shall we feed our people with game in time of
famine?"

"It is because famine looms that Geordie has slain deer
to feed his people," Rod countered. "But money will serve
to buy food as well as a bow and arrow will. Might I suggest a fine—say, a thousand pieces of gold?"

The lords gasped in horror and began to talk furiously
among themselves.

"Very wise, Lord Warlock." Diarmid nodded slowly. "A
fine that would build a manor house—or feed fifty villages
through a hungry winter! Yes, so high a fine would make
even a duke think twice about hunting out of season, and
would surely deter any lesser lord."

"I shall give you all I possess!" cried Rowena. "All my
dowry, land, and jewels worth a hundred gold pieces!"

"Rowena, no!" Geordie cried.

"What use is a dowry without a husband?" she retorted,
and turned back to Diarmid. "I can offer no more than that!"

"I can!" One of the earls shot to his feet. "I offer one
hundred pounds and ten!"

"And I a hundred and fifteen!" A baron leaped up beside
him.

"A hundred and twenty!"

"A hundred and thirty!"

Rod stood, amazed, as the auction mentality took hold.
Diarmid only nodded, keeping mental score, and when the
bidding stopped, called out, "That is eight hundred fifty,
my lords, but not enough!"

"Then I shall offer a hundred and fifty of gold!" Anselm
cried. "Remember, my lord, you said it would go to feed
the hungry!"

"And so it shall!" Diarmid stood up. "I shall lock it in a
separate coffer and shall open it as soon as Squire
Geordie's folk find themselves short of bread!" He turned
to the assembled noblemen. "My lords, I thank you! May
we all show as much generosity and care for our fellows as
you have shown today!"

The lords stared at one another; charity had certainly

been the farthest thing from their minds when they set out
on this trip.

Diarmid turned to advance on Geordie, drawing his
dagger.

Voices shouted in anger, but Diarmid only stepped behind Geordie and severed his bonds. Geordie raised his
hands, rubbing his wrists in amazement, and the shouting
died. Then Diarmid reached up, shook the chain to unhook
it, caught it as it fell, and handed it to Geordie. "Use this to
buy food for your people—and if they are ever in need
again, tell your duke rather than taking up your bow!"

Rowena ran to throw her arms about her husband, and
the crowd cheered.

In the midst of the shouting, Anselm stepped up to Rod
with his hand on his sword. "If my son had been slain,
Lord Warlock, I would have rebelled—and this time, I
swear, I would have torn down my overweening little
brother and his arrogant Queen!"

"Even though they sent you a judge who had sense
enough to see that Geordie was an invaluable asset?" Rod
asked.

"'Tis not Diarmid who saw sense, but you who showed
it to him!"

"Why, thank, you, Sir Anselm," Rod said slowly.

Anselm stared, realizing that he had paid Rod a compliment. Then he recovered and demanded, "There may be
truth in that—but rumor says you have left your post to
wander the land as a doddering knight-errant! Who shall
temper the Crown's justice now, if the Lord Warlock has
left his position to roam at his pleasure?"

"Why, my son Magnus," Rod told him, "though I doubt
he'll be needed. Alain embodies all the mercy the Crown
will ever need. No matter what you may think of your relatives, Sir Anselm, your nephew has a positive genius for
sound judgement."

"Perhaps once he is King," Anselm allowed, brooding,
"but that could be twenty years or more. Who shall temper
the Queen's judgement until then? Surely she will not listen to her own son!"

Rod could have pointed out that Tuan had always been

the voice of moderation that had kept Catharine from turning into a tyrant, but he knew Anselm's resentment of his
brother's mercy and position were so intense as to only
make him erupt in anger—so he said instead, "She may not
listen to her own son, Sir Anselm, but she will listen to
mine. It's time for us to start trusting the children we've
worked so hard to raise wisely and well. Don't you trust
your own boy?"

"Aye!" Anselm said fiercely. "There's none better in all
the land!"

"But quite a few just as good," Rod countered. "Trust
your own boy, Sir Anselm—but trust mine as well. After
all, Geordie will."

"HE DIDN'T LOOK convinced," Rod told Diarmid as they
watched Anselm ride away beside his son and daughter-in-
law. The grandfather-to-be was leading a riderless palfrey,
because Geordie and Rowena, for some strange reason,
had decided to share one horse.

"Perhaps, but he did not strike out," Diarmid said, and
shuddered. "Till you mounted those stairs, I thought a rebellion would begin here and now!"

"One of the nastier little problems with being a duke,"
Rod commiserated. "In fact, Your Highness, I've always
had the impression that you hated administration."

Diarmid laughed. "You know I would far rather spend
the time with my books, Lord Warlock!"

"Yes, I do." Rod nodded. "Just like Gregory. But Geordie
would rather be out and about the estates, checking to make
sure his peasants are doing well and that everything is running smoothly."

"I wish I had some small share of that gift!" Diarmid
sighed.

"Comes from his mother, probably. Just think, if
Anselm hadn't rebelled, Geordie would be saddled with
running the duchy of Loguire now, instead of you."

"More's the pity he is not!"

"Yes, but the law is a funny thing," Rod said, musing. "I
know attainder is usually not only for the traitor, but for all
his descendants as well—but an exception might be made,

if there were cause to believe the son might be as loyal as the father was treasonous."

He waited.

After a few seconds, Diarmid nodded. "There is merit in what you say, Lord Warlock. I shall have to discuss it with my father."

He'd let Tuan discuss it with Catharine, though—after thirty years of moderating her harshness, Tuan had become a past master. Rod smiled. It might not be strictly according to the law for Geordie to become duke of Loguire, but it would surely be in the best interests of the people.

Including Diarmid.

"HOW COULD YOU!" Durer raged, pacing back and forth. "How could you let him stop it! We were on the verge of civil war, you could have seen it start right there, but no! You had to let that smooth-tongued villain talk you out of it!"

"I was doing all I could to goad Anselm Loguire to draw his sword," the agent protested, "but that blasted Gallowglass managed to pull the fuse on the bomb I had so carefully primed!"

"Blast Gallowglass! Blast him to bits! Draw and quarter him! Roast him over a slow fire!" Durer raged, then stopped dead, leaning on his desk, gasping for breath. Then, slowly, he raised his head. "We have to kill him. That's all. We have to—and be ready to rise the second he's dead!"

"We've been trying to kill him for thirty years," the agent protested.

"Yes, but now he's off on his own with none of his brats to protect him! Get a Home Agent, one of those Gramarye-born telepaths we've managed to raise and recruit! Surely one of them must be able to lay an illusion that will snare him! Get a telepath! Lay a trap! And when it closes, kill him where he stands!"

ROD SAT ON a fallen log by his campfire, plucking minor chords from his lap-harp and chanting (because he knew he couldn't stay on key) of a wanderer grown old searching for the woman he had seen once, then lost—but as he sang, he saw a low branch sway at the side of the clearing where there was no breeze and heard an owl call a challenge. Wondering why the elves hadn't warned him, he laid aside the harp and came to his feet, hand dropping to his dagger-hilt, and called, "Who lives?"

"A friend." The branch swung aside, and a tall young woman stepped into the firelight—very tall, more than six feet, with a staff even taller. "A friend seeking counsel."

Rod breathed a sigh of relief, then frowned. "The forest is scarcely safe for an attractive young woman. What in the name of heaven did you think you were doing, out alone in the woods at night?"

Alea's eyes flashed at the word "attractive," but softened amazingly as she smiled, seeming oddly pleased. "You need not worry for me, Lord Warlock. Your son has taught me well how to take care of myself."

"Has he really!" Rod smiled, proud all over again. Then he nodded at the staff. "I suppose you do at that. A healthy young woman doesn't really need an oaken pole to lean on."

"Not when I have Gar—I mean Magnus."

Rod laughed softly, then gazed up at her a moment in wonder. How had Magnus ever found a woman so right for him?

The same way Rod had, of course—by searching half the galaxy.

"I really am a friend," she said, "or would like to be."

Rod smiled and held out a hand. "Come sit beside me, friend, and share my fire." Then as an afterthought, "There's still tea in the kettle."

"Tea would be welcome." Alea came to sit by him. "The evening is brisk."

Rod took the second mug from his pack, filled it from the camp kettle, and set it in her hands. As he sat, he said, "You choose a strange place to look for advice—or have you lost your way?"

Alea was slow in answering, staring at the fire. "I thought I had, for several years—but it was really scarcely two months."

"Something horrible happened," Rod said with concern.

"What could make a young woman lose her sense of direction so?"

Alea was silent, clearly torn.

"You don't have to answer," Rod said gently, "and don't worry, I won't read your mind. It doesn't come as naturally to me as it does to some others."

"Magnus doesn't either," she said quickly, "no matter how badly he wants to. He has never betrayed me for an instant, not in the slightest way."

She was silent, staring at the fire again. Rod decided she needed prompting. "You had expected him to betray you?"

"Everyone else had," she snapped. "There was . . ." Her words dried up.

"A seducer?" Rod said gently. "A young man who said he loved you but left you?"

She turned to him, glaring. "How did you know!"

"It's too common a story for young women," Rod said with a sigh. He turned away, admitting, "I tried it myself, once."

"Tried?" Alea was intent again. "It didn't work?"

"No," Rod said, "because I really had fallen in love with her. Took me a while to realize it, though."

"I can't understand anyone not realizing they were in love right away," Alea said.

"Can't you?" Rod looked directly into her eyes until she caught his meaning, then blushed and turned away.

"Not first love, though," Rod said softly. "You can ask yourself day and night, 'Is this love?' but it isn't. When it is, you know it—you find yourself saying, 'So this is love!' But if that love ends badly and hurts you terribly, something within you will equate love with hurt and deny romance forever after."

"Not 'forever,' " Alea said slowly. "For a long time, yes, but not forever."

"If you meet a man who's worthy of your love?" Rod smiled. "Tell me, lady—how did he prove his worth?"

Alea sighed and tilted her head back. "By patience. Time and again I lost my temper with him, but he never yelled back at me, only nodded and looked very serious. Mind you, I'm not saying he didn't argue—but it was more a matter of trying to persuade me to explain myself, of seeking to understand what I meant."

Rod felt another surge of pride in his son but asked nonetheless, "When he understood, did he still argue?"

Alea sat still a moment, frowning and searching her memories. Then she said, "He usually ended up agreeing with me." Then, "I don't suppose we ever argued about anything really important. Looking back on it, I'd have to say those quarrels were really his explaining his ideas to me three different ways and telling me all his reasons for them—and once I understood why he wanted to do a thing, I found he always made sense. Well, almost always," she amended, "but the other time or two, I was willing to go along with him and let him find out for himself how mistaken he was."

Rod's smile fairly glowed. "But you didn't realize you loved him."

"No, just that he was my shield-companion." Alea turned to him with a frown. "You don't mean that kind of patience can only come from love!"

"Not always, no," Rod said, "but usually. How long did it take you to realize it?"

"Four years." Alea's gaze strayed back to the fire. "It was only a few months ago, really. We were on a planet where the colony had deteriorated into a set of warring clans. I realized that I wanted him to hold me, to kiss me, to . . ." She broke off, blushing. "I still wasn't willing to call it love, though. That didn't happen until his little brother . . . until Gregory sent him word that . . ." She remembered why Rod was out in this forest and changed her wording. ". . . That his mother was ill. He became so worried then, so sad and solemn, and I knew that it was no time to pick a fight, that all I could do for him was to be quiet and wait for him to talk—then listen." She frowned, puzzled by her own behavior. "I suppose that was the first time I'd been so worried about him that I only thought about his needs, not my own—and he had done it for me so many times!"

She was silent, staring at the fire. Rod sat and waited.

"Yes, that was the first time," Alea said. "Come to think of it, it was the first time I'd ever been sure that he was so preoccupied that I didn't need to be on my guard, that I let myself be really open to him. He was so vulnerable, hurting so badly, and it would have been so very wrong to do anything that might have wounded him then."

Rod waited again, but she stayed silent. At last he said, "So you finally caught a glimpse of him as he really is."

"Yes." Alea nodded. "The inner Magnus, the little boy inside the man, the very young man who'd been hurt so badly by love." She turned to Rod with a slight frown. "That's why I had to come find you, you see—to learn why Allouette hurt him and how the hurt could have stabbed so deeply that the boy inside would have been afraid to love again, no matter how fearless the man might have become."

Rod gazed at her a minute and longer, then closed his eyes and nodded. "There are others who know him well enough to tell you that."

"Not any longer," Alea said. "His brothers and sister told me that themselves. He's changed so much, they said, that they don't really feel they know him any more."

"But they do know who hurt him, and why," Rod said gently.

Twenty-Three

"WELL, SO DO I," ALEA SAID. "IT WAS ALLOUETTE, I've learned that much—but I don't know how she hurt him, don't really understand how she could have cut him so deeply." She scowled, anger gathering. "I don't think I can ever forgive her for that!"

"Don't be sure," Rod pleaded. "It wasn't the Allouette we know now that scarred him. The woman you've met still has to be distracted from hating herself for her crimes."

"I'll agree with her every word," Alea said bitterly. "How could Cordelia and Geoffrey forgive her? How could Gregory *fall in love* with a woman who could do that to a man?"

"Because he didn't have much choice." Rod turned away to gaze at the fire. "Of course, they all think they know what Allouette did, but Gregory was too young to understand. Even Geoffrey didn't, though I'm sure he thought he did. Cordelia, though, she was old enough to know. In fact, it was she who helped patch him up."

"But she won't talk about it," Alea said. "She won't

violate his confidence, she told me. That means you're the only one who knows Magnus well enough to tell me what I need to know, and who might be willing."

"He won't tell you himself?" Rod's brow creased with sadness. "There was a time when he was very open."

"Was there really?" Alea stared into his eyes with an intensity that was almost frightening. "When he was a boy? Tell me of him!"

Rod studied her a few minutes, then smiled with nostalgia as he looked away. "He was bright and quick, though always with that exaggerated sense of responsibility that comes with being the eldest . . ."

"There must have been a time when he wasn't eldest," Alea pressed. "Cordelia is three years younger than he, isn't she? What was he like when he was an only child?"

"Bold." Rod smiled back over the years. "A sunny disposition, always happy, somewhat mischievous—and very bold. It never occurred to him to be afraid." He turned to her, a wrinkle forming between his eyebrows. "He was blond then, you know—golden-haired."

"No." Alea stared wide-eyed, drinking in every bit of information. "How could he have grown to be black-haired?"

"That was the result of a little family trip we took," Rod said, "an excursion into a land of faery, where magic really worked, and where we discovered that we each had an analog, a person very much like us fulfilling a role very much like the ones we hold here on Gramarye."

"This is only a story, isn't it?" Alea asked.

"No, it's quite a bit more." Rod told her how three-year-old Geoffrey had been kidnapped through a dimensional gate and how the whole family had gone after him and how, years later when all four children were in a predicament that went beyond even their powers, Magnus had reached out to that alternate self and borrowed his talents—but had gained more than he expected, for his hair had turned black, as his analogue's was, and his sunny nature had developed a somber side that was usually hidden but surfaced when he was distracted.

"Too fanciful to believe," Alea breathed, but Rod could see in her face that she did.

"I came back from it with a temper that was absolutely vile," Rod admitted. "It took years for me to expunge it—and that, only with Gwen's help."

"Is that what Magnus meant when he said you were cured when he was cursed?" Alea asked.

"Did he say that?" Rod asked in surprise, then, "Yes, I can see how he would. Not then, of course—years later. I'd lapsed into mental illness, you see—the aftereffects of an attempt at poisoning, but it's past now . . ."

Alea remembered what Magnus had told her and reserved her own opinion on the issue.

"I've always felt very guilty about that." Rod stared into the fire. "If I hadn't gone crazy just then, if I could have been more patient and understanding, maybe I could have protected him . . ." His voice trailed off; his stare intensified.

Alea saw his pain and reached forward to rest her hand on his in sympathy. "You can't blame yourself for being ill," she said softly.

"No. No, I can't, can I?" Rod turned to her with a bleak smile. "Or if I can, I shouldn't. But the timing was absolutely deplorable—a cursed coincidence, if you will."

The word struck an alarm inside Alea. She stiffened and said, "Magnus told me that you taught him to be wary of coincidence."

Rod stared at her.

After a minute, he turned back to the fire, nodding. "Yes, I did teach him that. Should have remembered it myself. Odd that I didn't see it till now—but the female viper who hurt him might very easily have reached into my mind and kicked off the madness again, to keep me from helping him."

"Who was that female viper?" Alea demanded, and when Rod sat silent, looking guilty, she said, "It *was* Allouette, wasn't it?"

"Her name was 'Finister' then," Rod told her, "almost a different person. 'Allouette' is the name her real mother had given her, before she was kidnapped—only a baby." He turned to her with a very earnest gaze, covering her hand with his own. "You mustn't blame her for what she did—she does enough of that herself. She'd been reared by a pair of emotional assassins who brainwashed her into paranoia, crushed her self-esteem, twisted her natural goodness into a thirst for blood and for mayhem, and left her an emotional cripple. Curing her was the hardest job Gwen ever tackled—but also her proudest accomplishment, next to the children she'd reared herself."

Alea noticed he didn't mention his own role in that upbringing but was prudent enough not to ask why. "All right, I'll try not to blame Allouette, even though I can see how hard Magnus has to try not to. Why? What did she do to him?"

"Promise you won't hold it against her."

"I'll do my best," Alea said, "I'll try my hardest to be kind and understanding and not judge. I can promise not to take revenge, but I can't promise not to want to."

Rod gazed into her eyes a minute, then gave a short nod. "Good enough. That's all I have any right to ask. Well, then, here's what she did." But he turned back to gaze into the fire as he told her of Allouette's gigantic capacity as a projective telepath, of her ability to make people who met her think they saw someone quite different—more beautiful or more ugly, depending on what she needed of the situation—and her talent of instant hypnotism, of bending her victim's mind to fall in love with her even at her ugliest. He told her of Finister's pose as the young unfaithful wife of an old knight, who enticed Magnus into her bedchamber and arranged for her "husband" to burst in upon them. Then he told of Finister's posing as the ugliest witch in the north country, of her compelling Magnus to fall in love with her anyway, of his resistance, and of her compulsion making him believe he was a snake bound forever to crawl around the base of a tree—then of Cordelia's breaking that spell and restoring her brother to humanity. He went on, telling of the wild, fey beauty who led Magnus on a wilder chase and, when he had fallen in love with her, leaving him cold, plunging him into despair, into a depression so deep that he couldn't even see that it wasn't real, couldn't wrestle his way out of it—but had, at his parents' urging, ridden to find the Green Witch, who had cured him of the worst of that depression, though she couldn't relieve him of the residual self-contempt deep within.

"So the Green Witch left him in such condition that he could be healed, but wasn't yet," Alea said slowly.

"That was beyond her," Rod said, "maybe because Magnus needed to let time dim the pain, or because he had to reach the emotional point at which he could realize, not just with his mind, but deep within, that those seemingly-different women were really only one in three disguises, and that not all women were like them."

"That not all of us seek to enslave him or degrade him, you mean?"

"That." Rod nodded. "And more."

"Then you think he can still fall in love?"

"Oh, yes," Rod said. "He was reared in a very warm and loving home, you see, even if he did have a father who might fly into a rage without warning. That was certainly enough to let love happen."

"In spite of what he's been through?"

"His ordeal will certainly make it harder for him to love again," Rod admitted, "especially since those experiences, as well as being the son of two exceptional people, has left him with low self-esteem. That doesn't mean he can't fall in love, though—it just means that it's going to take time— plenty of time with a woman he can trust who never turns on him no matter what kinds of opportunities she has."

Alea sat very still.

"Lost your temper with him a few times, did you?" Rod said softly.

Alea tensed but managed a curt nod.

"That wouldn't matter," Rod said, "so long as it was open and honest, not a matter of throwing every insult you could think of to try to hurt him, or accusing him of things he didn't do and making him try to guess what they were."

"No," Alea said slowly. "I've been open, at least—con-fronted him squarely—though what I was quarrelling about wasn't always the real cause."

Rod waited.

"I wasn't really angry at him," she said in a voice so low he could hardly hear it, "but I didn't realize that then."

"I expect he did," Rod said. "I wouldn't worry about fights like that—especially if they've passed."

"Oh, yes," Alea said. "There were a few years when I was jumping on him every time I felt angry or scared—but there's less of that, now. Much less."

"Because you know you don't have anything to fear from him?"

She nodded—then said, irritated, "Except his ignoring me!"

"I thought he talked with you all the time."

"Well, yes—but only as a friend!"

Rod waited.

"You can't make somebody fall in love with you if the love's not there, though, can you?" Alea asked.

"You mean if you're wrong for each other? If your chemistry doesn't react, if the magic doesn't happen?" Rod shook his head. "No—but I don't think that's the case with you two. I've seen how he leans on you now and then, seen the admiration in his eyes when he looks at you."

"Admiration isn't enough!"

"No," Rod said, "but it's a good clue that there's something more."

This time it was Alea who waited, and when Rod didn't go on, she asked, "What else does it take to heal him?"

"Devotion," Rod said. "Complete loyalty. His learning he can depend on you no matter what."

"He's had that!"

"Then wait."

"How long?"

Rod shrugged. "Shouldn't be much more than a year. He's home now; he has a lot to get used to—and meeting Allouette has probably made him freeze inside again."

Alea turned to him with a frown. "You mean being home will thaw him?"

"After he gets used to it," Rod said. "After he realizes, deep down, that Allouette isn't Finister, that everything Finister did was based on her illusion-spinning."

"He has to learn what reality is again?"

"Yes—and learn that he can turn to you to help figure it out."

"So Magnus is only attracted to my reliability and ability to fight?"

"That," Rod said, "and your concern for others. Magnus has told me of your nursing and teaching." He shook his head sadly, gazing into her eyes. "But lass, you're daft if you can't see that Magnus, at least, thinks you're beautiful. So do I, for that matter, and most other men you meet—but that doesn't matter, does it?"

"Not a bit," Alea snapped, "because I don't believe it for a minute!"

"Then believe how delighted Magnus was to meet a woman who didn't make him feel like a great lumbering oddity," Rod said. "Once you've thought about that, look down and see that your figure could set a young man dreaming."

"I'm a beanpole!"

"A beanpole with excellent curves," Rod corrected. "Not spectacular, maybe, but after what he's been through, Magnus would be repelled by the spectacular."

"Perhaps," Alea said reluctantly, "but my face is dreadful! I look like a horse!"

"Actually, your features are classical," Rod said, "with fine, strong bone structure."

Alea glowed within, so she glowered without. "I'm not convinced!"

"Magnus is," Rod countered. "You only need to see the truth of that."

"And not pay attention to the truth about my appearance?" Alea asked bitterly.

"You can't see that truth," Rod said simply. "Most of us are our own worst critics, after all. Besides, does it really matter what I think about your looks, or what Geoffrey thinks, or any handsome young man?"

Alea stared at him a moment, then admitted, "No. I only care what Magnus thinks."

"He'll let you know," Rod said, "sooner or later."

Alea was quiet again, then said, "Quarreling won't work, will it?"

"If he could understand it as a form of love-play, yes,"

Rod said. "If he could see it as a sort of game, the way Geoffrey does—but he can't."

"Why not?"

"He lost his sense of fun, somewhere along the way," Rod said sadly, "his sense of play. I understand it's something you have to learn as you grow up, and he did—but he lost it during his teens. I failed the boy there."

Alea felt his pain, wanted to reach out to him—but all she could do was say, "It wasn't your doing."

"No," Rod said, "but I failed to protect him from it."

"You had to let him stand on his own some time," Alea said softly.

Rod flashed her a smile. "Do as much for him as you're doing for me now, and the rest will take care of itself."

Alea stared at him, then laughed—but she sobered quickly. "You mean love will take care of itself, if the magic's there within us, waiting to come out."

Rod nodded. "And you can never know that until it happens."

"IF it happens," she said darkly.

"If," Rod admitted. He took her hand again, smiling. "But you can clear the obstacles that hold it back."

Alea stared into his eyes. Then, slowly, she smiled.

"THIS TIME, YES, the Crown showed mercy," Sir Orgon said, "but only because the High Warlock happened by and lent his influence!"

"Sir Orgon." Anselm fought for patience. "I have been listening to your cries of doom all the way home from Castle Loguire and all this long evening, and I grow very weary of them."

They sat by the fire in the main room of Anselm's manor house, the walls in shadow, their barely-seen tapestries rippling. A bottle and two cups sat on a small table between them, untasted.

"That arrogant prig Diarmid would have hanged your son in an instant!"

"Remember that you speak of my nephew!"

"Nephew or not, he would have hanged his cousin

without a second thought and never have let it trouble his slumber in the slightest! My lord, you must call up all the lords who owe you fealty and march on the Crown while there is still time!"

"I am no longer duke; none owe me fealty. Those whom I failed will certainly not rally to me now!"

"But their sons will! Their sons are exasperated with this Queen and her high-handed government. They have nothing but contempt for her lapdog King . . ."

"Sir Orgon," Anselm said between his teeth, "you talk of my brother."

"Did he think of brotherhood when he sent his son to hang yours? My lord, you must rise now! The moment is now! Delay even a day longer to begin your march, and it will be too late!"

"Too late for what?" Anselm turned to him with a frown.

Twenty-Four

SIR ORGON STARTED TO ANSWER, THEN CAUGHT himself.

"Too late for what, Vice of Betrayal?" Anselm stood and stepped over to Sir Orgon's chair. "Too late for other lords whom you have subverted? Too late for a mine you have dug beneath the castle?"

Sir Orgon glared up at him.

"Speak, worm of doubt!" Anselm seized the front of Sir Orgon's doublet and yanked him to his feet.

Sir Orgon's hand flashed; pain coursed through Anselm's arm; he cried aloud, holding his wrist in his other hand.

"I have spoken to good purpose all this long day," Sir Orgon said angrily, "but since it boots me not, I shall burden your hospitality no further." He turned on his heel and stalked toward the door.

"Seize him!" Anselm cried, and his two men-at-arms leaped to capture the knight. Sir Orgon snarled, whipping

out a sword and turning on them, and they backed warily,
lifting iron-banded staves.

Geordie came running into the room, his own sword
drawn. "Father, why all the . . ." He saw Sir Orgon with a
naked blade and knew all he needed to know. Dropping
into a fighter's crouch, he advanced on the knight.

The men-at-arms circled Sir Orgon, stepping apart as
they did. He couldn't follow both and knew that one was
working his way behind—so he whirled, slashing out as he
did. Geordie leaped in, and Sir Orgon's sword rang off his.
As it did, Anselm stepped up and swung a fist at the
knight's head. Sir Orgon reeled, stumbling, and the men-
at-arms were on him, pinioning his arms. Sir Anselm
turned back to the fireplace, yanked loose the rough rope
that had held the latest bundle of logs, and tossed it to his
men. "Oh, for a proper dungeon! But we shall have to
make do with the cellar. Bind him there and watch him
closely." He turned to Geordie. "Timely come, my son."

"You are hurt!" Geordie stepped forward, taking his father's arm.

"Only numbed for the moment," Anselm assured him.
"The snake knows some underhanded fighting tricks. At
dawn we shall take this traitor to your uncle and let the
King decide his fate."

Bound tightly to a cellar post with a man-at-arms giving
him a stony glare, Sir Orgon bowed his head in dejection.
The peasant army would reach Runnymede the next day
and would no doubt do an excellent job of distracting the
royal family—but there would be no cadre of lords to seize
the royal castle and bring down the Queen. One more
chance to win Gramarye for SPITE would slip away—and
with it, Sir Orgon's career. He would be stuck on this
dreary medieval planet forever, and would never again
know the pleasures and luxuries of the future metropolitan
capital his colleagues were working so hard to subvert!

FALSE DAWN FILLED the sky; the horizon glowed over
the river, about to explode with sunlight. Diru stepped out
of the woods and looked for the witch-sentries the minstrel
had sung about—the crown's tame warlocks, set to guard

the river to keep anyone from inviting the monsters out. There, he saw one, high atop the cliffs! But the woman only paused a minute or two, looking down over the river meadow, then turned away and paced out of sight.

Now would be the time, while she was gone! Diru dashed out across the meadow toward a huge boulder that stood twenty feet from the water. He crouched beside it, waiting for the mist to rise. Tendrils curled up from the water, thicker and thicker; the first ray of sunlight turned them golden as they merged into a swirling wall.

Now! Diru called out, "Monsters of the mist, come forth! Enter my land, and revenge me upon my enemies!"

For a minute, nothing moved, and Diru's heart sank— but that movement in the foggy wall turned into a whirlpool that opened, wider and wider. A giant tuft-eared cat leaped out of it onto the turf of Gramarye with a yowl of victory.

For behind it came a horde of them pouring out behind the giant cat, wailing and howling and chittering and bellowing, and the sight of them made Diru's blood run cold—a huge stiff-legged thing that looked to be some kind of giant insect with sharp hooks on the ends of its arm, and another with gleaming sickles for a mouth. Crowding behind them came creatures that were part wolf and part lion, great lumbering shaggy upright things grinning with multiple rows of razor-sharp teeth, huge lizards with fangs as long as his hand, and in the center of them all, riding a dragon with tentacles instead of wings, came a man gorgeously clad in robes of midnight blue and silver, grinning through a neatly-trimmed black beard as he shouted his triumph.

Then the huge cat came bounding over the meadow straight toward Diru. For a moment, he thought he was going to be praised, thanked, honored—but its mouth yawned wide showing teeth like scimitars, and Diru had just time to realize what a horrid fool he had been before he died.

THE PEASANTS CAME trooping into the meadow outside the walls of Runnymede, brandishing their scythes and flails but seeming nonetheless uncertain. Knowing they would be, agents circulated among the men, saying, "Remember your children! Do you want them to grow up to a life like yours?" And, "Why should the ladies dwell in marble palaces, wearing silk and surrounded by tapestries, when your wives wear homespun and walk on dirt floors?" or, "Bring down the lords, or your wives will forever sneer at you for cowards, and your beds will be cold all your lives!"

The men heeded and, little by little, began to remember their anger. The crowd began to churn into a restless and wrathful mob. Someone began shouting for blood; others took up the cry. Soon thousands of voices echoed the call: "Down with the King! Down with the Queen!"

The gates of the city opened, and the mob surged toward them, howling—but a score of armored knights rode out, each followed by a hundred armed and armored soldiers. The crowd began to slow, and their shouts gained an uncertain tone.

Then someone bellowed, "Yonder!" and everyone looked up to see another score of knights riding down into the valley from the west with two thousand soldiers behind them. Another panicked cry turned the crowd to the east to see yet another army advancing. The crowd's tone took on a note of fear. One voice shrilled above the others: "They're a long way away! We can still run for . . . AIEEE!"

With a gasp of horror, peasants pushed backward, leaving an open space around the fallen man, blood flowing from the dent in his skull. Before they could recover from violence within their own ranks, a voice cried, "Thus be it ever to traitors!" and others took up the call, "Face the knights and chop down their horses!" Still another called, "We'll be forever shamed if we go home empty-handed!"

"The King!" a dozen voices cried, and the whole mob turned to see three men riding out from the gate, flanked by palace guards. A golden crown glittered around the helmet of the middle one.

"I AM LOATH to strike down my own people, Father," Alain said.

"I am even more loath to let them strike down *you*," Geoffrey said from Tuan's other side.

"Is it kill or be killed, my son?" Tuan asked. "Do you see no other way?"

"Let me talk to them, at least," Alain urged.

Tuan thought a moment, then nodded slowly. "They are your people now and will be your subjects soon. Test their loyalty."

Alain nodded and kicked his horse into a trot. Geoffrey stared, then sped after him—but Alain heard the hoofbeats and turned back with a radiant smile. "I thank you, my friend," he said, "but this I must do alone."

Geoffrey reined in, exasperated. "Do you speak as my liege lord?"

"As your future liege," Alain qualified.

"Then I shall do as you bid," Geoffrey had to force out the words, then cried, "If they harm a single hair on your head, I'll see every one of them hang!"

Alain beamed at him in answer, then turned to ride alone toward the crowd.

They murmured in awe as he rode up to them—and in among them. They parted, scarcely able to believe they were so close to their Prince—or that he dared come into their midst when they held weapons. Then a voice shrieked, "Haul him down!"

Three men turned on the rabble-rouser and clouted him cold.

"I am your Prince!" Alain called out. "Why have you come? Tell me your grievances, that I may address them!"

"Don't trust him!" a voice shrilled. "He's a lord! They only want to use . . ."

A meaty thud cut him short.

"We will hear you!" a dozen voices shouted.

"Nay, it is I who shall hear you!" Alain called in reply. "Speak! Do your lords' soldiers beat you? Do your lords starve you or force you to work so long on their lands that you cannot tend your own? Tell me!"

The crowd milled about for a few moments, muttering to one another; then a man called out, "Why must we live in mud huts while your kind live in castles?"

"There will always be rich and poor, alas," Alain answered. "Were I to forsake my castle and give you all I own, it would be gone in a fortnight, and some other man would fight his way to owning that castle and making you work for him."

"Not if we killed all the lords!" another man shouted.

"Some of your own would gather more and more bullies about them," Alain answered, "and seek to make you all their slaves. Their grandchildren might begin to think they have some obligation to you, but how many of you would have died in misery by then?"

"How many of us shall die in misery now?" demanded another.

"Well asked," Alain replied, turning toward the voice. "Tell me who lives in misery, and I shall give him food and clothing of my own. If you know any old folk who dwell in poverty and are like to die in misery, give me their names and places, and I will send helpers to them."

The crowd muttered in surprize. Then someone shouted, "We should not have to come to the King for that! There should be assurance!"

"Your lords should provide," Alain returned, "but if they do not, you can seek redress from me."

The crowd erupted in amazed conversation.

"I pledge it!" Alain cried. "I shall swear it if you wish!" Then, in a lower voice, "At least with me and mine, you already know us, and know what to expect."

CORDELIA STOOD WITH Gregory and Allouette on the battlements, fingers clutching the stone, ready and braced for an enemy telepath to lash out at the royal family—and on edge, waiting to twist weapons out of hands by telekinesis if anyone tried to strike at Alain. "How can he have had the stupidity to ride among them, one man in the midst of so many enemies!" Cordelia cried.

"It is wisdom, and a calculated risk," Gregory told her. "More to the point, though, with your husband, it is compassion for the poor and a sense of what is right."

"Must he be so devoted?" Cordelia instantly answered her own question. "Yes, he must. I would not love him so if he were not."

Allouette touched her hand. "Sister, he is even more devoted to you."

Cordelia stood in silence a moment, then gave her a smug smile. "Yes. He is, is he not?"

"Who comes?" With a frown, Gregory pointed toward a small party who came riding out from the eastern slope.

The women turned to look. Cordelia frowned. "A lord and his retainers, from the look of them, with an escort of royal men-at-arms from the eastern wing. Sir Nabon must think them important indeed to send them to Their Majesties in the mist of a battle! But why is that one man bound?"

"I think, in these circumstances, a touch of mind-reading would not be inethical." Gregory frowned a moment, then stared. "'Tis your Uncle Anselm and your never-seen cousin!"

ANSELM RODE ON one side of Sir Orgon, Geordie on the other—but the young man's gaze was fixed on the crowd. "What passes here? A parley?"

"A parley between your arrogant cousin and a mob of thousands!" Anselm said. "Does he think to fight them all single-handed?" But he put on a respectful, though scowling, face as they rode up to the King and Queen. "Majesties."

"Well met, brother." Tuan couldn't help staring. "What brings you to me on the brink of battle?"

"To your wife, not to you!" Anselm snapped. "We bring you a traitor who urged me to rebellion again. These last few days his exhortations have grown quite urgent, and I could not think why—but now I see." He turned on Sir Orgon. "You knew about this, didn't you? A peasant uprising, and you knew when it would happen, which is why you said there was little time left!"

"If that is so, leave him to me," Catharine said in an executioner's voice.

Sir Orgon looked at her and shuddered.

"Does your son not have manners enough to greet his aunt, let alone his Queen?" Catharine demanded.

Anselm bristled—but before he could answer, Geordie

cried, "I see them! Dickon and Ned, two of mine own peasants!" And with no more ado, he was galloping down toward the meadow.

Down, and in among the peasants, who parted in sheer astonishment, then closed around the rider with dark and angry shouts—but Geordie swung down from his horse and ran to his men. "Dickon! Ned! What do you here? Do you mean to lose your lives?"

"Good day, squire." Dickon had the grace to look shame-faced. "When the guardsmen took you away, we were angered indeed by the duke's high-handedness. We heard men were marching to tear down this arrogant Queen and her supercilious sons, and we came seeking revenge for you."

"Well, you no longer have need! The Lord Warlock pled my case, and that 'supercilious son' sent me back to care for you all as well as I may!" He spun to Alain. "Your Highness! No matter who else must be punished, I beg you spare these! They sought only justice for their squire, nothing more!"

"You are loyal to this lordling?" one of the other peasants asked, incredulous.

Dickon's face darkened; he took a firmer grip on his staff as he stepped up beside Geordie. "We will defend this man to our deaths."

"Aye!" Ned stepped up on Geordie's other side. "Our squire and his lady have done all they can to see that we and our families are well fed and well housed! If we lack anything, 'tis only because he has no more money! Indeed, the duke's men arrested him for seeking food enough to take us through the winter, though he had to shoot the Queen's own deer to do it!"

"This is the best reason I ever heard for poaching," Alain said.

"But how is this?" asked another peasant. "You do not mean to say the lords can be our friends!"

"I am no lord," Geordie said hotly, "for my father is attainted! I am only a squire!"

"But he is a lord by rights!" Ned proclaimed. "A lord, and our friend!"

"As I will be, too." Alain gazed at his cousin for a second, then smiled. "We are of one blood, after all, though we have never seen one another. Well met, Cousin Geordie."

Geordie gazed back at him, then decided to smile, too. "And you, Cousin Alain."

"How very touching," another peasant sneered, "reunion at long last—but they are lords nonetheless, and our enemies by nature!"

All about Alain, confused talk sizzled—until a voice shrieked, "We have come for blood! We cannot leave with nothing to show for our pains!"

"You shall have my blood if you wish it," Alain said gravely. "Choose your champion, and I shall fight him with his own weapons!"

HIGH ATOP THE north tower, Alea hovered beside Magnus, worried about the tension evident in every line of his body. "You mustn't, Magnus! Mustn't interfere! There's no cause yet!"

"My prince and childhood friend is surrounded by thousands of enemies," Magnus grated, "and you tell me there's no cause?"

"Of course there isn't! You know he has the situation under control, no matter what it may look like! You've done something like it yourself! How many times have you gone among hundreds of enemies?"

"Yes, but not to defy them!"

"Neither does he! Interfere now, and they'll lose the faith in him that he's building! I know it's the most difficult thing in the world to do nothing, but that's what you must do!"

"Unless they jump him," Magnus muttered, and almost wished they would.

THE MOB ROARED around the two cousins, who stared, each marvelling that the other could be his kinsman. The ocean of sound washed about them until one voice pierced it: "Don't trust him! It's a trick!"

"Is there none who dares fight me?" Alain called. "Surely there must be, or you would not have come! Find at least one!"

But the crowd churned about him, their noise incredulous—then died suddenly, and a channel opened as men pressed back. At the end of that channel stood a man like a wall, six and a half feet tall with shoulders like a bull's, arms thick as an ordinary man's leg. "I dare!" he bellowed, and shook a seven-foot staff. "This is my weapon! Do you dare to fight me, princeling? Do you dare shed your armor and fight me with nothing but a staff?"

Twenty-Five

AT THE CITY GATE, CATHARINE TURNED IN A FURY.
"Are you mad, Tuan? Our boy shall be slain!"

"I doubt it," Tuan returned, but his own face was taut
with strain. "There is far less chance of death by staff than
by sword—and our lad is well-trained."

"But if he were . . ."

"Then Diarmid would never forgive his slayer," Tuan
said, "and the peasants would have far more to fear when
you die, from a King who seeks to avenge his brother's
death."

"They have not the wisdom to remember that!"

"They shall have no need to." Tuan took off his
gauntlets and took her hand. "We must risk his hurt in this,
as we had to risk it when he rode off to help his friends.
How can he ever be King if he cannot rely upon himself?"

"But those were mere bandits and woodsrunners!"

"Is this opponent any more?" Tuan stroked her hand.
"Courage, my sweet. The boy is well-trained and has faced
worse enemies than this—and amazingly, he has reduced

this conflict from a battle between armies to a bout with a quarterstaff."

Catharine stared at her son, stalking toward the huge peasant, and said, with a touch of awe, "So he has."

Then, tense with worry, she sat holding her husband's hand fiercely as she watched her son step forth to an apparent slaughter.

THE SENTRY WASN'T the only one by the southern river—a SPITE telepath stood within the forest border nearby. She heard the cacophony of the monsters invading and ran out of the trees—then froze, staring, horrified by the sight of the invading nightmares. She closed her eyes, shaking her head to free her from paralysis, and sent a thought north to Runnymede, to her fellow SPITE espers.

One of those telepaths was in the midst of the peasant army, right by the Mocker's elbow. "They've done it, chief! The dupe has invited the monsters in!"

"Then the telepaths will be too busy with them to help out in the battle."

"I dare fight you," Alain told the strapping peasant, "and I am delighted to see that at least one of my subjects has the courage to stand against me."

It was too much for Geoffrey. With a howl of anger, he charged the crowd. They pressed back with cries of alarm.

The Mocker raised his voice, calling out, "Treachery! Charge him! Bury him! All of them, before they bury us all!" He knew his own psis would hobble any defenders, no matter how well armed.

The peasants answered with a roar of anger, and as Geoffrey rode in among them, dozens of hands seized his horse's harness. The brave beast screamed, trying to rear, but the weight of many peasants held him down. More peasants pressed in, hands reaching for Geoffrey—but the blades that thrust at him slowed and stopped inches short of his sides.

"Why can't they stab him?" the Mocker hissed. "What are our psis doing? Tell them to block the espers who are protecting him!"

"We're trying, Chief," the man at his other side said,

face taut with strain, "but the royal psis are fighting us for all they're worth. We're deadlocked!"

"It's the Gallowglasses!" the Mocker hissed. "Why haven't they teleported south to fight the monsters?"

"I thank you, Sir Geoffrey!" Alain called out. "I had need of a squire. Will you unbuckle my armor, then?"

Geoffrey looked at the angry faces around him and swallowed. "Your highness, I shall."

Men pressed back to leave room as the knight slid down from his horse's back. He took a step or two away, then lifted his vizor to look at them impatiently. "Well, will none of you help me doff my own armor? How can I assist my prince with this weight of tin about me?"

The peasants stared in surprize. Then ten willing hands reached to help him unbuckle.

"Do not trust him!" a voice shrilled. "He is a warlock! He shall fell you with a thought!"

"I shall do no such thing!" Geoffrey shouted back in indignation. "I would be disgraced if I interfered in a duel!"

"If not him, the prince's wife!" another voice cried. "The High Warlock's daughter, the Princess Cordelia! Surely she shall not stand patiently to watch her husband slain!"

Geoffrey frowned, stilling, his gaze unfocused, and the men unbuckling him paused, staring in alarm at his face. Then his eyes came alive again; he gave them a curt not. "She gives her pledge that she too will withhold her power. She rages at me, but she will abide."

"You cannot trust him!" the voice screeched. "You cannot trust any lord."

Geoffrey stilled again, only his legs now armored. "Let him who would call me a liar come forth to meet me man to man, with our hands bare!"

The crowd was still, waiting expectantly, but the owner of the voice was silent. Geoffrey nodded and leaned down to unbuckle his greaves. Then, clad in only shirt and hose, he went to help Alain.

A few minutes later, Alain, too, stood in only shirt and hose. He looked about him, calling, "Who will lend me a staff?"

A dozen poles thrust at him. He tested one after another, nodding, and chose a stick of dark dense wood and inclined his head courteously to its owner. "I thank you." Then he stepped forward toward the big man with the seven-foot staff.

Geoffrey swallowed and remembered his word.

"THERE IS NO cause yet!" Allouette insisted. "I know it looks as though there is, but trust me, sister, this is truly a battle for men's minds, not their bodies—and your husband fights it like the expert he is!"

"How would you know?" Cordelia asked through clenched teeth.

"Because I was trained for this! Because I worked at it for five years! Trust me, sister—and trust him!"

Watching the woman he loved, Gregory marvelled. She didn't seem to realize the contradiction—that Cordelia should trust her because she had been trained to be a subverter—but she was right.

"If they harm one hair of his head," Cordelia said, "I shall burn their minds out where they stand!"

"Wait for more than one hair," Gregory advised.

"It is true." Allouette nodded. "He must let the big peasant strike him once, twice, or more, to win their respect!"

"How shall I know when he is truly in danger?" Cordelia cried.

"If they strike him down and he does not rally," Allouette explained. "So long as he rises again, he has them under his spell."

"You know a lot about spells, do you not?" Cordelia snapped, and instantly regretted it.

But Allouette seemed to take it as a mere statement of fact. "I do, so trust me in this. Withhold your might!"

FAR TO THE south, a telepathic sentry stood atop a cliff and saw a score of monsters burst from the morning mist over the river. They bounded straight for the young man who had called them. The sentry was only a telepath; she had no other mental powers to help protect the poor idiot who had trusted the monsters' promises and invited them in. She turned away with a shudder and, with all her strength, sent the mental alarm north to the rest of the Royal Witchforce. *The monsters have broken out of the mist! The monsters are loose!*

IN RUNNYMEDE, CORDELIA stiffened with a gasp— and so did Allouette and Gregory.

"I dare not go!" Cordelia wailed. "Not while my love is in danger!"

"We dare not go either," Gregory said grimly, "while the Crown may need us. Pray the monsters do no harm before this is ended!"

None of them believed that for an instant—but they knew they had to stay and watch.

ON THE FIELD below, Geoffrey stiffened with alarm, but knew even better than his siblings that he dared not disappear—especially among a crowd who feared witches.

High in the tower, though, Magnus's eyes widened. So did Alea's, the alarm blasting through her mind, too. Then Magnus's eyes lost focus, and she cried, "Not without me!" She seized his hand, wrapped his arm about her, and tucked hers as far about his waist as she could. His arm tightened about her, lifting; then an explosion echoed and the world disappeared in a sickening slide of colors that churned all about her. An instant later, the earth jarred up against her feet, and she clung to Magnus until the dizziness passed, sure that she would never again envy his ability to teleport.

Then she looked up and saw the monsters bearing down on them.

THE BIG PEASANT jeered, "Will you stand there and wait all day, princeling? Have you the courage to strike the first blow?"

"Marry, that I have," Alain answered, "for I will not have it said that you attacked your prince. Still, I admire the courage of any peasant who dares fight a belted knight, and would know the name of so valiant a fellow."

"I am called Bjorn," the peasant returned, "and I must

honor the courage of any man so little as you who dares
stand against *me*!"

Alain took a step closer, smiling up at the man who
stood a head taller than he and outweighed him by eighty
pounds of muscle. "We fight with respect, then. Defend
yourself!" He swung his staff like a baseball bat, up high
and down at Bjorn's head.

Bjorn laughed and swung his own staff to block. Alain's
cracked against it and, on the rebound, swung at Bjorn's
ankles. He dropped it to block, then chopped down in a
short hard blow that glanced off the side of Alain's head.

At the city gates, Catharine screamed.

Alain staggered backward, shaking his head, and Bjorn
followed, tight-lipped and plainly disliking his work, but
swinging at Alain anyway.

Somehow, the prince leaned aside at just the right moment, and the staff whistled past him. He gave his head one
last shake and leaped high to swing a roundhouse blow at
Bjorn.

Too late, Bjorn recovered and lifted his staff, but Alain's
blow cracked on his collarbone. He howled in pain and
swung the butt of his staff at the prince's belly. Alain
blocked both that and the next blow at his head, then gave
ground, blocking every blow as Bjorn grew more and more
angry, then swung a two-handed blow at his head. Alain
ducked and, before Bjorn could recover, advanced on him
with three-strike combinations. Now it was Bjorn who fell
back, trying frantically to block—until he missed, and one
swing connected. Alain's staff cracked squarely against
Bjorn's skull, and the big man's eyes glazed.

Alain leaped back.

Bjorn began to lean from side to side, dazed but managing to hold his balance—barely. Alain could have struck
him down with impunity. Instead, he thrust with the staff as
though it were a lance and struck Bjorn's breastbone. The
big man overbalanced and fell like a tree. He slammed into
the ground, and Alain was at his side in an instant, dropping to one knee to feel for the pulse in the man's throat.

The peasants held their breath.

Then Alain looked up grinning. "He lives!"

The peasants cheered and lifted him up bodily.

Geoffrey forgot his pledge and dashed forward. Then he saw that Alain was sitting on the broad shoulders of two peasants, while the others danced about him, cheering and waving their flails and scythes in triumph. They bore the victor back to his parents, chanting a war song.

Geoffrey started to run after them, then remembered and turned back to help Bjorn to his feet.

The crowd bore the grinning Prince before the King and Queen, then suddenly fell silent, shocked by the enormity of what they had done. Into the silence, Alain cried, "They are a people of whom we may be proud, my liege! And the one who dared fight me is surely a hero!"

"That he is," Tuan said gravely, then turned to the guardsman beside him. "Bid the castle cooks bring out food and ale for all these men, that we may celebrate my son's victory!"

The crowd stared, unable to believe they were to be rewarded, not punished. Then they let loose one massive cheer, and the dancing began again.

In the midst of it, Alain managed to slip down off the shoulders of his bearers and turned to face the still-dazed peasant who came before him with one arm slung about Geoffrey's shoulders. "Bjorn," said the Prince, "you are an honorable man who has had the courage to stand before his Prince this day, and fought a fair fight, cleanly and honestly. Will you take service with me?"

Bjorn blinked, coming out of his stupor. Then he bowed, albeit with Geoffrey steadying him. "Your highness," he said, "I shall."

"Lend me a groat, will you?" Alain asked the nearest soldier. The man stared, then fished in his pouch and held out a coin. Alain took it and pressed it into Bjorn's hand. "You have taken my pay," he told the big peasant. "You are my man."

"And you are my lord!" Bjorn grinned from ear to ear. "Hail, Prince of Gramarye!"

There was a commotion at the gate and people pressed back to let through a wagon bearing the first three casks of ale. The peasants cheered and pressed forward.

* * *

ALEA SAW MAGNUS standing poised for battle, glaring
at the thousand monsters who raced to see who could be
first to rip him open.

For a moment, she stared in horror at the nightmare
army, shrinking in terror—but beside her, Magnus stood at
bay, the man who had given her back her life, and she mastered the fear as she had mastered every fear that she had
faced since her parents had died, and stepped up beside
Magnus, clasping his hand to give him what strength she
could, turning toward the horde of horrors that bore down
on them, knowing that if she was going to die, she would at
least meet death by the side of the man she loved.

ON THE BATTLEMENTS, Cordelia sagged with relief.
"My love is safe!" Then she straightened, turning to her
brother and clapping her arm about his waist. "Now, leaping wizard!"

On his other side, Allouette seized hold of him, too.
Gregory threw an arm about each and teleported. The
women heard two thundercracks—one for the implosion
of air rushing into the space where they had stood, another
from the explosion of the air they displaced as they arrived. Dizzy for a moment, they clung to Gregory and to
one another, then looked up and saw a nightmare bearing
down on them, a horribly distorted cow with talons instead
of hooves and barbed horns that glinted with poison.

ROD SEEMED TO have inherited some of his son's talents, but teleporting wasn't one of them. He had to ride to
the riverbank—but he had a steed with a tireless gait. Robots do break down occasionally, but Fess was in excellent
repair.

"Okay, slow down, we're coming to the top of the sea-
cliff."

"It is thirty-six meters away, Rod." Nonetheless, Fess
did begin to slow. He went up the last few yards to the
brink of the cliff at a trot and stopped.

Rod stared down in horror. Horns, whelks, talons,
saber-teeth, tentacles—horribly distorted creatures filled

the meadow, parodies of animal forms, some combining two or three beasts, some part animal and part human. More poured out of the mist, rushing up the slope of the beach toward the grass at its crest. Thankfully, the rising sun was already beginning to burn away the fog.

That thought brought Rod out of his paralysis. Scanning the plain, he saw his son standing on the grass at the top of the beach with Alea beside him. Anger and fear shot through him. "Elves! Isn't there an elf around?"

"Here, Lord Warlock."

Rod looked down, staring in amazement at fifty elves who appeared from the grass, one standing head and shoulders above the rest. "Puck! I might have known you'd be onto this. Quick! Knock them over"

"We cannot." The elf's face was taut with strain, sweat trickling from his brow as he glared at the monsters. "Fierce magic protects them; all our power is brushed aside."

"Then feed your power into Magnus! Added to his and Alea's, it might be enough to make the difference."

"We have tried, Lord Warlock."

Startled, Rod whipped his gaze to the other side of his horse and saw Brom O'Berin. "Save your grandson, Brom! He doesn't have the good sense to leave this alone and wait for the army!"

"Only magic can prevail against this horde," Brom said, tight-lipped, "and that which gives power to them is too alien from ours."

"Maybe Magnus . . ."

"We cannot send our power into him," Brom said, never taking his eyes from the man who was his grandson. "He has been too long from the soil of Gramarye. We cannot feed him."

"I can!" Rod cried. "I'm his father! He has my genes in him no matter where he goes, and they're not made of the substance of Gramarye! Funnel power into me, and I'll channel it to him!"

Brom stared at him a moment, then gave a taut nod. "Come down."

Rod dismounted and knelt in the grass. Brom seized his

right hand, Puck his left, and the psi power of hundreds of elves coursed through him, almost making him faint—but he held on to consciousness, waited until his system adjusted to the flow of energy, then stared at his son, reaching out mind to mind, and channeled the flow of psi power into Magnus, adding all of his own, bringing it up from the very depths of his being.

MAGNUS REELED WITH the sudden influx of power thrilling through him; he could only think, *So this is how a high-voltage line feels!* Alea looked up in alarm, thrust her shoulder under his arm as he staggered and held him up. Magnus steadied and straightened, still feeling so full of psi energy that he must burst. Steady on his feet, he glared at the manticore that charged up at him and thrust Alea behind him. They had fought back-to-back many times before; her staff came up even as she pressed her shoulders against his, still feeding her psi power into him, but ready to defend.

She hadn't anticipated a living mace, a monster the size of a truck but bristling with spikes, with a curved and gleaming horn thrusting from its nose. The nightmare charged her, lowering its head to aim the glittering point at Alea's heart.

THE PEASANTS CAVORTED around Geoffrey, quaffing long drafts of ale and singing ballads praising the Crown. Geoffrey raised his mug with them, forcing laughter as he went from group to group to raise his mug in a toast. Finally he stumbled out of the crowd—and found Quicksilver waiting for him, hands on hips, with a huge warhorse behind her. "There is small time! Can you not move more quickly?"

"Let us hope I can!" Geoffrey went around the equine barrier that would block him from the sight of the party.

"We, you mean!" Quicksilver was right behind him and threw her arm around his waist.

"I fear you may be injured." But Geoffrey wrapped an arm around her shoulders a second before he teleported with a bang.

The warhorse stamped nervously and whinnied his disapproval.

The blast of their arrival echoed in their ears; they found themselves on the bank near the river-mist they had entered once before—and saw a beast that looked rather like a rhinoceros, only bristling with spikes all about and with a very sharp horn, trotting wide around Magnus to get at Alea.

"Upon it!" Quicksilver cried, and dashed to help her new friend.

Two swords stabbed the beast's flanks.

WITH A FEELING she was doomed, Alea set the butt of her staff in the earth, aiming the tip toward the horned monster who hurtled toward her—but at the last second, it screamed and swerved, whirling about. She stared, disbelieving her own eyes—then saw the streaks of dark blood on its flanks just before she heard a muffled explosion, and the beast stumbled and fell to show her Geoffrey and Quicksilver, swords bare and bloodied. Alea gave a glad cry. Grinning, Quicksilver leaped to stand by her side, sword ready for whatever might come.

Geoffrey stepped up back-to-back with her, beside his brother, just as the manticore's head disappeared in a cloud of mist. Geoffrey turned his glare on the giant snake with knife-like fangs, coiled to spring at them. It exploded. "No time for finesse," he snapped, then turned to see a scaly tail whipping toward him with a spike on the end. He ducked; as it flashed by overhead, he swung his sword up high to chop it off. Its owner shrieked like a steam whistle, but the tumbling tail slashed Magnus's shoulder on its way to the ground.

There were more scaly ropes coming toward them; a snake-headed woman with four spider-legs whipped a tentacle at Geoffrey as he straightened.

"He is mine!" Quicksilver snapped, and chopped with her own sword. The tentacle went flying as its owner screamed, but another slapped around Quicksilver's ankles. Still screaming, the monster jerked, sending Quicksilver tumbling to the ground, where a spider-leg reached with a dripping talon.

Geoffrey chopped it off, then swung his sword in a
figure-eight; the monster didn't stay to find out where it
would strike but backed off quickly. She had distracted Geoffrey long enough, though; a feathered monster struck
from above, laying open Geoffrey's forehead, then reaching for his eyes. Quicksilver sprang to her feet and skew-
ered the bird, then swung her sword snapping out in a line;
the carcass flew off to strike the next attacker in the face.

They were all around now, a solid wall of fangs, tentacles, and talons. Alea struck again and again with her staff
even as she channeled her psi power into Magnus; claws
laid open her arm, and her grip weakened, but she didn't
even look, only swung her staff all the harder, straight between the monster's eyes. It exploded, and she knew Magnus was still fighting with his mind.

High above, on a sea-cliff, Allouette, Gregory, and
Cordelia held hands, merging their power as they glared
down at the beach. Halfway across it, a line of fire leaped up,
and most of the monsters shied away in terror. A few jumped
through, though, and charged blazing and shrieking into the
melee around Magnus and Alea—and there were certainly
enough horrendous shapes crowding in about them.

Twenty-Six

PUCK APPEARED WITH A POP AMONG TREES that lined the river, where the cat-headed alien watched the battle with detached amusement. "If you truly have the power you boast of, Catface, use it now! Send it to those who can use it well!"

"I did not boast," Evanescent said, "but I shall send my power to the woman."

A sudden burst of strength filled Alea, making her stagger, but she straightened and used some of that amazing new power to make the monster who swung its mace-tipped tail at her explode before she channeled the rest to Magnus.

A force far stronger than anything he had ever felt charged Magnus; he reeled, dizzy with power for a moment—just as an explosion rocked the giant human-headed ants at his left. Gregory stood there, arms around his sister and his wife. They staggered, catching their balance, then lashed out at the surrounding horde with psi power, making bodies explode and tentacles strike at their owners. Even so, they couldn't fend off all the fangs and stings and horns; they were soon bleeding in several places each, but they fought on with their minds, winnowing the horde. As soon as they felled one monster, though, another thrust through in its place.

Back-to-back, the Gallowglass siblings and their spouses fought hundreds of monsters.

Magnus recovered, looked about him, and realized that Alea and his siblings could hold off the enemy for the moment. His eyes lost focus as he concentrated on the mental world, sending a thought questing ahead through the mist, seeking the mind that had organized and supported this obscene army. It was almost as though a cable of pure malice stretched from the monsters back into the mist. Magnus followed it—but before he found its source, a bolt of mental energy rocked him. Another followed, driving him to his knees.

A giant wolf burst through the line and leaped on the wizard, jaws gaping wide to engulf his head.

Alea screamed in anger and jammed her staff into its maw, knocking the beast backward—but a huge paw flailed at her and dagger-claws shredded her gown, slashing lines of pain down her left side as the beast fell, knocking her to the ground with it. It scrambled to its feet, jaws reaching for Alea—but Quicksilver's sword pierced its heart and the beast fell again, this time for good.

Anger and sullen determination made Magnus gather and concentrate the titanic power he held, building it into a mighty weapon of true force, but knowing with sickening certainty that it would not be enough—not quite enough.

Then, suddenly, a jolt of power flowed into him—not so very much by itself, but enough and more than enough to equal and overcome the mind of malice that directed the horde of monsters about him. Magnus narrowed his eyes, reached way down deep within and found strength there that he had never known, brought that force up from the bottom of his being to strike back with every bit of power he possessed, every ounce of anger and rage and fear, directing at the unseen malignant mind all his longing for revenge, all the outrage at everything he'd suffered and not deserved.

Something shrieked in anguish, some long trailing, dying, cry as the force opposing Magnus lessened. The shriek faded and was silent, and the cable of force uniting the monsters, dissolved.

A keening cry of despair rose all about the Gallowglasses, piercing their heads with pain, immobilizing them for a moment. When they looked up, though, the monsters were backing away.

Magnus lifted his head, eyes terrible with more power than he had ever known. He reached, lifted, and threw. The monsters exploded outward in a wave. Those farthest away turned to flee toward the mist, saw the line of fire and shied back screeching.

Allouette lifted her head, and the fire died.

The monsters raced for the mist, but their movements had slowed strangely, as though they fought their way through molasses.

Still on his knees, Magnus whirled to Alea to find her struggling back to her knees. He stared at the blood flowing down her side, reached to staunch it, but she pushed his hand away. "Only a scratch, Gar, though a long one. Finish what needs to be done."

Magnus stared at her a moment, then nodded and turned back to the fleeing remnants of the horde.

"We could slay them all." Quicksilver lifted her sword, mayhem in her eyes.

"Why slaughter even such abominations as these if we need not?" Gregory asked. "Send them home."

Geoffrey nodded reluctantly. "That is the chivalrous course."

Fire erupted from the beach again, right behind the last of the monsters. It trumpeted in panic and fled.

Rocks shot from the ground nearby, striking at monsters on the other flank.

Courses of rocks, sheets of flames, barrages of invisible stings—steadily they herded the monsters back into the mists.

Magnus realized he could leave the mopping-up to his siblings and their spouses for the moment, and turned to scan the cliffs and trees, wondering where that titanic force

had come from, that and the extra last jolt that had that
saved himself and his sibs and given them victory. He saw
no one standing under the trees, no one in the long grass—
but when he lifted his gaze to the cliff-tops, he saw a solitary rider looking down at him. For a moment, their eyes
met, and he knew his father.

Then Rod gave a single nod and turned away. He disappeared from sight, and Magnus gazed after him, stunned
that the man who begot him, the stranger to Gramarye,
should have gained so much power in his old age.

THE PARTY WAS in full swing, and it looked as though
the peasants were going to make a night of it. Catharine
and Tuan left their generals to watch over the field with
ranks of soldiers encircling the celebrants and most of the
off-duty troopers mingling with the peasants, helping keep
the party merry. The king and queen went back into the
castle, chatting as they went, marvelling over how well the
day had ended and the wisdom their son had gained.

As they came through their own huge portal, Catharine
said, "How amazing to have seen your brother and his son!
But where did they go?"

"Here, Mother."

Startled, Catharine turned from her husband—and saw
her younger son standing with his uncle and cousin, and
before them, the strange knight who stood with his hands
bound.

Catharine stopped, staring in surprize, but Tuan went
past her, arms wide, a smile lighting his face. "Well met,
brother! How wonderful, after so many years, to have you
visit my home!"

Taken aback, Anselm stared, then managed a small
smile. "I could wish it were for a happier occasion,
Majesty."

"I too—but you did not attend my son's wedding, and I
missed you sorely."

"I am an attainted traitor, Your Majesty!"

"Here at home, I am your brother Tuan and nothing
else! Except, perhaps, your nephew's uncle." Tuan turned
to Geordie and took his hand. "Welcome, George."

Geordie winced. "Please, Uncle! I am called Geordie now, a name I heartily prefer."

Tuan laughed. "Then well met, Geordie." He turned to the stranger knight with a frown. "But what is this gift you have brought me?"

"I am maligned!" Sir Orgon cried. "I am hauled here against my will, for no greater crime than . . ."

"Incitement to treason," Anselm finished grimly. "This man requested sanctuary at my home, Maj . . . brother, then sought to persuade me to lead another rebellion against you—and if the High Warlock had not spoken for my son, and your Diarmid not pardoned his poaching, I would have led the lords against you indeed!"

Catharine turned on him indignantly, but before she could speak, Tuan said, "Instead, you have brought the traitor to me—but what is this about poaching?" He turned to Geordie with a frown.

"The crops failed," Diarmid explained.

"My tenants would have starved in the winter!" Geordie protested. "I could not wait until their faces turned gaunt before I sought remedy—and why see them hungry when there was a forest full of game?"

"Then you should have asked your duke for permission to hunt," Tuan said. "I am sure he would have given it."

"Still, he broke the law," Anselm said, "but it was the Lord Warlock who convinced your son Diarmid that that law did not intend people's starvation."

"Of course it did not!" Catharine said indignantly. "It meant only that there should be deer for the lords to hunt."

"An unjust law," Sir Orgon cried, "but no reason to rebel."

"That is not how he spoke when my son stood in chains," Anselm said grimly.

Tuan turned to the man impatiently. "We shall hear your case on the morrow. For now, I wish to talk with my brother. Guards! See this man accommodated in our finest dungeon!"

"I am a knight!" Sir Orgon protested.

"We shall discuss the truth of that statement tomorrow, too." Tuan nodded to the guards, and they hauled Sir Orgon away, protesting every inch of the way.

"So you pardoned your cousin," Tuan said.

"I was overwhelmingly relieved that the Lord Warlock gave me good reason," Diarmid said, "for I was caught between the evil of favoring a kinsman, and the greater evil of hanging him."

"So instead of hanging," Catharine said to Geordie, "you came to join us for battle—and played the peacemaker!"

"I could not see my own peasant folk slain only for asking justice, Your Majesty," Geordie answered, "but I would never have fought against you."

"Instead, you stood by your cousin and helped him turn a bloody battle into a celebration." Catharine nodded and turned to her younger son. "It is well you were able to mete out justice instead of blind adherence to the law."

"Thank you, Mother." Diarmid smiled. "I, though, must thank the Lord Warlock."

"So I shall, when next I see him." Catharine turned back to Geordie with a frown. "You hold your lands enfeoffed from your father?"

"I do," Geordie said, "though I think myself only his steward."

"Far more, surely!" Anselm protested.

"Well, I think I do the job well enough," Geordie said with a smile for his father, then to the Queen again, "My tenants, at least, call me 'squire.'"

"I am sure your father has given you the warlike training that title requires," Tuan said.

"Of course," Anselm said impatiently. "He can fight as well as any knight—or any peasant, as our father taught us, Tuan." He forced a smile. "Perhaps I should not have taught him skill with the bow."

"Then he would have slain his deer with a sling," Tuan said. "He has certainly proved himself worthy of the title."

"He has proved his courage in battle this day," Catharine said with a smile, and caught Tuan's hand.

"Aye," Tuan agreed. "Running into the midst of the fray to defend your own was indeed a brave act."

"But all there were my own!"

"Well spoken," the Queen said, and gave her husband a

meaningful glance. Tuan nodded and turned back to his nephew, drawing his sword.

"How now, brother!" Anselm cried, his hand on his own hilt.

"You stand as his sponsor, do you not?" Tuan asked.

"His sponsor? What . . . ?"

"I am sure he does," Diarmid said, "and so do I."

"Then kneel, Squire George."

Geordie winced but had the good sense not to protest the use of his full name as he knelt.

Tuan touched his left shoulder with the flat of the blade, then arced it over his head to touch the right as he said, "I hereby dub thee knight." Then he lifted the sword and stepped in to give his nephew a clout that rocked his head.

Through the ringing in his ears, Geordie heard his king say, "Rise, Sir George, and be as loyal as you have been, loyal to both man and master forever more."

Geordie stood, dazed, and Anselm stammered, "Brother . . . my Queen . . . I had not thought . . ."

"Do so," Catharine advised. "We shall repeat this ceremony with greater pomp, but it shall not change his nobility." To Geordie, she said, "You shall bring your wife to meet us as soon as you may."

"Majesty," Geordie said with a gulp, "I will."

"There is another matter to consider, Mother," Diarmid said.

"Yes, my son?" Catharine frowned.

"He has proven his courage but also his concern for his people," Diarmid said. "Might I suggest he should have a title greater than knight?"

"Indeed!" Catharine said. "And whose estates should he hold—yours?"

"Exactly," Diarmid said.

Catharine stared, stunned.

Tuan smiled. "You really do wish to spend your days among your books, do you not?"

"Administering a duchy takes so much time," Diarmid complained.

"Be sure, sir, that I shall not let you fritter your time away!" Catharine said indignantly.

"Still," Tuan said, "there are other positions than duke that our Diarmid could fulfill, but that few others can."

"Majesties—I did not come here seeking preferment," Geordie protested.

"No, you came to serve your Queen," Catharine said, "and so you shall." She turned to Anselm with a frown. "I cannot restore an attainted traitor, even one who has proven his loyalty—but I can restore the son to the rank that should have been his by birth." She turned to Geordie. "Kneel again, sir."

Stunned, Geordie knelt.

Catharine stepped forward to lay her hand on her nephew's head. "Henceforth be as true and loyal to both Crown and people as you have proven yourself this day—but next time you think the law unjust, appeal to your Queen!" She lifted her hand. "Rise, Duke of Loguire."

As Geordie stood, wide-eyed and amazed, Anselm stammered, "Majesty . . . I assure you, I had never expected . . ."

"A simple 'thank you' would suffice, Anselm," Tuan said, with a grin.

Anselm swallowed any other words he had been about to say. "Majesties, from the depths of my heart, I thank you!"

"But I cannot steal my kinsman's title, nor his lands!" Geordie turned to Diarmid. "How would you feel if I did, cousin?"

"Relieved," the former duke told him. "Vastly relieved."

EVERGREENS CLOSED AROUND Rod as he rode into the forest, closing off sight of the sun—but since it was midday, enough light filtered through to let him see quite well. It was eerie and lonely; Rod shivered and hoped he and Fess could plough through to oak and ash again. He frowned as he looked around.

Then he saw a white speck drifting down. He blinked his eyes, not believing what they showed him—but sure enough, there was another and another. "Fess, I have to be mistaken—but I could swear I'm seeing snowflakes."

"You are not mistaken, Rod."

"But how can that be? It's barely October!"

"An early snowfall, perhaps? I know that the land slopes upward as we come to the western duchies; we are already at four thousand feet."

Rod shivered and told himself it was because of the cold. He blew on his hands and reached for his gloves—but stopped; had he seen movement? "Fess? Did you see something move?"

"Only the snowflakes, Rod."

"I could have sworn I saw something larger." He looked down to pull on his left glove—and froze; there it was, at the corner of his eye, and if he kept his gaze on his hands, he could see it. It was tricky, focusing his gaze on his hands while he focused his attention on the moving thing, but he managed it. It might have been only a cloud of flakes that he saw, sinuous and wavering on the wind—but there was a face atop them, indistinct as though made of drifting particles, a face with snow-white hair, eyebrows, and beard, a ghostly white, translucent face atop long flowing robes, but an arm separated from the blowing curtain of snow, a long and bony hand reached out toward Rod. He cried out and ducked, but the hand followed him and the forefinger touched his forehead.

Rod shivered, wiping at the spot of chill. "Serves me right for going out without a hat!" He frowned. "I do have a hat, don't I?"

"At home, Rod. Not here."

"Home? Where's that?" Rod's face cleared. "Oh yes, Maxima! But that must be an awfully long way away, Fess."

"Very far indeed, Rod—but Castle Gallowglass is only a few days' ride."

"Castle Gallowglass? What's that?"

"The castle where you lived with Gwendylon and your children, Rod."

"Children?" Rod frowned at the mantle of evergreen in front of him, then shook his head. "Don't remember any chil . . ." He broke off as a vague picture flitted though his mind, an image of a golden-haired laughing toddler shooting through the air while a red-headed woman held up her arms to catch him—but the vision faded and he shook his head. "I'm not old enough to marry."

"You were forty-nine when Catharine and Tuan insisted you occupy the castle for them."

"Who are Catharine and Tuan?"

"The King and Queen of Gramarye, Rod—your life-long friends, once they forgave you for the manner in which you brought them together."

Rod frowned, trying to remember, then shook his head. Movement at the corner of his eye distracted him, but when he looked, all he saw was blowing snow. "Why did we come to Terra, Fess? Mom and Dad are going to be worried sick."

The robot was silent a moment; then it said, "We are two hundred thirty-seven light-years from Terra, Rod, on a planet named Gramarye."

"We are?" Rod looked around at the mass of green needles. "Funny—it looks just like Terra."

"That is because it has been terraformed, Rod."

"Terraformed?" Rod frowned. "Seems I remember that, from a book I read—what? Last year?"

"You read *Terraforming Earth* when you were thirteen, Rod."

"Well, I can't be much older than that now, can I?" Rod frowned at the back of the horse's head. "How did we get here?"

"By spaceship, Rod. You were on an exploratory mission for SCENT and found Gramarye."

"What's Gramarye?" Yes, there was movement at the corner of his eye, but again, when Rod turned to look, there was only blowing snow. "Who's that guy in the long white robe, Fess, and why does he go away whenever I look at him?"

"He is no doubt a figment of your imagination, Rod."

"Who's a figment of imagination?"

"Rod—can you not even remember what you said only moments ago?"

"I don't know, Fess." Rod pulled up on the reins and slid off the horse's back, "I only know that I'm awfully tired. I'll just lie down and take a nap."

"No, Rod, not in the snow! You will die of cold!"

"No, I'll just sleep for a little while." Rod shivered but knew the cold would go away—it always did when he got into bed.

"Rod, get up! You will die of hypothermia, you know that!"

"What's hypoth . . . whatever?" Rod closed his eyes and rested his head on some fallen boughs. "Just half an hour. Wake me up, okay?"

"I will waken you now! Rod, get up! Remember who you are!"

"Yeah, yeah, I'm Rodney d'Armand, I know, I've got to keep up the family name." Rod snuggled down, hands under his head. "I'll do it after I wake up. Right now, the cold's gone away and I'm beginning to feel warm again. G'night, Fess."

"You are beginning to feel warm because you have begun to freeze! Rod, no! You must rise now!"

Rod only grumbled and burrowed deeper into the soft stuff beneath him. His eyelids fluttered, and he saw a face hovering over him, an elongated white face, all white, beard, hair, skin, with a gloating smile that bothered Rod, but he couldn't remember why. It didn't matter, though. It wouldn't keep him from sleeping. He closed his eyes firmly, telling himself he had to wake up in time for dinner or Mama would be very upset. Biting cold touched the center of his forehead, making him shiver, but it too warmed, and he nestled down into the soft, cocooning darkness.

Twenty-Seven

SOMEWHERE IN THE DISTANCE A VOICE WAS calling, "Magnus! Cordelia! Geoffrey! Gregory! Come! Your father needs you! Elves! Wherever you are, come out and waken him! Call for help!" That voice didn't matter, though, not when sleep was so close.

Then tiny little pains broke out all over Rod's body. He sat straight up, saying, "Robert, cut that out! Why did I have to have a big broth . . ." He broke off, looking at the foot-high people all about him. "Who're you?"

"Elves come to keep you awake," said one, "and do not dare to seek sleep again, or we will pinch you sorely."

"That's not nice." Rod shivered. "It's cold."

"This will warm you," said a deep voice, and sure enough, something warm and soft settled around Rod's shoulders. Looking down, he saw it was dark brown fur. He rubbed it, delighting in the feel, then looked up to see a man who stood as high as Rod—except that Rod was sitting. The man was very muscular, wearing a dark green doublet and brown hose under a cloak that looked very warm. There were streaks of gray in his hair under the bowl of his fur hat. "Waken, Rod Gallowglass," he boomed, and touched Rod's forehead with a forefinger.

"I am awake." Rod swatted at the forefinger, then froze. "I am Rod Gallowglass!" He looked about him. "A snow-drift! I was about to go to sleep in a snowdrift!" He looked up at the little man. "Thanks, Brom."

"You will never lack for friends, Rod Gallowglass." Brom smiled. "What brought you to seek sleep in snow?"

"I don't remember." Rod pressed a hand to his forehead. "Yes, that's just it—I didn't remember, didn't remember anything." But he did now and looked up round-eyed. "A man, ten feet tall at least, made of snow, but drifting and blowing like a curtain in the wind! He touched my fore-head and I started forgetting things!"

"Father Frost," Brom said grimly. "He comes as the year ages—but he is early."

"No, this pocket of evergreens has aged faster than the rest of the country." Rod shivered. "So have I. It's the frost of age that touched me, not of the year." He looked up at Fess, pulling the fur robe closely around him. "Thanks for calling for help."

"I rejoice that there was help at hand, Rod."

"We will always be close at hand," piped an elf.

"Be sure that they will," said Brom O'Berin, King of the Elves. "On your feet, Lord Warlock, or you will freeze sitting!"

Rod tried to rise but almost fell back, his legs refusing to straighten—but Brom levered him up somehow, and Fess stepped close so that Rod was able to lean on him as he began to force his legs to move, walking in place. "What did Father Frost do to me, Brom?"

"Froze your memories," said the elven king, "froze the flow of thought so that the ones you treasure could not rise."

Rod nodded. "And you thawed them?"

"Yes, but that will do little good if you stay in this freez-ing vale." Brom made a stirrup of his hands. "Mount and ride!"

Slowly and with great difficulty, Rod managed to lift his left foot and place it in that stirrup. Brom heaved, and it

was even harder to swing the right leg high enough to clear
the saddle, but an elf on Fess's hindquarters caught Rod's
foot and pushed it over his head, then leaped down as Rod
landed in his saddle. He looked down, holding out a hand.
"Thanks, Brom—again. Seems I always have something to
thank you for." His face tightened. "Especially Gwen."

"Ah, you have remembered your love," Brom said softly.
"Let that memory warm you, warlock—but not here. Ride,
and rejoin the world of the living." He reached up to swat
Fess's hindquarters, raising a resounding BONG!

"High-quality alloy," Rod explained. "Rings just like a
bell."

"I am sure Brom knew that, Rod."

Rod looked ahead at Fess. "Yeah, it was his idea of a
joke." He looked back at the elven king but saw only a
snowdrift churned by dozens of miniature feet. He shivered, as a sudden gust bit through the fur robe, and turned
back to Fess. "They've disappeared again."

"Yes, Rod," Fess said, "but the elves will never be far
from you."

"I suppose that's good to know." Rod hunched his
shoulders against another sudden gust. "I think Father
Frost is still trying to get into my head, Fess. How fast can
we get down where it's warm again?"

ALEA WENT THROUGH the doorway first, waited for
Magnus to clear it, then turned back, closed the door, and
dropped the latch. With their suite secure to themselves
alone, she turned back to her shield-mate and said, "You've
done it again."

Magnus turned, startled. "Done what?"

"Succeeded," Alea said. "Done as your father asked—
protected the people of Gramarye from three different
threats, all in a matter of days."

Magnus shook his head, still smiling. "It was Alain who
turned a mob into a loyal crowd—though Geoffrey's support, and his knights and footmen, might have had something to do with it. It was Dad who showed Diarmid a way
to spare Geordie's life and make peace with Anselm and
his would-be rebels—and all of my siblings and their

spouses who stood against that horde of monsters. Even then, it was Dad who lent that final surge of psionic strength that defeated them."

"And you who drew them all to that riverbank, by going to fight the monsters single-handed—well, with your living shield."

"That was not entirely by my choosing . . ."

"If you had managed to leave without me, I would have raged at you through eternity! But you knew very well that once you leaped to confront the monsters, your family would follow to save you."

"Not *knew* it," Magnus protested.

"Don't split hairs with me! Knew or suspected, it came to the same. Besides, it was you who told Geoffrey the peasant army was on the march . . ."

"He would have found out eventually . . ."

". . . you who saw to it that Gregory and Allouette and Cordelia stood ready to block the anarchists' espers . . ."

"No one could have kept them away."

". . . you who drew word of Geordie's peril out of your sister . . ."

"After you had told me of it."

". . . and you who told your father of Geordie and Rowena's danger."

"He needed something to occupy him, to interest him in this world again."

"Deceive someone else, if you must." Alea stepped close. "But don't try to hoodwink me—I've seen you do it on three planets! You arranged, you manipulated, you orchestrated—and you won!"

"We all won."

"Yes, especially the folk of this planet! You have set another people more firmly than ever on the road to their own form of government."

"My father's form of government, rather," Magnus said with his sardonic smile.

"Not any more," Alea said. "You protected them from the enemies who tried to conquer and subvert them, but you didn't try to lead them down your own road. You left them free to choose their own way."

"Yes," Magnus said, "and by some coincidence, that turned out to be the way Dad chose for them thirty years ago."

"Was it?" Alea demanded. "Or did he, too, only leave them free to work out their own system?"

Magnus was still, eyes widening. Then slowly, he nodded. "Perhaps," he said softly. "Perhaps he did." Then the sardonic smile came back. "Even so, he knew what he was doing, knew it very well."

She heard the bitterness in his voice, stepped even closer, said softly, "He's proud of you, Magnus. You've done what you said you would, and not a jot more."

"Yes, I have, haven't I?" He looked into her eyes, and the sardonic smile turned rueful. "Whether I wanted to or not, I've proved myself to be a true son of the old agent!"

ALLOUETTE CAME DOWN the hall toward the chamber she shared with Gregory while they were in the royal castle. As she placed her hand on the latch, a steward came up to her, stopping and bowing with an ingratiating smile. "My lady?"

Allouette frowned, repelled by the man's obsequiousness. "What would you, goodman?"

"A word of warning." The serving man straightened, and the ingratiating smile turned mocking.

Fear and anger chilled Allouette; she scowled. "Why should I need warning?"

"So that your husband does not learn the truth about you," the man said. "I am Durer."

Allouette frowned, puzzled, then remembered that before she was born, Durer had been the chief of a mission whose palace revolution had failed.

Durer saw the recognition in her widening eyes and laughed softly. "Yes, when my commanders learned that the High Warlock had . . . retired, and become disabled by grief, they sent me into the future to this time, to finish what I had begun."

"So you are unaware what passed in the thirty years since you left." Allouette hid her gathering anger.

"Oh, I know the history, never fear!" Durer said. "I

know that you became Chief Agent, for example—far too young, and that you used the post only to contract a noble marriage for yourself and turn on your own organization! Tell me, what would happen if your husband learned all that you had done?"

Allouette felt a chill strike to her heart.

"And he will learn, be sure of that," Durer said softly, but with a sneer nonetheless. "He will learn that you slept with whomever you were commanded to corrupt—and whomever would gain you advantage in your frantic desire for power. He will learn of your murders and subversions, of your seductions and betrayals. Do you think he will still love you after that?"

"What would you have me do?" Allouette asked through lips gone wooden.

"A minor invitation," Durer said breezily. "Only family hospitality. Find some excuse to invite all the Gallowglass brats and their spouses—yes, even the Heir Apparent, most especially the Crown Prince! Find some excuse for gathering them in the Great Hall at Castle Gallowglass. That is all you need do—nothing more than you ordinarily might."

"What will happen then?" Every word seemed leaden.

"Oh, you need not concern yourself with that!" Durer told her. "What hostess would ever think of unpleasantness? No, simply gather your guests—I shall see to the rest!"

Allouette's skin crawled at the menace in his tone, but she understood instantly what she must do. "When am I to execute this plan?"

"Oh, there is no rush." Durer waved the question away. "As soon as you can, that is all—and when you have set a date, tell Maud the scullery maid. Even twenty-four hours' notice will be enough." His voice sank into a threatening tone. "But do not wait overlong, or your husband shall learn all."

"As you say." Allouette turned away. "I shall do it. Now leave me."

Durer made a mocking bow and retreated.

Allouette opened the door, went in, then closed it forcefully and leaned back against it, trembling. A torrent of thoughts spilled through her mind, but one emerged clearly—that no matter what she did or did not do now, her marriage was over.

AS THEY RODE out of the forest onto the uplands, Rod was saying, "So I've done one more thing to help out people in a predicament and kept the country on track while I did it. Feels good, Fess."

"You seem to have solved predicaments for several people, Rod, not only Geordie and his wife."

"Yes—I pulled Anselm back from the brink of rebellion and helped save a few thousands peasants and soldiers from civil war by doing it." Rod nodded. "Not a bad day's work, Fess—or a bad life's work, either."

"It is certainly worthwhile devoting your life to people, Rod."

Rod smiled fondly at the back of the horse-head; Fess had deliberately misunderstood again. Then he frowned as the horse came to a stop. "What are you waiting for? We can make three more miles before sunset."

"We could not, Rod—the sun is setting. Besides, there is no more land."

"No more land?" Rod craned his neck, looking forward and down, and saw the turf end abruptly. Below it, he saw a blue and rippling expanse—then realized that those ripples were really waves; they were so far below that they seemed much smaller than they really were. "So." He sat back in his saddle. "We've come to the western coast of Gramarye."

"We have, Rod. We stand atop the sea-cliffs."

Rod looked into the setting sun—and saw a form emerging from its glare. He frowned, shading his eyes, trying to separate sun from object. "What's that coming toward us—a ship?"

"It is far too large to be a ship, Rod."

"No, nor tall enough either, not considering how wide it is."

The object seemed to swell, separating itself from the sun-glare, and Rod stared. "Fess! It's a floating island!"

"Surely only an illusion, Rod."

"If it is, it's a mighty convincing one! It's not just floating, it's sailing—and its coming right at us!"

It did indeed. The island loomed larger and larger, swelling till it filled half the horizon, then three-quarters, then blocked all of the western vista, becoming a whole land of its own, its cliffs crowned by a meadow of thyme and lavender. Behind it rose a forest—but surely no forest like this had ever existed, not in any world Rod had visited. The trunks of its trees were of silver and ivory and gold, and the leaves that adorned them were all the colors of the rainbow; the fruits that hung from them were crystals and gemstones. Birds fluttered among their leaves, birds of extravagant and gaudy plumage, like birds of paradise only far more various.

And a human form moved among those trees, moved and came forward, stepping through lavender as though it scarcely touched the earth, drifting closer and closer until it revealed itself as a woman.

Rod stared, spellbound, and his heart began to ache.

Then she was only thirty feet from him, for the island had drifted closer still until only a yard separated its cliffs from Gramarye's, and the woman paced closer still, smiling and reaching out toward Rod.

"It's Gwen," Rod breathed. "It's Gwen as she was when I met her, Gwen not yet thirty!"

"I see nothing, Rod," the robot's voice said in his ear.

"I do, and that's all that matters! Fess, I've found it! I've found Tir Nan Og, the Land of Youth—and Gwen!"

"Do not lose yourself in illusion, Rod. That has been your abiding struggle."

"Fess, this is no illusion! She's there, she's real!"

Gwen's smile was radiant.

"Let's go!" Then Rod paused, frowning. "No, that's not right. Once I cross that gap, I can't come back. Not that I want to—but I have no right to take you with me."

"Where you go, Rod, I will bear you."

"But you don't belong to me, you belong to the family! Magnus should inherit you after I've left!" The heartache sharpened, and Rod pressed a hand to his chest. "They'll have need of you, all the kids—and their children, too!"

"They shall endure, Rod." Fess turned his head to look at his master. "If nothing else, Magnus has the computer

Herkimer, who guides his ship—and has all my memories."

Rod gave him a quizzical look. "You want to come with me, then?"

"Gwen has been my friend, too, Rod, for thirty years— and the more my friend because she has made your life joyous."

Rod smiled. "Then let's go see her."

He gazed at Gwen and everything else seemed dim and unimportant; she *was* Tir Nan Og, a wonderland in which he could lose himself. His heart twisted as he gave the robot a nudge with his knees. Fess paced forward to step across the gap into Tir Nan Og, and Rod rode with him. For a moment, there was resistance that gave way, a searing pain in his chest, and a feeling as of a tearing veil; then Tir Nan Og was all about him, its colors even brighter now that he was a part of it, and Gwen was lifting her arms and he was swinging down from Fess's back and running the last few steps to sweep her up and whirl her about. As he did, he saw his hands, and they were unwrinkled and young again, as he knew his face and all his body were. Desire hammered hot and strong within him, and as Tir Nan Og once again moved away from the world of the living, he found her lips. They were soft on his, they tasted like the sweetest wine, and he drank deeply, as he would do forever.

WORD CAME TO the High Warlock at his seat in Runnymede, and Magnus d'Armand came to the western shore to gaze upon the body of his father where it lay broken on the shingle above the tide line. Nearby stood Fess, as faithful as he had ever been, but when Magnus spoke to him, he could not say what had happened, and he seemed changed. The robot was never the same again; there seemed to be something missing in him, as though he were indeed only a machine.

Then his brothers appeared about him, his sister came spiraling down from the sky and with one touch read the massive heart attack that had taken Rod's life before his fall. Together they knelt by their father, each immersed in his or her own thoughts and prayers. Then together they lifted up his body and bore it away.

* * *

"SO WE ARE bereft of mother and father in the same year."

"It's not supposed to happen this way. Papa wasn't supposed to die until we were in our fifties, and Mama was supposed to outlive him by ten years."

"I was prepared to console her and help her out of her grief, but not for this!"

"We will have to help each other, then," Magnus said gravely.

No one said anything. The silence was enough for him to feel the tightening, the resentment of his seeming assumption of authority, especially after his long absence. Then the mood relented, and Cordelia allowed, "At least we have each other—and there are more of us."

"There are," Magnus agreed, "but for this first night, perhaps we each need to be alone with our grief, to take the first step in coming to terms with it." He rose and turned away to the door. "Good night, my sibs."

"Good night," several voices said.

Alea stared at Magnus's back, turned a questioning glance to Cordelia, who could only shrug. Exasperated, Alea rushed to catch up with Magnus.

"What was that all about?" she demanded.

"I'm not one to stay where I'm not wanted," he answered.

She could hear the hurt and anger in his voice. "But she's your sister! They're your brothers!"

"I think it will take a few years for us to re-establish our relationships," Magnus said. "After all, when I left home, I was still the font of wisdom to Gregory, and Geoffrey was still testing himself against me."

"And Cordelia?" Alea was glad she asked, because the question brought a smile, albeit a small one.

"Well," Magnus said, "Cordelia and I were always squaring off as to which had the authority—unless someone attacked us, of course. Still, she does seem to resent my coming back." He came to a stop, frowning into the darkness. "Perhaps that's it. Perhaps I'd be welcome as a visitor, if they could be sure I would leave." His face darkened. "And perhaps I should." He began to walk toward their suite again.

"Perhaps not!" Alea hurried to catch up with him. "Perhaps you should stay and wait until, inch by inch, they've moved over and made room for you again!"

"Perhaps," Magnus admitted, but didn't sound as though he believed it.

ALTHEA PUSHED ASIDE her peasant bonnet to ask Raven, "Do you really trust any of them?"

Raven cast a quick glance at the VETO agents carrying sacks of provisions into the kitchen of Castle Gallowglass and said, "Not for a second. They'll turn on us the moment we've finished executing the Gallowglasses."

"Then why did Durer call the Mocker for help?"

Raven shrugged. "Common enemies. We both need to eliminate the Gallowglass family if we're to have any hope of taking over the government—but the second the brats are dead, start shooting the VETO agents."

Althea started to say that the totalitarians must be planning the same fate for them, but she shivered too badly at the thought.

Dressed as peasants and carrying sacks of provisions, the SPITE agents trooped into the castle beside the file of VETO agents.

THE AMUSEMENT AT dinner was muted, but the Gallowglasses and their spouses were managing to smile and enjoy the reassurance of one another's company.

"The kingdom still stands, at least," Gregory observed.

"Yes, thanks to your valiant efforts in fighting off the monsters." Alain raised a glass. "To my friends and guards!"

"To the Prince who had the good sense to talk before he fought." Geoffrey raised his glass in return.

"Aye, and the brave knight who spoke on his peasants' behalf." Cordelia raised her cup, too. "To your cousin Geordie!"

"Yes, well met at last!" Alain said with relief. "Now the family can heal—I hope."

Magnus watched with a half-smile, but Alea sizzled beside him. Didn't any of them realize how much Magnus had done to fight off all their enemies? Deliberately, she raised her own cup and said loudly, "To kin and friendship!"

"To friendship!" the others chorused. All their cups rose, then all drank.

Alea blinked in surprize, amazed that her toast had been accepted.

"To enemies!" said a voice.

The Gallowglasses looked up in polite surprize as men and women in peasant garb stepped out of doorways, moved from behind tapestries, appeared in the minstrels' gallery—all levelling crossbows that bore ominous gems beneath the bolts.

A man who appeared aged and emaciated stepped forward before all the rest with a mocking smile. "Your servants salute you."

"You, then, are the one called Durer?" Gregory asked.

"He is—and I am the Mocker." Another lean and wrinkled man stepped forward with a bow. "Your parents' ancient enemies—and your own."

"Do not think to attack us with your psi powers," Durer said, "for both our organizations have enlisted locals who are very powerful espers."

"And you think they are stronger than all our powers joined together?" Gregory asked, amused.

The Mocker frowned. "I assure you, you have very little to smile about."

"Surely seeing our enemies face-to-face at last is cause for delight," Cordelia said.

"Then at least you will die happy." Durer raised his weapon and pulled the trigger—then pulled it again and again, his look of triumph transforming to horror.

"Fire!" the Mocker yelled, and all the agents squeezed triggers and pushed firing buttons. Only two of the crossbows loosed bolts—but those nosedived into the flagstones. A few of the jewels glowed brightly with rays that gathered, but never burst out.

"We have telepaths of our own, you see," Cordelia said, her face taut with strain, "to aid us in restraining your weapons."

"And soldiers to disarm you," Alain said.

Loops of rope dropped down and around each of the agents; the soldiers who held them pulled tight. The agents shouted in alarm and anger, struggling to twist free, to turn their weapons on their captors, but the soldiers kicked their feet out from under them and forced them to their knees.

Durer glared at Allouette and hissed, "Traitor!"

"Traitor!" Allouette was on her feet, face burning with anger as she advanced on him. "You dare call me traitor, you whose agents stole me from my cradle? You who sent me to false foster parents who twisted my sexuality and smashed my self-esteem deliberately and methodically? Whose successors debased me and abused me and shaped me into a weapon to strike at their enemies? *You* dare call *me* traitor?"

"They housed you and fed you!" Raven cried. "They changed your diapers and bandaged your cuts!"

"And called me whore and told me I had been born corrupt!" Allouette raged. "Nay, you have fashioned your weapon—now feel its sting!" She glared at Raven, eyes narrowing.

Raven screamed, clutching her head, then fell to the floor writhing in agony. "Cut it off! Cut if off to stop the pain!"

Allouette's mouth opened in a rictus of anger and effort, and Raven went limp. Then Allouette turned that awful glare on Durer.

"She betrayed you!" Durer shouted to Gregory. "She is our agent! She won your heart only so that she could be here within your midst to destroy you—as she maimed your eldest brother!"

"Fool, do you truly believe we do not know that?" Gregory stepped up beside his wife. "By titanic effort, my mother managed to undo the worst of the damage your agents had done to Allouette. Then my love told us all she had done, all the malice she had borne toward us."

Durer stared at Allouette, then bared his teeth in a snarl. "Betrayed from the moment I talked to you!"

"Oh, be reassured sir," she said bitterly, "for you have destroyed my life for the second time and disintegrated any chance I might ever have held for happiness!" Her eyes narrowed, and everyone in the hall could feel the power building in her, the mental power with the rage of years behind it.

Gregory touched her shoulder. "Leave him to the Crown, my sweet. Do not soil your hands with his corrupted blood."

Allouette's gaze snapped to him, staring in incredulity. "Do not mock me, sir! Well do I know that you cannot remain married to a woman who is as treacherous as I!"

"Remain married!" Gregory stared back, stricken.

"Aye! Miracle enough it is that you took a serpent to your bosom once, who knew so many of your enemies that she was the obvious choice when they sought one to betray you! How could you ever trust me again!" She turned to march to the doorway, sheer leashed rage radiating from her so intensely that soldiers and prisoners alike flinched away.

Alea stepped between Alouette and the doorway, looking down at her in exasperation. "You fool! You absolute total fool! You have the richest love a woman could hope for, you have a man who loves you to distraction, who couldn't even dream of blaming you for the slightest flaw, can't even recognize that there IS a flaw, and you're ready to leave him because you don't think *you're* worthy of *him?*"

"Step away, virago!" Allouette's rage cut loose. "Frozen spinster who is eaten up by envy of the love you cannot find, who seeks revenge on the world because you think yourself unlovable! I have withstood your silent condemnation for months, I have endured your silences and slights, but I will bear them no longer, nor let you bar me one second from the fate I deserve! Stand aside, amateur, or learn what true psi power really is!"

Alea didn't budge an inch. Tense and white-lipped, she said in a low and venomous tone, "And this is the woman who claims she has abandoned the ways of cruelty!"

Allouette froze, turning pale—and in that moment, Alea stepped back as Gregory stepped between them, staring into his wife's eyes, then dropping to one knee. Gazing up, he caught her hands between his own and said, "You are everything that is good and right, you are all that is completely loveable, not only for your beauty but also for your warm and generous nature—and above all, for your loyalty. How could you ever have thought that I could believe you a traitor?"

The blood drained from Allouette's face; she stared down, still frozen, aching to believe but unable to.

"Trust him, lady."

Turning, Allouette found Magnus gazing down at her—but the grave look he gave her was full of sympathy, not enmity. "Those of us who think ourselves unfit for love must look now and then at truth."

Alea stared at him, thunderstruck.

"You proved your loyalty by telling Gregory at once of the ambush Durer planned," Magnus said, "loyalty that is so titanic it stuns me, now that I realize that, from the moment Durer approached you with his blackmail, you have been sure you would lose your marriage and your love!"

"How could you doubt me so?" Gregory rose, staring deeply into her eyes. "How could you doubt me when you have only given me cause to love you more?"

Still Allouette stood frozen, eyes darting from one to the other. Then belief and relief broke through her anger, and she fell sobbing into Gregory's arms.

He soothed her and caressed her, murmuring, "Nay, sweet love, 'tis done, and the monsters shall be banished from your sight. Never again shall they rise to hurt you. Nay, my jo, my dear, my precious, be sure that I love you with a love that shall never vary, never swerve, for I know you for what you truly are, and 'tis for that I do love you."

His brothers and sisters looked on, beaming fondly—but Alea whirled and ran from the chamber.

Twenty-Eight

MAGNUS STOOD STARING AFTER ALEA, STUNNED, then started after her, walking quickly, even now careful not to come too close too quickly.

He came out into the courtyard just in time to see her run into the stable. Knowing she was unlikely to leave, he followed slowly and came in carefully, searching about him in the gloom, then following the sound of weeping.

He found her leaning against the post between two empty stalls, head on her arms and weeping with the deep, racking sobs of true heartbreak. Magnus came up as near as he dared, then asked gently, "Why do you weep, companion of my bosom? Surely you cannot think that anything Allouette said in a moment of despair might be true!"

"But it is, it all is!" Alea groaned. "Go away, Gar! Let me be miserable in peace!"

"I cannot leave you sunken in lies."

"Lies?" Alea whirled to face him, face blotched, eyes red and swollen, tears still running down her cheeks. "She told only truth! I've always known I was awkward and gawky, too ugly for any man to love!"

"That is not true, not a word of it!" Magnus still dared move no closer, but he reached out. "But your feeling that way means that every word Allouette spoke went straight to that most vulnerable point in your heart."

"You can't deny that I'm awkward and gawky!"

"You are the soul of grace and deftness," Magnus countered. "Your movements in battle are a symphony; every step on the road or in the forest is sheer poetry. Oh yes, I deny most heartily that you are in any way awkward—but I can believe that you were in your teens."

Alea's eyes widened. Suddenly conscious of them, she made a quick swipe at her tears. "I'm far too tall to be graceful!"

"You're the perfect height," Magnus contradicted, then amended himself. "Well, perhaps an inch too short."

"Don't mock me, Gar!"

"I wouldn't dream of it." Magnus stared steadily into her eyes. "You want truth, and that is all I'm giving you— or honesty, at least; truth as I see it."

"You can't really believe I'm beautiful!"

"I've believed it since the first day I saw you," he said, "covered with briar scratches and smudged with dirt, your hair wild with two days' flight through a forest. I believed it then, but I knew it two days later, when you were clean and neat, and I thought I had never seen so beautiful a woman in my life!"

"All right, maybe I'm plain, not ugly—but you can't expect me to believe you find me beautiful!" Hope had crept into her voice, though.

"You must believe it," he said, "for it is true—believe that in my eyes, at least, you are beautiful." At last he stepped closer, lifting a hand to touch her cheek but not quite daring. "Come, you know you've caught me looking at you with admiration time and again—the times you caught me by surprise when you turned to look at me, and I hadn't been quite quick enough to look away."

"With admiration, yes." Her heart was pounding with hope that she tried to thrust down. "But desire? Never!"

"You've never caught me at it, no," Magnus said. "I hid it well, knowing you would see it as the worst sort of betrayal."

Alea stared at him, startled, then said, "For the first few years, yes, that was true—but not any more!"

"I could not take that chance, though, do you see," Magnus said, "could not take the chance of frightening you and hurting you and undoing all the progress you had made toward healing. So as to being repressed and frustrated, I most certainly am—but I will continue to be so, as long as that is what you need from me."

Alea only stared at him, wondering how so intelligent and sensitive a man could be so stupid, then said, "That's not what I need from you any longer. I need the final stage of healing now."

Magnus's eyes glowed; he stepped closer, but he only asked, "What could have wounded you so badly that it has taken so long to heal?"

"Only a careless, selfish lover." Alea tried to make light of it, but a sob caught in her throat. "Only a man who swore he loved me, told me his desire for me caused him physical pain, and begged me to assuage it. Flattered beyond words, I let him bed me—but when he had taken his pleasure, he called me a whore and went away, then never spoke to me again." She couldn't hold back the tears as she said it.

Face all tender concern, Magnus held out his arms, and Alea stood rigid, then swayed into his embrace and let the sobs go.

Magnus held her firmly, and when the weeping had slackened, he said, "Even after five years of my safekeeping and devotion, it still hurts you so badly."

"Nowhere nearly as badly as it did." Alea looked up at him, wiping tears from her eyes. "But you—it's been ten years now, and the wounds Finister gave you still fester."

"Well, yes." Magnus's embrace loosened; he stepped back a little, but still gazed into her eyes. "There was reason, though. She induced my love not just by allure, but by projective telepathy—total, abject devotion—then shamed me and humiliated me in every way she could. She even

convinced me I was a snake doomed to crawl forever
about the base of a tree, and I understand that I did just
that, though everyone else saw a naked man curled about
that trunk."

Alea gasped in horror, hearing it again, but from his
point of view. "How . . .?"

"My father found me and called Cordelia, who was able
to banish the worst of the spell—she's a strong projective
herself. But the witch came back again to compel my love
and shame me one final time, leaving me mired in a morass
of depression. My father found me again and called my
mother this time, who knew she must not cure me herself
and sent me to the Green Witch, who healed the worst of
my pain."

"Healed the worst, but it has taken you ten years to heal
the rest?" Alea gasped.

"Yes—for the only true healing I could have was to fall
in love with a woman who was absolutely trustworthy . . ."
Magnus touched her face, ever so lightly. ". . . a woman
who might disagree with me to my face but who would
never speak against me behind my back, and would certainly never, ever humiliate me or shame me."

His face was so near, but he was not, could not be, saying what she had so longed to hear. "It's too bad you
couldn't fall in love with me, then," Alea said with a catch
in her voice.

"No," Magnus agreed, "I grew into love with you, instead."

She stared at him, riveted, frozen, though her lips parted
ever so slightly—and ever so slowly, he lowered his own
lips over hers in a kiss that melted her and lasted far longer
than either of them intended. They broke apart, gasping
and staring at one another, wild-eyed—but when they had
caught their breath and the wildness had faded from him a
little, Magnus breathed, "Marry me, beautiful woman—I
beg you to marry me, for if you don't, I'll live a lonely man
all my life."

"But—but there are a thousand women more beautiful
than I am," she protested.

"None," Magnus said, with total conviction, "and none

who could even begin to understand me as you do. Will you marry me, for love?"

"Yes," Alea said, in a voice so small that even she could scarcely hear it.

Then Magnus lowered his lips to hers again, and the world went away for a while.

Epilogue

THE ORGAN PEALED THE "WEDDING MARCH," and Alea found herself walking down a rose-petal-strewn aisle on the arm of the King of Gramarye, in the cathedral of Runnymede, draped in white bunting and festooned with roses, just as Gwendylon Gallowglass would have wished—and at the end of the aisle stood Magnus, resplendent in a gold-figured doublet, white-lined golden cape, and white hose, staring at her in awe, as though she were a goddess come to Earth—and she almost melted at the sight of him; she had never known he was truly handsome.

Then King Tuan handed her to Magnus, the archbishop questioned them severely as to their realizing what they were getting into, and satisfied that they meant it, asked for their vows. She stared at Magnus as he swore lifelong love and loyalty, then found herself stammering as she repeated the same vow, felt his ring slip over her finger, then placed hers on his hand. The archbishop allowed them a kiss, and she meant it to be chaste, she really did, but three weeks of waiting in increasing tension welled up, and the only reason she finally broke away gasping was because cheering rang in her ears.

Then the archbishop intoned his way through an interminable Mass, but Alea was only aware of the masculine presence that seemed to burn beside her. At last the priest blessed them one more time, and the trumpets blew, the organ crashed the first chords of the recessional, and she and Magnus found themselves pacing down the aisle, grinning into one another's eyes like a prize pair of idiots.

Then, of course, came the feasting, and the greeting of guests, and the circulating among them—so when at last the door of the bridal chamber closed behind them, she was stumbling with weariness—stumbling straight into Magnus's arms, and he held her up, but also held her tight against him.

Alea stared up at him, riveted, frozen, though her lips parted ever so slightly—and ever so slowly, he lowered his own lips over hers in a kiss that began quite chastely. But the brushing of his lips electrified her, and she returned it with ardor, her own lips opening, and the feather touches of the tip of his tongue sent fire racing her veins, and her lips opened farther almost without her knowing. The kiss lasted and lasted as her blood grew hotter and hotter, banishing weariness. Finally Magnus lifted his head to catch his breath, gasped, and said, "You must be exhausted. We'll sleep in the same bed, but I'll leave you alone."

"Don't you dare!" Alea snapped. "Not after that kiss!" And she pressed close for more.

Magnus lowered his lips again, and kiss led to caress, and caress to undressing, then to more caresses that led to the final intimacy that had been so long delayed, an intimacy that loosed raging passion in them both, passion that built to wave after wave of ecstasy.

IN THE WOODS beyond, Evanescent lay with her eyes closed, purring, as she read the amazement and joy of her two humans, and decided that living on Gramarye could make her choose to prolong her life indefinitely. Then her eyes opened, and she lent just a little more power, a little more energy, to a darkened corner of Magnus's mind.

*   *   *

ALEA AND MAGNUS lay naked and stunned in the light
of a single candle, gasping in the aftermath of passion,
gazing at one another with wide and wondering eyes—but
as they did, an image grew in the flickering shadows, a
presence, one that only Magnus could see, for it came from
the depths of his mind—a tubby red-nosed man in a fusty
bottle-green tailcoat and battered top hat, who shook his
head and sighed, then stepped forward.

Magnus stared, then caught the blanket to pull it over
himself and Alea.

"What is it?" She darted a glance that followed his but
saw nothing and turned back, caressing his face as she
asked in a voice soft with concern, "What is it, love? What
could affright you so?"

But the rag-and-bone man dropped a bit of glittering
metal into the hollow of her throat, then turned away, sighing and shaking his head, to disappear forever into the
shadows from which he had come.

"Tell me!" Alea seized Magnus's face in both hands, really alarmed for him now. "Whatever phantom assails you
is my enemy too!"

"But you have already defeated him." Magnus laughed
softly as he relaxed beside her. "Fought off my old nemesis, and he has given you what he knew you already had."

Alea frowned. "What riddle is this? What did I already
have?"

"Only a key," Magnus said, and kissed her again.

Stayton Public Library
515 North First Avenue
Stayton, Oregon 97383

The novel that launched the
epic Warlock series

THE WARLOCK IN SPITE OF HIMSELF

BY

CHRISTOPHER STASHEFF

The interstellar romp that proves
science and sorcery CAN mix—

Only hard-headed realist
Rod Gallowglass can save the people
of Gramarye from their doom by
becoming a warlock.
Now, if only he believed in magic...

0-441-87302-2

AVAILABLE WHEREVER BOOKS ARE SOLD OR
TO ORDER CALL 1-800-788-6262

A521

10/04

SF

STASHEF

Penguin Group (USA) Inc. Online

What will you be reading tomorrow?

Tom Clancy, Patricia Cornwell, W.E.B. Griffin,
Nora Roberts, William Gibson, Robin Cook,
Brian Jacques, Catherine Coulter, Stephen King,
Dean Koontz, Ken Follett, Clive Cussler,
Eric Jerome Dickey, John Sandford,
Terry McMillan…

You'll find them all at
http://www.penguin.com.

Read excerpts and newsletters, find tour
schedules, enter contests…

Subscribe to Penguin Group (USA) Inc. Newsletters
and get an exclusive inside look
at exciting new titles and the authors you love
long before everyone else does.

PENGUIN GROUP (USA) INC. NEWS
http://www.penguin.com/news

Stayton Public Library
515 North First Avenue
Stayton, Oregon 97383